THE CARNAGE SERIES 1

CONTENTS

Marley 007

The letters... 354

A Different Kind of Christmas 478

MARLEY

carnage book three
LESLEY JONES

PREFACE

IF YOU ARE EASILY TRIGGERED, PLEASE TAKE NOTE...
I write books that are about more than just the romance.
I've lived a life, an interesting one. It hasn't always been rainbow farting unicorns, in fact, rarely has it been that. Like most of you, I've loved, and I've lost. Sometimes I'm a nice person, sometimes I'm a bit of a cunt.
All of this is reflected in my stories and my characters. If you choose to stay around, you won't always love the journey we take you on.
Remember, you're reading a work of FICTION!
My characters don't always represent or reflect my views.
Shitty things happen to good people, and all of that is reflected in my stories.
So, if you're happy with all of that, buckle up mother fuckers and enjoy the ride!

Copyright 2013 Lesley Jones
All Rights Reserved

This book is a work of fiction. Any references to real events, real people, and real places are used fictitiously. Other names, characters, places, and incidents are products of the Author's imagination and any resemblance to persons, living or dead, actual events, organisations or places is entirely coincidental.

All rights are reserved. This book is intended for the purchaser of this e-book ONLY. No part of this book may be reproduced or transmitted in any form or by any means, graphic, electronic, or mechanical, including photocopying, recording, taping, or by any information storage retrieval system, without the express written permission of the Author. All songs, song titles and lyrics contained in this book are the property of the respective songwriters and copyright holders.

Model Edition
Cover and Formatting by Lou Stock LJDesigns
Proofreading by: Ashley Williams, AW Editing

GLOSSARY OF TERMS

The following is a glossary of terms that are used throughout this book. These euphemisms and slang words form part of the United Kingdom's spoken word, which is the basis of this book's writing style.

Please remember that the words are not misspelled. They are slang terms and are part of the everyday, United Kingdom and Australian lifestyle. This book has been written using UK English.

If you would like a further explanation, or to discuss the translation or meaning of a particular word, please do not hesitate to contact the author – for your convenience, contact details have been provided at the end of this book.

I hope you enjoy a look into the United Kingdom/Australian way of life.

Arsed
Can't be bothered doing something.

Bespoke
Created especially for someone, in the same way that you say custom

Bird
A young woman

Bib/Bibbed
To honk your horn

Bloody
Swearword originating in England, used in the middle of words/ phrases to emphasize meaning - be it good, sarcastic or bad

Blower
Telephone

Bog
Toilet

Bogies
A piece of dried mucus discharged from the nose

Bollocking
When one is lectured, criticised or reprimanded

Bollocks
Generally indicates contempt for a certain task, subject or opinion, also used in place of bull shit.

Brass
Prostitute.

Charlie
Cocaine

Divvy
A fool or idiot.

Faffing
To spend time on a non-productive activity
"to waste time".

Fuckeration
The meaning is that whatever you have gotten yourself into, it is one holy fucked up, fuckeration of a mess.

Gaff
House or place.

Gissit
'Give Us It' or just 'Give It'.

Gobby
Talkative.

Gregory
Cockney rhyming slang: Gregory Peck – neck.

Give us a bell/ I'll bell ya
Call me/I'll call you

Hark
Look at you, or listen to you.

Mate
Buddy or a friend.

Motor
Car

Narna
To get very angry or to lose it.

Mildred
Vagina

Fanny
Vagina

Off My Tits
To be VERY much under the influence of a substance. Most commonly used as either an excuse or a conversation starter.

Off License
A shop licensed to sell alcoholic beverages for consumption off the premises.

Plonked
Meaning to put something down, unceremoniously.

Scooby
Clue.

Shag
To have sex, or get your fuck on, to score, get some, hit it, tap it, do it.

Shitfaced
Under the influence of drugs or alcohol.

Skin Up
To make a cannabis cigarette.

Soundo
This is London slang for asleep. It derives from the phrase "sound asleep" thus "soundo".

Stellar
A word used when something is outstanding or immense.

Summit
A lazy way of saying 'something'

Swanning
Posing or posturing around.

Take/ing the Piss
To take liberties at the expense of others, or to be unreasonable. To mock or make fun of.

Tarted Up
To improve the appearance of something.

Telly
Television.

Tits Up
Something that is no longer functioning or working.

Tuppence Worth
Phrase used when someone has brought all the evidences to support his point of view.

Vest
Tank Top/Singlet

Whaz
Urinate

Whizz
Speed

DEDICATION

For my brother.
I hope in death, you've found the peace that eluded you in life.
I'm sorry that as your big sister I couldn't save you.
I'll love you forever, but I'll never understand why.

ACKNOWLEDGMENTS

This has been the hardest book I've ever written. So many times my heart told me to walk away but my head kept telling me 'you've got this'.

I didn't want to just write words, I wanted to do Marley justice and write him the story that he deserved. It was all there, just stuck in my head, not wanting to escape. I would open my lap top on a daily basis and just stare at the screen. So for a little while, I walked away. I forgot about getting Marley and his words down and instead retold and rewrote his story in my head, all day, every day, until he just would not shut up. Then I went back to my lap top and suddenly five thousand, eight thousand, even twelve thousand words a day started happening, until one day, it was done.

I hope I did him justice. I know that not everyone is gonna be happy. I know that some will want more. More Marley, more Maca, more Georgia, or more Cam but this is Marley's story and he told it the way that he wanted it.

Thank you to all of my readers that have waited so patiently for this book. Thank you for your words of sympathy on the death of my brother and your words of encouragement when *my* words just weren't happening.

I've been fortunate this year to travel around the world and meet so many of you. Your passion for my writing will never cease to blow me away. You humble me each and every day.

Thank you to all of you that take part in our crazy discussions in my groups and my amazing admin team that run them, making sure that everyone plays nice and that we manage to keep both the spoilers and the spammers away.

To my beta's, I thank you for your time and your feedback. I know I don't listen to all of it but I am getting better at taking constructive criticism and direction … sorta.

To all of the other authors I have had the pleasure to meet and connect with over the last year, thank you for letting me be a part of your community, I'm truly honoured to be considered a colleague and to some, a friend.

To all the bloggers out there that have my back a million and one percent, I thank you. My career would not exist without you.

Last but by no means least, thank you once again to my family. You should all be pretty used to dealing with the crazy unwashed lady that can quite often be found tapping away on her keyboard, locked away somewhere in your home, but I thank you regardless. Thanks for muddling through and getting on with things in my absence and dealing with my trips overseas.

To my husband, my rock, my Tiger, thanks for holding the fort and allowing me to travel and meet so many of my readers this year. Thank you for mopping, vacuuming, grocery shopping and doing all of the other things I fail miserably at while hiding away in my cave or flying around the world. Most of all I'd like to thank you for putting up with all of my bull shit and bollocks and for dealing with life when I can't face it. I love you.

PROLOGUE

I wipe the steam from the mirror with the palm of my hand, clearing it enough to see my reflection. I rest my elbows on the granite counter and lean forward, taking in my image. I rake my hand through my hair, then over the stubble on my chin. My eyes are bloodshot from the weed we smoked earlier, the after-effects of which have also left me feeling decidedly depressed.

I stood in the shower and cried tonight for the first time in a long time over the death of my best friend, my bandmate, and my brother-in-law, Maca.

So pointless.

So tragic.

So unfair.

Drawing in a deep breath, I leave the steamy solitude of the bathroom and head for our dressing room, passing the sleeping form of my wife—my rock—on the way.

I smile at the thought of having a dressing room, feeling like a stupid fuck as I do. Of all the material things that fame and fortune have blessed our lives with, this dressing room makes me feel like a horny teenager in a sex shop. It's the sort of room I dreamt of as a kid, back when I was thirteen or fourteen, trying to imagine what it would be like if Carnage made it big. I never imagined having one like this though, on property that I never thought I would be able to afford … to *own*.

Ashley's clothes are lined up along one side and mine along the other, with everything broken down by style and colour. In the middle, we both have a mechanical shoe carousel that moves from floor to ceiling. Ashley's shoes take up her entire carousel, along with three-quarters of my space. I've also notice that a few of her winter coats have managed to sneak their way over to my side. The woman has fifty feet of wall space for hanging her gear, and another twenty for all her knickers and bra's she insists she needs and still, she needs more room.

It's not that I mind. She can have whatever she likes. She's my world, and I would give and do anything for her.

At the end of the room there are two full-length mirrors that tilt and unfold so that you can see yourself from all angles. In the centre is a tacky, Hollywood-style mirror, complete with lights around the edges. In front of it is the kind of sink a hairstylist would use, with a chair that leans back. All of Ashley's crap surrounds the surfaces on either side of the sink: make-up, face cream, hair shit. I have no idea what ninety percent of it is, or what it does—nothing, as far as I can tell. You can't improve on perfection, and my wife is perfect. She's stunningly beautiful, has curves in all the right places, and she's so much more than I could ever deserve—so much more.

I pull on a pair of boxers and the automatic lighting turns off as I leave the room. I laugh to myself at the full-on description I've just run through of our dressing room. In case you couldn't tell, I love that fucking room.

As quietly as I can, I take my sneaky stash pack of cigarettes and lighter from the chest of drawers next to my side of the bed.

Ash will give me shit if she catches me smoking. She makes an allowance for a few joints on occasion, but she hates me smoking cigarettes. It's been an emotional few days and I need one, maybe two, to calm my nerves.

Ash has never smoked and thankfully, neither do any of my kids … well, not cigarettes at least. I've caught Joe with a joint a couple of times, but the boy's twenty-four so what can I do? I've given him the talk—warning him of the dangers of hard drugs—but I don't know how much more I can do. I know, considering my past, that it's highly hypocritical of me to lecture him, but at the end of the day, I'm his dad and it's my job. Besides, what I did when I was younger is irrelevant. He does as I say, not as I do, or did. Yeah, I'm a pretty strict parent— who'd have thought?

I slip quietly out onto the balcony, closing the doors behind me and light up. I lean one hand on the railing and bring the cigarette to my lips with the other, drawing in the much-needed smoke into my lungs. I know it's a filthy habit. I know the toxins and chemicals can kill me, but the pleasure I'm receiving from the little stick of poison right now, I couldn't care less.

Ash has never been a nag. She's never really got on my case about things, but she hates me smoking.

Fifty. I'll be turning fifty next year, and I'm grateful for every day that I've managed to stay alive. I let out a long breath as images of the life I've led, the things I've seen, people I've met, and places I've visited rush through my mind. I've done some stupid shit in my time, and I mean some *really* stupid shit.

Goosebumps erupt over my skin, and I shiver. It's a beautiful warm summer's evening—the kind that reminds me of the long school summer holidays we enjoyed as kids—days when the sun always seemed to shine and the air smelt of fresh cut grass. We thought we were invincible back then. All that mattered was the music, practising our next cover, and attempting to write our next song. We thought we knew everything—thought that we would live forever, but obviously we knew fuck all.

The damn breaks again and I grip my hair, trying to quiet the loud sobs that are escaping. I hear the door click behind me and turn to see Ash staring at me.

"Babe?"

I turn away from her, gripping the rail as another sob escapes.

"Oh Marls, I knew this would happen. I warned you, didn't I?" She's not accusing, just stating a fact. She did warn me. She knows me better than I know myself and I love her for it. Her naked front pushes into my bare back and her arms slide underneath mine, wrapping around me.

"Talk to me, Marls. Please, don't shut me out."

I turn and face her, pulling her in tight and breathing in the scent of the woman I've loved for twenty-five years. She's one of the very few things that I haven't fucked up in my life, not since the early days anyway. She's loved me at my worst, stood by my side, and pulled me back from the brink so many times I've lost count, but she still doesn't know all my deepest, darkest secrets—most, but not all.

"It hurts, Ash. It still fucking hurts so much," I say into her hair. The smell of her shampoo calms my racing heart.

"Of course it does, especially on nights like tonight when you've been talking about him and remembering all the good times." She pauses for a few seconds and I know she's struggling not to cry herself.

"It's normal, Marls. You just need to let it out. Don't bottle it up like you used to. Just let *me* in and the *tears* out."

She takes my hand and leads me back inside to the bedroom and over to our bed.

"Get in and give me a cuddle. You've shut me out these past few weeks and I've missed ya."

I let out a long sigh as I climb into bed, feeling guilty because she's right.

I've spent the last few weeks practising for this year's Triple M concert with Conner Reed, lead guitarist for Shift. Because of the tragedy his band has recently endured, we thought it would be a good idea to collaborate and bring in some extra revenue for the charities we support while at the same time, commemorate and celebrate our lost bandmates.

This will be the thirteenth year we have held the event and it's gone from strength to strength. The diversity of the charities we raise awareness and money for keeps a broad selection of the public interested. Despite Maca being gone fourteen years this December, there are still a lot of Carnage fans out there who turn out every year to support the cause, and I couldn't be more proud of what we've managed to achieve between Georgia, Len, and myself.

Georgia, George, G, or to Maca, Gia, is my little sister and the bravest person I've ever met. How she has held her shit together and clawed her way back to becoming a functioning human being again, I will never know. I couldn't have done it, but *she* did, and with the help of Cam, she's in a good place. She still has her moments. I still get the odd call from her in the middle of the night when she can't sleep, or because she's had a bad dream, but they are few and far between now and I'm glad—glad that she's found her place in the world. Her family and this charity pretty much take up all of her time, and despite the fact that her job is to promote a charity that was set up to honour her dead husband, Cameron King has been on board and one hundred percent supportive since the very beginning.

Despite my doubts about their relationship when it first began, he has been a bigger man than I ever could have been, and I'm not just talking about the size of the man's dick here—which is apparently legendary. No, I'm talking about his capacity to love my sister the way that he does. I might even go as far as to say he loves her more than Maca did. Don't get me wrong, Sean loved George, but their relationship was borderline obsessive of each other.

I let out another long sigh as I pull Ashley back into my front and she grinds her arse against me.

"What are you thinking about?" she asks me quietly.

"Anal mostly—*Humph*," is the noise I sorta make as Ash elbows me in the ribs.

"We were being serious, Marls." I kiss the top of her head and give her nipple a squeeze.

"I've got a hard-on now. I don't wanna talk, I wanna fuck."

"Don't try and deflect. I wanna know what's going on in that head of yours right now."

"I just told you and it earned me a crack up the ribs," I complain.

"You either talk to me, Marley Joseph Layton, or I go and find another bed to sleep in. Don't shut me out, I'm being serious."

"George," I tell her honestly.

"Well, that's disturbing. Anal and your sister in the same convo. I've always thought you two were overly close." I bite her shoulder.

"Ow! I'm joking you arsehole. What about her?"

I shrug my shoulders, "How far she's come."

I feel Ash nod her head. "She's in a good place, possibly the happiest I've ever known her to be."

We're both silent for a few moments before Ash asks, "Have you thought any more about the book?"

My stomach does a few backflips and I instantly feel too warm.

"I can't do it to her, Ash. She's been through too much already. Fuck, I've caused her enough shit in her life … I can't do it."

She wriggles around and faces me, reaching out to stroke the stubble on my cheek with the palm of her hand. Her soft fingers rubbing over my whiskers instantly calms me down.

"Will you still not tell me what's so bad? Is there stuff about you? You scare me when you won't even discuss it with me. We've been together a long fucking time, babe. What's past is past."

I raise my eyebrows as I look at her. We both know full well that she's full of shit.

"So, if you read something about me shagging someone way back when and we just happen to bump into that person, you're gonna be fine with it?"

She pulls her head back so she can look me in the eyes. I notice that hers are shining like she's about to cry.

"Did it happen since we've been together?" She asks me quietly and my fucking heart breaks for her.

"What? No, babe. You know everything that you need to. You knew about it back then, when shit happened." I sit up in bed and pull her up to straddle my lap. I feel ashamed. I treated Ash like shit when we were first together, mostly because I was terrified of what I was feeling for her, but also because I'm a complete dickhead.

"See? This is why I can't do it, not even for charity. If I write it, I want to be honest. I want to tell the truth, and if I do that…" I trail off as I think about the damage it would do. "If I do that, then I'm gonna hurt a lot of people, including my sister. I've fucked up her life enough and I'm not gonna be responsible for doing it again."

Ash looks up at me from under her lashes. "But you're not gonna tell me what it is that might upset G?"

"No," I reply without hesitation. "I don't want you having to keep things from her. I don't want you knowing shit about Sean and worrying that she needs to know the truth because she doesn't." I press my forehead against hers. "We were young. We fucked around and we fucked up and then, even when we got a bit older, we still sometimes fucked up." I meet her gaze and continue. "I'm still here, Ash. I can justify and explain my actions, but Maca's not and I'll never do that to him. I won't hurt my sister and I won't ruin Maca's reputation. It's just better for everyone involved if the book doesn't get written."

This whole argument has been going on between us since a publisher asked me to write my life's story. They would cover the costs involved in editing, promotion, and whatever else needed to be done to bring a book to print and digital. All the proceeds would go to Maca's Music & More charity. It would probably bring in a lot of coin, but I can't lie—if I'm gonna put it out there and publish the fucker, then I'm gonna want to be honest and tell the world the truth. And if I do that, people are gonna get hurt, especially my wife and sister, and I can't do that to them.

"What if you just wrote it and made the decision after you finished it? Write it all down and then decide if it's really as bad as you think it is."

I smile at her. "You only want me to write it down so you can read it. I'm not fuckin' stupid, Ash."

Her brown eyes sparkle as she smiles back at me. "I'd never do anything to hurt you, baby," I tell her, "and if I was to write this book with honesty and from the heart, I can't guarantee that I won't do just that. There's things that I'm not proud of—things that I don't want you and the kids to read about."

"Well that fuckin hurts in itself," she says, her smile now replaced with a frown. "The fact that you're keeping secrets from me fucking hurts, Marls."

I can't win. "Fine, have it your fuckin' way. I'll write the book so you can read about my life—the good, the bad, and the fuckin' ugly, but don't you dare complain to me that you're not happy with some of the life choices I've made. I don't wanna hear you complain about how ugly things have been for me.

I expect her to climb off my lap and storm off, but instead she surprises me by wrapping her arms around my neck and kissing me. "Shut the fuck up and stop behaving like a martyr. It's all in the past, but if it's gonna help you, write it. If it's gonna leave you miserable and depressed, walk away, babe, walk away."

If only she knew that it's already too late. The book has already been written. The second the publishers came to me with the suggestion, I couldn't get the idea out of my head. I laid awake every night for weeks, going over past events in my head: the good, the sad, the bad, and the bits that are so fucked up, I don't think I want anyone to know about … ever. In the end, I decided to write down all of it—the truth about my life, Sean's, my sister's, and Carnage. I've been brutally honest throughout the whole process to the point where I've actually begun to see things in a different light. I've finally accepted the part I played in fucking up and fucking with the lives of my little sister and of my best mate. Now, I just need to decide what the fuck to do with all these words that have the potential to break hearts, maybe even minds. Do I leave it as it is and tell the truth, or do the kind thing and leave bits out? I've hated lying to Ash, but I know that if she knew it's already been written, she'll force my hand either way and want to read it. I'm not sure if I'm ready for that. I'm not even sure if I'm ready for anyone to know the ugly truth, especially Ashley.

* * *

Later, after making love to my wife, I abandon her sexy sleeping arse and slide out of bed and head silently down the stairs to my office. I fire up my laptop, pour myself a glass of my favourite single malt and sit back on the leather sofa. I begin to read what I've spent the last six months writing behind my wife's back.

I skim through the prologue, which covers the early years, and jump straight into the part where things take off for us, and at the same time, fall apart.

Carnaged

BY

MARLEY LAYTON

ONE
1985

I tilted my head back to let the ice-cold beer slide down my throat.

Fuck Len and his rules.

I wasn't a fucking child, and I wouldn't be treated like one. Yeah, we played like shit the other night … one night out of the whole tour so far. We didn't sound our best and Lennon kicked off like a fucking lunatic, trying to keep us locked in our rooms and banning phone calls. We were in Paris, and I was gonna enjoy myself. We'd worked bloody hard on this tour and we'd more than earned the chance to have a bit of fun, so yeah, fuck him.

I turned around on my stool at the swim-up bar and watched as Rocco waded through the water towards me, waving a little plastic bag in the air.

"Big bro let you out to play today, Layton? Where's your buddy?

He too pussy-whipped by your sister to be allowed to join us?"

He wafted the bag of cocaine in front of my nose as he spoke. I was eighteen and stupid, and I thought Rocco Taylor was a god.

"My 'big bro' can go fuck himself, and I have no idea where Maca is—probably loitering around the nearest payphone so he can ring George."

He shook his head. "Dude, I know she's your sister and all, but seriously, that shit could end your careers. You need to show him that single is the way to go. Just look at what Yoko did to the Beatles."

I'd never thought of that before. Maca had not stopped complaining about how much he missed G. He even mentioned that he was gonna ask her to marry him as soon as she left school so that my mum and Dad would have no objection to her touring with us.

She was sixteen, for fuck's sake. Who got married at sixteen? I loved my sister, and Maca was like a brother to me, but they were far too young to be thinking about all that shit.

"You wanna line? This is good shit. I've got an Algerian contact who gets me whatever I like at a moment's notice.

He had one of those waterproof, plastic coin storage tubes hanging from a cord around his neck, containing the contents of a small chemist's shop.

"Try one of these. When the girls get here, you will be able to fuck for hours."

He handed me a small white pill, and without even thinking, I swallowed it down with the last of my beer, then snorted a line of coke up each nostril from the bar.

I wanted to obliterate my thought process—I was sick of thinking and feeling. I just wanted to be numb. I'd just endured three days of watching my brother and my best friend behave like they were in fucking heaven, just because their birds had flown out to see them.

I wasn't jealous as such ... *fuck* ... yeah, actually I was. I was jealous because Maca always chose George over me and I was jealous because Jimmie had chosen Len over me. I didn't even really fancy her that much, but I'd always assumed that one day, Jim and I would get it on. We'd always flirted around each other. Even as kids, there'd been a little something between us, and I think I just felt like I was entitled to claim Jimmie as mine. I never for a minute considered that she would be interested in someone else. Then when she was just fourteen, it all came out that she was seeing my eighteen-year-old brother. Everyone but me seemed to know about it and it *hurt*. It hurt a fucking lot. I felt stupid, like Jimmie had led me on, just to get to my brother, but of course she hadn't. We'd been mates, Jimmie and I, and nothing more. What I saw as flirting, she saw as teasing. It was no different to what Maca did with her, but back then, my head needed a bit of a wobble, so instead, I sulked like a little kid and allowed Rocco and his poison to get under my skin.

"He's talking about proposing to her," I stated after a few minutes of silence.

"Maca … to your sister? How fucking old is she?"

"Sixteen. She's still at school," I told him.

"Seriously? Why the fuck would he wanna do that?"

"Because it's the only way my mum and Dad will let her come on tour with us."

"What about her education? College? Do your parents not want all of that for her? I mean no disrespect, dude, but they're both so young. What if in a few years from now they split up? What's your sister gonna be left with then?" he asked with a serious, concerned tone to his voice, and me being the idiot that I was, I took it at face value. He was, after all my friend, and was just showing concern for my sister.

Yeah, right.

"Relationships are hard to hold down in this industry. You guys are just on the verge of making it big. There's gonna be tours, worldwide TV appearances, long hours in the studio, and women. Fuck, there's gonna be women throwing themselves at you every which way you turn. How long till he can't resist? After a month, or even a few weeks away from home, he'll start feeling lonely, and there will be warm, wet pussy available everywhere he goes, willing to keep him company. How many times will he be able to say no, especially once the babies come along and your sister can't travel with him all the time? I'm telling ya, man, he'll either cave, cheating on your sister, or he'll wanna quit the band and stay home with her and the kids. Either way, it will bad news for you—bad, bad news."

I hung on his every word, absorbing them all like a sponge. I let them soak into my bloodstream like the coke he fed me for the rest of the afternoon. They settled like poison in my chest, my belly, and my brain.

A few hours later, I was a mess. I was high as a kite from the coke, horny as fuck, and loving anything and everything, all from the little white pill that Rocco had given me. I'd never experienced anything like it. I felt euphoric, like I could take on the world. I wanted everyone to try one of those little white pills so that they could feel as amazing as I did.

I looked up as a crowd of girls started to make their way towards us. Haley White was at the front of a group I recognised to be band slags that had been following us around from gig to gig.

I had to hand it to Haley, she was a resourceful little thing. From following us around the pubs and venues of Essex and East London, she was always there, sucking and fucking her way through the members of each band we played with, just so they'd keep her around.

At the time, she was Rocco's favourite plaything, but I'd watched her, and I knew she had her sights set on Maca, who she'd always been obsessed with. It was something we joked about and took the piss out of him for. However, none of us had any idea of the lengths she would go through to split him and Georgia apart.

I watched as the group of about twelve girls threw down their towels and bags on the sun loungers. Some of them started to remove their tops before jumping into the pool to join me, Rocco, Wayne Allen,

Kombat Rock's drummer, and Riff Reynolds, their guitarist. I slid off my stool at the swim-up bar and dipped farther down into the water to hide my hard-on. I was eighteen, snorting cocaine, popping what I later found out was ecstasy, and drinking beer with three members of one of the biggest bands of the time. In addition to that, I was in a pool with a swim-up bar, surrounded by a dozen women wearing little more than a smile and a 'come fuck me' look. Of course I had a fucking hard-on.

Things slowly began to spiral out of control from there. A few minutes later, I watched all heads turn as Maca walked out to the pool area, looking thoroughly pissed off. He pulled his T-shirt over his head, threw it on a chair and dived in. He swam almost the length of the pool, underwater, surfacing in front of me a few moments later. The water was just below his hips as he stood up and you could almost hear the collective sighs of every woman, and some of the blokes, as he pushed his hair back off his face.

Even I had to admit he was a good-looking fucker, almost verging on the side of too beautiful for a bloke. He was always a bit skinnier than me, but we had both been hitting the hotel gyms hard while on tour and even had a set of weights we regularly used on the bus, so we were both looking pretty ripped for a couple of eighteen-year-old kids.

I don't know exactly what happened in those few moments I spent watching him wade through the water towards me—the drugs and alcohol I'm pretty sure played a big part—but I'd readily admit there was something else. I don't know if it was his presence or the effect he had on everyone around him, but something made my dick stir as I watched him.

I'm not gay. I've never fancied blokes or had any desire to fuck or be fucked by another man, but for the first time ever, as I watched Sean McCarthy walk through the water towards me, I got hard for a man. It fucked with my head big time, making me feel angry and that, combined with Rocco's words from earlier about Sean splitting up the band to be with Georgia, made me resentful. He was my bandmate, best mate, and like a brother to me, but at that moment, I was confused about exactly what it was I was feeling for him.

"Maca, glad you escaped the chains that being in love have wrapped around you and decided to break free to come and join us," Rocco called out from the bar stool he was sitting on, Haley straddling his lap with her bare tits pressed against his chest. Despite being in that position, I'd noticed she hadn't taken her eyes off Maca since he'd walked out to the pool.

"Fuck off, Rocco," Maca replied as I passed him a beer.

"Cheers," he nodded towards me as he spoke.

"You need to chill the fuck out. What's up?" I asked him.

"Your fucking brother, that's what's up. G's gonna be going mental that I haven't phoned and it's all because he suddenly thinks he's God and can tell us when we can make fucking phone calls. I'm not a fucking child and I won't be treated like one. Between him and the label saying she can't come backstage, I'm just about ready to fuck off home and fuck the lot of them."

My stomach churned as I listened to his words. I looked over to Rocco who was shrugging his shoulders and shaking his head in an 'I warned you' gesture.

"That's a lot of fucks you just threw out there. Drink your beer and try one of Rocco's party smarties. They'll make you feel better, I promise," I told him.

Rocco, listening to the conversation, unwrapped Haley from around him, calling Maca and me over to the bar.

"You need to chill out and enjoy the party, man," Rocco said.

"Your girl loves you, right? She'll understand when you explain that Lennon had you all on a curfew, surely?" Maca shrugged.

"Well, if she don't, then you two are gonna have some serious issues in the future. Like I told Marley earlier, you guys are heading for the big leagues. You'll be playing in places where trying to get a call out is impossible and life's gonna get so crazy, you'll barely have time to take a dump. So, she best get used to going a few days without talking to you." He patted Maca on the back as he spoke, coming across all brotherly and caring.

"Now, try one of these and enjoy your night off. In fact, take two and a couple lines of this. I promise, life will feel good again, my friend."

Maca looked at me, "What you had?" I shrugged and smiled as I danced to Dead or Alive's, *'You Spin Me Right Round.'*

"What've I had? A good fucking time, that's what I've had. All while you've been running around, trying to find a payphone so my sister doesn't kick off when you eventually speak to her."

I watched him as he looked at the drugs lined up on the bar—two E's and two lines of coke. He shook his head, bent down and snorted the coke, then washed the two pills down together with a swig of his beer.

"Shit," I exclaimed, "you should've done those pills a couple of hours apart, not together like that."

"You just told me to chill so bring it on, I'm ready to party. I'm sick of feeling like I'm being pulled in every direction." He wiped his mouth on the back of his hand. "I've asked G to marry me," he announced out of nowhere.

I closed my eyes for a long moment. Everything was tilting sideways around me and I felt panic rise in my belly. It was all gonna come true … everything Rocco said would happen was gonna happen. I took a deep breath in through my nose and looked at my best mate.

"You must want your fucking brains tested."

"I love her, and I want her with me. I knew you wouldn't get it."

"Why, Maca? Why do you want her with you? So she can witness all this?" We both looked around the pool area. Everyone from the tour had taken over the space, from roadies, technicians, riggers, even backing singers. Tears for Fears, *'Everybody Wants to Rule the World'* started playing and everyone joined in, apparently knowing the words to the song. We were a collective—a group of strangers that had bonded after travelling, living, and performing together, and for once,

I felt like I was a part of something. I didn't feel like a loner or the odd one out, and I didn't want it to end. At that moment, I realised how much I truly loved my job, my band, and being on tour.

We had a whole day and night off, spending it in a hotel and not on the road, so everyone was making the most of it and partying hard.

"Well, you gonna answer the question? What d'ya think George would say to all this?" I gesture with a nod of my head to the scene unfolding around us. "There's topless women, for fuck's sake. Maca, some of them are naked. There are girls kissing each other, girls kissing boys, and I swear there are at least two couples over in the middle of the pool having sex. Everyone is either drunk, stoned, high or like me, a combination of all three." I made sure to point out everything that would make George hate it here. "If she sees this first-hand for herself, she will never trust you when you're on tour again," I told him straight. I knew my sister. I knew exactly how she would react to what was going on around us that day.

"She won't have to worry if she's with me. Your mum and Dad are never gonna let that happen unless we get married, or until she turns eighteen."

"Then fucking wait—wait until she's eighteen. Let her finish her education so we can enjoy these next few years on the road." He raked his hand through his hair as I spoke.

"Marls, I can't. I need to have her near. What if she goes off to college and meets someone else? What if she decides that this isn't the life she wants?" Was he serious?

"Maca, I know she's my sister, but Georgia's a good girl. She's only ever had eyes for you since she was eleven-years-old."

"What if you propose and she *is* allowed to travel with us? She's gonna see shit like this happening all the time. What if she *still* decides that this ain't what she wants, that this life isn't for her? What'll you do then?" He closed his eyes and tilted his head up to the sky as I spoke.

"I don't know ... I don't fucking know. She's so young, Marls. She thinks she knows it all, but she has no idea. She'd hate this, and she'd hate knowing I was around this shit." He gestured with his chin towards the debauchery going on all around us.

"You need to let her go, Maca. I know you love her, but you need to let her finish her education, and you need to concentrate on the band. Then, in a coupla years, maybe think about settling down with her. We've got plenty of time for wives and babies. Let's just focus on making Carnage the biggest band ever first—that, and enjoying what it brings with it."

"I can't let her go and I won't ... not for the band, not for anyone. I'll tell you straight up, Marls, if it comes to the band or G, she'll win every time ... *Every. Fucking. Time.*"

My heart rate accelerated. I needed to do something to make him see that the band was more important than the fucking fairy tale he thought he had going on with my sister.

Please bear in mind I was eighteen, stupid, and selfish. We'd worked so fucking hard to get the band to where it was and we were so close to seeing all our dreams come true. I just couldn't see beyond that. I'm not trying to make excuses for how events unfolded that night or the part I played in them, but I was manipulated as much as Maca was. I may not have been innocent, but I was set-up the same as he was, and I've never forgiven myself for what happened over those next few hours.

If I hadn't behaved like a selfish little prick, I have no doubt that Sean and Georgia would've been happily married with a family, years before they ever were. Everything would've been different. They would never have been out on that icy street on that freezing cold December afternoon, and I sure as shit know that my best friend and my nephew would still be alive today. I live with this every single day of my fucking life, but being the wanker that I am, I will never let my sister know the part I played in changing the course of her life. I lost her once for a few years, and if she knew the truth, I know without a shadow of a doubt that I would lose her forever.

TWO

1985

A few hours later we got kicked out of the pool area after numerous complaints to the hotel's management, and we ended up crammed into Rocco's hotel suite.

Maca was dancing on a table, sandwiched between a very naked German girl, and a little Spanish girl who was grinding her bikini-clad arse onto his dick. I watched as the fräulein reached around, trying to slide her hands into his shorts, but he pulled them away and placed them on the Spanish girl's hips, who in turn grabbed them and placed them over her tits.

Maca's eyes caught mine as I watched. He winked and smiled, raising his beer bottle in a 'cheers' gesture and in that moment, I made the decision that ultimately changed my best mate's life.

We were about to make it big as a band. The last thing we needed were girlfriends or wives around us. I loved my sister, but I wouldn't let her bring an end to it all. And at the end of the day, ultimately I'd be doing her a favour. It would gut her to see what her Sean was doing right then. He loved her, but with that much fanny on tap, I knew that at some stage he'd get shit-faced and end up shagging one of the band slags, or some other random that would offer it up to him on a plate. So yeah, I was totally doing my sister a favour and saving her a lot of heartache by showing Maca exactly what he'd be missing out on if he kept George around.

I found Rocco and got a couple more pills from him. I slipped one into Maca's hand with a wink and popped the other into my mouth, washing it down with the cold beer.

'Relax' by Frankie Goes to Hollywood started to play and the whole room started to move as one to the music.

Haley White appeared from nowhere and wrapped her arms around my neck, moving her hips to the beat of the music against mine. I was hard in an instant. She was wearing an oversized Kombat Rock T-shirt and when I slid my hands underneath to squeeze her arse, I realised she wasn't wearing any knickers.

The effects of my second ecstasy tablet hit me harder and much quicker than the first, and I suddenly felt like I could hear in colour. My dick was throbbing and Haley White was the most beautiful thing that I'd ever seen.

She kissed along my jaw and whispered in my ear, "Get Maca. I want to feel you both inside me at the same time."

I nearly came in my pants as she followed her request off with a kiss that involved her tongue licking every part of the inside of my mouth.

"Tell him I've got some great blow, but I don't want to share. We need to go back to your room and just keep it for ourselves."

She kissed me again and I had to push my hand down flat on my dick to hide my boner while walking over to where Maca was still dancing on the table. I pulled him down by his hand and he stumbled as he landed beside me and laughed. He was as fucked up as I was, which worked for me. I would have no problem convincing him to join in on a little three-way fun with Haley and me.

"Let's go back to our room for a bit. Haley's got some high-grade coke that she only wants to share with us."

He struggled to focus while looking at me.

"I dunno, Marls. I'm pretty fucked up already."

"That's coz of that pill, but once you come down off it, you're gonna crash. The stuff she's got will keep us going for the rest of the night, and we don't wanna miss out."

He looked around the room, raking his hand through his hair, obviously debating with himself on what to do. "Your sister never gets to hear about this, never. You hear me?"

"Of course not. I'm not fucking stupid, dude. What happens on tour stays on tour."

We did our 'boys in the hood' type handshake and started to leave the suite, heading to our room. As we got to the door, Haley was there with Rocco. I gave her a 'What the fuck is he doing here?' look, which he saw.

"Don't worry, dude, she's all yours. I just want a line of the high grade, and maybe watch what unfolds. Maybe even take a few photos for posterity. You've seen the videos; you know how Haley likes to perform."

Fuck yeah I did. Rocco's videos had been our wanking material since the tour started, but the latest one of him and Haley with another girl had been the best. For some perverse reason, the thought of him watching what might happen and even filming it, turned me on big time, but I knew Maca wouldn't be happy.

"Listen, you can't let Maca know you're taking photos. He will flip if he thinks that there's any way Georgia will find out," I told him.

"No problem, man. By the time Haley gets him worked up nice and good, he won't even remember you have a sister. And any thoughts he might be having about quitting the band will be gone for good."

I would like to be able to tell you that at that moment, I had some doubts about what we were about to do, that I felt some kind of guilt or compassion towards my sister, but I didn't.

My drug-fucked brain totally believed that I was doing G and Maca a massive favour. He would realise how much he would be missing out on if he married George anytime soon and end things. Yeah, she'd be a bit upset, but she'd throw herself into her school work, pass her exams, and get a good job. Then perhaps in a few years, when we'd made it, maybe then they could get back together and think about marriage and kids. Everybody could then live happily ever after. In my head, it all sounded easy, and so fucking perfect.

"You go back with her first and get her warmed up. I'll walk back with him in a while, and he won't know what's hit him once he sees her in action."

My dick twitched at the thought. I grabbed Haley's hand and dragged her out of the room and along the corridor to ours.

As soon as we were inside, she pulled her T-shirt over her head. She turned and faced me, naked, except for the little waterproof tube that hung around her neck between her tits; the same kind that Rocco had earlier. Hers was pink and a bit bigger than the yellow one he had though. I watched her while I leaned back against the door.

"Nice room, Marley. You've done well. Just think how much better things are gonna get. You'll probably be headlining your next tour, not supporting." She opened her legs and put her hands on her hips, adding, "*If* you're still together, that is."

"Oh? And why wouldn't we still be together?" I asked her.

"Well, from what I hear, Maca's thinking of giving it all up coz your stuck-up little sister don't approve of the rock and roll way of life." She licked her lips when she finished talking. I don't know if she thought it was a sexy move, and I really didn't give a shit. She was naked with holes that needed filling, and that's all I was concerned about.

"Well, we'd better put on a show that convinces him that the rock and roll way of life is exactly what *he* wants, even if my sister doesn't."

I walked toward her and kissed her hard on the mouth. I'd fucked Haley before, a couple of years ago, after we played for someone from schools sixteenth. It was hard, fast, and pretty uneventful, but this time we were in a hotel room and not up against a van in a pub car park. I'd planned to give her a time she wouldn't forget.

With all the sex I'd been getting before, and especially after the tour had started, I'd learnt a few moves, and I'd planned on trying every one of them out on Haley White. *Every. Single. One.*

At the end of one of the two double beds was a two-seater sofa, and in front of that was a long, wooden coffee table.

"Take that off from around your neck and lay on the coffee table, legs facing the door," I ordered her.

Her eyes flicked over me from head to toe, and then up and over my face as she thought about my instructions.

She swiped the magazines off the table and lied down on it. She was short, around five foot two, at most. If she hadn't worn so much make-up, I would've gone as far as saying that Haley was a pretty girl: blonde hair, blue eyes, curvy little body. She had a nice arse and a great pair of tits too. It was a shame, really, that she was such a little slut. I could've quite fancied her if it wasn't for that. Don't get me wrong, I have no issue with girls that like sex, none at all. What I do have an issue with are girls that use sex, or their sexuality, to manipulate and get what they want. Perhaps I'm a hypocrite, I don't know, but they're just my thoughts.

Haley bent her legs and put her feet on the edge of the table. Unhooking the pink plastic tube from around her neck, she held it out to me and as I took it in my hand, it gave me an idea.

"Open," I told her. She opened her mouth and I slid the pink plastic capsule inside.

"Suck," I ordered.

Haley deep throated it like a pro while I took off my shorts and started to stroke my cock. I pulled the tube out of her mouth with a pop, and she turned, trying to get her face level with my dick.

"Not yet. Let's give you some fun first."

I knelt at the end of the table and swiped the pink plastic through her cunt, then pushed it inside of her. It was about seven or eight inches long, and about as thick as three fingers, so even a bucket crutch like Haley should be able to feel it.

"Fuck, Marley. That feels good."

Yeah, she felt it.

Just as I started to work my thumb over her clit while fucking her with the plastic tube, the door opened.

I turned to watch as Rocco and Maca came to a stop, just inside the room. Rocco smiled as Maca raked his hand through his hair, his eyes all over Haley's naked body.

The self-closing door shut with a click behind them and Maca jumped.

"Shit," he said quietly.

"Carry on, children, don't mind me," Rocco said before moving over to one of the beds. He sat with his back against the headboard, in a prime position to watch whatever was about to unfold.

Haley sat up and faced Maca. Her legs were wide open and straddling the coffee table. She pulled the capsule out of her cunt and stood to go towards Maca. Dropping to her knees in front of him, she sucked the capsule into her mouth and started to work it in and out while stroking Maca's obviously hard cock through his shorts.

"Want me to suck your dick, just like I suck this?" she asked him.

He looked at me, then back down to Haley.

"I-I don't…" He laced his fingers together and pressed them to the top of his head. Closing his eyes, he swayed gently and swallowed hard.

That moment right there was when I should've shut things down.

He was young and horny, yet he was also unfocused, swaying on his feet, pumped full of drugs. But despite all that, he knew where his heart laid. He knew he loved Georgia, his English Rose, and as the song said, *'No bonds could ever tempt him from she.'*

And I shit all over that. I took what they had, what he felt for my sister, and kicked it right in the gut. I kicked until it couldn't breathe—until their love was a crumpled heap on the floor, gasping its last, dying breaths.

All I cared about was the band staying together and making it big. What Sean and Georgia had going on was inconsequential to me ... irrelevant. There were plenty of willing women out there, so why get stuck with just one?

"No Haley, I don't," he told her, opening his eyes and looking down at her.

"But ... I thought you might—"

"Get your fucking hands off me."

She stood up and turned from him to look first at me, then at Rocco, sitting on the bed.

"Well, you're no fun, Sean McCarthy. Let's see if some of what I have here loosens you up a bit."

She unscrewed the pink tube and just like Rocco did at the bar, she pulled out a small plastic bag full of charlie and shook it in the air.

Rocco pressed play on the boom box and Paul Hardcastle's *'19'* began blasting out the speakers.

"On your back, Haley. Serve it up properly, just like I showed you."

Without a word, Haley was back on the coffee table, tipping the contents of the packet through her cleavage, as far down as her belly button and then over each of her nipples.

"Come and get it, boys," she said with a giggle.

The music got louder as I looked across to Maca. He looked fucked, and I mean wasted.

"Last hit of the day," I said.

He gave me a small nod before we both moved to either side of her and started snorting the coke from her tits, cleavage, and belly. I watched as she grabbed at Maca's hair, trying to kiss him, but he pulled away and crawled over to the bed. She started asking me to fuck her, but I stuck my dick in her mouth and let her suck me off instead. I can't even remember if I came.

Then she was gone. Maca was lying face down across my bed and Rocco was nowhere in sight. I could hear the Rah Band singing about clouds across the moon and I instantly thought of Georgia. She loved that song. Ever since we were little kids—whenever we went away, whether it be abroad, or just to my parents' caravan in Clacton, G always had to have a holiday song—a song that would remind her of our time there, and that song had been played everywhere we went when she was with us that past week. G had loved it and declared it her holiday song, the song that would always remind her of Spain.

The image of my beautiful smiling sister punched into my heart like a fist-wielding blade. What the fuck was I thinking? I sat on the end of the bed and held my head in my hands, letting the guilt wash over me. She could never know about Maca being in the same room with Haley, and she could never know that I instigated the whole thing.

I'm not sure what was in those last few lines we snorted, but it couldn't have been cocaine. Maca had passed out cold, and I was starting to feel sleepy too. That drug usually had me going for hours, feeling like I could take on the world, not dizzy and disoriented like I was feeling then.

Sounds became fuzzy while images seemed to bend and look distorted. I looked up, thinking I could hear screaming, but I wasn't really sure; it could've been laughter, I didn't know. Noises faded in and out, and all concept of time was lost to me.

There was movement all around us, but it was fractured and disjointed. My name was being said and my face was being slapped, but no matter how hard I tried, I couldn't focus.

The next thing I remember very clearly was throwing up in the foot well of a car and someone shouting in a foreign language. Not being able to move my arms was the only cognitive thought I could process before I drifted off again.

I had no sense of the time over which the following events played out. I later learnt it was only a period of just over 48 hours.

I woke up alone in a cell as a tray of food was slid through a hatch.

I shouted and screamed, asking for someone to tell me what the fuck was going on, but I was shouted back at in return, only in French.

I was taken to an interview room where I was told by a policeman wearing a very crumpled suit and about three days' worth of stubble on his chin that I had been accused of rape.

I was taken back to my cell where I tried to get my shit together. For the past six or so weeks, I'd taken some kind of drug at least once a day. My body and my brain were reacting to the substance abuse it'd been enduring and the lack of its daily fix. I was hot, cold, and I couldn't stop vomiting. The shaking and shivering was unbearable.

I wasn't an addict, but my system had become somewhat used to its daily fix, and it was gonna take me at least a few days to get myself straight.

Lennon arrived with another bloke I later learnt was from the label.

I'd never seen Len so angry in my life. He punched me hard on the chin, but then he demanded that I have access to a doctor. I was hooked up to a drip and given another blanket, but once again, I was left alone to try and work out what the fuck had happened.

I slept for what felt like a very long time, finally waking to the sound of the drip bleeping because the bag of saline being pumped into me was empty.

Apparently, I'd been taken to a hospital. I had no recollection of how I got there or how long ago I'd been moved.

Len arrived with my dad and a lawyer, then everything was explained to me. Haley White had accused Maca and me of raping her. My first thought was of G.

What did I do … What the fuck did I do to her, to Maca, to the band?

I told the lawyer, who'd now been joined by the police, everything

I could remember.

I wasn't a good person. I wasn't a good friend or brother, but I was *not* a fucking rapist.

Again, the concept of time was alien to me. I was allowed to leave the hospital. I didn't go back to the hotel we were staying in because we'd been kicked out and had to go somewhere else.

Finally, I got my head around the fact that it was Friday.

I was silent in the car as my dad ranted and threatened all kinds of physical violence to me, Maca, Rocco, even Haley.

Lennon explained that the band would be practising for a few hours during the day and we'd be expected to perform that night and the next in Paris, as our shows were sell-outs. His tone told me he was pissed off and not to be argued with.

My dad and Len entered the hotel room in front of me and the instant my eyes met Maca's, who was lying back on the bed with his hands behind his head, he flew from the bed, coming right for me.

Maca was one of life's most laid back people. He always looked for the good in everyone and found the positive in any negative situation. He could fight, but he rarely did; it just wasn't his nature. He was the opposite of George and her fiery temper, but at that moment, he looked like he wanted to kill me.

"You cunt! What the fuck did you get us into?" My dad grabbed him, pinning both his arms to his sides.

"What did you do? Did you set me up for that?" He actually tried to fight my dad. Yeah, we laughed about that over the years a lot.

Maca, being the skinny fucker he was, wriggled his way out of my dad's grip and made another move towards me. Lennon stepped between us, but he swung around him and landed a punch on the side of my head. My dad grabbed him by the shoulder and spun him around, and lamped my dad on the chin.

The room fell silent. *Maca just punched Frank Layton.*

"Shit," my Uncle Fin said. He was sitting, unnoticed by me, in an armchair in the corner.

"I'll give you that one, son," my dad said to Maca, "but I'm telling you now, you need to calm the fuck down."

Sean's breathing was heavy when he turned back around to me to say, "Get the fuck away from me. I can't be near you right now."

I didn't say a word. I mean, what could I say? He didn't even know the half of it, and yet he still knew I was to blame for what we'd been accused of.

THREE
2014

I read over the words that I've typed a few more times, pouring myself another drink in between. I think what I've written is the truth, but in all honesty, so much of that night and what happened afterwards is a blur, so I really can't be sure.

The only part of it I know for sure as the absolute truth is that it was all my fault.

I continue reading…

1985

After playing our Paris concerts Friday and Saturday night, we finally got home to my parents' house in the early hours of Sunday morning.

The flight home was made in almost complete silence. Maca

chatted with my dad on the plane, but he'd barely spoken a word to me since we'd been released by the police. Despite our lack of communication, our performances during the last two nights of our shows had been pretty spectacular.

Lennon, Billy, and Tom weren't speaking to Maca or me. Maca wasn't speaking to me, and I wasn't speaking to anyone, but the anger, emotion, and frustrations of those last few days' events had everyone performing at their unbelievable best. The crowds were insane and the label and promoters were over the moon.

When we walked into my mum and Dad's house, my mum was curled into my dad's armchair, while George and Jimmie were sleeping at each end of the sofa.

I pulled out a stool at the kitchen worktop and sat, looking at everyone in the living room.

Maca knelt down next to a sleeping Georgia and kissed her gently. I held my breath as her eyes fluttered open, my heart feeling like it had actually stopped as she backed away from him, getting as far into the corner of the sofa as her skinny frame would allow.

For a few seconds, her face crumbled and I thought she was going to cry from the hurt I'd caused, so obvious in her expression. Maca closed his eyes and I heard him whisper, "Georgia, I'm so sorry."

I closed my eyes as the room swayed. I needed to put everything right, but I had no idea where to start. When I opened my eyes, both my parents were looking at me, but I couldn't meet their concerned stares.

Georgia stood and gave a cuddle to my dad and Len. Totally ignoring me, she said, "Well, now you're all home safe, I'm going to bed. Night."

"Georgia, wait," I could hear the absolute panic in Maca's voice as he told her that they needed to talk, and I almost choked on the guilt that was rising higher in my chest. Why didn't I feel it that night? Why did I think that what they had was so unimportant?

I slipped out through the laundry and into the back garden to smoke a cigarette, shutting out the sound of Maca asking my dad's permission to go up to G's room.

As I headed back in through the laundry door, my mum's house phone started ringing. "Leave it!" Len shouted as I went to pick it up. I held my hands up in surrender to show him I wasn't gonna touch it and watched my dad pick up the extension in the living room.

"Frank Layton," he answered with the kind of authority that only my dad could at three in the morning, especially after the few days we'd just experienced.

He stayed silent for a few seconds, then his brown eyes slid to meet mine as I walked from the kitchen towards the sofa where Jim and Len were sitting.

"Excuse me?" my dad said into the phone. I watched as he pressed his left hand, palm down, to his forehead and dragged it down his face. My heart was beating so hard, it jolted everything inside of my belly and I felt like I was about to throw up.

The phone was suddenly ripped from its cord, flying across the room, bouncing off of the worktop I was sitting at earlier. "You fucker! You stupid, stupid fucker!" my dad roared. "You let someone take photos?" He took a step towards me, my mum and Len jumping up between us. Jimmie turned and looked up at me with her mouth hanging open and shook her head.

"What the fuck is wrong with you, boy? Did I teach you nothing? There's photos ... evidence, Marley, of you and that other skinny prick upstairs, snorting charlie off that little cunts tits and she's sold them to the fucking papers."

Jimmie stood and smacked me across the face. I flinched, but I didn't actually feel any pain. Aside from the guilt, I was numb.

"Th—this is too much, Marls. This is gonna kill your sister," Jimmie said quietly. "I hope you two are fucking proud of yourselves." She sobbed through gritted teeth, then turned and headed towards the stairs.

"Don't tell her, Jim," I pleaded, reaching out and grabbing her arm. "*Please*, don't tell her."

I'd managed not to cry so far, but the thought of my sister seeing pictures of what we were doing and with who ... *fuck*! I couldn't control my lip from trembling, just thinking about what it would do to her.

"Get your fucking hands off her," Lennon yelled, knocking my hand from Jimmie's arm.

"Are you gonna tell her Marls? Are you gonna go up there and tell George that there are pictures?" Len asked me.

"Well, someone needs to. The papers will be out in the next few hours, so she's gonna find out one way or another," my dad informed us.

Jimmie drew in a breath and headed up the stairs, Len following.

There was shouting. My dad, then my mum, rushed up the stairs next while I stood there alone for a few moments, too much of a coward to go and face my little sister.

When I got to her room, my dad was shouting at Maca to get out of our house while my mum was trying to calm him down. Jimmie was screaming at Maca, and all the while, George just sat on her bed, tears rolling down her cheeks.

She was too young for all this. She was sixteen, but at that moment, she looked like a little girl of about ten; frightened, bewildered, and overwhelmed with what was going on around her, and it was all my doing.

What could I do to make it better?

I was an eighteen-year-old kid, living in a grown-up world and I'd made a fuck up of adult proportions.

I could barely breathe. I'd never felt as alone as I did in that moment. I merely stood in G's bedroom doorway and sobbed.

Len dragged Maca out, kicking and screaming past me and finally, my eyes landed on hers. She'd been broken, and I swore to myself that I would never fuck up like that again.

Oh, how little did I know!

FOUR
1985

The following days were a frantic mess. Georgia didn't leave her room. Maca wouldn't stop ringing the house or knocking at the door, eventually deciding to sit outside all day in his car because Dad wouldn't let him near my sister. Then the press arrived, along with the fans, and I couldn't leave the house without them chasing me up the street.

Georgia had a week of exams and had to be escorted to and from school. I went up to her room with an apology all prepared in my head, but she just closed the door in my face without saying a word.

That Thursday, we flew off to Sweden for the last two shows on the European leg of our tour. They were a complete sell-out. Kombat Rock celebrated with a massive after-party on the final night, but we got on a plane and flew home in silence. Billy and Tom had their girlfriends with them while Lennon, Maca, and I were alone, none of us talking to each other or anyone else.

We got a much-needed break from each other the following week. Maca rang the house a couple of times for G, but Dad threatened to string him up by the balls with the phone cord if he didn't stop. I went to stay with my Uncle Fin for a few days because it was so hard being at home. The press were still hanging about outside, George still wouldn't speak to me, and then there was the guilt. Fuck, so much guilt it was eating me up. Watching Maca withdraw was bad enough, but standing in my sister's doorway, listening to her cry herself to sleep at night, just about broke my heart. She wasn't just dealing with the split from Maca. The fuckers at the newspapers had written some god-awful things about her, all of it bullshit. My parents had kept a lot from her, but the bitches at school took great pleasure in filling her in on what they were saying. Then there were the pyscho fans with their constant phone calls and hate mail, but one day came the blow that really broke her—a padded envelope full of dog shit, wrapped in a plastic bag. It arrived with a note…

For breaking Maca's heart, you little slut.
We hope the rest of your life is full of dog shit!

I was in my bedroom when she must've opened it. I ran to her room when I heard my mum shouting, reaching it at the same time as my dad got to the top of the stairs. G just sat on her bed, tears rolling down her face, her blue eyes wide as she looked between my mum and Dad.

"Why?" she cried. "Why? What did I do? I was a good girlfriend. I loved him—I loved him so fucking much!"

"Oh Georgia," my mum cried.

"Why do they hate me, mum? He fucked up, not me." She turned her eyes to me. "You … you and him. You did this, but it's me they hate. Why?" She cried even harder.

"Go downstairs, get Len on the phone. The label needs to pull their finger out and do something. I'm not having this. I'm not fucking having it," my dad spoke through clenched teeth as I watched mum rock Georgia in her arms.

"Move your fucking arse, boy, before I kick it down them stairs," he shouted.

The following day we were all at the record label, listening to the final cut of the album. It was releasing Monday, and our UK leg of the tour started off on Wednesday at the Palais on Shepherd's Bush Road. It wasn't a particularly large venue, but over the years, Maca and I had seen a lot of our favourite bands play there, including my all-time favourite bands like The Clash, The Jam, and we'd even managed to get in to see The Sex Pistols when we were far too young.

Watching The Clash perform '(*White Man) In Hammersmith Palais'* is a memory that would always stay with me. It's the reason my son is called Joe.

Maca's eye caught mine as our meeting was ending. We were all heading over to the BBC to do an interview to be aired on Sunday, and then to Capitol Radio for a live interview.

"Can we talk?" he asked me with a slight tilt of his head, which I'd assumed meant that he didn't want to do it in front of everyone.

Len watched our interaction and steered everyone out of the room, leaving me to face my best mate. My mouth was suddenly dry and my insides were not happy.

"Whatever issues you two have got going on, you need to get them sorted. Next week is the biggest in the history of this band. It's what we've all worked so hard for all these years, and I'm not letting the fallout from your fuck up affect the rest of us. Say what you've gotta say to each other and let's move on. I love you both, but could happily bang your heads together right now." Len looked at both of us, then left the room, calling out, "Sort it out, children. The limo leaves in fifteen minutes."

Len had just turned twenty-one, but he managed us like a seasoned pro, and I was so glad that he was a part of what we were about to embark on. I'd been so swept away with being a rock star while we'd been touring Europe that I'd not taken any notice of the legalities and formalities of releasing our first album; the rights, the royalties, or the obligations. I'd let it all slide, but not Len. He'd spent hours with Marcus, who worked for my dad, going through contracts and paperwork, finally getting us a better deal than we were initially offered.

One day, I'll thank Len properly, but right now, I need to let my best mate know how sorry I am.

"I'm sorry, Mac. I fucked up. As soon as George will let me talk to her, I'll explain everything."

I looked at him, and I mean *really* looked at him. He had dark circles under his eyes, his hair looked straggly, and he almost had a full beard going on. He'd even lost weight, all since we'd gotten home from France.

He took in a deep breath and shook his head. "We both fucked up, Marls. I should never have gone back to the room knowing she would be there. You're single, so what you do is up to you, but I should've known better. I've got G, and I love G. The last fucking person I should've been anywhere near is Haley fucking White."

I didn't agree with what he was saying, but I nodded my head anyway.

"Have you spoken to her?" I asked. He blew out a long breath that made his hair move, and I watched as his eyes filled with tears.

"Na, I can't get past your parents on the phone. I've sent her a couple of letters, but I don't know if she's read them."

He leaned back on the table we were all sitting around earlier; his knuckles white where he was gripping the edge so tightly.

"Did you hear what happened the other day, with the dog shit?" I asked him. It was a low move. I was trying to deflect the focus onto our crazy fans and away from my wrongdoings.

"Yeah, Jim told me. I put out a statement saying that what Georgia and I are going through is a private matter and in no way are events that happened in France her fault." He looked up at me and shrugged his shoulders. "Hopefully, that'll be enough to make the pyscho fuckers leave her alone." I nodded my head, but I doubted his statement would help. Our fans seemed to be out for George.

"She should be here, Marls. She should be by my side, by our sides. These are the biggest events of our lives, and she should be a part of it. I miss her so fucking much." Tears rolled down his cheeks, and I swallowed around the ball of emotion lodged in my throat as I watched him wip them away with the back of his hand.

"I don't know what to do. I'm so fucking lost without her. How the fuck could I be so stupid? The one person, possibly the only person G hates in the world, and I do something like that."

I close my eyes, blocking out the sight of my broken mate, the damage I'd caused, and the pounding in my head that hadn't stopped for days.

"She'll come around,"I eventually say. "You know what she's like when she's pissed off. Just give her a chance to calm down." I tried to reassure him, but he shook his head at me.

"Thing is, Marls, she's not pissed off or angry, she's broken. I fucking broke her … I broke us. She trusted me and I fucked it all up."

"She's hurt and she's angry, but she loves you—we all know that. Perhaps give her a bit of space to get her head around it all. Stop calling and just write the letters. Let her read them and take them in at her own pace. She'll get there, it's just gonna take her a while."

"I've got no fucking choice, really, do I? She's there and I'm here, about to head off around the country. I'm gonna ask her to come and see us play in Liverpool on my birthday. It's still a few weeks away and I'm hoping that she'll hear me out by then. Even if she can't forgive me, I still need to know that I can have her in my life—that she'll at least talk to me." His eyes were once again full of tears. "Coz this…" he gestures around the empty room, "this big fat nothing—this blank where she should be—is killing me, bit by bit, day by day. I'm fucking dying."

I felt like the biggest cunt on earth. My mouth watered a little bit from the sick feeling I had inside.

"I love you man, and I'll do everything I can to help put this right." I stepped towards him and wrapped my arms around him. It wasn't awkward, we'd done it before. We were artists; expressing our feelings came natural to us.

"I think you're gonna need to, mate. I think it's gonna take more than just me to convince your sister just how sorry I am."

FIVE
2014

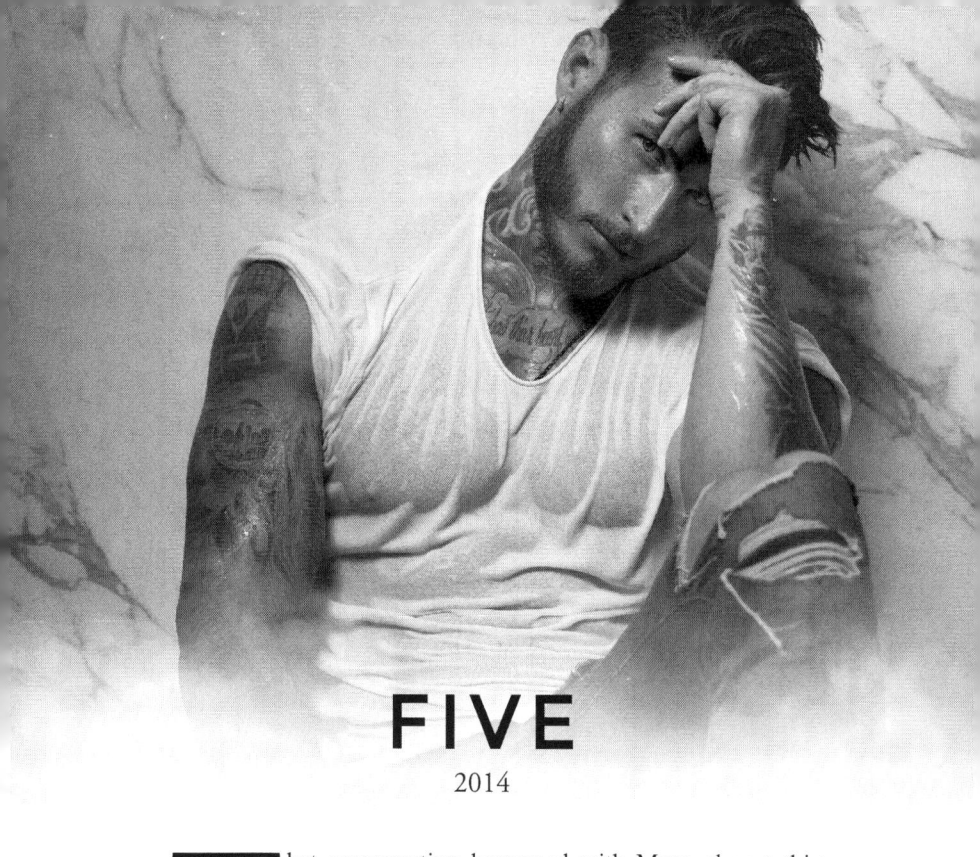

That conversation happened with Maca almost thirty years ago, but I remember every word, and I'll never forget the defeated look on his face.

The sun's up. I really shouldn't be drinking whiskey at this hour, but I can't be bothered to get up and go make coffee, and I doubt that Ash'll be up anytime soon.

I pour more of the amber coloured liquid into my glass, taking it and my laptop, over to the sofa. I sit with my legs stretched out in front of me, the computer on top of a cushion and sip on my drink as I start to read more of what I've written. When the early morning sun hits the crystal tumbler my drink's in, it occurs to me that the colour of the single malt appears pretty close to the colour of Sean's eyes. I get that usual stab of pain in my chest, which happens whenever I think of him. I stare at the computer screen in contemplative silence, wondering what sort of level my sister's pain is at these days. Does she feel that swift, sharp pierce with each memory of him, or has Cam done such a good job of putting her back together that it's more of a dull ache these days?

As happy as she is with her life right now, I know she still has the odd moments where she struggles. We were at a function for one of the charities our foundation supports a few weeks ago when a woman asked her how many children she has …

"Six," George replied. "Four growing up rapidly, and two angels in heaven with their daddy." I couldn't meet her eyes for a few seconds. After I swallowed down the lump in my throat, I looked up to find her staring at her plate while everyone else at the luncheon conversed around her, no one sure of the correct response to her reply. I reached out and took her hand.

"I don't know how you do it."

She gives me a half-smile and her blue eyes shine with tears as they meet mine.

"I have a family that gave me no choice. I have a husband that holds my hand every step of the fucking way, four beautiful children that make me fight for every breath I take, and I have Sean, Baby M, and Beau to make proud. I'm just doing my best."

"And he would. He'd be so fucking proud of you, G." She wipes a tear from under each of her eyes.

"You have no idea how often I question that Marls," she whispers.

"Well, you shouldn't, not ever."

"Shit," she says quietly, leaning down and pretending to look for something in her bag while blowing her nose.

"Subject change Marls, please?"

She sits back up and smiles at the blonde sitting across from her, "So, Gwen. How's the fashion line going? I bought a beautiful bag of yours the other day."

I think George has learnt better than any of us, how to hide the pain memories of Sean and her babies must inflict.

The door of my office slowly opens and my wife blinks her way through it. Her blonde hair is a bed-headed mess and she looks sexy as fuck. She squints through her brown eyes at me and licks her lips.

"Marls? What are you doing? It's not even six yet. Have you been down here all night?"

Her voice is croaky from sleep and my dick likes it. Fuck, I love her. I had no idea about being in love or relationships when I met her, and my feelings scared the crap out of me, but we'll get to that later.

"C'mere." I hold out my hand to her but she shakes her head no.

"What's that?" She gestures with her chin towards the laptop.

I arch my back in an attempt to stretch and I yawn. Putting my glass down on the floor, I look up at her. My wife owns some of the most expensive bits of silky and satin shit ever created on this earth, but she's standing in front of me wearing a white Ed Sheeran T-shirt of mine, her long legs crossed at the ankles as she leans on the door frame.

"Are any of the kids home?" I ask, not that that's going to stop me from doing what I want to do to her.

"No. Connie stayed at Annie's last night. I don't think any of them are coming home this weekend."

Joe has his own place in Hoxton in East London, and Annie and her boyfriend, Fletcher, have just moved into Sean and mine's old place in Docklands.

My kids are all doing well. Joe, despite starting an engineering degree, just couldn't stay away from the music and his band, Paywall, are just about to start a world tour as a supporting act to some big American band I can't even think of the name of ... Date The Parson or Pastor, or something like that. They're a little too grungy for me but have a considerable following.

I've lived a relatively quiet life since Carnage split up. We never wanted the press attention when we were together, so I definitely didn't want it once we parted, especially around my kids.

People eventually worked out who they were, but they'd all grown up to be well adjusted young people.

Our three, and Len and Jimmie's four had all gone to the same school out in the Essex countryside. They were a tight little bunch and always looked out for each other; pretty much the way I grew up with my brothers and sister. All of them had gone on to various universities around the country, except for Paige. She'd dropped out and had been modelling since she was sixteen. I'd often see her face on a billboard if I were out and about. Even at home, she'd pop up on the telly in an ad occasionally. Paige was the absolute spitting image of George and Tallulah, her devil child daughter. Don't get me wrong, I love Lu—we all love Lu, it's impossible not to. But she's Georgia's child and shit, don't we know it. My ol' man just laughs when Lu is having one of her 'moments.' He shakes his head and tells George, "Well, you've finally met your match, George—got the daughter you deserved there. Good luck with that one."

I don't pity Cam one little bit when the hormones kick in with that one.

"Marley?" Ashley's voice brings me back. "What are you reading on the laptop, and why are you drinking whiskey this early?"

"I've written the book," I admit, and her eyes widen.

"What, already? You've written a book in just one night?" She takes a step towards me. I stare up at her, my mouth hanging slightly open as I think about how I'm going to explain this.

She stops and folds her arms across her chest, her tits moving up and I must look like a goldfish as I open and close my mouth a couple of times.

"You'd already written it, hadn't you? All this time and you'd already done it."

It's not a question, her voice is accusatory. Her eyes fill with tears, and now I hate that I went behind her back.

"C'mere. Please, Ash. Just come over here, sit on my lap and let me tell you about it."

I need to hold her, feel her warmth and breathe her in. She shakes her head, and a tear hangs from her bottom lashes.

"What's in it Marls? What've you kept hidden from me?"

Nothing.

Everything.

I close the laptop and swing my legs around, planting my feet on the hardwood floor. Ash takes a step away from me, and I don't like it, not one bit.

"Don't fucking step away from me," I tell her. She raises her eyebrows and gives me the look.

I've pissed her off, big time.

"Are you fucking kidding me right now Marls? You've secretly written a book about *your* life behind *my* back, and you want me to come and sit on your lap?"

I shrug my shoulders and smile my best smile. "Well, I'd rather you sat on my face, but you might not be able to understand what I'm saying through a mouthful of fanny, so lap will do… or dick. Dick would work." I wiggle my eyebrows.

She ain't having it … *Not. At. All.*

"What did you do? What happened that's so terrible you've never told me?" her jaw trembles as she asks.

"No, no, baby. Nothing, I just …" I lean down, pick my glass up from the floor and start to drain the contents. Before I finish, Ash knocks it from my hand and it spins through the air before hitting the floor, bouncing once and cracking into pieces as it lands.

"Don't fuck with me Marley. If you've done something …" She pauses and swallows. I regard her in somewhat stunned amazement.

She's so fucking beautiful when she's angry. She's stunning, and she's mine.

"If you've fucked about and then written about it in this book before telling me, I'll walk. I'm telling you now, straight up. I'll fucking walk."

"No, Ash, it's nothing like that. I swear on my life that's not it." I rub my hand over my stubbled chin, keeping my eyes on hers as she moves and flops down on the sofa next to me.

"Then tell me what the fuck is going on, coz right now you're scaring the crap out of me."

I let out a long breath. "I've included lots of stuff, lots of things that no one but me and Maca knew about; private conversations with my family, with you. I just found it easier to write it how it actually happened, and now I have to read it all back and decide what parts to take out."

I turn and look at where she's sitting beside me, her long legs curled underneath her. She tilts her head back and stares up at the ceiling for a few seconds, then turns to look at me.

"Well, why don't you read through it, let me read through it, then take out the parts that you think should never be seen by anyone but your wife, from whom you keep no secrets if you like your balls being attached to your body." She raises her eyebrows and leans slightly towards me for emphasis as she says this and I fight not to smile.

"Then, let everyone who this may affect read it and let them have the final say in what *should* or *shouldn't* be made public."

Ash looks at the world from such a simplistic viewpoint. She's always so good at coming up with a practical answer to things. I'm an over-thinker where Ash is a rational thinker. Did I mention that I love this woman?

I lift her onto my lap so that she's straddling me. Sliding my hands under the T-shirt she's wearing, I hold her naked bum cheeks in each of my palms. "What would I ever do without you?" I ask, rubbing my nose against hers as I talk.

"Don't let me read that book, Rock Star, and you'll soon find the fuck out."

I raise my hand, and my fingertips skim over her bareskin until I find the parts of her I really want to touch My thumbs brush across her nipples. She leans into me, arching her back so that her tits push forward. I kiss her throat, grinding my hips into her as she gives out a small moan.

"Stop trying to distract me," she fake complains, while really, she's loving everything that I'm doing to her.

"Baby, I need you to be perfectly clear about something," I tell her.

She gyrates against my cock, and it takes all of my willpower not to pull it out of my boxers and bury myself balls deep inside her, but I need to tell her the truth first. I can't have her hurt and upset, worrying that I'm hiding something from her.

"Eyes, Ash, look at me."

She instantly meets my gaze. We look at each other in silence. "There are things that I've said and done in my life that I'm not proud of. I've been in denial about some of them since the moment they happened, while others I've tried to justify by convincing myself that I was young, stupid, and didn't know better."

I tilt my head slightly and break our connection for a few seconds. "Writing this book, reliving these situations, has helped me come to terms with…" I take a deep breath. "To take ownership of some of the shitty things I've done in the past. I just need to make sure that I'm ready for the rest of the world to see me for what I am … who I was." I shrug and let out a long sigh.

"There's a lot of sex, drugs, and rock and roll in there, babe. There's some explicit shit, but you know all that, about all of that."

"Is there stuff about us?" she asks. "I don't think, I mean, the kids, Marls. I don't want them reading shit about me." She leans her forehead against mine.

"No, I wouldn't share stuff like that. Our life is our life, and it's got fuck all to do with anyone else." I look up at her and smile. "There is a bit about when we first met though; about what I thought, what I was feeling, and even about the shitty way I behaved in the beginning."

"You were a prick—a flash fucker."

"Yeah, I was, and then you happened, baby," I tell her, unable to contain the smile that memories of our first encounter evoke.

"Pffftt, you were a prick for a long time after that too."

"Cheers, babe." I feign offence but know that what she's saying is probably true.

I tuck her hair behind her ear on one side. "It's not a pretty story, Ash. My life before you was exactly what you might expect from a single bloke in a successful band, but it's not just that." I stroke her cheek with the back of my hand. "There's other people's secrets in there and they're the things that I need to decide what to do with, but you have nothing to worry about. There may be a few things I've written about that may come as a surprise to you," I shrug my shoulders, "and some you may have already guessed at, or even known before me. Just give me this weekend to get it read and then I promise I'll let you take a look." She nods her head.

"So, we gonna fuck, Rock Star, or go back to bed for a bit?" she asks.

Did I mention that Marley loves Ash?

SIX

After the exertion of giving my wife a couple of orgasms and her returning the favour by sucking me dry in the shower, I go back to bed while she heads out for a day of shopping with Jimmie and George.

I eventually wake up just after noon. After a quick coffee and the bowl of porridge Ash insists I have to eat every day, I go back to the study and start reading…

1985

The next few weeks were the stuff of dreams. Our album broke into the top ten on the Tuesday charts, just a day after its release. It was number one by the following week.

The entire UK tour was a sell-out, and extra dates were added where possible.

Maca's birthday arrived, but there was no sign of Georgia.

Until that point, we had been on our best behaviour—back to our hotel rooms, or just to the bar for a few quiet drinks, but not Maca. He just went back to our room alone as soon as each show ended.

Kombat Rock were still the headline act, but everyone knew it was us that people were turning out for, and that pissed Rocco off on a nightly basis.

He had kept his distance since Whorely-Gate but was still partying up in his room or backstage after each show.

On the night of Maca's birthday, the entire crowd sang an impromptu rendition of 'Happy Birthday' as we returned to the stage for our encore. After Maca said a few words, thanking the crowd for turning out, buying the new album and their support in general, it meant that KR started their set about fifteen minutes late.

As we left the stage and they headed on, Rocco called over to Maca.

"Hey, birthday boy." We all turned to look at him.

"You want me to call up Haley so you can celebrate with some coke and a side of rape later?"

Maca never got a chance to reply. Tommy stuck the nut on him and put him straight on his arse. For anyone Non-English reading this, Tommy head-butted Rocco, knocking him onto his backside.

The fight that ensued after was just what we needed as a band. We once again became one, a unit, all looking out for each other. It was over as quickly as it began, but I landed one punch right to Wayne Allen, KR's drummer's jaw, and dodged all that were thrown my way. Maca was dragged away by Len before he had a chance to do anything. Rocco tried to stand, but Tom caught him in the gut and sent him to the floor again. Billy ended up the worst, with their guitarists both landing punches to his pretty face before one of our roadies stepped in and broke things up.

We were all eventually hauled back to our changing room where Maca was pacing and shouting at Len that he'd had enough and wanted to quit.

Tom pulled a bottle of bourbon from somewhere and we passed it between us, each taking a swig.

We were silent for a few minutes. My hand hurt, but I wasn't about to admit that in front of Len. Billy's nose was bleeding and Tommy had a wet towel wrapped around his knuckles. The door flew open and Jim walked in. She'd sort of fallen into the job of Len's assistant since she'd joined us and the label had put her on a wage. She mainly dealt with the press and booked our hotel rooms so everything was ready when we arrived at the next town.

"What the fuck just happened?" Her eyes met Lens, "You okay?"

"I'm fine. It's this lot that think they're Rocky."

She lifted my hand and looked at the split skin on my knuckle. "Go run that under the tap and I'll get some ice. Otherwise, you won't be able to play tomorrow night."

She followed me into the bathroom and placed a small hand towel under the running cold tap, then shoved my hand under the flow.

Jim and I didn't talk much anymore. Things hadn't been great for years, but they'd been even worse since Paris. We both stared down at my hand as I held it under the running water.

"Have you spoken to George at all?" I eventually ask. She shrugged her shoulders before answering.

"A few times, but it's hard, ya know?" She gestured with her chin out to where the boys were.

"She doesn't want to hear anything about him, the band, or—"

"Me," I finished for her.

"Look, Marls. She's hurt, and she's angry. She'll come around eventually. She's just really struggling right now and dealing with all this shit in her own way."

I nodded my head as my belly did continuous forward rolls.

"I don't think she's ignoring you as such," she continued, "it's just that talking to you, it's like talking to him and she's not ready for that." I licked my bottom lip a couple of times to try and hide the fact that it had developed a wobble.

'Don't cry. Don't you dare fucking cry.' I repeated over and over in my head.

"This is George we're talking about, Marls. She's never experienced things not going her way in life." She swallowed and I knew she was struggling not to cry too. "Just give her time, yeah?" I wasn't entirely sure who she was trying to convince at that moment.

"I'm gonna go and clean Billy's face up before Linda gets here and freaks the fuck out. I'll get you some ice once I've done that." She leant up on her tiptoes and kissed my cheek.

"You know you can ask me about George anytime, Marls. If you want me to pass on a message or anything, just let me know, yeah?" Her brown eyes looked over my face while her hand rubbed up and down my arm in what I assumed was a gesture of reassurance, understanding, and friendship? Who knew, but at that moment, I felt that it was more than I deserved.

We all ended up back in our room, blind drunk that night. Even Jimmie and Len joined us, as well as some of the crew. Maca spent a lot of the night drinking whiskey and crying on Jim's shoulder, while I joined one of the lighting engineers in the bedroom with a girl he had picked up. He willingly shared her and his illegal substances with me.

Things changed after that night. We were tighter than ever musically, despite the celebrating we did after each show. Our days were filled with television, radio, magazines, or newspaper interviews. On our nights off, we tended to go off and do our own thing, but it was getting harder and harder to do anything or go anywhere without being recognised.

I loved the attention, the women that threw themselves at us, but the rest of the band, not so much. Tom and Billy were still with Cheryl and Linda, the girls they'd been with since school. They were with us most of the time, both of them forgoing careers to travel with the band. The label insisted they keep a low profile around the fans and the press, but when we were back at our hotels, they were there, waiting for their boys. They partied with us sometimes, but usually they'd just disappear off to their rooms.

Since the success of the album and the fact that the tour was a sell-out, Len had negotiated for us to each have our own rooms and after a few drinks, Maca usually disappeared off to his alone, every night.

We spent some of our days writing, but because the UK was so small, we didn't use the tour bus like we had in Europe, so the opportunities to collaborate didn't present themselves as often.

Spending so much time alone, Maca was writing a lot, and although a lot of it was a bit mushy for me and obviously about George, by the time we had worked on it together and tweaked a few things, we were coming up with some fantastic stuff. We knew that it wouldn't be long before we had enough new material to write another album.

Our UK tour was due to end in late July. A couple of festival dates were added to our schedule in August, and studio time was booked for the beginning of September.

Maca finally cracked and ended his self-imposed exile and celibacy on Georgia's birthday.

I had been home a few times during the tour, but she still refused to speak to me, closing the door in my face every time I went to her room. I don't know if Maca was still trying to contact her, he never said, and my dad never mentioned he was still being a pest when I spoke to him.

The label rented us a flat to live in close to the studios when the tour ended, so we spent the end of that summer making music, eating, drinking, and partying together.

We had found a quiet little pub around the corner from our flat in West London and had turned it into our local. It was the last place that anyone would think of looking for England's biggest band, so we could spend our evenings having a few drinks, a game of pool, and even grab some lunch or dinner if we hadn't previously eaten.

I'm not sure how word got out, but when Maca and I arrived at the pub one night, there were four girls standing at the bar and we knew that it was us they were waiting for.

Tom and Billy had headed straight off as soon as we had finished recording. We had a day off the following day, so they had driven back to Essex to see their girls.

I stood at the bar, waiting for our drinks while Maca racked up the pool balls. I watched as one of the girls approached him. She was tall. Even without the shiny patent leather heels she was wearing, she had a cracking pair of legs. Her dress was a royal blue colour, skin tight, and made from this stretchy waffle patterned material. Funny how after all these years I should remember all that. I think it's because Jim had a similar type of dress and we had all commented on how good her arse looked in it, earning me a smack upside the head from my brother.

"They've been asking what time you usually get here." Jock, the landlord told me, placing two beers on the bar. "I told them I didn't know what they were talking about," he said with a nod as I handed him a tenner.

Jock knew who we were. His daughter had recognised us when she was working behind the bar one night and sent him over for autographs. We'd asked them to keep it quiet, donated to buy the pubs football team a new kit and given Jeannie, his daughter, a pile of signed merchandise and an album.

"Cheers, Jock. How long they been here?" I asked.

He looked at his watch and gave a small shrug. "Since about six. There were two more, but I had to throw them out for being underage," he said quietly in his soft, Scottish accent.

"Those four have got ID's, but they've all only just turned eighteen, except for the brunette talking to Maca, she's older. You boys watch yourselves."

"We will. Cheers again, Jock."

I headed towards the pool table, smiling at the three girls trying to artfully prop themselves at the bar and note that they all looked a bit … soapy, as my dad would say. That didn't mean they were covered in bubbles if that's what you're thinking. It meant that they looked like they could do with a good wash, and I don't care what ID they'd flashed at Jock. Not one of them seemed to be more than fifteen or sixteen.

Now I know I was only just nineteen myself at that stage, and a bit of an animal, but jailbait was not my thing, and something I was extra careful about after Whorely Gate. Not that she'd been underage or anything. She was actually a few years older than us, but after that incident, the label had sent one of their female execs to give us 'The Talk.' Basically she told us to always practise safe sex, always make sure we were aware of the age of consent, depending on which country we were in, (especially places like the US, where it can vary from state to state), and never, ever let anyone film or take pictures of you in the act.

It hadn't slowed down the amount of women I'd slept with, but I was very aware of *who* I slept with and tended to go with the girls that looked older rather than younger, just to be safe.

I passed Maca his drink and held mine up so we could say cheers. We both knew what the date was. He'd been very quiet and looked extra sad. I silently wished my sister a happy birthday and took a swig from the bottle.

"This is Siobhan," Maca introduced her, tilting his beer bottle towards her, then to me.

"Siobhan, this is Marley." She looked me over, every inch, with the most amazing blue eyes.

"Siobhan." I nodded towards her. "Isn't that Irish? Sounds like it should be spelt S, H, E, V, O, N, but instead has a B or some random letter in it?"

"That's right," she said with a smile and proceeded to spell out her name. She was definitely older than the other girls were … much more groomed and better put together. Having a guess, I would've said she was about twenty-five. Older than most of our fans, but an average age for a groupie, although I wasn't sure if that was what she was. I was suddenly on alert.

"So, what's a nice girl like you doing slumming it in a pub like this?" I asked her.

"I could ask you boys the same thing," her reply was followed by a nervous laugh.

"Press," I said to Maca as he leant across the pool table to break.

His head swung up to look from me to the woman standing between us. He looked back along the pool table and potted a stripe. Standing up straight, he gripped the cue with both hands.

"Fuck off," he said to her, gesturing with his head towards the door.

"Wh-what?" She looked between us, her mouth hanging open.

"Oh come on, boys, give a girl a break," she pleaded.

"Give you a break?" I asked. "Do you have any idea the damage you lot have done to us, my family, and our band?"

She looked down at the ground for a few seconds, then back up, looking back and forth between Maca and me.

"Look, I know some of it was a bit rough on your sister, but that wasn't me. I'm not that kind of reporter."

"There's only one kind of reporter," Maca told her, "the cunt kind. Now, fuck off before I get Jock to throw you out."

She held her hands up as if she was surrendering.

"Look, I'm gonna go to the bar and get a drink. I just want a few words from you. I don't wanna ask questions about what happened in France or anything to do with that." She looked between us. "Just a little something about the success of the album, the sell-out tour, and how you're coping with it all. Maybe something about what you've got coming up next year? Please, just think about it?"

We both stood and watched her hips sway as she walked to the bar. I had to adjust my dick in my jeans. I hadn't had a shag since the tour ended, and I was more than a little desperate.

"She's got a nice arse," I said quietly.

"What the fuck has that gotta do with anything?" Maca turned back around, taking his second shot and missed it. "Your spots."

"I know. What if we do her a deal?" I pot one spot, followed by another.

"What type of deal?" he asked, his eyebrows drawn together.

I stood up straight and passed him the cue back after missing my third shot. "I dunno ... a blowie or summit? I'm gagging for a shag."

"*You're* gagging for a shag? How d'ya think I feel? It's been four months and three countries since your sister left Spain, and I last got my leg over."

I took a step back from him. "Dude, do you know how seriously happy my life would be if I never had to talk, or even think about you shagging my sister again? Like, ever?"

He laughed and took his shot. It was good to see him smile. I know that he'd made a point of making sure that Jimmie knew the phone number and address of our new flat, but there had still been no contact from George.

"Was she doing anything special tonight, d'ya know?" He took his shot while asking. I knew it was so that he didn't have to make eye contact with me as he talked about her.

"My mum said that she didn't want any fuss made. She has college tomorrow." I tell him what I know.

"How's college going for her?" He took another shot, still not looking my way.

"All good, I think. You know George. She and Len are the brains of the family."

Unable to avoid me anymore, his eyes met mine. "She seeing anyone?"

"I honestly don't know, mate. She's not spoken to me since she left Spain. Jim, Len, Mum, and Dad, only tell me what she wants me to know."

He looked down at his feet before picking up his bottle and finishing the contents.

"I really fucking miss her," he stated, his eyes shining with tears.

"I know you do, mate, but without sounding harsh, she's getting on with her life and I think it's time you moved on with yours."

He nodded his head before potting every stripe on the table, and then the black. "Yeah, I'm beginning to think that too."

Game over.

SEVEN

1985

Siobhan appeared beside us at the pool table with drinks for all. I'd watched her as she spoke to the little group of fangirls while she was waiting at the bar, and they were trying to edge closer.

"Where'd you pick up your posse, Mothercare?" Maca asked.

She shrugged. "They're not my posse, they're yours," she replied, winking at him. She let out a long breath and pointed to a table away from the bar.

"Look boys, I'll be totally honest with you here." Maca pulled out a chair for her at the table, ever the gentleman, despite calling her a cunt before, but whatever. "I'm still earning my stripes for this game and I get sent out on all the shitty jobs. One of them is to have a wander past all the big recording studios, see if there's anyone interesting coming or going." She sipped from her bottle and I couldn't help but watch the way her lips wrapped around it, the way her throat moved as she swallowed.

"Swallowed … *fuck*. Just that word was making me hard. Maca kicked me under the table.

"Anyway," she wiped her mouth on the back of her hand and I thought I groaned, or even came just a little teeny, tiny bit. She frowned and looked at me, shaking her head.

Head. See, that's how my brain would function. I needed sex on a regular basis. I'd gotten used to sex on the regular, so to go without for four weeks was a long time—a long, long time.

"I've learnt over the past few months that the little teenybopper fans also do the same thing, hang about outside the studios, I mean." She looked between the both of us again. "Now I don't know where they get their info, but I'm telling ya boys, they're better than MI5 or the CIA, or whoever the people are that know about shit."

I watched as Maca ran his hand over his beard, then his thumb over his bottom lip. Siobhan watched him and fuck if she didn't make a little noise like I'd just done watching her swallow.

"Anyway …" She turned from him to me, her cheeks flushed, so I deliberately licked my lips, seeing as she seemed to have a thing for them. Her eyes traced the path of my tongue.

"So," she said a little too loudly, before clearing her throat, "that little lot were all hanging about outside the studio you've been using this morning. They told me it was you boys that were in there and that they had it on good authority that you had been using some pub on a regular basis." She looked over to where the girls had moved to the next table over. "I offered to buy them all a drink if they told me the name and just took a chance that you'd come in here tonight. Getting a few words from you boys could be the break I need. Just a few words—"

"Get your gang over here," I told her.

"What?" she asked, frowning in confusion.

"Call them over here. We'll sign some stuff for them and then I want them gone. I don't know what ID they showed Jock, but there is no way any of those girls are eighteen."

Maca remained silent, sipping on his beer and observing, the way he often did.

"Yeah, I think they all have older sisters or friends, or whoever they borrowed their ID's from. I don't think the landlord looked at it too closely, apart from the two that were obviously only about twelve." I watched as she chewed nervously on her bottom lip. "So, if I get rid of them, you'll talk?"

I shrugged my shoulders. "Maybe we could come to some arrangement," I told her.

She nodded her head, licking her lips and looking between us again. "I'd be happy with an arrangement."

"Good, now call them over."

We signed autographs, kissed cheeks, and posed for pictures. Then we gave them twenty quid and told them to go to the corner shop and buy some sweets and lemonade, and to stay out of pubs until they were eighteen.

We spent the next couple of hours drinking beer with whiskey chasers, and I even played Siobhan at pool, beating her arse while Maca stared at it.

I know that it wasn't very gentlemanly of me, but I'd been buying her doubles every time I'd been to the bar, and I knew that she had to be at least a little bit drunk.

"So, let's talk business. This arrangement, I'm assuming sex will be involved, and that's the reason you've been plying me with doubles?"

Maca spit out his drink and I laughed. I liked her. She was up-front and surprisingly honest for a journalist.

"Which paper d'ya work for?" I asked.

"The Sun," she replied with a hint of apology in her voice. "Look, I tell ya what. Don't tell me anything, forget about all that. I've had a drink and I'm horny. I'm not one of your stupid little fifteen-year-old fans. I'm a grown woman, I'm twenty-eight years old, and I haven't had sex in nine weeks. I fancy a shag and I fancy shagging both of you, at once."

"Fuck," is what came out of my mouth.

"If you're twenty-eight, how come you're only just starting out as a journalist?"

Seriously, that's all that Maca got from what she said? Her age, and not what was on offer?

She slumped back into her chair before continuing. "I did a teaching degree, got a job teaching at primary level, and just found that it wasn't my thing. I've always loved English, I have a degree in both language and literature, and I have a passion for music. Music journalism seemed like an option and now here I am, trying to earn a name for myself with that *one* big story."

"By fucking your way through every band?" I asked her.

"No, I've never done this before … well, not with anyone in a band before. Not anyone famous, at least."

"So you've had a threesome before?" I asked, looking across to Maca as I did. I was trying to gauge his reaction, but of course I couldn't, he was completely neutral.

"Yes, I've had a threesome before. Two girls, one bloke, and me with two blokes. Had a foursome once too. I've been to uni, boys; weed, whiz, trips, they all help to lower your inhibitions."

We were still teenagers. A threesome was being offered up on a plate. What would you think the end result was gonna be?

"Jock, can you come over here a second please?" Maca suddenly called out to the landlord.

Jock threw the cloth he permanently had in his hand over his shoulder and walked over to our table. "What can I do for you boys?"

"This is Siobhan," Maca said, pointing to the girl. "She wants to come home with me and Marley. I need her to tell you right now that if she comes home with us, she knows it's gonna end up with us having sex with her."

Well fuck! My boy was back and he was finally zipping up his pussy and bringing his balls to the party.

Siobhan's mouth dropped open while Jock raised his eyebrows and tilted his head. He gestured towards her with his chin. "You know what you're letting yourself in for if you go home with these wee rascals lassie?"

She nodded her head. "It was me that offered, Jock, so yeah, sex is what I'm hoping will happen with both of them."

"Well, there ya go. I'm your witness, boys," he shook his head as he spoke. "I'm in the wrong fucking game here. I can hold a tune, ya know? Does that get me an invite? Go, have fun," he said over his shoulder before heading back towards the bar.

We bought a bottle of whiskey on the way back to our flat. It was actually more like a house, being the top two floors of a converted three-story house in Notting Hill. We all had a bedroom each, as well as two full bathrooms and a third toilet on the lower floor, just off the open plan; living, dining, and kitchen.

We'd only just started to see the royalties coming in from the tour and album sales. The figures were blowing us all away.

Maca and I were off to buy new cars the next day and we'd all look for our own places to live once the album was finished. We were hoping to have it released in time for Christmas, and a tour had already been lined up for Australia, Asia and the US, starting in February of the following year.

All that, and what was about to happen with this woman, seemed surreal. It was all more than we could ever have dreamt of, but for myself and Maca being the youngest, I sometimes felt a little overwhelmed at the speed with which things had moved.

"Take her to my room," I told Maca. I knew that all his lyrics, notebooks, and diaries were usually spread everywhere in his room, and he was pretty private about all that shit.

I felt a sudden twinge of guilt as thoughts of George flashed through my mind. Most of the new album consisted of songs about her, or heartache in general, but both musically and lyrically, it was our best work to date. Angst seemed to equal hits.

I gathered three glasses from the kitchen and headed upstairs. When I walked into the bedroom, Maca was sitting with his back against the headboard, legs stretched out in front of him. I put the glasses down on the chest of drawers and poured us each a drink.

"You know, Len will flip if he finds out about this," he stated the obvious.

"Then we won't fucking tell him," I replied. "I've lived like a monk since we came off tour, and you've behaved like a nun since George, so fuck it. What's the point of being in Britain's band of the moment if we can't get the occasional shag now and then?" He looked back at me, glassy-eyed. Shit, I shouldn't have mentioned George.

I turned to pass Maca his drink, just as Siobhan walked out of the bathroom that he and I shared. She was stark bollock naked. Taking the glass from my hand, she looked between Maca and me. "Chop chop, boys. Clothes off."

I pressed play on the boom box sitting on my clothes chest and '*Orgasm Addict*' by the Buzzcocks blasted out. We were all silent for a few seconds before bursting out laughing. Well, at least it broke the ice a little bit.

I poured more whiskey into the glass that Siobhan just emptied and passed her another. She kissed me, full on the mouth, and I ground my already hard dick against her. She broke away and walked over to the bed where Maca was sitting with his fingers laced together, hands behind his head. He didn't take his eyes off her as she stalked across the room towards him. He reached out his hand and took the drink from her, knocking the lot back in a few gulps.

I unlaced my Doc Martens and kicked them off, pulled my jeans down and my T-shirt over my head. By the time I looked up, Siobhan was straddling Maca on the bed and he was sucking on her tit while digging his fingers into her arse cheeks. She broke their kiss so that she could pull his top over his head. I downed my drink and brought my empty glass, along with the bottle, over to the bedside table, placing them down before crawling up behind Siobhan to join the party.

'Lavender' by Marillion played as I lifted Siobhan from Maca and turned her around to straddle me. He climbed off the bed and turned the light off, keeping the lamp on, before taking off the rest of his clothes and joining us.

I've seen Maca naked countless times before now. We've crossed swords pissing in the same toilet and fucked different girls on the same bed at the same time in the past, but we'd never shared a girl. I was fine with it, I just hoped that he was too.

He kissed along Siobhan's shoulder from behind, his hands slid around to cup her tits. She continued to grind into my naked lap. The length of my dick was between her pussy lips, the tip pressed against her clit. She broke our kiss and turned her head towards Maca and I watched as their mouths collided, tongues tangling. I lowered my head and took her nipple into my mouth, Maca pulling on it at the same time. My tongue lapped at his fingers. It wasn't intentional. I had never in my life done anything like that before, and I knew with one hundred percent certainty that I wasn't gay. Writing this doesn't make me uncomfortable, as I'm clear on that. We were just three people enjoying each other's bodies, caught up in the moment and just going with it.

I drew Maca's middle and index finger into my mouth and dragged my teeth along them and Siobhan's nipple. She let out a groan and when I looked up, they were both looking down at me.

"Fuck, you two are beautiful." She sounded almost reverent in her tone. She moved her hands to the backs of our heads and simultaneously pulled both of our mouths to hers.

Lips, teeth, and tongues clashed, tangled, danced, and assaulted. My hands instinctively rose and I gripped each of them by the hair.

My heart was racing and my stomach felt like a Russian gymnast had taken up residency inside it. Backflips, forward rolls, it was all going on. And my dick? Fuck, that thing was like steel.

Siobhan shifted and suddenly I was chest to chest with Maca, dick to dick. Her legs were open, and we had a thigh each between them while she rubbed her wet pussy against us. Our heads were both turned towards her, our mouths still on hers, and each others.

Simply Red was singing about money being too tight to mention when Siobhan reached between us, taking our dicks in each of her hands, then wrapping her hands around both, bringing them together.

Maca watched as she lowered her head, taking us both into her mouth at once. My hips thrust forward of their own volition, and Maca slowly raised his head to look at me. His chest was heaving, eyes shining brightly. I reached out and pushed my hands through his long hair, pulling on it so that his head tilted back slightly.

"It's just sex," I told him. "It's just sex. Fucking. It means nothing, it changes nothing." I was trying to convince him as much as I was trying to convince myself.

He twisted his head, forcing my fingers to give up their grip on his hair. Grabbing Siobhan by the back of hers, he pulled her up to face us. She had spit or jizz, or a combination of both, all over her chin and around her plump lips. We both dove in at the same time to kiss, lick, and suck it off.

"Jesus, you two are good." The girl was amazing for our egos. She had no idea that we'd never done this together before.

"You got condoms?" Maca asked.

"Yeah, in the drawer." I gestured with my chin. Maca reached over, refilled, and passed us our drinks over before pulling a box of condoms from the drawer.

"Do you have any KY?" Siobhan asked.

"You want anal?" The surprise was obvious in my voice. Girls had been a bit reluctant to give that up the last few years, since AIDS had reared its ugly head.

"Don't you?"

"As long as I'm giving, baby. Don't do the taking."

"What about you, pretty boy?" She looked over to Maca.

"I'm a giver, not a taker, sweetheart. Nothing gets past my chocolate starfish unless it's exciting."

I spit my drink.

"Dude, you seriously just called your arsehole a chocolate starfish? Have you inspected it that closely to know that's what it looks like?"

"Well, I was gonna call it Marley, but I thought that might cause confusion."

"Ha, you're funny." I couldn't think of anything to come back with before Siobhan interrupted.

"So, you two … you've never … with each other, I mean?"

"Fucked?" I sounded all high-pitched and indignant.

"No, love, never," Maca answered. "Although he is known as cuntface to many, so I suppose it would be understandable if I was to stick my dick in his mouth one of these days."

Ha, so my best mate's suddenly got his balls back and became a comedian.

Fucker.

"You're spoiling your image as the dark and brooding member of the band, Maca. Fuck off, and stop trying to be funny," I told him. He flipped me his middle finger and blew me a kiss.

I turn to Siobhan. "No, darling. In answer to your question, we don't fuck each other. What you saw just then was us putting on a show. The girls love it. You loved it, right?"

"Fuck yeah."

"Well, let's move things along then. "You up for DP?"

"I just asked for the KY, didn't I?" I liked this girl … woman, actually. I kept forgetting that she was eight, nine years older than us. She knew what she wanted and wasn't afraid to ask. Why couldn't all women be like that? It'd leave them satisfied more often and make blokes lives so much easier.

"You fuck her, Marls, I'm happy with a blow job," Maca said.

"You've not got a dose of anything, have you? I just had your dicks in my mouth. If there's any chance you have, I need to know."

"Sweetheart, despite what you might read about me, I've had just one girlfriend in the past few years," Maca admits with a pissed off edge to his tone.

"Don't mean you weren't fucking other people."

"I was only fucking *her*, and she's *never* fucked anyone but me."

Okay, la, la, la. I didn't need to be hearing that.

"So what? Me and what happened at the hotel in Paris, they're just one-offs, are they?"

Maca reached out and grabbed her by the hair, pulling her face towards his. "I never fucked anyone in Paris, but because of the bullshit you and your mates printed about me and what supposedly happened, we're no longer together. I'm now single, so whatever goes on here now, between us, it's of no consequence to anyone." He threw me a condom. "Now, you gonna suck my dick or what, Siobhan with a B?" he laid down on the bed as he asked.

We were all silent, just the sound of Annie Lennox, singing about angels in the background.

I fought with Ash over giving our daughter that name because I didn't want it tainted with the memory of that night, but if you'd ever tried to argue with Ashley about anything, then you'd understand why I always lose.

I watched as Maca started to stroke himself and I did the same before sliding the condom over my dick.

Siobhan leaned forward and wrapped her hand around his dick while I reached around her body and with my middle finger, started rubbing circles over her clit.

"Move closer to him," I said into her ear. I was kissing, licking, and dragging my teeth over the curve of her neck and across her shoulder. "Open your legs wider and lean forward." She turned her head towards me. Her porcelain skin was flushed and her blue eyes were shining.

"I want you in my cunt."

For a boy who was only nineteen, hearing those words caused me to nearly come all over her back, but instead, I pushed her face first onto Maca's dick and rammed inside her from behind.

We saw Siobhan on a regular basis after that. Sometimes it'd just be me and her, sometimes just her and Maca. She brought her friend Julia along occasionally and all four of us would end up in bed together. Jules was a budding photographer, so as a thank you to them both for the no strings sex, we did an exclusive interview and photo shoot on our last day of recording at the studios. Jules went on to become one of the world's biggest rock photographers, and Siobhan an editor of a celebrity magazine. Our paths crossed many times over the years, but our arrangement never lasted beyond that year and our meetings after that were always friendly and professional. Siobhan sadly died of ovarian cancer in 2010, and it was the reason the UK's biggest ovarian cancer charity received a large donation from the Triple M event every year. Maca liked Siobhan, and I know he would've wanted money raised in his name to be sent in that direction.

Despite the album and a single from it being the UK's Christmas number one, the actual day that year was horrible. I asked my parents if Maca could still come for dinner, same as he'd been doing since he was about fourteen, but they'd said no. My mum actually seemed surprised that he even wanted to because by that time, unknown to all of us, Haley the whore had already started to weave her web of deception and my mum truly believed he had moved on.

Maca refused to spend the day with his mum and her husband, so instead, he stayed alone at our flat, writing songs.

He gave me a gift for George before I left to go to my parents'. It was odd, not waking up at their house on Christmas morning, but I just couldn't face the atmosphere. The less time I spent around my sister, the less guilt I felt. The last time I'd seen George, she was painfully thin and looked almost drained of life. She spoke when spoken to, but treated me like I was invisible.

I slipped the present under the tree when I got there, not wanting to make a big deal of it in front of my parents. Later, when Jimmie, Len, and Bailey arrived, the last of the presents were given out, but it wasn't there. I found out years later that my mum had removed it and hidden it from George, thinking it would upset her. It was a silver bracelet with a 'G' hanging from it, matching the necklace he'd bought her a few years before. When it came out that my mum had played a hand in keeping them apart all those years, she admitted that like the letters and everything else Maca had sent, she'd returned it with a note, once again asking him not to send her gifts or attempt to make contact. He finally took notice after that. My mum returning his Christmas gift was what made him stop sending the letters and parcels, but it didn't stop him from buying her things or writing her letters, he just never *sent* them.

Georgia has a huge crate somewhere, full of Maca's letters to her that were either never sent, or returned. It also contains his diaries that he always kept, the notepads he always had with him, and old video cassette tapes of interviews and performances where he either directly or indirectly mentioned her. There were music tapes of songs that we'd never heard, and songs that he wrote but never allowed anyone else to read or see.

Ash told me that after a few previous attempts, George has finally decided to start working through and cataloguing the contents of the old packing crate. I'm hoping that one day soon, she'll want to share anything that's relevant, but at the same time, I'll totally respect her decision if she wants to keep it all private.

I sometimes wonder how Cam copes with it all. My sister is obviously head over heels in love with the bloke, but at the same time, we all know that nothing or no one would ever be able to replace Maca and what they had together. I think her and Cam work because he's never tried to do that. Where George and Maca's love was intense, bordering on obsessive, their love is different, much easier to be around. It was like her and Maca needed each other more than air. I don't know how to describe it, really, but that's how it came across as an outsider looking in.

All of this is probably going to get deleted from the book. It's just my thoughts and really fuck all to do with anyone else. I'm writing it because it helps me sort shit out in my head. It helps me make sense of thoughts and feelings I had about certain situations back then, all these years later.

Maca had the right idea, keeping a diary and always scribbling in those notebooks of his, but when we meet again, I'll never admit that to him.

After sitting through a strained Christmas dinner, mostly spent watching my sister move food around her plate, rather than attempting to put any of it into her mouth, I made my excuses and left. As I was putting my coat on in the hallway, my mum came out and asked me what Maca had done that day.

"He's at our place alone, mum. You said he couldn't come here, remember?"

She nodded and sucked in her cheeks as she swallowed.

"Marley," she said my name as if it were almost a plea. My sister's obvious heartbreak was taking a toll on her, like Maca's was on me, and I suddenly needed a cuddle from my mum.

My mum had always been tiny, but she felt frail when I wrapped my arms around her. I breathed in the Dior perfume that she'd always worn and held her close as she rested her head on my chest.

"I miss you, Marley. I hate what your sister's breakup has done to our family." She said quietly, her voice humming through me.

"I know, mum, I know, but Maca's as much of a mess as G is. I just wish there was a way we could get them to talk to each other."

She stepped back so that she could look up at me. For a few seconds she looked like she was going to say something, but she didn't. If only she had let me know that Whorely had been to see her, the truth would've come out so much sooner. Maca and G would've sorted their shit out, got married, had babies, and gotten the happily ever after they both deserved.

"I don't think your sister is ready to see him yet. She leaves the room if his name even gets mentioned on the telly. It breaks my heart to watch her, Marls. I'm her mum and I don't know how to fix this, to fix her. I just want to wrap her in cotton and protect her from the world. I'm so bloody angry with that boy." She was crying as she spoke, and I was struggling not to.

"Mum, please don't be angry with Maca. It was my fault more than it was his," I pleaded with her.

"Yeah, well, I'm angry with you as well. Drugs Marley? All those drugs, and what about that AIDS that they're all dying of. Sex and drugs ... I don't like it, not one little bit. I know you're a big rock star now, but you're still my baby boy. I wish you were all little again, all here with me, tucked up in bed at night by seven so I knew exactly where you were and what you were up to." She swayed from side to side as she spoke, reminding me of when she rocked me as a kid and I loved it.

"I'm sorry, mum. I've been good lately, I promise, and I'm always careful. No condom, no shag. The label has given us the talk about AIDS, unwanted pregnancies, girls trying to trap us, all that stuff, and we follow the rules." My cheeks burned as I spoke that way to my mum. It was Christmas day, and that wasn't really a conversation I wanted to be having with her ... ever.

"Is Sean really at your place all on his own?" She was obviously happy to change the subject too.

"Yes, mum, he really is."

"Well, just you wait a minute while I plate up a dinner for the boy. I hate to think of him not getting a proper Christmas lunch today."

Less than an hour later, I pulled onto the drive of the place I currently called home. It wasn't not home, but now, neither was my parents' place. As long as there was animosity between me and my sister, I wouldn't feel comfortable there. I felt a pang of loneliness uncurl from my belly and snake its way into my chest. I didn't belong anywhere then.

I turned off the engine of my new car and looked across at Maca's black version of my red Escort XR3i. We had the colours custom made to match the band's logo. His was black with a red trim and interior. Mine was red with a black trim and interior. Maca had an older version, one that my dad had recently sold for him, but our babies were brand spanking new.

I banged my head on the steering wheel of my brand new car and decided to stop feeling sorry for myself. I was better off than a lot of people, and if I felt lonely then, how the fuck would Maca be feeling?

When I let myself in the front door of our place, it seemed to be in darkness, but I could hear the faint sound of a guitar strumming. I put Maca's dinner and dessert in the kitchen and made my way up to our bedrooms. His door was open and he was sitting on the bed with his legs out in front of him, back pressed against the headboard, strumming on his acoustic.

There were papers spread all around him, lyrics and music sheets, and a pencil tucked behind his ear. He had shaved off the beard that he'd had most of the summer, but his hair was still long. My heart sort of hurt as I heard my sister's voice in my head, always telling Maca how much she loved his hair longer.

He sensed me watching him and looked up at me.

"All right?" I asked him.

"I'm good." He leaned across and reached for a bottle of Jack sitting on the chest of drawers next to his bed. He took a swig straight from the bottle then offered it to me. I stepped forward and took it from him and brought it to my lips.

I watched as he pulled the pencil from behind his ear and crossed something out on a piece of paper, then wrote something else. He then picked up a music sheet and made changes to that.

"There's a dinner downstairs for you if you're hungry. My mum sent it. I have a present for you too, probably the usual."

His eyebrows shot up. "Shit, I didn't think I was your parents' favourite person. I wasn't expecting a present … I didn't get them anything."

I shrugged my shoulders. "They think of you as family. Families fuck up, and they know that."

He nodded his head. "Shame your sister didn't see things that way." I remained silent, not knowing how to reply.

"What's that you're working on?" I asked and gestured with my chin towards the papers spread all over the bed.

"Something new I've written, but I just can't get the tune right. I need you for that."

Maca was great with the lyrics, but I was just as good, if not better than he was with the music. It was why we worked well together over the years. Billy and Tom never wrote lyrics, but they were both amazingly talented musicians and could turn my humming of a tune into an intricate musical masterpiece within minutes. We'd grown and evolved over the years, and although we'd improved massively, we still had a lot to learn.

"You wanna work on it now, or d'ya wanna eat?" I asked.

"Go get your guitar. I'll eat later."

I carried the Santa Sack, (my mum still insisted on putting all our presents into it), to my room and emptied the contents onto the bed.

Despite the money I was earning, my parents still bought me the usual socks, underwear, and aftershave, as well as a checked Ben Sherman shirt. I had a vintage looking, Small Faces T-shirt from Jim and Len, along with a rare European import copy of *'That's Entertainment'* by The Jam. Bailey had given me a bottle of bourbon.

As I reached for Maca's gifts from my mum and Dad, I noticed another gift, still wrapped. I recognised Georgia's handwriting on the tag instantly and I was shocked to see that it was for me. I tore apart the wrapping and opened the cardboard pouch, tipping it upside down and shook it over my bed. A black leather guitar strap slid out. It had red stitching and the heart-shaped crying eye, which was the bands logo,

stitched into the leather, along with the letters B B M.
I read the message on the tag properly.

> *To my Big Brother, Marley,*
> *Merry Christmas!*
> *Your Little Sister, Georgia*
> *XXXXX*

I ran my thumb and finger over the leather, my emotions at war inside my head and my heart. I wanted to be angry at my sister for shutting me out, for not being prepared to talk to me or hear Maca out, but at the same time, when I saw her, it was then that I understood how hurt she was and I knew that she just needed time to heal. The small gesture from G gave me hope that one day I'd have her back in my life.

I folded up the strap and placed it carefully in my drawer, grabbed Maca's presents from the bed, and headed back to his room.

I sat on his bed and rolled a joint as he unwrapped the standard socks, boxers, and aftershave that my mum and Dad got him every year.

When I'd finished rolling and lit the spliff, Maca passed me a sheet of A4 paper with words written all over it. I moved up the bed and leaned back on the headboard next to him so that I could use the light from the lamp and start to read the words to the song that he'd written.

Seaside Heart

My heart, it's like a seaside town.
On a dark, winter's day,
The shutters are down. The crowds stay away.
Its beat it resounds, resembling a military tattoo.
But devoid of all feeling, since there wasn't you.
My heart, it's like a seaside town, when the wind blows hard.

And lightning strikes, all emotion charred.
It's bleak and it's lonely.
It's cold and it's bare.
The sun doesn't shine.
Now that you're not there.
I miss you so much,
That I can barely breathe.
Without your warmth, taste, and touch,
I'm brought to my knees.
Like a seaside town,
I'll wait for my sun.
Keep my love boarded up
Till the day that you come.
I'll wait and I'll hope.
I'll beg and I'll plead.
Worship at your feet,
If that's what you need.
Just like the sunshine,
I know you'll return.
Our bond too strong,
For you not to be mine.
Until that day happens,
When the sun shines bright,
I'll keep your heart in my hands,
My memories held tight.
Like a seaside town,
I'll always believe
In the love that we share,
Of you and of me.

I ran my hand over my face, struggling to find the right words to respond. I took a draw on the joint before passing it to Maca. I scratched at my head and let the effects of the weed slalom through my brain.

"I don't know what to say," I mumbled on an exhale. "Fuck, mate, that's fucking brilliant. I—I honestly—I have no words."

We sat in silence for a few long moments. I'd had one question going around in my head and although I wasn't scared to ask it, I was terrified of the answer.

"Is this really how you feel?" I eventually asked, already knowing what the answer would be.

"Every second of every day."

"Fuck, Mac ... how? I mean, shit. How do you get through a day? How can you live your life feeling like this?"

He took a long draw, then passed the joint back to me. I stared up at the ceiling as I waited for his answer. I heard him blowing out the smoke he'd inhaled.

"I can't, not anymore. I'm done, Marls. I love your sister, I'll never stop loving her, but I need to let her go. If I don't, it's gonna kill me."

I turned my head towards him, my mind racing with what that meant.

"You've not ... I mean, you wouldn't? Shit." I sat up and tried to get what I wanted to say straight in my head.

"You wouldn't do anything stupid though, would ya, mate?" Despite feeling boneless and light, my heart was racing as I asked.

"You mean top myself?"

"Yeah. Yeah, that's exactly what I mean, Mac. Please tell me that's not something you'd do." I smoked the joint down to the roach and put it out before turning to look at him.

"Do you never think about dying, Marls?" The gold and amber in his brown eyes apparent as the light from the lamo caught them. I laughed, rather than answer his question.

"What are you laughing at?" he asked. "I thought you was asking a serious question, ya dick."

I laughed again. "Sorry, sorry. I was just thinking that your eyes look pretty in the lamplight."

"My eyes look pretty?" he asked on a chuckle, and it felt good to see him smile for a beat.

"Yeah, sorry," I tell him with a head shake.

"You're fucking mad. You're not gonna make a pass at me or anything, are you, Marls? Coz no offence, mate, but you're just not my type."

"No, Mac, I'm not gonna make a pass at you. Sorry, I'll just shut up."

"Yeah, I think that'd be for the best."

"Although, we've never spoken about what happened with Siobhan that time."

He let out a long sigh and turned his head to look at me, raising first his eyebrows, then his shoulders in a shrug. "What's there to talk about? Like you said, at the time it was just sex. We were both fucking the same person at the same time. It's happened since then, and I'm sure it'll happen again, but it's not like we fucked each other. I love ya, Marls, but I have absolutely no desire to fuck you. No offence, mate."

I smiled at him. "None taken. Your eyes still look pretty in the lamplight though."

"Fuck off being a dick," he said with a grin. The mellow from my joint now superseded by the buzz I felt at making him smile.

"And stop avoiding the question I just asked."

"What was the question?" .

"Do you ever think about dying?"

I decided to go with honesty.

"Not often, no. It's crossed my mind occasionally, especially when we were on tour and I was using a lot, but now that I've stopped all that ol' bollocks, no, not often." I paused for a few seconds, actually thinking about my own death.

"I could never put my family through the consequences of me doing something deliberate. I hate to think what that might do to them," I tell him honestly.

"Yeah, well, that's probably the difference between me and you."

"What is?"

"You've got people that give a fuck. Who gives a shit about me?"

"Oh, charming. So what about me and my family? What about Tom, Bill, all of our fans? Dude, how can you lay there and even say that?" Anger started to boil away at his crass comment and I actually wanted to punch him. "I know things have been shit between you and my family lately, but they still love you the same. Even George, despite everything, still loves you."

"Yeah, perhaps they do, perhaps she does, but not enough to get me an invite to Christmas dinner and not enough to reply to one of my letters, or to pick up the phone and say 'let's talk.' Not enough for much, really."

"I'm not defending her, but she's hurt and angry, and perhaps we all have to accept the fact that she's never gonna forgive us. I hope that's not the case, but I don't think George is gonna be getting in touch anytime soon, but that's not to say she wouldn't care if anything happened to you."

I didn't want to tell him that she gave me a Christmas present, as I thought he'd take it one of two ways. He'd either be really hurt that she didn't get him anything, or he'd see it as G's walls coming down. And as much as I would've hoped that'd be the case, I didn't know if she'd ever be ready to give Maca another chance.

"Think about it. If she's this devastated at the thought of you with another bird, can you imagine what state she'd be in if anything ever happened to you?"

He shook his head. "Probably the same way I'd feel if anything ever happened to her."

"Well, there ya go then. Now, stop talking shit and let's get a tune going for this lyrical masterpiece you've spent the day writing."

Seaside Heart was the fastest and biggest selling single of 1986 in five countries.

EIGHT

1986

Our tour of Australia, Asia and the US kicked off in February of 1986. We started in Melbourne for four nights, then up to Sydney and Brisbane. Because of the demand for tickets, we agreed to fly back to Sydney and Melbourne and played an extra two nights in each city. I paid for my parents to fly out and they watched us play in Sydney. I arranged for them to also tour the rest of Australia, staying in the Blue Mountains—Melbourne and Surfers Paradise. It felt good giving back and they seemed to love Australia as much as we all did. It does, in fact, remain one of my favourite places on earth to visit.

Asia was hot and sweaty and the fans were crazy, but still, we loved every moment. It was our first tour as the headline act and we were having a blast.

The label had sent Milo to be our minder and we were under strict instructions to stay out of trouble, which we managed to do, at least while in Australia and Asia, but then we got to the good ol' US of A, and things went downhill rapidly.

We arrived in April and played the East Coast first, then snaked our way across the country, playing inland and then back down to coastal towns.

The crowds were insane and the after-parties rocked. No offence to any American college girls reading this, but shit, ladies. You girls are just insatiable. I don't know what happens to the females of America when they're let loose at college, but let me tell you, they do not hold back. Every time we played at a venue where there was a big college nearby, we had the best of times. The amount of sex on offer was off the charts. Hell, even our tour bus driver was getting in on the action.

The further West we travelled, the more the girls wanted to party with us and by party, I mean fuck with us, with each other, in front of us. Whatever way there was to fuck, they wanted to try it and we were *very* willing to oblige. I mean, we were only too happy to represent our green and pleasant land, and that we did!

We rolled into San Diego on a warm and sunny Thursday morning. We were due to be playing at Qualcomm Stadium both Friday and Saturday nights so we were booked into The Grant Hotel, in what we were told was Downtown San Diego.

The hotel had been newly refurbed and felt like a palace after so many weeks on the tour bus. Maca and I shared a two bedroom suite; Tom and Billy, another.

Jim hadn't joined us yet in the US. She'd been with us through Asia and Australia, but was running our offices while Len joined us on tour, and quite frankly, he was a fucking nightmare to deal with when Jim wasn't around. They were engaged now and planning on a big wedding in a couple of years' time, when things would hopefully quiet down a bit for the band. They were good together, really good. Len was generally a nice bloke and a great manager, but he did tend to get a bit stressed about things, mainly mine and Maca's antics when we weren't performing. Well, it was just our serial fucking that pissed him off. He worried all the time about girls going to the press and selling their stories. We had so many talks about Carnage being a brand and we were ruining its reputation with our behaviour. We knew he was just doing his job, but at the end of the day, what was the point of being in one of the biggest bands in the world if we couldn't behave like the rock stars we were? Maca and I were busy building our reputations and the more we fucked, the more drink and drugs were involved in the wild parties we were either attending or throwing in each town we visited. The more people talked about us, the more the women wanted a piece of us. This was the last few months of my teens. I was living the dream and I had every intention of seeing them out with a bang ... several bangs, actually.

We checked into our rooms, had a quick shower, then headed off for a game of golf with Len and a couple of suits from our record label. We had slept on the bus as we travelled through the night and were feeling pretty fresh that morning. The label execs talked about how our plans would fit into there's for the next two years, and where they thought changes could be made. We ate lunch with them at the course's club and talked more business. This side of things bored me senseless, so I left most of the talking to Len and a little to Maca. We signed a few T-shirts for them and a few for some blokes who'd just come off the course and had kids that were fans, but mainly we drank.

We had a night off that night and we fully intended to enjoy the day and whatever the night would bring. As Milo drove me, Maca, and Len back to the hotel, Len began to lecture us.

"I know you have a night off tonight, boys, but I think it'll be best if you just stick around the hotel. You have a photo shoot and an interview to do at eleven tomorrow and you'll need to be fresh for it."

I watched the traffic pass by from the back of the enormous four-wheel drive SUV we were being driven in. I didn't want to argue with my brother, but there was no way we were staying in tonight. I remained silent, expecting Maca to do the same, so I was surprised when I heard him ask, "Best for who, Len?"

I looked over at my brother as he turned around in the passenger seat to face us in the back.

"Do what?" he questioned.

"Us staying in on our night off ... who will it be better for?" Maca expanded on his previous question.

"I think it'll be better for everyone, Maca. I'm not saying don't kick back and enjoy a few drinks—"

"Then what are you saying, Len?" he asked again, his tone sharp.

"What's your fucking problem, mate?" Len asked him. I remained silent, catching Milo's eye in the rearview mirror. We both raised our eyebrows in surprise at Maca's vehemence. I was usually the one who argued with Len. It was me and him that Milo, Maca, and the rest of the boys were continually separating before we could do each other any real damage.

"You're my fucking problem, Len. Just coz Jim's not here, don't take your shitty attitude out on us."

"That's fucking rich coming from you. George has been missing from your life for almost a year and you've never heard me complain about the shitty attitude you've had since then."

Maca kicks the back of Milo's seat, once, twice, three times.

"Stop the car. Stop the fucking car! I need to get away from this cunt," Maca shouted.

"Pull over," I told Milo. "Nice one, dickhead," I said to my brother.

Milo pulled over, double parking, causing drivers behind to pull around us. A few of them bibbed and I gave them the finger in return as I climbed out of the car after Mac.

I followed him along the street for a little ways, pulling my cap down low so you couldn't see my face. It was two in the afternoon and hot as fuck.

"Slow the fuck down, Mac. I'm melting here." He turned around, lifted up his sunglasses and looked at me. Before he could say anything, I jumped in. "Don't frown at me with them big bushy eyebrows. You seriously need to get plucked or shaved, or whatever before the photoshoot tomorrow, dude." His frown deepened.

"Fuck off, Marls." He looked over my shoulder and his frown became a smile. I turned and followed his gaze to a bar across the street. "I need a drink," is all he said before making his way across the road.

The place was busy for a weekday afternoon; a mixture of construction workers, blokes dressed for the beach, as well as a few girls in shorts and vests.

We ordered a pitcher of beer and a couple of whiskey chasers from the pretty barmaid and sat ourselves at the bar, thankful that we hadn't been asked for ID. This being twenty-one to drink nonsense had caused us issues since we'd been there and I blamed that law entirely on the reason why so many parties ended up back on the bus or in hotel rooms.

After knocking back the whiskey, followed by two glasses of beer each, Maca finally spoke.

"Your brother's a dick."

"No," I replied. "My brother's a good bloke, but our manager is the dick."

"Either way." He let out a long sigh and raked his hand through his hair. "She's been out of my head. I've *kept* her out of my head for these last few weeks at least, and then he has to go and say shit like that."

"I know, mate, it was wrong. He shouldn't have said that. I'm sorry."

He poured us each another beer and held his fingers up at the barmaid who I'd noticed had been watching us for a while, and asked her for two more whiskeys. She came over with a bottle and topped up our glasses.

"You boys are asking for a headache in the morning if you keep going at this rate." She said with a smile, looking between us.

She was pretty, in an all-American kind of way; tall, blonde, tanned, perfect teeth, and clear blue eyes. My cock twitched and I smiled back at her.

"Well, is there anything that you can suggest that's gonna give us less of a headache and make us feel equally as good? Maybe something a little less legal?" I asked her.

That wiped the smile off her face and I watched her throat move as she swallowed, hard. *Bingo.* Miss USA knew exactly what I was after and where I could get hold of it.

We'd smoked a lot of weed and popped a few pills, even tried some LSD while we'd been on tour, but we'd stayed away from the marching powder. Yet right now, we needed a quick fix and couldn't afford to be hungover in the morning, making cocaine the perfect drug of choice for the evening.

"You guys cops?" she asked me outright.

"No, love," Maca said. "We're tourists on holiday, over here from London, and we'll make it worth your while for a few grams of good quality white stuff." He made a point of being nonspecific about what we were after, just in case she did recognise us and went running to the papers.

She flicked her hair over her shoulders and looked up and down the bar.

"I get off in ten minutes. I'll make some calls then, but it'll cost ya." She narrowed her blue eyes at us, probably trying to work out if we had money or not. We showered and changed after our game of golf and were both wearing cut off jean shorts—don't judge, it was the 80's remember—T- shirts, and flip-flops.

"Not a problem, love," Maca told her. "We got a really good pound to dollar exchange rate, so we're feeling flush," he told her with a wink. I watched in silence as she visibly melted a little and then leaned across the bar towards us.

"Flushed enough to share with me when I get off?" she asked quietly while we both stared down her vest at her tits.

"We'll share with *you*, if you share with *us*?" Mac told her. She smiled her Hollywood smile and looked up at both of us through her lashes.

"What would you like me to share?"

"Yourself," Maca said bluntly.

"Well, I could, or I could call some friends up and we could all have a good time together."

I was suddenly very hot, and very hard. I took off my cap and ran my hand through my hair. It was either that, or I pulled out my dick and wanked myself off all over her face from across the bar, which I was pretty sure would've been an offence in America, and probably the rest of the world. So, I decided to keep my dick in my pants, at least for a little while longer.

An hour later, we were the proud new owners of five grams of class A. We'd done two lines and played three games of pool, and we were flying high and feeling fine.

Like I'd said before, don't judge. It was the 80's, and we were rock stars living the dream. Underage drinking and snorting coke was practically written into our job descriptions.

Almost.

The barmaid approached the table we were sitting at with two friends in tow—one blonde, one brunette. "Hey, boys. I called up some friends. A few more are on their way."

Being the perfect pair of shit-faced English gentlemen that we were, we both stood up. "Ladies," Maca bowed slightly for effect.

"Holy fucking shit," the brunette yelled. "It's you! I'm, I-I mean, you're them," she continued to stutter.

Keen to shut her down and not draw attention, I stepped in. "Indeed, we are *them*, ladies, but we'd like to keep that between *us* if you don't mind."

"Who are you?" The barmaid asked.

"That's Marley Layton and Sean McCarthy from Carnage," the blonde that had just arrived said with a smile.

"Shit, I knew I recognised you from somewhere. I can't believe I asked if you were cops," she laughed.

"Neither could we," Maca told her.

"So, what are your names, ladies?" I asked.

"I'm Cindy," said the barmaid.

"Of course you are," I replied, "And I bet you two are Tressy and Barbie." They all look at each other, confused. "If I press your belly button, does your hair get longer?" I asked the brunette.

"Dude, how high are you?" Maca asked from beside me, but the girls start to laugh as the penny dropped.

"Barbie, Cindy, and Tressy are all dolls." The brunette explained to Maca.

"How the fuck do you know that?" Maca gave me a confused look.

"Because my sister had one of each when she was a kid."

Shit.

He let out a breath as if he'd been punched. Fuck, why did I mention my sister?

"And my eagle-eyed action man used to kidnap them on a regular basis, making them strip off and shag him before he would let them go," I add for the sake of some humour.

"You're sick," said Cindy.

"Actually, I'm Marley, and that's Maca. You're Cindy and you two lovely ladies are?"

"I'm Mel," said the brunette.

"And I'm Dawn," said the blonde that wasn't the barmaid.

They were both pretty—not as pretty as Cindy, but good looking enough. Mel was short and curvy with dark hair, skin and eyes. Dawn was tall and slim with broad, athletic shoulders—a swimmer if I'd had to guess. She had zero curves and not really my type, but right then, sex was sex.

"So, ladies. How'd you fancy coming back to our hotel for a few drinks?" I asked them with a smile.

After waiting around for three more of Cindy's friends to arrive, we made it back to our room in two taxis. Word must've gotten out on where in town we were staying. There were a few fans and a couple of photographers waiting outside. For some reason, Maca decided to put on a show for the snappers and posed with his arms draped around two of the girls.

After signing some autographs, I eventually dragged him inside and up to our room, where we found Milo sitting on a chair outside.

"What the fuck you doing here?" I asked.

"Len's orders," he grunted, apparently not happy. Milo was big, and I mean a huge bloke. There was no way that his arse could be comfortable on that chair he was sitting on.

"What exactly were Len's orders?" Maca inquired.

"That you two go to your room, alone, and don't slip back out later tonight." I looked across to Maca and we both started to laugh.

"Tell Len to either come join the party or go fuck himself," Maca told him as I let all eight of us into the room.

"You coming in, fat boy?" I asked Milo.

"I'll give you fat boy, you little prick. Fat or not, I'll put you on your skinny white arse."

I shook my head. "You've gotta catch me first," I said with a smile and slammed the door shut in his face.

He knew I didn't mean it. It was the usual banter that went on between the two of us. I was fully aware of the fact that Milo Williams could probably kill me with one hand tied behind his back.

Maca was on the phone when I turned around, ordering up room service and less than five minutes later, two bottles each of Dom Pérignon, Smirnoff Vodka, and Jack Daniels bourbon arrive.

Maca pressed play on the music system. Run DMC and Aerosmith's *'Walk This Way,'* blasted out and the party got started. Alcohol was consumed, coke was lined up on the coffee table and snorted, weed was smoked, and less than an hour later, I had my fingers inside one girl while another rode my face, and a third sucked on my dick. After pulling my fingers out of Cindy, I lifted the girl off my face by her hips and looked around the room. Despite having two bedrooms, we'd all ended up spread over the two Queen beds in my room.

Maca was flat on his back, two girls kissing his mouth and stroking his cock simultaneously as a third girl sucked on his balls. I sat back against the padded headboard and lit a joint.

"You girls ever fuck each other?" I asked Cindy.

"All the time," she said with a lazy smile. She was lying next to a girl named Lori at the end of my bed. Without taking her eyes off me, she pulled Lori in for a kiss. Mel moved from beside me and crawled between Cindy's legs. I watched as Lori straddled her face and Cindy's arm snaked around her as she slid two fingers inside her arse.

"Mac! Maca, you seeing this." He sat up and blinked a few times before looking at me with a smile.

"Fuck," he said with a laugh.

Without interrupting the rhythm Mel had going with her tongue and her finger inside Cindy, I pulled her hips up in the air towards me and opened her legs. She was wide open, wet, and glistening. I needed to fuck her. Before I could move and get into position behind her, she stopped what she was doing and looked over her shoulder at me, shaking her head.

"No, I want you both at the same time." My eyes darted to Maca who was still watching. He nodded his head ... of course he would.

Van Halen was asking *'Why Can't This Be Love'* from the other room and I smiled, thinking to myself that the world would be a much happier place if they all just took a few drugs, had some good sex, and chilled the fuck out.

Maybe that's what Len needed in his life.

"Come over here, sweetheart," Maca said, holding his hand out to Mel.

"Ladies, you wanna go join the party on that bed for a while." It wasn't a request, and the three girls, whose names I didn't know that were all over him a minute ago, stood and made their way to my bed as I took Mel by the hand and walked over to where Maca was lying flat on his back, waiting, stark bollock naked with his dick hard on the other bed.

"You done this before?" he asked Mel. She shook her head no.

"Me and Cindy with other guys, but never me with two guys. I want to though."

"You got lube?" He asked. She shook her head no again and his eyes turned to me. I shrugged my shoulders and headed into the bathroom. The only thing I could find that might be useful was the complimentary hand cream. I headed back out to the bedroom where Mel was sliding a condom onto Maca, who was now sitting back against the headboard. I threw him the hand cream and he laughed.

"I'm improvising," I told him as I climbed onto the bed.

Mel tore open a condom wrapper and slid it over my rock-hard dick as I watched.

"Turn around," Maca ordered her. "Get on all fours, face the end of the bed and open your legs so that you're straddling both of us." She did as she was told, putting her in a position that meant she was wide open to both of us.

"I fucking love being me," I said to no one in particular.

I watched as Maca pushed two fingers inside her cunt and she instantly pushed back on them.

"You got any preferences, sweetheart? Do you care which one of us fucks what?" I asked her.

She looked over her shoulder at me. "You in my pussy, Maca in my ass."

I took the hand cream and unscrewed it, squeezing the citrusy smelling lotion onto the crack of her arse. Maca watched me as I dragged it down and circled my fingers around her arsehole. Again, she pushed back, wanting more. Maca adjusted his position and pushed all four of his fingers inside her at the same time I slid my index finger into her arse.

"Oh. Oh god," she moaned. "Fuck, it's too much. I'll come if you keep doing that."

"That's okay," I told her. "We'll soon make you come again."

We both worked our fingers inside her at a faster pace. The harder we finger fucked her, the harder she pushed back. I watched as her spine curved and arched.

Her skin was beautiful, flawless, and the colour of a milky coffee. I added another finger and she let out a hiss, but still pushed back, taking all that we were offering her.

"That's it, baby, let it go," I encouraged her. She was moaning and sighing things that we couldn't quite make out. We didn't look at each other, our concentration solely on making the girl come, and when she did, it was with a loud groan and convulsions that we felt move through her whole body. I leaned forward and kissed her arse cheek as I slid my fingers out of her.

"That was beautiful, Mel. I'm gonna go wash my hands and then we're gonna fuck you senseless, make you do that all over again."

When I came back from the bathroom, she was kneeling between Maca's legs and kissing him on the mouth. I climbed onto the bed next to them.

"Turn around, baby. Hook your legs over Maca's." She turned around as if she was sitting on his lap and opened her legs, hooking them over each of his, which were bent and raised at the knees.

"Can you feel his dick, baby?"

"Yeah."

Maca sat up and adjusted his position slightly, looking down into his lap.

"Oh fuck," she sighed, tipping her head back and biting down on her bottom lip.

"You all right?" he asked her.

"Yeah, yeah, I'm good. More, give me more."

He moved again and this time, it was him that let out a groan.

"Fuck, that feels good," he said through gritted teeth. Mel curled her arm around his neck and pulled him in for a kiss.

"So good, so fucking good," she whispered.

He laid back, taking her with him; her back to his chest. His knees were still raised, legs spread apart, with Mel's legs hooked over his thighs. He gripped her hips for leverage and moved her slowly up and down.

We'd never done it like that before. We usually took the girl on her side or with her face down, us in the same positions as we were in then, but her with her arse in the air? That was different.

I climbed between both their legs and sucked on the nipples that Maca was pinching, before kissing her on the mouth. I held myself up with one arm and guided my cock inside her with my free hand.

"Fuck, you're tight." I hissed. All I got in response was a moan from both her and Maca. Maca moved and I could feel him, just a thin layer of skin and latex between us. I moved again, sliding inside her till I was balls deep.

"You okay?" I asked her.

"Move," she said quietly. "Both of you, move. Fuck me."

I didn't need any more encouragement than that. I thrust and ground against her hard. It took a few attempts, but we got our shit together and found a rhythm that worked. We were musicians, for fuck's sake. We had it covered. Maca thrust so hard that his hips were lifting off the bed. I was grinding back until I got that all too familiar tingle at the base of my spine.

My eyes met his and I watched as he bit down on the curve of her neck. His hands cupped her tits, like he was offering them up to me. I raked my teeth over one, then the other, returning to lick and suck them and Maca's fingers as I did. It was the most intense sexual encounter of my life. I felt it in every fibre of my being.

Mel reached around to my arse with one hand and up around to Maca's hair with the other.

"Fuck," She screamed. "Harder, harder ... oh god, oh god." Her fingernails clawed into my lower back and arse cheek.

"Oh, fuck—yes!" Maca roared, her nails digging in harder. I made a noise that didn't even sound human as I came and came and came, experiencing, what was at that time, the best orgasm of my life.

And then suddenly, in an instant, everything changed.

"Oh god, Georgia, yes," Cindy cried out.

My head spun around and I watched as she pushed one of the other girl's head between her legs, her hips bucking up and grinding into her mouth. She stilled and went ridged before panting out, "You are so fucking good at that, George, so good."

I turned to look down at Maca. He was staring up at the ceiling, breathing hard.

I slid out of Mel and pulled off my condom.

"Ow," she complained as I pulled her ungraciously off of Maca.

He slid off his condom before he even stood up. He walked over, grabbed the bag of coke and a couple of joints that had already been rolled from the chest of drawers, and stormed out of the bedroom, across the living room area of the suite and into his own room, slamming the door behind him.

NINE
1986

I gave him an hour before I went and checked on him, but I just got told to 'fuck off' from behind his locked door.

I left him to it and headed back to my bed and the six needy young ladies that couldn't get enough of me, or of each other.

I woke to the sound of Len shouting. Fuck knows how many hours later.

"Get up, get dressed, and *get out*!" he shouted.

Without opening my eyes, I reached down to scratch my balls but instead came into contact with a head full of long, silky hair. I dragged my fingers through it and with my other hand, I guided my semi-hard dick into the mouth that belonged to the hair.

"Marley, get her lips off your dick and get the fuck in the shower. It's nearly nine o'clock, and Jimmie lands in half an hour. I want you up and looking lively when I get back from the airport."

"Fuck off, Len ... Oh yeah, just like that baby, don't stop." I told the girl whose face I was fucking. I had no idea which one of them it was because I had yet to open my eyes.

I heard Len move around the bedroom. "Up, ladies. Get up and get out, else I'm calling Milo in to throw you out and believe me, you don't want that."

I heard the girls groan and complain, but I still didn't open my eyes. The mouth that my dick was inside continued to suck and my hips continued to thrust. A fingertip slid along the seam under my balls and travelled along until it started to circle my arsehole before slowly pushing its way inside. I had women do it to me before, and I knew that if she hit the right spot, I'd be done in seconds.

Bingo.

My balls tightened and my hips thrust forward.

"*Marley!*" My brother shouted right in my ear. I opened my eyes and watched, horrified as he grabbed the girl by the hair and pulled her mouth off my dick. Jizz shot out of me and hit the girl in the face, along with Len's nice navy blue Pierre Cardin polo shirt.

"What the fuck, Marls? What the... You dirty bastard. You dirty fucking bastard," Lennon ranted. "You *spunked* all over me. I actually have your *spunk* on me, Marley," he whined.

"Chill the fuck out, dude. What're a few bodily fluids between brothers? We both slid out the same vagina, remember."

Lens eyebrows raised and his mouth hung open. He was finally silent for a few seconds.

"What the fuck has that gotta do with anything?" His voice was starting to sound all girly and high-pitched. I ignored him.

I could see that the girl that had just given me a knee trembler was Lori. She looked from my dick to Lens T-shirt with wide, blue eyes. Scooping my spunk off her cheek with the back of her finger, she proceeded to suck it into her mouth.

"Good girl," I praised her with a smile and leaned forward to kiss her. Len lifted her up and stood her on her feet.

"Good girl? Good fucking girl?" Len continued to shout, his face red—purple, almost. I thought he was a bit pissed off … just a bit.

"You, get your clothes on," he shouted at Lori. "And you, you dirty fucker. Go and get in the fucking shower before I do you some damage."

"Bye, Marley. Thanks for a great night," Lori said as she was about to head out my bedroom door.

"Anytime, babe. Don't forget, there'll be six tickets at the door for Saturday night under the name of Cindy. They'll get you backstage passes too, so I'll see you then."

"Cool. Tell Maca I said bye."

Shit!

Maca!

My eyes met my brothers, which were looking a bit like they were about to bulge out of his head.

"Please tell me he's not in there with six birds too?" Len asked through gritted teeth.

"No, he's on his own."

"Well, thank fuck for that."

"He just had three grams of coke and two spliffs for company."

Lennon made a sort of choking noise, but I didn't look at his face. I was too busy jumping off the bed and pulling on a pair of boxers to watch his reaction.

I banged on Maca's door. Nothing. I tried the handle, but it was still locked.

"Maca, c'mon, get up," I shouted, then continued banging with my fist.

"Where's Milo?" I called to Len over my shoulder.

"In his room I s'pose. Why?"

"We need to get this door open. He was a fucking mess last night. I checked on him once, but forgot to check back," I explained.

Len was already on the phone, calling down to Milo's room. I continued to bang on the door, then used my shoulder to try and break my way in, but it didn't budge.

I looked around for something to unscrew the handle with and took in the empty bottles when another realisation dawned on me.

"Oh fuck, Len."

"What?"

"I think he might have a bottle of Jack in there with him as well."

"For fuck's sake, Marls." He moved and in an instant, he was beside me.

"After three," he ordered. We counted, then threw our shoulders against the door, but we didn't stand a chance against the heavy hotel, standard fire door.

There was a knock and Len moved to let Milo into the room. He promptly pulled a small leather case from his pocket and opened it up to reveal a set of alum keys and small screwdrivers. He had the door unlocked in less than a minute. Milo and Len rushed in, but like a coward, I hung back.

I've never told anybody this, but in that moment, I knew. Don't ask me how, but I just knew that one day, we would lose Maca.

"For fuck's sake," I heard Len say. Seemed to be his favourite phrase for the day.

"Get him up, Mi. Marls, get in here."

"Fucking hell," was the first thing I said as the stench of vomit hit me.

Maca was, luckily, face down in his own puke, lying across the bed.

"Is he breathing?" my voice sounded as terrified as I felt.

"Yeah," Milo grunted. "Go and put the shower on. You can hold him up in there."

I headed into the bathroom and turned on the shower. It was one of those that sits over the bath, so no room for both of us.

Milo dragged him in with his back against his chest as he held him under his armpits, lifting him and lying him in the bath. I took the showerhead off the slide rail it was on and sprayed water over Maca's head, face, and chest, washing the puke away. He opened one eye.

"Morning, Princess. Wakey, wakey, rise and shine. Don't you know it's breakfast time?" I repeated the greeting my mum had woken us up with all our lives.

"Fuck off, Marls," he croaked out.

"Get showered, Maca. Get some coffee and some food inside ya. You've got a photo shoot in an hour and then a live to air interview. You go straight from that to the venue for a practice and a run through with the light techs," Lennon barked at him. Maca proceeded to lean forward and throw up into his own crotch.

"Dude," I shouted as the smell hit me. "You have puke in your pubes. Not a good look man. *Not. A. Good. Look.*"

Milo shook his head as he left the bathroom. Len paced the confined space, raking his fingers through his dark hair while Maca continued to dry-heave. He and Maca were gonna have one fucked up day, that was for sure.

The photo shoot was being done in Lennon's room and by the time I got Maca organised, we were twenty minutes late. Billy, Tom, the photographer, and two make-up artists, as well as a hairdresser, were already there, waiting impatiently.

Len had gone off to the airport to collect Jim, which was probably a good thing. It meant he didn't get to witness our lead singer vomiting into a waste paper bin while having his make-up done.

We were only five minutes into the shoot when Maca had to vomit again. He looked like shit and probably felt worse. The snapper followed him into the bathroom and I panicked, afraid that he was going to call off the shoot. Instead, he pulled out a bag of coke and offered him some to help liven him up.

After borrowing Len's toothbrush and downing a glass of water, along with a line up each nostril, we got our singer back. He still looked like shit, but at least he could keep his eyes open.

By the time the photographer wrapped things up, the TV crew was there, along with the two presenters, waiting to interview us for some US afternoon chat show.

The presenters were called Gary and Lisa, who had a talk with us first about the way they'd like the interview to go. I personally didn't give a fuck what they asked, but the label and Len had pretty strict guidelines, and what happened in Europe the previous summer was a definite off-limits subject for any interviews. Luckily, Len got back before we went to air and made it clear that that topic would not be discussed.

Maca had spent most of the previous half hour in the toilet, and I had a feeling that he bought the rest of the coke the photographer had from him.

I caught Len turning to look at me, eyes wide and once again, looking like they were about to bulge out of his head. He twitched his nose like he was sniffing the air, just as the smell hit me.

"Fuck!" Billy and I said in unison.

I shook my head at Len and headed into his bedroom, banging on the door of the bathroom. Maca opened it and the smell of weed almost knocked me down. He stood in the doorway with a shit-eating grin on his face.

"What the fuck, Maca? The people are here for this interview. You seriously need to get your shit together." Even my patience was wearing thin at that point. Len must've been about to have a coronary, and if he'd seen Maca's glassy-eyed expression, he probably would have.

I sprayed some of Lennon's aftershave over Maca and lead him back out to the living area of the suite where everyone was set up and waiting for us.

We were directed to sit on the sofa; Tom on one end, Billy the other, me and Maca in the middle.

The interviewers started by introducing the show and talking through the day's topics. The camera turned to us as they announced that we would be interviewed shortly.

The whole thing was a pain as we had to sit quietly while they talked to the camera, but were allowed to speak when the show cut and ran a pre-recorded piece to air.

I had to nudge Maca a couple of times when I saw his eyes start to close. He'd barely spoken a word the entire day, and I knew that he wasn't in a good place. Fuck if I knew how I was going to get him through rehearsals and a show.

Lisa and Gary finally started their interview with us and asked the usual questions to start: How did we meet? How long had we been together? Then she asked us about our musical influences and what made us want to become musicians ourselves.

As usual, Billy and Tom kept their answers short, both explaining that it was all they'd ever wanted to do.

"And you, Marley. I understand your dad's a big music fan, and that you, your brothers, and your sister, all have music-related names. Can you tell me about that?" Lisa asked.

I was a little taken aback at first because we weren't usually asked about our families. All anybody wanted to know about us was who we were dating, and when was the next song gonna be released. I suppose because the show went out to an older audience, they'd mixed it up a little to what we weren't used to. I cleared my throat.

"Yeah, my dad's a massive music fan. He loves all music and plays the guitar and piano pretty well himself. He always encouraged us as kids."

"There's four of you, right?" Gary asked next.

"Yeah. Bailey's the eldest. He was named after some bloke that makes or designs guitars. I think my dad met him at some folk music festival or something back in the sixties, and I'm pretty sure that Bailey was his surname. Bails can play guitar, but doesn't often. He runs the family building firm back in England with my dad. Lennon, my other brother, is our manager and I think his name, and mine, are both pretty self-explanatory." I stop there, my eyes darting to Len's who was standing behind Lisa off camera.

"And you have a sister too, right?" Lisa continued.

Fuck.

"Yeah, my sister's the youngest. She's named after one of my dad's favourite songs and singers." I swallowed hard, hoping that I'd given them enough.

"Which is?" Gary asked, looking amused.

Lisa was leaning back in her seat, looking smug and I got goose bumps. Call it a sixth sense or just an acute awareness of arseholes, but my guard went up with where this interview was going. I'd not looked at Maca once during their line of questioning. I could feel the heat radiating from him as he sat next to me, but other than that, he sat so still and quiet that I wouldn't have known he was there.

"Her name's Georgia, after the song, *'Georgia on my Mind.'* Her middle name is Rae, spelt with an E, but after the great Ray Charles."

Lisa's green eyes slide catlike to Maca.

"And how is Georgia doing these days, Maca? Have you guys kissed and made up? Must make things awkward, dating your best friend and bandmate's little sister?"

Bitch.

I watched Len cover his mouth with his hand and close his eyes for a few seconds as we all waited for Maca's response.

"From what I know, Georgia's doing great and continuing with her education back in England," he informed her.

"So, you guys never got back together? That's such a shame, but I hear that there's no shortage of ladies who are only too keen to be seen on your arm. Are you seeing anyone right now?"

"I don't see what the fuck this has got to do with you or any other fucker," Maca snarled at her before standing up and pulling off his mic and earpiece.

Lisa and Gary scrambled to apologise, cutting to an add break. I got up and walked towards her.

"My sister is a little girl of seventeen, trying to put her life together after you cunts shredded it to pieces. Maca is still trying to come to terms with their breakup and the trouble he brought to her door. Their split has been very well documented and that was a spiteful thing to do to him on live television. I hope you're fucking happy with yourself," I told her, letting my voice rise with every word.

Len was standing beside me. I thought I was about to get a bollocking when he simply said, "Not cool, Lisa. Seriously, not cool." He turned to Billy and Tom who were still sitting on the sofa. "C'mon, we're done here. They're getting no more from us." Len told them. Turning back to the two presenters, he continued, "Pack your shit up and get out of here."

"Now wait a minute," The shows director, or whoever the fuck he was, stepped in. "We still have another twenty minutes of the show to broadcast."

"I don't give a fuck. Play some music, show some ads, I don't care. Just get the fuck outta my room," Len shouted.

"Boys, go back to Marley's room, now. Milo, stay here and make sure they pack up and go," he ordered everyone before heading out the door and up the corridor towards my room.

"What the fuck is going on, Marls? Maca's a mess," Billy asked.

"Yeah, thanks for stating the fucking obvious, Bill."

"Fuck you, Marls. Tell Len I'll be in my room. I'm not going back to your room to watch Maca fall apart. I love the boy like a brother, but he seriously needs to put his hand up his arse and pull himself together."

"Thanks for your sympathy. I'll be sure to pass it on," I spat out as Billy let himself into his room.

Tommy put his hand on my shoulder as I stopped outside my room to take a few breaths before heading in.

"Sorry, Marls. You can count me out too. My Mrs. is in my room waiting for me. I don't need to watch Len burst a blood vessel over the state of Maca. Tell him to call my room if he needs me. I'll see you at rehearsals." Tommy patted me on the back before he too deserted me.

"Yeah, see ya in a bit, Tom."

I remained standing outside my room for a few more seconds. I felt helpless. My best mate was a fucked up mess and I didn't know what to do about it. I wanted to get drunk and off my face right along with him, but I knew that what he needed was for me to look after him. Perhaps it wasn't a bad thing that he'd finally reached his breaking point. The timing couldn't have been worse, but maybe he was ready to allow his head and his heart to move on, and not just his dick.

I could hear shouting from inside the room and the door swung open. Jimmie stood there, tears rolling down her cheeks.

"What the fuck, Jim? What happened?"

"Your brother, that's what fucking happened," she sobbed.

I stepped forward and wrapped her in my arms, still holding the door open with my shoulder. Len was standing, looking out the window as I looked into the room. His fingers were laced together, hands behind his head.

"Come back in here," I said to Jim, guiding her back into the suite. "What the fuck's going on?" My question was aimed at whoever wanted to answer me. Apart from Jimmie's soft sobs, I was greeted with silence.

"Where's Maca?" I asked.

Len swung around from the window.

"Ask that silly cow. She let him go storming off." Len stated.

Jimmie pulled away from me and turned around. "He's a grown fucking man. He doesn't need my permission to go anywhere. How the fuck was I supposed to know to keep him here?" she shouted back at Len.

"You weren't. Don't talk to her like that, Len. None of this is her fault."

Len tended to lash out at everyone when he was stressed. Jimmie was usually the calm one, but she'd just gotten off a flight from London, so I didn't think she'd be feeling too chill.

Len looked from me to her, then around the room. "I'm sorry.

Come here." He stepped towards her. "I'm so sorry, babe. I shouldn't have shouted at you like that, and I'm sorry I was late picking you up." I stood there and watched as my brother wrapped his girl in his arms as she cried, at least until they started kissing. That was when I decided it was time to go.

"I'll go and look for him. I doubt he's gone far." Again, I spoke to no one in particular.

"Don't leave the hotel, Marls. We've got a car coming at three to take us to the venue. I'm not having you go on the missing list too."

Without another word, I left them to make up.

I didn't need to leave the hotel. I found Maca sitting on a stool at the hotel bar. He had a tumbler full of whiskey, or bourbon, in his hand.

"I'll have a Jack and coke, please, mate," I tell the barman as I sit down next to him.

"You doing all right?" I asked.

"What *d'ya* reckon?" Maca replied.

"To be totally honest, I've no fucking idea what's going on in that head of yours these days, Mac. I thought you were getting over things. I thought you were moving on, but apparently, the only thing that's done that is your dick. Your head and your heart seem to still be stuck firmly in Georgia territory."

"The same, please," he told the barman as he put my drink down.

"We've got a car coming to pick us up at three for rehearsals." I felt like Lennon now, getting on his case, but fuck. If he carried on his drinking, on top of the night and the morning he'd had, he wouldn't be fit to fart, let alone perform for an hour and a half.

He turned his brown eyes on me and I just knew he was about to give me shit, so I was shocked when he said, "If I was just to turn up now, just turn up and make her listen, what d'ya reckon she'd do? Would she listen? Does she even *care* what this is doing to me?"

"Mate, whatever you're going through, she's feeling it too, but you've gotta remember…" I trailed off, trying to think of how to word it. "Not only is she missing you and the rest of us, even being a part of this, but she also feels betrayed, and I'm so sorry about that. I really am sorry that this has all been caused by my stupid, selfish actions, but from what I'm hearing, she's getting on with her life and like I keep telling you, it's time for you to do the same." My heart was pounding in my chest as I waited for his reaction. My stomach twisted in knots at the guilt that I felt, but I couldn't change things. If I could've, I would've in a heartbeat.

He gave a small laugh. "Ya know, I swing from hating her, and I mean really, really hating her, to loving her so much that I can barely breathe at the thought of living the rest of my life without her." He knocked back the contents of his glass and gestured to the barman for yet another. I say nothing. I'm his mate, not his manager. He'd get enough shit from Lennon later so he didn't need it from me.

"I wanna walk away right now, Marls. I wanna walk away from all this and just go to your sister and make her listen to me." He looked me square in the face. "If I thought there was the slightest chance that she'd listen, I would be on the next plane home."

I wanted to tell him no fucking way, he can't. I wanted to tell him that he didn't have a chance … that she wouldn't listen to him and that she sure as shit wasn't ready to forgive him. But I didn't. I said nothing. It was my interfering that caused it all in the first place. As much as I loved my band and the life that I was leading, I'd sacrifice it all to make the two people I loved most in the world happy again.

"Go then. If you feel that's what you need to do, then go."

At that moment, Jimmie appeared at the bar and moved herself to stand in between us.

"Boys, how are we?" she asked.

"Jim," we both acknowledged her.

"Who's gonna buy me a drink?"

Maca nodded in the barman's direction and Jim ordered a Diet Coke. We were all silent for a few seconds before Maca asked her,

"So, how's everyone back home?"

"They're good ... everyone's good."

Maca twisted his whole body around on his bar stool so that he was facing Jimmie.

"How's Gia, Jim? How's she doing, and no bullshitting me."

Jim tucked her long brown hair behind her ears. "She's doing great. She's just finishing up for the summer at college and she's working hard at the shop with Bernie when she's not studying or at the gym."

"She's going to the gym now?" he asked.

"Yeah, she is. Though fuck knows why. There's nothing of her," she told him. He nodded his head, not that he knew how skinny she was those days. My sister had never been curvy, but when I saw her at Christmas, she was painfully thin.

"So the shop, it's going well then?" I asked. My dad had bought a dress shop in the High Street, and my mum and sister had taken it on as a project, which seemed to have taken off.

"It is. George and your mum have set themselves up as a business and are already looking to expand. They're selling all high-end designer labels and people can't get enough. They're off to Italy in a couple of weeks to a fashion show and to meet with a couple of new suppliers."

I watched as Maca once again finished his drink in a few gulps. He looked over Jim's head at me.

"You're right, mate, it's time to let go. Let's get to rehearsals. We've got a show to put on later."

Maca asked for the tab and I noticed he signed the docket, *Lennon Layton,* and put Len's room number down. Len was gonna have heart failure when he found out.

TEN
1986

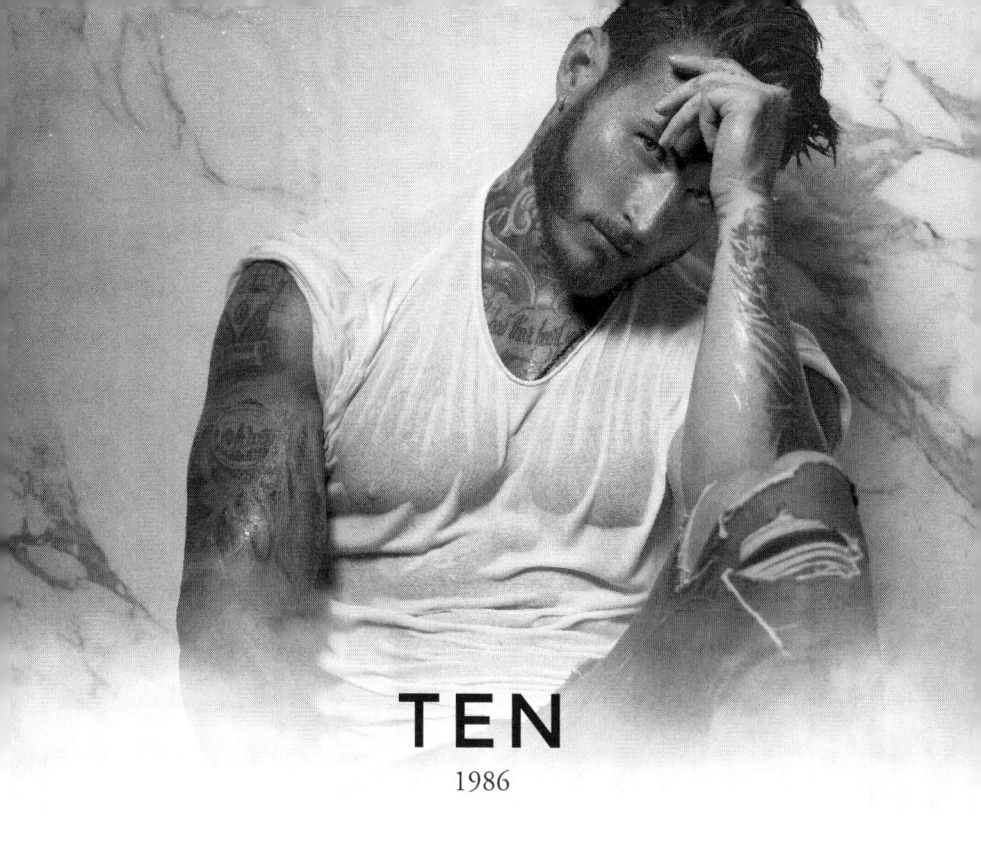

The concert that night was one of our worst and best ever. Maca was drunk, shit-faced, and highly emotional. He constantly changed the set list. As his bandmates, we knew the songs and quickly fell into stride along with whatever he decided to sing, but the sound techs and lighting blokes must've been majorly confused.

He broke into one of the best versions of *'Train In Vain'* by The Clash that I'd ever heard, then a sombre and random cover of *'Denis'* by Blondie, changing the words *'Denis'* to *'Georgie'* and *'King'* to *'Queen.'* He followed this with a haunting version of *'River'* by Joni Mitchell. His song choices were erratic, he went from sad and slow into a manic version of the Buzzcocks, *'Ever Fallen In Love,'* then slipped into a bluesy version of Dylan's *'Don't Think Twice,'* which he played and sang alone with his electric acoustic. This was followed by our own *'Seaside Heart,'* his usual raspy-voiced version of *'English*

Rose,' and then *'Georgia.'* It was possibly the best performance of his life.

He left me to say his 'goodnights' and 'thank yous' as he exited the stage without a word.

Tonight, there would be no encore.

I watched as he walked straight into Jimmie's arms and sobbed so hard he could barely stand.

She held on tight, stroking his hair and his back. She kissed his cheek and the top of his head, speaking words to try and comfort and soothe him while at the same time, encouraging him to let it all out.

Jimmie managed to coax and steer him out of the venue and into the back of the car that was waiting to take us back to the hotel.

I sat in silence and watched my best mate fall apart. The pain from the guilt and anguish felt as I witnessed Maca break into a million pieces was like being eaten alive from the inside out, but so much less than I deserved.

So much less.

2014

My eyes fly open and my heart skips a few beats. I must've fallen asleep while reading. My laptop obviously got bored of waiting for me to scroll down the page and has joined me for a nap.

I hear a giggle and realise it must've been the noise that woke me. Ash must be home.

The door to my office flies open and my sister falls through it. Yeah, she actually falls, or more like collapses in a heap.

"What the fuck, George?"

She looks up at me with her blue eyes and blinks a few times.

"Big brother, Marleeeeeeey," she grins as she calls from her position on the floor. She starts to crawl towards me on all fours.

Ashley appears behind her in the doorway, frowning as she looks at me.

"Georgia drunked," she slurs, swaying as she tries to speak. I realise then she's not frowning at me, but trying to focus. "G, she got—she got drinked."

My sister is now lying flat on her back, looking up at the ceiling and laughing her head off at what? I really don't have a clue.

"No," Ash says. "No, no, no. Not drinked, she's not got drinked." She shakes her head, slides down onto the floor and joins G, laughing at whatever it is that's so amusing on my office ceiling.

"How the fuck did you get in this state?" I ask them as I stand up and look over at my wife and sister, who are now doing a bang on impersonation of a couple of hyenas.

On meth!

"Y-you, Marley Layton, are my favouritist big brother called Marley. The best—my very bestest one." George points her finger up at me as she speaks.

"I'm your only big brother called Marley."

"This true, this is vrery, vrery true," she slurs.

I continue to watch the pair of them lying there. Ash is now curled on her side and crying with laughter. I still have no clue what she's finding so funny though.

"Be smiley, Marls," George says. "Don't be a Lennon face, be a smiley Marley face."

I hear a crash from up the hallway, just before Jimmie appears in the doorway.

"Oh great, here's another one," I say to anyone interested.

Jimmie is staring at me, well, at least trying to. She squints her eyes and sways as she holds something up to me. "My Louboutins, I brokeded them."

What is it with women talking like three-year-olds when they get pissed up?

"Noooooooo," Ashley screeches from the floor, attempting at the same time to sit up.

"Not the Boutins, that's just so sad." I give her a hand and move her to sit on the sofa I'd been sleeping on before the drunk circus arrived in town.

"Love you, Rock Star," she whispers, making my heart do its usual little happy dance when I hear her say those words. That shit never gets old and my smile is instantaneous.

"Love you, baby." As always, that's my reply.

"Who said Len?" Jimmie asks. "Someone said Len, Lenny, Lennon. Where's my baby? Is he here?"

She looks around with a smile on her face, as if Len's hiding from her and about to jump out from behind the sofa and shout 'ta da … sur-fuckin-prise.'

They've only been invading my space for five minutes but they're already giving me a headache. I know these three women better than I know my own dick, and I know full well that this is highly unlikely to end well.

"How the fuck do you go clothes shopping and come back in this state?" I ask again. They went to buy dresses and shoes. I'm pretty sure at no time was alcohol mentioned.

"S'er fault." Ash and George say together, both pointing at Jimmie who I'm guessing is the least likely to blame for this.

Jimmie opens her eyes and mouth wide and looks around the room. Whether she's still expecting Len to appear, I've no clue, but I wish he would. I'd welcome any kind of backup right now.

"Was Paige," Jimmie states, vigorously nodding her head.

"Yeah," says George, still speaking from her prone position on my office floor.

"It was her what done it. Lunch, she said, didn't she girls?" They all nod.

"Where's Paige now?" I ask in the hopes that one of them are capable of giving me an answer, and praying that they didn't leave my niece drunk and wandering around Bluewater Shopping Centre.

"S'gone," Ash sings and they all nod in unison, then she suddenly starts to laugh. "She's not famous…" She gasps for breath between laughing and talking. "She's not as famous as us." All three of them are now howling hysterically.

Jimmie slides to the floor and takes off her other shoe and crawls over to lay beside George, whose wiping tears from under her eyes.

"My daughter's a bigger diva than your sister," Jimmie informs me.

"Fuck you."

Here we go.

"No one's a digger biva than me," Georgia declares, much to the delight of the other two drunkards.

"You said digger biva, not bigger diva." Ash laughs and gasps at the same time.

All three of them are now cackling like witches, and as much as they're annoying the shit outta me right now, it's an absolute joy to watch my sister like this.

"I'm Queen Diva. Paige is only Princess Diva, and anyway, I'm more fame—shit, famouser," George declares.

"But she's a model," Ashley says in a stupid voice, which appears to be so funny that I worry for a moment they've all stopped breathing as their amusement takes their breath away.

"Ohmagod," Jimmie pants. "I need another drink."

"Yessss." The other two agree.

"Yeah, not happening, ladies. I think you've had enough."

"Fuck off, Marls," George and Ash say together and yeah, apparently that's funny too.

I walk over to my desk, retrieve my phone and call my brother.

"Little brother Marley."

"Got summit of yours here, mate. It's currently flat on its back in my office, pissed as a fart and cackling like a deranged hen."

"For fuck's sake." Yeah, it's still one of Len's favourites. "Wife or daughter?"

"Wife, although I would be tracking your daughter down right now as I can't get any sense out of these three as to where Paige is."

"She's a model, don't cha know?" Ash shouts out in her best Little Britain, 'I'm a lady' voice, reducing the three of them to sound again like a small pack of hyenas that have now mixed their meth with crack.

"What the fuck's all the noise?" Len asks.

"That, mate, is the sound of The Priory's next three detox patients."

"I'll be over in a bit. You eaten?"

"Na, I need to ring Cam. I'll call you back and let you know what to pick up. We'll need to double the order if the big man's coming."

"All right, I'll call Paige. Try and get some water into those three."

"Will do," I assure him.

I end the call and realise the room is quiet. When I turn around, I see that Jimmie and Ash are gone and there's just me and George left. She's still lying on her back. I follow her gaze to a photo of me and Maca on the wall. It's from some awards ceremony or other. We're both in suits, but it's obviously the end of the night as our ties are missing and top buttons are undone. Maca has a bottle of champagne in his hand. We look young and cocky, probably because we were.

I stand in front of my sister, blocking her view of the picture and hold my hand out to her. She takes it and I pull her up to a standing position. She's kicked off her shoes and stands barefoot in front of me, swaying slightly.

I know what's coming. I mentally square my shoulders in anticipation for it. She's strong most of the time, I'd say ninety percent these days, but she carries her losses with her on a daily basis. I see that ten percent of sorrow that never leaves her eyes, and I think Jimmie, Ash, and Len do too. I'm not sure if Cam sees and accepts it, or if he purposely chooses to remain oblivious.

I notice her breathing change and I know that she's fighting not to cry. Crying for her dead husband and their children overwhelms her with guilt because she's now happily married to Cam and they have four babies of their own. That, in turn, makes her feel guilty about Maca, Beau, and Baby M. I don't think any of us will ever truly understand her struggles and the demons she fights every single day of her life.

I see her sway, watch her legs start to buckle and pull her into me. The sound that tears from her insides and escapes is primal and can only be described as grief in its most basic form—raw and gut-wrenchingly painful.

I hold her to me as I move us both to the sofa. I sit her down in my lap and let her cry into my chest, the way that I've done so many times before. She's my sister, I love her, and I hate with a passion that there's nothing I can, or will ever be able to do, to take away this pain.

"Why, why Marley? Why *them*? Why *my* husband? Why *my* babies? Oh God, Marley. It hurts so much, so fucking much. It hurts. It hurts. It hurts," she chants, almost choking on her words, she's crying so hard.

"I miss him every day," she sobs and that, combined with the way she slurs her words, I have to listen hard to what she's saying, but I already know the gist of it. It's what happens every time Georgia drinks and old memories are stirred up. Her guilt and self-doubt about the life that she's gone on to lead are never far from the surface and when she drinks, everything goes to shit when there's a trigger.

"With every, every breath and every heartbeat, Marley. Every fucking beat of my heart, I miss him. Does that make me bad, Marls? Does that make me a bad wife to Cam? A bad Mumma to my babies?"

I remain silent. I've heard her ask these questions so many times, and I really have no answers. Some would say yeah, it's terrible that you still mourn your dead husband when you're married and have children with another. But others, probably those that have been through or witnessed someone else going through what she has, they would totally get the concept that Georgia missing Maca and their children in no way detracts from what she has *with* and feels *for* Cam and their children.

"They're my mife, Larls—Fuck—my life. You know what I mean. I'm a bit drunk." She blinks as she looks up at me and all I see is the little girl she used to be. Her big blue eyes are wide with tears hanging from her lashes. I swallow down the lump in my throat before I even attempt to speak.

"You're drunk, George? I'd never have guessed that one, babe." My sarcasm goes right over her inebriated head.

"Yeah, yeah I am. Just a bit," she says in all seriousness, and I can't help but kiss her temple.

"They're my world, Marls. My kids and Cam are what keep me going, but there's always this piece of my heart ... this piece, this big fucking piece ..." she lets out another heaving sob that shakes her whole body as she punches herself in the chest, her heart. I respond by pulling her in tighter to my chest. I have nothing else to offer, no words that will ever be able to make this better for her.

"This piece," she says again, this time slapping her palm flat over her chest. "It will always be his, always be theirs, but I do, I do, do, do love Cam, I truly do. He's my rock—my Tiger."

"I know, George. You don't have to explain, you really don't," I try to reassure her.

"Do you still feel it Marls? Do you still miss him?" She tries to focus and look me in the eyes when she asks.

I take in air and try to free my lungs and chest of the sensation of being crushed.

"More than I could ever put into words. I miss him so much."

"I get scared, Marls. So, so scared. What happens when we're gone? Who's gonna remember him? Who's gonna talk about him and miss and love him like we do?" She starts to cry again.

"There'll always be the music, George. He's one of the best songwriters this country has ever produced. The music will outlive us all. Elvis has been dead for nearly forty years. I bet all of our kids know who he is though."

"I hope so, Marls, I really fucking hope so. He has no babies. They're the only things left of him, his songs. Our babies died, Marls, they fucking died." Her crying is agonising, the pain palpable.

"Why? Why, why, why did I have to lose it all, every part of him?

I get so angry. Oh God, I get so angry. Why couldn't it have been me that died? I'm no one, nothing. He was special, so special and talented, and people all—all around the world love his words and music and his voice, and I'm just no one, nothing."

I try and be the strong one when George has these breakdowns. When it's my turn, we both tend to cry together, but when it's her, I try and stay strong, but tonight's different. I hate hearing her say this about herself. It breaks my heart that she feels that she's so worthless.

"Fuck, G, don't ever think for a minute that you're not important. If you had died that day, then there'd now be no George, Kiks, or Lula. Harry would have no mum. Without you, those little people wouldn't exist today. Would you deny them the right to life George?"

I feel her shoulders shake as she silently cries, but she manages to shake her head no.

"If you had died that day," I continue, "Maca would never have survived. He could never live without you in this world."

"He would. He would've come to terms with it. Event—eventually, just like I've had to."

"You came to terms with it because you've had Cam to hold your hand and help guide you through. He's been there. He lost his wife, unborn baby, and his dad under horrible circumstances," I tell her. "I'll be totally honest here and tell ya, George. I don't think you would've made it without Cam. I'm not religious, I don't believe in fate, destiny, or that things happen for a reason. Life is what it is. Shit happens to good people because that's just the way life is. You and Cam, you really are just perfect for each other, and what happened in both of your pasts made it that way. There's no one else on this planet that could've put you back together the way he did, George, and I mean no one. It goes against everything that I believe in, but it's almost like you two were destined to be together." I tell her from my heart.

"I love him. He's my Tiger," she explains matter-of-factly.

I smile at her because I can see the smile in her eyes as she talks about the man that saved and rebuilt her the best that he could. We never got the old Georgia back, how could we? None of us were the same after Maca's death and the loss of Beau. Our whole family was, and will be, changed forever because of those events. But Cameron King gave us back a version of Georgia that we never thought we'd see again. Step by step, day by day, I got my beautiful, funny, mouthy, diva of a sister back, and I'll never be able to thank him enough for that.

Jimmie appears in the doorway, a full champagne flute in hand.

"I told you no more drink."

"And we told you to fuck off," Jimmie replies.

"Actually, you didn't. It was your two mouthy mates that did that," I remind her.

"Yeah, I did. I just said it in my head, so that counts double." She smiles at me and gives her eyebrows a little raise, as if to say 'so there.'

"How fucking old are you?" I ask.

"Old enough to know when I want another drink." She narrows her eyes and smiles.

I give in. It's three against one until the boys arrive. Which reminds me, I need to ring Cam. I slide Georgia off my lap and stand to get my phone out of my pocket.

Ashley arrives with a bottle of Moët and two more flutes. "No more for her," I tell Ash, pointing at George.

"Fuck off, Marl," I get from all three of them, followed by "Love you, Rock Star," coming from Ash.

"Love you, baby," I tell her back. I know I sound like a wuss, but it makes my wife happy and horny when I call her baby so I do it as often as I can. Because at the end of the day, I like my wife happy, horny, and knowing that I love her.

I head out to the kitchen to ring my brother-in-law. "Marley, you heard from the girls? I was just about to call you. Georgia's not answering her phone."

"She's here, mate," I reassure him. "The three of them are here, a little worse for wear, and very emotional."

"What, pissed you mean?"

"Yep, and as much as I've tried to stop them, they've just opened a bottle of Moët and seem determined to carry on the party."

"For fuck's sake."

"Funny, Len said those exact same words."

"Right. Let me get the kids sorted and I'll be over."

"Bring them with you if you want. Len's on his way, and I was gonna ring him back with a food order if you fancy staying and eating."

"Yeah, sounds good. Marian's here, actually. I'll get her to stay with the kids. What were you thinking of eating?"

"Whatever you fancy, mate ... Chinese?"

"Yeah, sounds good. Tell Len to get plenty and I'll sort him out the money when I get there."

"Will do."

"Does Georgia need anything?"

"Just you, mate."

"What's that mean? How drunk is she?"

"Yeah, they're all pretty gone and about to get worse."

"She cried?"

"She has."

"Right. You got any decent bourbon or single malt?"

"I've got Jack, Jim, or Laphroaig. Take your pick."

"Good, I think we're gonna need it."

"I think you're probably very right."

"I usually am, ask my wife."

"Yeah, don't know if I'll get much sense from her right now."

"Great," he replies sarcastically. "I'll see you in a bit. Try and get them to slow down." He hangs up before I can reply. *Well, good luck to me then.*

I call Len back and ask him to order everything off the menu from our favourite Chinese takeout and to pick up some mixers for the bourbon as Ash doesn't allow fizzy drink in the house as a rule.

The girls have taken the party out to the deck by the time I get back to them. For some reason, best known to themselves, they have Right Said Fred's, *'I'm Too Sexy'* playing from one of their phones and are doing their best 'model on the runway' walk.

It's bad.

I watch as my sister struts the length of our deck; hand on hip she turns, looks over her shoulder, total duck face going on, and then starts walking/swaying back to where the other two pair of idiots are still laughing.

Georgia actually walks the walk pretty well. She's modelled a few times at various charity events over the years, so she has had some practice.

I stand and shake my head before giving in and asking what the fuck they're doing?

"Paige." They all say together.

I raise my eyebrows in expectation and hold my hands up, gesturing for them to elaborate.

"In the bar ... the man ..." Ash laughs as she attempts to explain.

Jimmie is now up and attempting 'the walk,' but she's wearing the shoes that George has just taken off and they're obviously too big. She only makes four strides before going down like a sack of shit and landing in a heap on my Tasmanian Oak decking.

I actually join in the laughter this time, regretting only that I'm not filming this so I can show Len and Cam when they arrive and play it back to the girls tomorrow.

I help Jim to her feet and sit her on a chair. "Why are you taking the piss out of Paige? I don't understand?" I question, although really not expecting a coherent answer.

"Oh my God, Marls, we told you," Ashley whines.

"Actually, babe, you didn't."

Jimmie knocks back the last of the champagne from her glass and tries to top it up from the bottle, but it's empty. They've drunk the lot.

"S'gone. Gononother, Marls?" Georgia asks.

"Not till you tell me why you're taking the piss outta Paige." They said 'man' and 'bar.' Not that I'm green-eyed or anything, but I want to know what that's all about.

"The man in bar ... bar, the bar," Ashley starts. This could take a while.

She tilts her head and looks up at the sky before looking back at me and my stomach goes over. What the fuck happened today? I grow concerned for my wife because she's suddenly looking like she's about to cry.

I watch her throat move as she swallows before continuing with a shaky voice. I'm not sure if it's the alcohol or some kind of trauma that's caused this, and panic sets in as she looks at George, Jim, and then me. Taking a deep breath, she starts talking.

"A bloke in the bar, he... he started ch—chat—chatting with Paige. We thought he recognised her, but it was ... it was George, and then me." She's slurring but making sense, sorta. She blinks and looks down into her lap, and when she looks up, I watch as she brushes a tear from her cheek.

"Ash, baby?" I draw in a breath as I start to feel the panic rise, not having a clue where this story is going. Ash shakes her head, hopefully to let me know that she's okay. Taking a deep breath and speaking slowly, she continues.

"He spoke to Paige so that she—he, I mean. So that he could ask her if G was Georgia McCarthy. He was a massive Carnage fan, Marls." Her voice rises and she sobs and then nods her head, silently composing herself before continuing. "He had all your albums on his playlist and told us all about the times he'd seen you live. He asked for mine and G's autographs and we posed for pictures with him." The tears run freely down her face as she speaks and cries now. "He bought us all a drink and then he just got a bit emotional and overwhelmed. He cried, Marls." She sobs again while still trying to speak. I look across to Jim and George who are both just staring out at nothing as they listen to her.

"He cried so hard. This man, he knew exactly where he was when he got the news about Sean and he started to tell us, but he just broke down." She wipes her nose on the back of her arm, coz my baby's classy like that, and I wouldn't change her for the world.

"It's hard. It was hard to watch. He's a stranger, a complete stranger and he cried. To see him, watch him cry like that was hard, and it just brought it all back." Her voice breaks into another sob before she takes a few deep breaths. "I love Cam. Honest to God, Marls, Cam, and the kids, I fucking love them, but why? Why did we have to lose Maca and Beau like that to get them? It hurts and it's shit, and I fucking hate it, but yeah, anyway." She shakes her head and I wipe at my own nose which is now running right along with the tears down my face. "Anyway, Paige's face was a picture when she realised he had no clue who she was, and he was only interested in her old aunties. It was funny. So, so funny."

She forces a smile on her beautiful tear-stained face as she ends her story. I stand and nod my head for a few seconds, not wanting to make eye contact with my sister right now, but not sure what to say either.

"So you all decided to get drunk to celebrate?" I go for the 'trying to be funny' angle.

"Ferzactly," says Jim, "but the shervice here is sit—too slow, so now we're nearly sober again."

"Oi. You can soon fuck off, back to your gaff if you don't like the service at mine." I tell her over my shoulder as I walk back to the kitchen to find them more champagne.

"Love you, Rock Star," I hear Ash call out.

"Love you, Baby."

"We love you, Butt," Jimmie and George shout out, and then proceed to cackle again.

Yeah, I'll explain that inside joke later.

The girls become a little more subdued for all of ten minutes, but once the champagne starts flowing again, the noise level rises, all except for George, that is. She remains quiet, staring out over the pool and the tennis courts.

My alarm system bleeps, letting me know that someone has punched in the gate code and is approaching the house. I check on the monitor and see Cam's Range Rover heading up the drive.

The front door is unlocked and I know that he'll just let himself in. Georgia doesn't notice as he stands, leaning against the doors that lead from the house to the deck. He gestures with his finger to his lips for me not to announce his arrival, and I get the pleasure of watching him look at George with complete and utter devotion written in his eyes as he raises his sunglasses to his head. G must sense she's being watched as she turns and looks right at him, her face lighting up.

I'm turning into such a sad ol' fucker. I can't help but grin as I watch the silent exchange between my sister and her husband.

He walks towards her, lifts her from her chair and sits in it himself, placing G on his lap.

"Kitten," is all that he whispers into her hair, kissing her head as he does.

"T," she greets him.

"Love the fuck outta you."

"You better."

"Heard we've had some tears. Tough day?"

"S'all better now you're here."

"I'm always here, Mrs. King, always."

"T.D.H! How's it hanging, dude?" My wife greets Cam, ending their moment as she leans in for a kiss to his cheek as she does.

They share a special bond, those three—well, the four of us, I suppose. We were all there to witness Cam and Georgia's twin girls that Ashley had carried for them, being delivered by caesarean section over eleven years ago.

I can honestly say that it was like watching my own children being born, and equally as stressful. But just like with your own kids, when the drama of the birth was all over and the calm set in, I had the pleasure of witnessing this giant of a man fall apart when first one, then his second daughter, was placed in his arms.

My alarm bleeps again, letting me know that Lennon is approaching with food.

The rest of the evening is spent with the girls being noisy and us blokes just sitting back and enjoying the show.

Nobody made it to bed before three in the morning and the last to leave were Len and Jimmie at around noon on Sunday. Georgia and Cam left a little earlier to get back to the kids.

All of this means that I don't get a chance to read again until Ash has gone to bed on Sunday night.

ELEVEN
1986

The rest of that American tour proceeded a lot quieter. Len made sure that alcohol on the bus was limited and any hotels that we stayed in were made aware that Maca and I were still under twenty-one.

When we arrived back in England in the very early autumn of 1986, we were called into Len's office for a diary meeting to go over what we had booked for the next six months. Len, being a control freak and megalomaniac that he was, liked to have everything planned well in advance.

When we got there, he was on the phone.

"Why, what does she want? ... A what? ... Why the fuck does she want one of them? ... Well, if you don't know, I certainly don't ... When did they stop making them? ... Yeah, well, good luck with that."

I continued to listen, wondering what the fuck was going on.

"Dad, what makes you think that she'd listen to me? ... Fine, I'll try, but Jimmie's got a better chance."

Len looked up at me.

"Shame things weren't better between her and Marley. It's him you need on board for this one."

I sensed Maca shift slightly in his chair next to me.

"Yeah, I know, Dad, I know. Listen, I've got a meeting about to start, so I'll call her or pop into the shop to see her when I get a chance. And I'll get Jim to ring her … Yep. See ya later, Dad."

"What was that all about?" I asked straight away.

"Hello, Len. How are you today, Len? Yeah, I'm great, Marls, how are you doing, mate?" My brother's tone dripped with sarcasm.

"Fuck off, Len. I only saw you last night. What's the ol' man want?"

He let out a long breath and threw the pen he was fiddling with on his desk. His eyes move from mine to Maca's.

"Georgia's being a princess about what car she wants."

"I thought Jim said he'd bought her a beamer?" I questioned. If my dad wouldn't buy her the car she wanted, then I would. It was the very least I could do.

"She doesn't want a beamer, she wants a Triumph Herald," Maca said from beside me, "with a sunroof."

Len's eyebrows shot up. "How the fuck d'ya know that?" He asked. Yeah, how did he know that?

"It's what she's always wanted. I always planned on buying it for her." He looked between the two of us as he talked.

"Burnt orange and black, Triumph Herald with a sunroof and one of those fake walnut interiors," he informed us.

"Well, where the fuck is the ol' man gonna pluck one of them from?" I asked.

"He can't, that's the problem," Len stated.

"I'll find one," Maca interrupted. "Call your dad and tell him I'll find one, even if I have to get it shipped from another country. I'll find one in the best nick I can, but check that his boys will be okay spraying it if I can't get the colour she wants."

Len and I looked at each other in silence for a few seconds. I was hoping he was thinking the same thing as me. I shrugged my shoulders to let Len know that I wasn't gonna be the one to tell him.

"Mac, look mate…" Len started and then looked to me for help.

"Don't tell her. I know she won't accept it if she knows it's from me, so just don't tell her."

Len and I mirrored each other's movements as we both sat back in our chairs.

"You sure, mate?" Len asked. "The ol' man's had his feelers out for the last month or so, and he's come up with nothing. You gonna have time to do the same? Sounds like a bit of a mission to me?"

"I'll find time," Maca said quietly. "She's not exactly my favourite person right now, but still," I watch as he shrugs and shakes his head, "I'd really like to do this for her."

I spent the next few weeks travelling the country, trying to find that poxy car for my sister. Maca was obsessed with getting one in time for my dad to present to her on her eighteenth birthday.

With four days to spare, we found the perfect car. The colours weren't right, but the interior was spot on. Maca paid for someone to drive it down from Northampton to one of my dad's blokes in Bethnal Green the same day. The boys worked on it 'round the clock and on the 24th of September, my sister got the car of her dreams.

Not invited to the birthday celebrations, Maca and I went to our local pub, got completely smashed and staggered home with just each other, two chicken tikka masala's, two keema naans, and a large rice for company.

It was after that night that I noticed a bit of a change in Maca. I wouldn't call it an improvement, really, just a change. Instead of seeming as though he was permanently grieving what he'd lost with my sister, for a while he just became angry.

We had some time off until the following spring, in which we took a holiday in Barbados over Christmas, rather than me going home, and Maca spent it alone like he had the previous year. We bought ourselves a building in the Docklands area of East London and contracted my dad's building firm to renovate the old warehouse for us and turn it into nine apartments. The entire top floor was being turned into the penthouse that Maca and I would share. We also started work on songs for our next album.

We were booked in for studio time in early March, but Maca had been writing as far back as the end of the US tour, so we rented a hall not far from the studio where we could leave our gear set up and create the music to go with the songs Maca had come up with.

Outside of the band, we rarely saw Billy and Tom. They were both married with babies on the way in the summer. We were all amicable with each other, but apart from the music, we just didn't have anything in common. Maca and I were both single and out and about at least four nights a week, attending events, parties, the opening of an envelope even. We were there, usually with a few pretty girls on our arms.

There was a never-ending supply of women, all nameless and faceless; one blurring much into the other. We still had the occasional threesome and the odd all-out orgy, but not at any stage did either of us meet anyone that made us want to go back for seconds. We were kings of the double F… Fuck and Forget 'em. It should've been tattooed on our foreheads, or maybe our foreskins because no matter how many times we told the girls, how clearly we spelt it out, they just wouldn't listen.

I arrived at rehearsals late one morning and when I walked into the hall, I could hear Tom and Billy in conversation.

"I'm not saying there's anything wrong with the lyrics, although I fail to see how it will ever get airtime on mainstream radio. What I'm saying is that Marley ain't gonna like it, neither will Len, for that matter," Tom stated before taking a long draw on his cigarette.

I breathed in deeply through my nose, enjoying the smell. Maca had been ordered to quit after having a chest infection after Christmas, so I'd done the same to try and support him, but it wasn't easy. That ol' nicotine shit was addictive. Kids, if you're listening, take note of what your Uncle Marley is saying. That stuff is bad, bad I tell ya. Save your money and invest in property instead. That don't stain your fingers or make your breath stink.

"What's Marley not gonna like?" I watched as they both jumped at the sound of my voice.

Feedback screeched through one of the speakers and we all look up to see Maca standing at the mic, his Fender hanging over his back. He was wearing a white T-shirt, leather trousers, and the scowl that I've gotten used to these last few months.

"Rock star much?"

"Twenty-four/seven, baby. Twenty-four/seven," he said without cracking a smile. He flipped his guitar over his shoulder and instantly started playing a tune I didn't immediately recognise until he began to sing, that is.

"The cleaning lady told him he reminded her of David Essex, but with brown eyes. It was this morning. I think it's gone to his head," Billy explained as he stood next to me, both of us watching our lead singer perform his own rendition of *'Rock On,'* which I had to say, wasn't fucking bad.

"Well, at least he looks a bit chirpier today," I said with a nod towards the stage where Maca's husky voice was still belting out a mighty fine rendition of a song I hadn't heard in years.

A short woman, probably in her sixties, appeared through a side door, pushing a mop bucket by the handle of the mop that was resting in it. A younger woman, about thirty, and not bad looking, appeared beside her and slung the cloth that she was holding over her shoulder.

"Told ya, Kell. David Essex, but with brown eyes and a better voice," said the older woman.

"Fuck. Me," the younger woman said.

Maca ended the song and winked at the two women who were now giving him a round of applause.

"Don't encourage him, ladies. His head'll be too big to fit through the doors when it's time for us to pack up later." I told them.

Maca licked his index finger, pulled up his T-shirt and circled it around his nipple. What the fuck had gotten into him this morning?

The two women fanned themselves as they left by the same door they came in through.

"You seem happy," I told him as I walked towards the stage.

He smiled and his eyes were shining. "That bird I brought home last night sucked like a Hoover. Three times, and she swallowed every drop. What's not to be happy about after a night like that?" He stared at me for a few seconds after he finished speaking and I could see that the anger was still there. He couldn't fool me.

"I've got a new song I wanna try," he said, jumping down from the stage and pulling a sheet of paper from his back pocket. "I've got an idea of how I want it to sound, but I wanted your input first."

"Mac, c'mon, man. I really don't think this song is a good idea," Billy said.

"Chill the fuck out, dude. It's just a song," Maca told him.

"No, it's not just a song though, is it Mac?" Tommy added his voice into the conversation.

I looked between the three of them, my eyebrows pulled into a frown caused by my obvious confusion.

"Yeah, *Tom*, it *is* just a song. What the fuck is your problem?"

"You're my problem, Mac. You've spent the last year bouncing between being catatonic with grief, drugs, and booze, and then pinging off the walls and trying to fuck anything with a pulse, all to try and get Georgia out of your system. You've changed all of that up the last few weeks and have been miserable as fuck, walking round with a face like a smacked arse and wanting to punch anyone that looks at you the wrong way. Then you turn up here this morning, cracking jokes like a fucking game show host and pull that piece of shit song out, knowing full well that it's gonna upset people."

I swear to God, still to this day, that was the most I'd ever heard Tommy say. He was seriously pissed off about the song, and I had no idea why.

"How about you fuck off and mind your own business, Tom? When was the last time you wrote us a song?" Maca asked.

"Never, Mac. I'm not a songwriter and I've never claimed to be, but if I was, I wouldn't pull a stunt like that." Tommy rubbed his hand over his shaved head and turned his pale blue eyes on me. "I can't be part of this, Marls. I'm sorry, mate," he said before turning and walking over to where all of our equipment was set up.

"What the fuck was that all about?"

Billy put his hands up, as if in surrender. Shaking his head, he said, "Nothing to do with me. I understand why he's pissed, but it's your shout whether you want us to put some notes down for this."

"Well, I've not even seen the fucking thing yet, so how would I know?" I told Bill as he headed in the same direction as Tom, who was now banging on his drums.

"You gonna show me what's got him so pissed off?"

Maca took a draw on the cigarette he'd just lit. "Why the fuck are you smoking? Len'll go ape shit if he walks in here and catches you."

"Fuck Len. In fact, fuck the lot of ya." He threw the sheet of paper with the song written on it at me. "Until you lot can come up with something better, we'll keep using my lyrics, and if any of you have got a problem with them, then I'll just stop writing and leave it to you three."

He could be such a fucking diva sometimes. Between him and George, I couldn't tell ya who wore the biggest crown.

I bent down and picked up the song sheets and started to read.

You called this on,
Now you've got your way.
Time for me to move along,

Tomorrow's another day.
Fuck you, baby, I did my best.
Fuck you, baby, now I'll go fuck the rest.

I tried to reason, make you see sense,
But you walked away... No recompense.
You gave me no chance to talk or say my goodbyes.
You ignored my pleas, ignored my cries.
So fuck you, baby, now I'll go fuck the rest.
I fucked you, baby... You weren't the best.

When you meet another, which I'm sure you will,
Just remember me and the way I can make you feel
When he slides inside you, and when he holds you tight.
I hope you think and dream of me, all through the night.
When he pushes in deep and looks into your cold hard eyes,
When he says and does those things that only I know you like
Don't you forget that I was your first, the first to hear your moans,
the first to hear your sighs.

So fuck you, baby, my time here is done.
I'm through with crying, time for me to have some fun.
Fuck you, baby, maybe see you around some time.
Then you can join all the others and wait your turn in line.

"You are fucking kidding me, right?" I looked up at him, then back down at the words.

"Why would I be kidding?" he asked. He was actually being serious. This wasn't a joke, he really meant for me to write music for this.

"You seriously expect me to write music, then get up on stage and perform a song that talks like that about my sister?"

"You've had no problem singing any of the other songs I've

written about your sister, and you've had no problem living off the royalties either."

I didn't hesitate for a second. I swung a punch that caught him square on the chin. Luckily, he hit a chair on his way down, preventing his head from cracking open on the concrete floor.

"Marley!" Jimmie screamed my name from the doorway. She dumped the brown paper bag onto the first table she saw and came rushing towards us. Len followed her through the doors, carrying coffees and a carrier bag.

"What the fuck is wrong with you?" she screeched, the sound echoed around the quiet warehouse.

"Me?" I actually pointed at myself as I paced in front of where she had Maca's head in her lap. Now that his eyes were open, any concerns I may have had that I'd actually hurt him were gone.

"Read this before you start accusing me of wrongdoing, and tell me you or Len wouldn't have done the same." I shoved the pieces of paper at her and she started to read.

"What the fucks going on ... what's that? Why's he on the floor?" Len fired off.

"Marley knocked Maca out." Jim held the paper up to him before moving and letting Maca's head hit the concrete. He gave a groan of complaint.

"Now it's your turn," she told Len. "And when you're done, I want first dibs before Bailey finishes him off."

Len read the words to the song, looking up at me and laughing a couple of times, then down at Maca, who was sitting up on his own.

"Wh-what is this?" Len laughed nervously as he asked.

"That's this pricks latest offering. He expects *me* to come up with a tune for this. He expects *me* to perform and record it. A song about *him* taking my sister's virginity, about some *other* bloke fucking her." Jimmie put her hand on my chest as I stepped toward the fucker again.

"Have you finally lost the plot, Maca? Stand the fuck up," Len shouted. Maca stood, still rubbing at his jaw. "What the fuck is going on with you, boy?" Apparently, Len turned into my dad when he was angry.

"It's just a song."

"Just a song? And you really expect him to get up on stage and sing a song like that, knowing it's aimed at *his sister*? You really think that I want to be the manager of a band who sings a song like that, about *my* little sister?"

"So as long as I write songs about how much I love and miss your sister, we're all good, but if I write something honest, about how she shut me out with no chance to explain or apologise, or I write about how she let me shag her when she was just fifteen, that's—"

He didn't get a chance to finish before Len flew at him, knocking Jimmie over in the process.

"He seriously has a death wish," Jim said as I was helping her up. We stood back and watched as Len and Maca rolled around on the floor for a few minutes before Tom and Billy separated them.

They were both breathing heavy, bleeding from the nose, and had split lips. Surprisingly, it was Maca that was trying to break free from Billy's grip and get at Len again.

"This is bullshit, fucking bullshit. How much money did you all make from the songs I've written about her the past couple of years, eh?" He looked around like a crazy man, still breathing hard. His white T-shirt was ripped at the neck, and bloodstained.

"She broke my fucking heart. She's a cold-hearted bitch who won't answer my calls or reply to my letters." He'd actually gone beyond shouting and was screaming at us.

Jimmie stepped up. "How *dare* you. How fucking dare you. *You* broke *her* heart ... *You*." She punched him, like a girl, with the flat side of her bunched hands on his arms and chest. "You broke her heart, you stupid fucker, and you almost broke her mind. She's shut you out because that's the only way she can survive. You've no idea, you have no idea what she's been through. She's hurt and humiliated. They wrote horrible things about her in the papers and she didn't ask for any of it. She gave you her virginity when she was just fifteen because she's loved you since she was eleven years old, since that very first day we set eyes on you in *their* back garden. She loved and trusted you and what did you do, Maca? You went off to a hotel room with that slut, that fucking oxygen thief of a human being, just a few days after proposing to George. You went into a hotel room and snorted blow from Haley White's tits. Of all the people in the world Maca, it was with her? Why her? Have you any idea what you've done to my best friend?"

Jim was breathing heavy through her tears. Len, Billy, and Tom were watching in stunned silence while Maca and I both cried.

Fucking tears. They just come from nowhere.

Guilt sat like acid in the bottom of my stomach, in my chest, and pumped through my veins, burning me from the inside out.

"It wasn't his fault," I said quietly. Jimmie's head turned quickly and her brown eyes were on me, sweat glistening on her light, cocoa coloured skin. I've never seen Jim so angry.

"Fuck off, Marley," she spat. "He went to that room willingly, knowing all the while that he had a girlfriend, an unofficial fiancé. He asked your sister to marry him and just a few days later, he's in a hotel room with the one and only person I've ever known George to hate. Yeah, you're as much to blame as he is, but he was the one with a girlfriend. He was the one that should've stayed away from that conniving little cunt, but he didn't." Her face crumbled as she looked at Maca.

"You broke my beautiful friend. You broke her sixteen-year-old heart and I don't know if I'll ever get her back. So don't you dare stand there telling me that she's a cold-hearted bitch. Don't you fucking dare stand there spitting the dummy because she shut you out. What you did was shut her down."

"So why won't she just talk to me? Why won't she just let me explain?" he pleaded. His voice was full of desperation. It hurt my heart so bad to watch him, to hear all of it and know that I was to blame.

"Because she's not ready to see you. You hurt her so much that she can't bear to even hear your name." She stood in the middle of all of us, but faced Maca, shaking her head. "She's just doing what she needs to do to get by, but never have I heard her say such spiteful things about you. Why would you want to do that to her? Why, after everything you've put her through, would you want to cause her any more hurt and humiliation? Just get over it, Maca. Move on and stop acting like a lovesick kid."

"But that's what I am. That's what you all forget. I may be twenty-years-old, but I'm still a lovesick kid. I always will be for her. When will you all fucking get that?"

We all remained silent, everyone realising in that moment that he was in fact right, even if he'd just behaved like a complete dick. We were still so young, stupid, clueless, horny, and emotional. Our lives had been turned on their heads in a short amount of time; cameras constantly going off in our faces, fabricated stories being written about us.

For us it was, and always would be, about the music first. I didn't want celebrity status. Yeah, back then I liked the amount of birds it led to me banging, but right from the very beginning, we all hated the intrusion. Billy and Tom had settled down from the very start of the bands fame so it was always Maca and myself the press focused on, especially as we were also seen as the two front men. But we weren't men, we were still boys—kids playing in a very grown-up world. We had no clue how to handle what we were feeling, and we didn't always handle things the right way. Unfortunately for us, every fuck up we made from the age of eighteen was reported on, documented, and sometimes photographed. It was just part of the deal, it came with the territory, and there was nothing we could do about it.

At the end of the day, I suppose all that Maca was doing with those lyrics was what came natural to him, letting it all out in a song.

Didn't stop me from wanting to put him on his arse again though.

I knew my sister was no angel. I knew her and Maca were getting up to shit when she was far too young, but I honestly thought that they'd be together forever, that they were *it* for each other. At no stage did I ever account for me and my own selfish motives being the instigator in their downfall.

Maca and I didn't speak for over three months after that. The album was delayed because we couldn't agree on anything and all our public appearances were strained. Billy and Tom were finally taking over the interviews, leaving me and Maca to blend into the background.

Our studio time was cancelled, the label agreeing to let us have the summer to ourselves; hoping that some time apart was all that was needed. As long as we agreed to regroup in September and get the tracks down in time for a Christmas release, they left us alone.

After our March fallout, we finally had to meet in June and make a few decisions on the interiors of the apartments Maca and I had invested in together. We actually agreed on most of what we wanted during the meeting with the design team my dad's builders had set us up with, and we went out and had a few beers together that night.

The place the label had set us up in, near the West London studios, were too big for us once Tom and Billy had moved out, so we had found places of our own. Both of us unknowingly bought penthouse apartments in the same building, just five minutes from where our own place was being built in the Docklands redevelopment area of East London.

We spent a bit of time together through the summer, working on new material, but things didn't really begin to thaw completely between us until we got back into the studio in early September. Maca was still pretty quiet and withdrawn. I knew just from the limited time I'd been in his company that he was smoking a lot of weed. I mean, don't get me wrong, I'm not trying to promote drug use. It was something I'd done since I was about thirteen, before I even met

Maca I think, but yeah, all things in moderation. You need to be able to function and when we first got into the studio, I really think he was only just hanging on.

And then he met Carla.

TWELVE

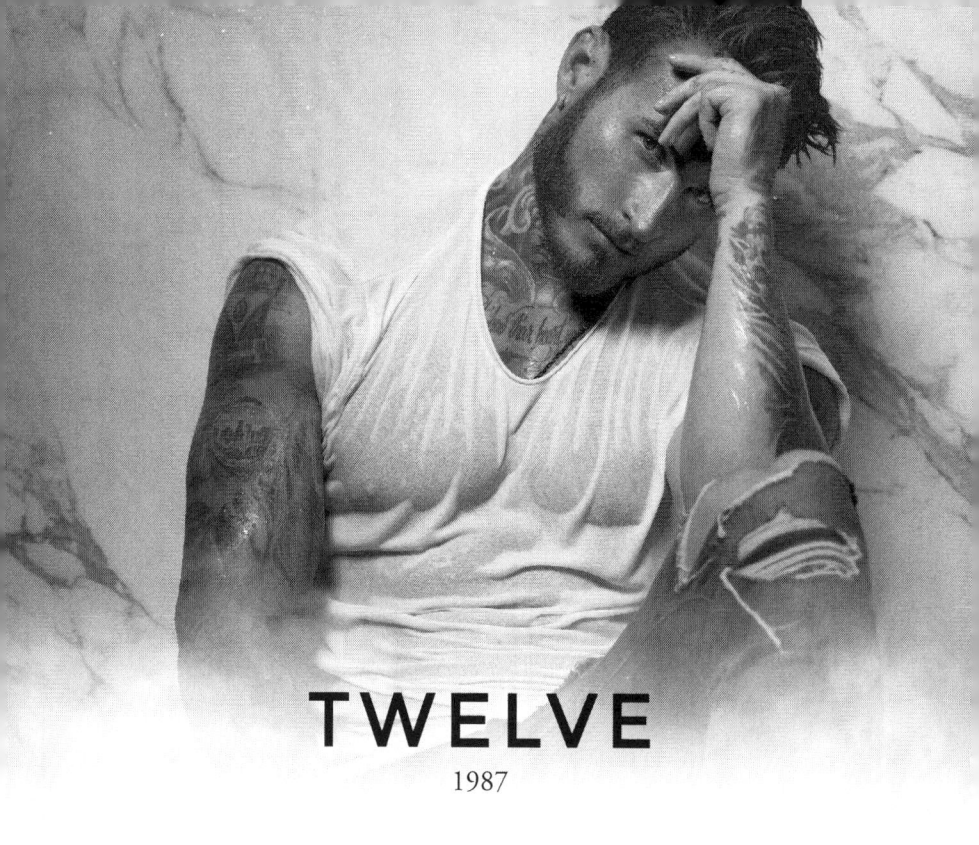

1987

The first day in the studio we were introduced to the team. The place Len had found for us was in a leafy suburb of London, not too far from Hampstead Heath. It was a brand new set up and we would be using state of the art digital technology, a lot of which was all new to us. The two sound engineers were a brother and sister team called Max and Lydia. We'd never worked with them before, but Len assured us that they knew our work and were the best in the business with the new equipment now available. Trevor and Nile were our usual producers, and we had every faith in them coming up with the sounds we were hoping to create.

We were introduced to a few office and backroom staff, and then we were introduced to Carla. She was a newly qualified sound and recording engineer who had been taken on by Max and Lydia. She was straight out of university and looked like a pixie.

No tracks were laid down the first week. They rarely were with us. We spent the time getting our sound tight, Maca working on his voice and listening to playbacks.

During that time, Carla was in and out of the live room with drinks and food for us, and I had noticed Maca watching her.

She was cute, don't get me wrong, just not my type; short, and really petite, with an almost androgynous body. No curves, no tits, and spikey blonde hair. She told us that she was twenty-three, but she looked twelve. As far removed from my sister as you could get, really. Perhaps for Maca, that was the appeal.

On the Friday at the end of our first week, Max suggested we all go to the pub together and we ended up at The Spaniards Inn. It was a beautiful evening and we were able to get a table out in the beer garden and enjoy some late summer sun.

Drinks were drunk, conversations flowed, and we all learned a little bit about each other.

Max and Lydia were in fact twins. Their dad was a well-known session musician who had played with some of the biggest bands in the world over the years.

Max, it turned out, was married to Nile's sister, Nicole, who joined us with their two kids an hour after we arrived at the pub.

It felt good to be in a crowd of people who just accepted you for who you were. No bullshit, no pretences. No one wanted to touch us or have us sign parts of their bodies. It was like being with family and I suddenly felt very homesick.

Over the coming weeks, it became a regular thing for us to all have a drink together on a Friday, and at first, I enjoyed sitting back, watching Maca and Carla get closer. After a while though, I noticed that she was a little bit flirty with all the blokes; single, married, she didn't care. It was almost like she was just after someone, anyone, even me, and it made me uncomfortable. Maca wore his heart on his sleeve and the last thing he needed was to get his heart broken again.

Max, Trevor, and Len had all given Maca the 'Don't shit on your own doorstep' talk. I still wasn't exactly sure what was happening between the two of them. I'm not sure if it was because of George that he didn't confide in me, but we could all see that Maca was happier. Despite that, I still had my reservations. Call it gut instinct. There was just something about the girl I didn't like.

That year, Georgia's birthday passed without a mention of it from Maca. I sent her a card and a Beastie Boys T-shirt that I'd managed to get signed for her. Jimmie passed on her thanks and a message to say that she loved it.

By mid-October, the album was finished and Maca and I had moved into our new place together in Docklands.

Although I knew he was seeing Carla, he never brought her back to our shared apartment. I'm not sure how serious things were between them at that point, but I knew for a fact he wasn't seeing her exclusively. She was a distraction, I got it, but I did feel a bit sorry for the girl, even if I didn't like her. By the end of our time in the studio, it was obvious to everyone that she had a massive crush on him, but I wasn't sure how deep his feelings went for her, or how at that stage he was feeling about Georgia.

We were lying in front of the telly at home one Sunday night when Jim and Len came around.

"Big brother Lennon, to what do we owe this pleasure?" I asked as he shoved a nicely chilled bottle of Bolli into my hand.

"Come to ask a favour, bro," is all he said before sitting down and muting the sound with the remote control.

"What the fuck, Len? Make yourself at home, mate." Maca sat up complaining. Jimmie sat down on the sofa next to him.

"Thanks, Maca, I will." Len winked as he spoke.

I got us all a beer from the fridge and called out to Jim, asking if she wanted me to crack open the bubbly. "Well that depends on your answer to our question," she called back. "A beer will do for now." I brought her a beer and went and sat on the opposite sofa with my brother.

"What's up then? Spill the beans," I told them both.

"The wedding's all booked for the 3rd of June, 1989," Jim said with a smile.

"Congratulations," Maca and I said in unison, all of us raising our bottles in a toast.

"I've asked Bailey to be my best man." Len added. I felt a little stab of jealousy, but that was just a long-held sibling rivalry issue. I knew that as the older brother, it was only right that Bailey was best man.

"But we'd like you two to be groomsmen." Len quickly added.

"Of course, it'd be my pleasure," I told them both, having no idea what a groomsman was, but happy to be given a role.

It was quiet for a few seconds and I just knew there was a 'but' coming. I watched Jimmie flick her dark hair over her shoulder and lick her lips. She was nervous. I'd known the girl since we were in playschool, and I knew when she was shitting herself about something.

"Maca?" She looked at him, waiting for his answer.

"It'd be my absolute pleasure to be a part of your wedding, but I totally understand if you change your minds about me being there. I don't wanna cause you issues with other members of your families."

Of course, Georgia.

"It's not a problem for Georgia. She understands that we obviously want you all there with us and she's good with that," Jimmie reassured him.

"That's not the sort of thing Gia would say. Tell me honestly, Jim, how's she really feeling about it?" Maca asked.

She looked between the both of us.

"She's promised to make an effort to get things back on track between her and Marley before the wedding." She smiled and looked at me as she talked, and I swallowed down the lump in my throat. I promised my mum I would go home for Christmas that year. Perhaps that would be a good time to start building bridges.

"And what about me?" Maca asked again. "How does she feel

about seeing me there?"

Jim takes a swig of her beer, looking at Len for guidance, and when he gave his head a small nod, she looked back at Maca.

"She said that for *me*, she could do it. To give me the day that I want, she would be able to deal with being around you, just for one day."

"Well that makes me feel wanted." I felt so sorry for him in that moment and pissed off with my sister.

"All I ask is that she doesn't take anyone else with her," Maca requested.

"What?" Len and Jimmie asked at the same time.

"A bloke, whoever she's seeing. Ask her, from me, if she could just come on her own." His eyes looked around to each of us. "I don't think I could handle seeing her with another bloke," he told us honestly.

"Maca, you have got to be kidding me? She doesn't go anywhere to meet blokes. She goes to work and the gym, that's it. That's her life. She goes nowhere, sees no one. She doesn't see any of her friends. Well, in all honesty, she doesn't really have any friends outside of us." Jimmie turned her gaze solely on Maca as she spoke. "When you did what you did, not only did she lose you and Marley, but in a way she lost me and Len too. Even Billy and Tom. The biggest part of her life, the part that she planned on being her *whole* life, her *world*, went too. I thought you got that? I thought you knew how isolated and alone she's been."

I watched him as he stroked the two middle fingers of his left hand over his lips. His eyes welled with tears, but he managed to swallow them down.

"No, Jim, I had no fucking idea that was the life she's been living. I don't know if *you* realise this, but you lot don't tell me much about what's going on in her life. You *can* talk about her around me, ya know? I'm fully aware that I'm a pussy where she's concerned, and that my behaviour's not normal for a bloke my age, but what we had— what I have with G, ain't normal. I don't know what love's like for others, but I've seen people go through breakups, I've listened to them declare that they're heartbroken, and then a month later they're seeing someone else, declaring their undying love for them, but that's not possible for me. I know that I shag other birds—"

He took a swig from his beer as Jimmie chimed in with, "Lots of other birds, lots and lots and—"

"Yeah, yeah, Jim, we get it." I cut her off.

"I don't wanna say that I'm glad she's as miserable as I am. You're her brothers and her best mates, but fuck. As much as it hurts me to hear that she's hurting, hearing it gives me the tiniest bit of hope, and shit yeah, in a weird and twisted way, it makes me fucking ecstatic."

He drained his drink and tilted his bottle towards me.

"Let's crack open the Bolli. Looks like we've got a wedding to go to, dude."

THIRTEEN
1987 / 1988

The Christmas of 1987 turned out to be a bit of a disaster. We had an album and a single sitting at the number one spot on both sides of the Atlantic, and in seven other countries around the world.

Maca and I celebrated all night on Christmas Eve, and I turned up at my mum's in a taxi, ten minutes after dinner was served. I was high as a kite, stinking of booze and perfume, and my family was far from impressed.

Any attempts at talking to George were blown out the window when she heard me telling Bailey about mine and Maca's exploits from the night before.

My parents had moved from the house we were raised in, and were now living in a beautiful barn conversion. My dad had added a soundproofed room out to the side of the property and I'd headed in there with Bails for a sneaky joint after our almost silent dinner. He had recently split up with Donna, his long-term bitch of a girlfriend, and was living back at home with Mum and Dad.

The conversation started off innocently enough, with me asking Bailey how he was handling living back at home with the 'rents' at twenty-six.

"It's actually not as bad as you think. You know mum; clothes are washed, ironed, and hanging in my wardrobe a day after I leave them on my bathroom floor. Cooked breakfast ready for when I get up and my dinner's waiting on the table every night when I get home from work. I've put on about five pounds since I've been here." He rubbed his belly as he talked.

I was lying with my back pushed into a bean bag on the floor, my legs stretched out in front of me, crossed at the ankles. My back was to the door as I faced Bailey, who was lying up on the old leather Chesterfield that had been in our family forever.

"But what about when you bring a bird back? What's the ol' dear have to say about that?" I asked him.

"Yeah, not gone there yet. It's either been back to their place, or a quickie in the car. Why'd ya think I drive a Land Rover?" he asked with a wink.

"Fuck that. I ain't had a shag in a car since I was about sixteen."

"Well, we've not all been lucky enough to have tits and arse handed to us on a plate like you have, Mr Rock God," he said with a smile.

I shrug my shoulders and laugh as I think about the night before.

"Yeah, it's fucked sometimes, mate. I'll tell ya, women just don't give a shit when you're famous. They're up for anything."

"Like what?" he asked, passing back the joint.

"Fucking hell, where do I start? We went to a club last night and got chatting with these girls. Bought them a few drinks and next thing I know, they're dragging me and Maca off to the toilets. One had her skirt up and was bending over the sink with her arse in the air as soon as we got in there. I didn't even bother to take her knickers off, just pulled them to one side and fucked her from behind."

"Hope you wrapped it up first?"

"Always, man, always," I reassured him.

"Anyway, this leaves Maca with three other girls all over him. One drops to her knees and starts sucking him off while he sticks his fingers inside the other two…" I trailed off as Bailey looked wide-eyed over my shoulder.

My skin prickled as I turned my head. I already knew what I'd find.

Georgia was standing with the door held ajar. Her eyes were wide, her mouth opened and closed, as if she was going to say something.

"George…" I called to her but before I could say any more, she was gone.

"Fuck, fuck!" I repeated to anyone that wanted to listen.

"I don't think she heard what you were saying," Bails tried to reassure me.

"Then why the fuck did she run away?"

"Coz that's what she does, Marls. She's got a screw loose. Trying to get a word out of her these days is fucking impossible. She's changed so much from how she used to be. It's fucking heartbreaking to watch, mate, I tell ya."

I stood up and paced, unsure of what to do.

"Leave her, mate. She won't talk to you anyway. She barely talks to me and I'm *not* in her bad books."

I heard the sound of a car start up and when I looked out the door, Georgia was heading up the drive in the little car Maca had bought for her.

I watched her go as Jimmie and Lennon walked across the gravel drive in my direction.

"She okay?" I asked them.

"Yeah, she just wanted to get home to her own little place. I think Ash is coming over tonight," Jimmie said.

"Ash? She seeing someone?"

"Noooo," Jimmie replied, sounding like I'd just asked the most ridiculous question ever.

"Ash ... Ashley Morrison? We used to go to school with her," Jimmie said it like I should remember her.

"Blonde hair, good looking girl?" She continued in a tone, suggesting that I should know who Ashley was.

"Well anyway, she went to school with me and George, then college with George. Now she's working at Posh Frocks for George. She's like the manager or assistant manager, or something like that."

"Well, that's good then. If she's got a mate coming over, that's good." My conscience eased somewhat.

"Yeah, she's a good girl, Ash is. Comes from a rough family, but she's got a heart of gold and always trying to get George to go out with her," Jimmie tells me.

"She still not going out?"

Jimmie shakes her head. "We all try, Marls. I'm not really sure what more any of us can do. It's just a case of waiting and letting her do things in her own time." She shrugged her shoulders, probably feeling as helpless as we all did.

"Where did Maca end up going?" Len asked.

Once again, I had asked that Maca be allowed to come for dinner, but George had told Len to tell me that she still wasn't ready to see him.

"He actually went to his dad's."

"Didn't think he had a dad," Bailey commented.

"Don't be stupid, Bails. Everyone's got a dad," Jimmie tells him.

"They've just gotten back into contact with each other," Len explained before I got a chance to.

"He's actually an all right bloke. He's been to our place a couple of times," I told them.

"So now Maca's made the big time and the money's rolling in, his ol' man has come crawling outta the wood work?" Bailey questioned.

"No, Bails. Believe it or not, it wasn't like that," Jimmie chimed in. "His dad had no idea where his mum had fucked off to when Maca was a kid. As soon as she got wind he was close to tracking her down, she moved him on again. That's why he went to so many different schools. In the end, she moved them from East London into Essex, and that's how he ended up at our school." Jimmie sat down on the sofa next to Bailey as she explained what Maca's dad, Kenny, had told Lennon on the phone when he contacted the record label's offices.

"Anyway, when his dad first realised Maca was his son, he was worried that Mac would just think he was after his money if he showed up unannounced. He left it a couple of months and then got in touch with the label and explained who he was. I spoke with him on the phone, then put him on to Len, who passed all of his details on to Sean and we left him to decide what he wanted to do." We were all silent for a few moments. My brothers and Jim probably doing the same as me, contemplating what they would've done in Maca's shoes.

"What did Maca say?" Bailey asked.

"Pretty much what you did," I told him. "Then they spoke on the phone a few times, met up at a West Ham game, and then went to see a band together. Things have just moved on from there."

"His dad is where Maca gets his love of music from," Lennon added.

"He plays guitar and piano, and apparently he's not a bad singer either. He's been in bands since he was a kid and still is now," I said.

"Well, I'm glad things have worked out for him, but I still owe the little fucker a good hiding for breaking my sister's heart," Bailey stated.

"Honestly, Bails. He beats himself up daily for that fuck up. There's no need for you to add to that boy's pain," Len informed him.

"So, apart from all the different birds he shags, is he seeing anyone?"

"Well, there's Carla." Jimmie's head swung around to face me, her eyes widened and her nostrils flaring.

Fuck, that girl misses nothing, and yet she had no idea about this until I opened my big fat gob.

Lennon shook his head as subtly as he could.

"Carla? The sound engineer bird?" Jimmie questioned.

"Yeah. I don't know exactly what he's got going on with her. I mean, he never talks about her and he's never brought her back to our place, but I know he's seen her a few times, at least I think he has," I stuttered and stumbled over my words.

"Wow. I'd never have picked her as his type. I actually thought she was into girls," Jim said.

"Perhaps her being so different to George is the appeal," Len added.

"Did you know?" Jim narrowed her eyes on Len.

"I thought the same thing." I tried to deflect Jim's question.

"Lennon, did you know?" She wasn't giving up.

"I had my suspicions," he stated matter-of-factly. "I noticed there was a bit of flirting going on when the boys were recording the last album and warned him to stay away until the business side of things were done." He shrugged his shoulders. "What they got up to once the album was finished, I have no idea. It's got fuck all to do with me anyway."

"So how many times has he seen her?" She was like a dog with a fucking bone and she wasn't letting go anytime soon.

"I don't know, Jim. He doesn't discuss her and I don't ask. I think it's just a convenience thing for him. Ya know, sometimes going home with a complete stranger every night gets a bit old. Sometimes, it might be nice to wake up to a familiar face in your bed," I explained to her, giving away more about how I was feeling than what Maca might be feeling.

"How the fuck would you know?" Len asked. "When was the last time you shagged a bird more than once?"

I had to think about that one for a few seconds.

"San Diego, last year. When Maca had his little meltdown."

"There were five other women involved, that hardly counts,"

Jimmie argued.

"Five other women?" Bailey almost shrieked from the sofa next to Jim. "You had a six-some with five birds?"

"Noooo." Now it was my turn to use the 'don't be ridiculous' tone. "Maca and I shared them, so technically it was seven-some, if you count me and him."

"Fuck me. I've gotta get out of this car dealership and nightclub running game and become a rock star," Bailey said with a huff.

"Believe me, dude, it's really not all it's cracked up to be."

* * *

Despite Georgia not being there, I enjoyed my Christmas night with my family. It felt like years since I'd spent time with both of my brothers, just chilling and chatting and shit. It just reinforced my determination to set things right with George, no matter how difficult she made it for me to get through to her.

Nineteen Eighty-Seven rolled into Nineteen Eighty-Eight. We toured with the new album for a large part of the year. As with every tour we'd been on, there were parties and there were women, but Maca rarely got involved. He got up on stage, gave the crowds the Maca they expected, but as soon as the show was done, he headed back to his room and when we were touring England, some nights he had Milo drive him all the way back home.

There were a couple of nights when he would show his face at an after-party for five minutes, but generally, because Billy and Tom never hung around, I was there alone.

And it was getting old.

I felt like something was missing from my life, but I had no idea what it was. I had the job of my dreams, more money than I could spend in twelve lifetimes, a family that loved me, and women at my beck and call, but something was off and I hated how empty I felt inside.

A large part of what we do for a living is showmanship. The Carnage that fans see on stage or in front of the cameras is not who me, Maca, Billy, and Tom are as individuals, or even when we're together out of the public eye. I was constantly putting on the persona of Marley Layton; womanising, hard drinking, drug taking lead guitarist of Carnage. It was wearing me out, and beginning to depress the fuck out of me.

I craved normalcy. I appreciated more than ever my family, and the fact my mum would still bollock me for leaving my cup on the side, or that my dad still questioned how I spent my money, and that my brothers were there giving me shit because I was the youngest out of the three of us and that just meant they could.

We had been living in the spotlight for around four years by that time and I was looking forward to next year, when we had been promised a break; no tours, no albums, just a few commercials to make and interviews to carry out.

We had Jimmie and Len's wedding to look forward to and time to spend with my family. I didn't know how I was gonna do it, but I knew I had to fix things with Georgia. I know that I'd said it repeatedly, but now with the wedding looming, I knew it had to be faced. I'm Marley Layton, Rock God, for fuck's sake. Georgia was my skinny little sister, so what was the problem?

The tour combined with television appearances, the filming of commercials, and magazine shoots, meant that it was August before we were back in England with time on our hands.

Len and Jimmie had bought their first house earlier in the year, but because of our schedule, Maca and I had yet to see it, so a few days after arriving home we were at Len's door with a couple of bottles of 'Rare Breed,' and a bottle of Bollinger to celebrate their purchase.

They had decided to remain in the Brentwood area and were fairly close to my parent's, and just up the road from where my sister lived, above her shop.

"Jimmie not home?" I questioned as I put the bottles down on the open plan kitchens worktop.

Len shot me a look I didn't quite understand before saying, "No, she's out with George, actually."

Maca turned around from where he was standing and admiring the view of the grounds from the back patio doors.

"Georgia's gone out?" I asked, "Or d'ya mean that Jim's just gone to G's for a drink?"

"No, G's actually going out with Jim and Ash, the girl that works at the shop for her."

He looked from me to Maca, who I was already studying to try and gauge his reaction.

"Don't look at me like that. It's been three and a half years. I can't fucking stop her from going out," Maca stated.

"Pour him a drink," I told Len. "Your house is cool, by the way. I love it—well done."

"Thanks. All Jimmie's hard work," he said with a smile. My brother had it so fucking bad for that girl. As much as I one day hoped to find what they had, I sometimes looked at Maca and thought, 'No thank you, very fucking much.' I didn't ever want a woman to have the ability to leave me in the state my sister had left him in for the past three and a half years. I was sure when, or if it ever happened, it would be out of my control, but at that moment I most certainly wasn't looking for anything beyond a one night stand.

Len poured us each a bourbon and we went and sat outside to enjoy the sunny summer's evening.

"What's up, Len? You look like you've got something on your mind, mate?" Maca asked.

My skin prickled when I looked at Len. Maca could read his tells as well as I could. He'd been as close as a brother to the pair of us for almost ten years, and he'd gotten it spot on that night. Len definitely had something bothering him.

"The four-city tour you're supposed to be doing in the States next year—" Len started.

"The one we asked you to get us out of?" I interrupted. I wasn't asking him, just reminding him in case he'd forgotten that the label had promised us a year off from touring and recording.

"Yes, fuckface, I'm aware that you did. Just hold your horses and listen to what I'm about to say, would ya?" I flipped Len my middle finger as he spoke. "The plan by the label was to bill this as a double headlining tour, featuring you and Kombat Rock."

"No way."

"No fucking way," Maca and I said over each other.

"Calm the fuck down, the pair of ya. Just listen to what I'm saying. It's like dealing with four-year-olds sometimes with you two, I swear."

Len got up and went back inside, leaving us sitting there.

"*Shit*! I thought he was gonna tell me G was getting married or having a baby or something. I thought I was gonna throw up there for a minute," Maca said, raking his hand through his hair as he spoke.

I was shocked by what he'd just admitted to me, especially after being so closed off for this past year. All the colour had drained from his face and he had sweat beading on his newly shaved top lip.

"You really worry about shit like that?" I asked him.

"Only every fucking day. Sometimes all day." I finished my drink, not really knowing what to say.

Len returned, carrying the bottle of Wild Turkey, a bottle of coke, and an ice bucket. He sat them all down on the table. "You might need refills by the time I finish telling you what Jim found out this week," he said, topping up our drinks.

"Spit it out then, Len. You're killing us here," I nagged.

"Marley just shut the fuck up and listen before I slap ya," he snapped.

"Just you try it, motherfucker. I'm not twelve anymore."

"Dudes, where's the love? We're all brothers here, so let's play nice," Maca interrupted. "Len, get the fuck on with it, will ya? And you, shut it."

"Kombat Rock are done—washed up old junkies that nobody wants to listen to anymore. The label planned to get them supporting you on this four-city tour of the US you're *supposed* to be doing." Len looked at me as he emphasised the word 'supposed.'

"That would hopefully bring them the publicity that they need to relaunch their careers. Apparently, Rocco is fresh out of rehab and has been writing again. Anyway, the idea was put to him and he's thrown a hissy fit, saying that he wants double headlining act for KR, alongside Carnage. Obviously, I've said no way is that happening and used it as my excuse to pull you *from* the tour." He looked at me again, driving his statement home.

"I'm gonna knock you the fuck out you keep on," I told him.

"Please, little brother, we all know that'll never happen."

"Get on with it," Maca jumped in, wanting to hear the rest.

"Anyway, Jim's been on the phone with Alix from the KR's management team all week and she's telling Jim that no one likes Rocco, and she can't believe the label would even consider putting them alongside Carnage after what he did to you two boys."

Maca and I turned and looked at each other at the exact same moment. We shrugged and turned back to Len.

"He set you up, boys … the whole thing with Haley White? He deliberately gave you the gear to get you off your nuts, plotted with her to get you back to your room, and for her to cry rape. The fact that you allowed him in the room with a camera was just an added bonus for him."

What the fuck?

My mouth opened and closed a few times, but no words came out as I looked at Maca.

"Well, we always knew it was his photos that ended up in the papers," Maca said before draining his glass.

"But why the rape allegations? What was that all about?" I asked.

"He thought it'd get you kicked off the tour," Len admitted.

"Fucker," Maca said through gritted teeth.

Len topped up our glasses again.

"Is there no way we can use this to bring charges against the pair of them?" I was curious.

"No. No fucking way am I having all of that dragged through the courts," Maca jumped in, guns blazing.

"What they did…" He took a few deep breaths, trying to compose himself. "That pair of cunts ruined mine and your sister's lives. I'll find a way to make them pay, but it won't be done publicly. There's no way I'm having all the details of what went on that day dragged through the courts and made public. G's been through enough—I've been through enough. No more. No fucking more."

I threw myself back in my chair like a sulky child, but frustration was my driving force, not sulkiness.

"I mean it, Marls. We'll get that fucker, but not in a way that's gonna hurt Georgia," Maca reiterated to me.

"Yes, Mac, I fucking heard you the first time."

"We'll get him, don't you worry, boys. We'll find a way and we'll get him," Len reassured us. "I'll call in every favour that I can and he won't see it coming."

Not long after that, we left, leaving Len with a video of an advert we'd just filmed in Japan for an energy drink. We headed home, and I was feeling a little less pissed off, thanks to the bottle and a half of bourbon we'd consumed.

Within the month, Kombat Rock had been dropped by our label. A plagiarism charge had been brought against them for some song they'd claimed to have written in the Early Eighties, and Rocco Taylor's Hollywood mansion had been raided, where an 'undisclosed' quantity of class A drugs had been discovered.

Did I mention that I loved my big brother Lennon?

FOURTEEN

1988 / 1989

Maca and I had invested in a holiday resort in the Turks and Caicos Islands in early '87. We were invited to the opening in December of that year and spent all of Christmas, New Years, and January of 1988 there. We hadn't planned on staying away that long, but the weather back home was freezing and the place was like paradise.

We played a lot of golf, snorkelled, and even wrote and composed four new songs. I returned to England feeling relaxed and centred, although I hadn't been able to shake the feeling that there was a hole somewhere. Something was just missing from my life, but I didn't know what.

In February we took a skiing holiday with Jimmie and Len, and finally settled back into life in England in early March.

Thinking back on it now, I know that I was just running away from the loneliness I was feeling inside, and I suspect that Maca was doing the same. It had been almost five years since we'd had this much time to ourselves, and if the truth be told, we had no one except each other to spend it with. What a sad pair of wankers we were.

Sundays, when I had nothing to do, were always a shit time for me. I knew that my whole family gathered on a Sunday at my parents' place, but I was usually travelling, busy, or too hungover to care. But that particular sunny March morning, I woke up feeling pissed off that I couldn't just turn up there for dinner with Maca in tow like I'd done hundreds of times before when we were growing up.

The girl I'd come home with the night before was still curled up and sleeping next to me. I laid there for a moment, trying to remember her name. I went through the alphabet, starting with A, recounting every girl's name that I could. I got to L and knew I was close; Laura, Lauren, Linda, Lesley, Louise. It began with an L, I was sure of it.

My bedroom door flew open and Maca stood there, drinking from a coffee cup.

"It's a beautiful morning. Fancy taking the bikes out?" he asked.

We had bought ourselves a couple Harley Softtail's last year, but had only been out on them a few times in secret, behind Len's back. Both he and the label would shit a brick if they found out, so we'd kept those particular purchases quiet.

The blonde sleeping next to me poked her head out from under the duvet.

"Talking of bikes," Maca said, "how was that one to ride? She made enough fucking noise."

"Ooooh, harsh dude, and a highly misogynistic assumption."

"You eat a dictionary along with her fanny last night?"

"Oi. Don't come in here with the hump, just coz you didn't get any last night. Fuck off back to bed and rub one out."

He'd left the club early the night before, getting pissed off with the way the women there thought it was okay to keep putting their hands all over him. I mean seriously, would you go up to a complete stranger and start rubbing their cock through their jeans? No, probably not, so why the fuck do women, and some men, think it's okay to do it to us, just because we're in a band? We're neither pieces of meat, nor public property, at least not once we're offstage. If we were to approach random women and grab them by the snatch, we'd be locked the fuck up for it.

Anyway, Maca jumped in a taxi and went home. He was going through another withdrawn and angry stage. As much as his mood swings gave me whiplash, he was my mate and I worried about him. I stayed for another hour, talking to a couple of mates when blondie, with the L sounding name, caught my eye and I ended up taking her home. If I remember rightly, she was short, cute, and had a massive rack. The sex was pretty good too, and I seem to recall bending her into a few interesting positions during the night, but what I'd liked most was that she had no fucking clue who I was.

L girl sat up and blinked a few times.

"Oh my fucking, shit, fuck—" She stared at Maca while trying to wipe her make-up from under her eyes and messing with her hair.

"Morning, blondie." I played it safe, seeing as I couldn't remember her name

L ... Li ... Le ... Lu ... Lucy! Fuck yeah, I'm good. Lucy. That was her name.

She turned to me and screamed. "Oh my fucking god, Marley Layton!"

I gave my best impersonation of her scream and in her voice, I said, "Oh my fucking god, Lucy."

She looks around the room, frowning. "Lucy? Who the fuck's Lucy? My name's Olivia."

Oops.

"Livy, sorry. I meant to say Liv or Livy, not Lucy."

"Ooh, nice backtrack, dude," Maca got in, shaking his head as he walked away.

"Shut the door on your way out, fucker," I called after him. "Don't want you getting all jealous coz your right hand is the nearest thing you've got to a Lu—I mean, a Livy this morning."

Shit, just shoot me now.

After another quick roll around with Lucy Livy Lou… yeah, that's what I'd decided to call her. It gave me a few more options at getting her name right and she was giving me the best blow job, all because she thought I'd given her a 'cute nickname.' Everybody won.

She headed off to my bathroom and showered while I went out to the kitchen to find Maca sitting at the breakfast bar, watching an episode of ThunderCats on the television. He had the sound muted, while sipping on another cup of coffee.

"You all right, dude?" I asked him.

"I'm gonna go and see your sister," he stated while staring at the television screen.

"Why?" I asked, honestly curious as to his reason.

He turned and looked at me. "I need to know, Marls. I need to tell her everything, and I need her to hear me out. Then I need to know if there's ever going to be a chance for us to sort this mess out."

I nodded my head, while debating internally as to whether it was a good idea.

"From what Jim and Len tell me, she's miserable, and I'm still fucking dying here without her." He rubbed his hand over the stubble on his chin.

"I can't carry on like this anymore. I'm existing, but I'm not living. Even if she says no, if she tells me straight up that there's no chance of us ever getting back together, at least then I'll know. It'll hurt … fuck, it'll be agony, but it can't be any more painful than what I've been going through these last few years."

"When?" I asked. "When you planning on going to see her?"

"This week. I don't wanna wait now that I've made up my mind, and I don't want Jim or Lennon to know, just in case they warn her. I don't wanna give G a chance to overthink what she's feeling, so I'll just turn up. I know her, Marls, I know her inside and out. I'll know what she's really feeling as soon as she sees me."

As much as I cringed with the knowledge of how well Maca knew my little sister, I also accepted that what he said was true. Those two were inseparable for five years, and were sleeping together for the last year or so they were together. Nobody knew George as well as Maca did, and being the big brother that I was, that was actually the way I'd like it to stay—him being her one and only.

I had no idea if she'd seen other blokes. Jimmie had mentioned that she'd finally started going out with this new friend, Ash, but she'd never mentioned her dating anyone. She did say that she didn't go to my mum's for Sunday dinner anymore because she was out most Saturday nights. That was something I hadn't yet mentioned to Maca.

"Whatever you feel you need to do, man. I won't say a word to anyone. Just let me know if there's anything I can help do to make this happen." I patted him on the shoulder as I spoke.

We both stare at the television in silence for a few seconds.

"Fuck, I need a shag. I'm actually sitting here with a semi because of a fucking cartoon cheetah cat woman on the telly," he stated.

"Oh, come on. What's not to get hard about Cheetara? It's when you start getting hard over Jaga you need to worry, or worse still, WilyKat. Now that would just be wrong, dude."

I watched as he smiled and shook his head.

"Seriously though. We have to fly to Ireland tomorrow for that charity, do the interviews Len's lined up, but we're back home next weekend. Perhaps I can try and find out what she's doing next week so you'll at least know where she'll be."

"I'd rather talk to her somewhere private, not at your mum and dad's in front of everyone."

"That's fine. I'll just find out when she finishes work. She's living in the flat above the shop now so it shouldn't be too hard to get her on her own."

"Thanks, mate, appreciate it."

"Least I can do, brother," I told him as I headed off back to my bedroom to shower and get dressed for our run out on the bikes.

By the time I'd showered and dressed, Maca and L girl were chatting and laughing like old friends in the kitchen.

"Olivia wants to know if we could collect her mate from where she stayed last night and give them both a lift back to Chelmsford?" I wasn't sure if Maca was asking on L girls behalf, or telling me that that was what we were going to do. He shrugged his shoulders before continuing, "I just thought it might give us a decent run out on the bikes."

"Can do," I replied. "I was actually thinking of heading out to my parents' place … ya know, to see what I could find out about what G's up to for the next few weeks," I informed him, trying not to give too much away in front of our present company.

"I'm not sure, Marls. Who's gonna be there?"

"By the time we get there, no one you'll need to worry about, but I'll check on whose cars are on the drive once we're there anyway. If there's a problem, we'll just keep driving and drop the girls off." He still didn't look too happy, but I continued. "Where's your mate want picking up from, sweetheart?"

FIFTEEN

Turns out that L girl's mate was actually her sister who spent the night at their brother's, just around the corner from us.

I sometimes wondered how stupid I was at that stage of my life. At the time, I thought I had my shit together, but my decision-making skills and the complete lack of thought I put into them were obviously something I had yet to master.

We picked L girl's sister up and drove out towards my parents' place with the girls on the back. It felt good. It was a Sunday afternoon and the traffic was light. Living the life that we did, the freedom of the open road—no cameras, no fans—just complete anonymity was something to savour and I decided as we drove, that that was something we should make time to do more often.

Maca was still not convinced that calling at my parents' place was the right thing to do, but I reassured him that if G was there, then we'd just keep driving. I didn't want to let him know that she wouldn't be and burst his bubble.

I left him at the gate while I went and checked if Georgia's car was on the driveway. As expected, it wasn't.

I signalled for Maca to follow me down to the house. Parking our bikes and removing our helmets, Maca asked, "You sure about this, Marls? If Bailey's there, I don't think he's gonna wanna see my face while he's eating his Sunday roast."

"It's after four o'clock, Mac. Dinner'll be done and everyone but my rents will be in the studio. Anyway, Bails'll be fine." I tried to reassure him, knowing all the while that Bails would probably not be fine and would have a few choice words to say to Maca, as he did myself after the Paris incident; most of those words being a variation of stupid, little, and cunt. But hey, I survived, and I'm sure Maca would too.

"Who's Bailey?" L girl asked.

"My older brother." I told her.

"And I just happen to not be his favourite person," Maca added.

"Aw, is the big bad rock star scared?" The sister whose name had escaped me, chimed in. Maca shot her, then me, a look, which I interpreted as, 'shut her the fuck up.'

"Chill, dude."

"Easy for you to say. You're not the one about to be fed your own dick for Sunday lunch."

I threw my head back and laughed at that statement and opened the door to the studio. I felt like every muscle in my body disconnected itself from my brain. I remained standing but was paralysed, unable to move another step.

My eyes didn't leave my sister's. I watched a spark of something flare in her eyes for a few seconds before a look of complete heartbreak marred her features as she took the four of us in. All too late, I realised once again what an almighty fuck up I had made, and that once again, I had caused my sister pain.

"No, oh God, no," Georgia sobbed quietly.

"*Fuck*, Gia," Maca said from beside me before making a move towards her.

Bailey started shouting at Maca to get out, while Maca begged George to give him chance to talk.

I watched my sister's eyes roam over the face of the man that I knew, that we all knew, that she loved.

"What d'ya want me to do, George?" I heard Bailey ask, the room silent. All eyes were either on Maca or G.

I silently begged my sister, with everything I had in me, I begged her to just give him a chance, to please hear him out.

Georgia had been my best friend from the moment she was born. I'd always felt responsible for her, was raised to always protect her. Until the last few years, I'd spent more time with G than I had with any of my other siblings and I knew every expression that girl could create. And I knew, in that moment, she was about to tell Maca to stay. I'd witnessed the hard look in her eyes leave, to be replaced with only love, shining brightly in them as she looked across to my mate.

As much of a pussy this might make me sound, I'd readily admit that I wanted to cry. Watching two of the people I loved most in the world, finally come face to face again, knowing the heartbreak they had both endured while apart, was finally about to be over. I stood there, rooted to the spot and held on to my tears, willing my sister to just do the right thing.

And then it all fell apart.

"Who the fuck's she, Maca?" L girl's stupid, stupid sister asked.

Georgia's eyes moved to take in the girl now standing right beside Maca and I knew in an instant what was going through my sister's mind. It had gone through mine when we picked her up. She was short and curvy, with big tits and blonde hair.

Haley White.

She looked like Haley White. I saw it and G sure as fuck saw it too. Whether Maca did or not, I'm not sure, but he shouted at her nevertheless.

"Get out!" he roared, making her flinch. "*Get out. Get out. Get out.*"

Whatever I thought that I'd witnessed in Georgia's eyes a few moments ago was now gone, replaced by a cold hard stare of indifference as she looked at Maca.

"G, please baby, just talk to me. I miss you so much, so fucking much." His begging tone hurt my heart because I knew my sister and I knew he had no chance of making her waiver from whatever decision she had now come to.

"Go," she whispered.

"No, G, no. Please, just five minutes. There's so much I need to tell you. I love you so much, Gia."

"*Go Sean,*" she screamed back at him.

Len and Bailey moved. Everyone shouted. There was chaos all around me as my brothers dragged my best mate out onto the drive as he called my sister's name and she just sat with her arms wrapped around her knees, which were pulled up to her chest, and cried. She cried the cry of someone broken, damaged, and in so much more pain than any human should have to bear, and it was all my fault. Once again, I'd fucked up and was the cause of my sister's heartbreak, and the devastating sound of my best mate calling her name.

I don't know what part of my stupid, stupid twenty-something-year-old brain thought it would be a good idea to bring Maca here with two girls in tow; two girls that meant absolutely nothing to either of us, and one of them we'd only just met. I wasn't an idiot, so what part of my brain thought that that would be okay? To this day, I have no idea … no fucking idea, but I knew I had to put it right.

No matter how many times I tried to explain to my family that it wasn't Maca's fault, that it had all been my idea, they wouldn't listen. By the time I'd headed outside, Len was pulling Bailey and Maca apart, and my mum was trying to get between my dad and the three of them.

By the time the shouting was over, there were ripped clothes, split lips, and bloody noses. My mum had put the girls in a taxi and sent them on their way. I was convinced we would be reading about this little debacle in one of the tabloids over the next few days, but was surprised to this day that those girls chose not to run to the papers about our not so friendly family Sunday.

Georgia had been given a Valium and put to bed. I went up and watched her sleep for a while. I told her I was sorry, that I loved her, and I hoped that one day soon she'd be able to forgive me for the fuck-ups that *I'd* made, but which had impacted *her* life.

My mum put ice on Maca's bruised cheek and my dad and Bailey finally listened to our side of the story, but my mum and Dad refused point blank to let him anywhere near my sister, even if she was sleeping.

After handshakes and manly back slaps all round, we finally drove home and went straight to bed, ready for our early morning flight to Ireland the following day.

I knew Maca was pissed off with me, but I wasn't expecting to be totally blanked for the following few days.

He was moody and distant. He insisted on having a room to himself and returned to it after every appearance that we made. He turned up, smiled for the cameras, said what needed to be said, and left. I tried over and over to tell him how sorry I was, but he looked right through me without saying a single word.

Lennon had told me that George had met someone new and being the coward that I was, I just let Maca continue to ignore me. It was easier than facing him and having to explain that this time, it really was over between him and my sister.

I'd never been in love at that stage, so I had no idea what he was going through, but could only imagine that once he found out George had finally moved on, it would feel a whole lot worse, and I didn't want to be the one to tell him, or even be around when it happened.

I'd called my mum daily to see how Georgia was doing and felt like the bottom had fallen out of my world when she told me that the doctor had described her condition as a 'minor nervous breakdown.' I really was the worst brother and best friend on earth. I felt even worse when she told me Maca had been calling every day, but my dad wouldn't let him talk to G. He'd sent her flowers daily too.

We had a break Wednesday evening from the TV, radio, magazine interviews and appearances we'd been doing, so I got Len to book me a flight home and a driver to collect me from the airport and take me to my mum and Dad's place.

I arrived just after eleven. My mum was at the front door, saying goodbye to a girl who she explained was a friend of Georgia's and worked for them at one of their shops. She was gorgeous—long blonde hair, sweet curve to her hips. Under different circumstances, I would've taken some time to say hello, but I didn't have long and I was there to see just one person.

I nodded my head and smiled hello, kissed my mum on the cheek and headed straight up to my sister's room, where I found her curled up and sleeping on the top of her bed.

Georgia had never carried much weight. She used to remind me of a foal when she was about eight or nine and started to grow head and shoulders above the other kids her age. She was all arms and legs, always walking around with her head down, probably hoping that it would make her look shorter. Somewhere between the age of nine and ten, her boobs started to grow. I hadn't noticed, she was my skinny little sister. I knew what boobs were, but I had no interest in hers, and it wasn't until my mates started to comment that I told my brothers that they needed to tell my mum to get her a bra. It was only about a year after that our parents sat us three boys down and told us that George was growing up and becoming a woman, and that her privacy needed to be respected. I had no idea what the big deal was until I walked into the local corner shop the following Sunday afternoon and my little sister was in there buying a box of tampons that the penny dropped.

I felt so sorry for her when she turned around and saw me

pretending to flick through a car magazine. Perhaps if it'd been a music mag, she wouldn't have blushed so much because we both knew that my knowledge and interest in cars was less than zero at that time of our lives.

"Marls," she'd said, while rushing past me.

There was no such thing as Google or the internet then, but I was a pubescent boy and was fully aware of the facts. My little sister was all grown up and could now potentially get pregnant, and there was no fucking way that was happening on my watch.

I'd always been protective of her. My dad had drummed it into us boys that it was our life's mission to look after our little sister and despite the few years that I failed big time, it's what I've spent the majority of my life trying to do.

I laid down on the bed next to where she was sleeping, stretching and crossing my legs out in front of me. I laced my fingers and placed them behind my head. "I've missed you, George. I feel like part of me is missing, not having you in my life." I turn my head to look at where she's still sleeping soundly. The landing light was shining in through the bedroom door and I could see her long lashes fanning out on her prominent cheekbones. Her face was drawn and gaunt looking, her dark skin paler than I'd ever seen it. I swallowed down the lump in my throat, caused by the knowledge that my actions on Sunday had done this to her. Whatever happiness she may have been experiencing with that new boyfriend, my thoughtlessness had caused her four years of misery, and I knew for a fact that whoever this new bloke was, she would never have with him what she had with Maca.

"I'm so sorry about Sunday, G. Those girls, they meant nothing. Maca was just doing me a favour and giving a lift home to the sister of the girl I'd brought home the night before. I fucked up, George. I always seem to fuck up where you and Maca are concerned." I took in a deep breath, trying to ease the tightness in my chest.

"I love you. You're my little sister and I would never do anything to intentionally hurt you, but I seem to do it so often that you must think I'm on a mission to keep you and Maca apart, when nothing could be further from the truth." I moved my hands from behind my head and laced them over my chest.

"He loves you. I mean, really fucking loves you. I'm not an expert or anything, but fuck." I shook my head as I tried to come up with how to word it without it causing any more damage than I already had.

"He's Sean McCarthy, George. Do you have any idea what that means now? Do you have any concept of how big Carnage has become? We're not just a bunch of kids playing the local pubs. We sell out stadiums. We have two platinum albums under our belts and untold awards. I'm twenty-two-years-old ... hang on, am I? Fuck, I'll have to ask mum, I've lost track." I laughed out loud as I gave up trying to work out in my head how old I was.

"That's how insane our lives are, George. I can't even remember how fucking old I am right now. How mad is that? But anyway, the point I'm trying to make is that despite all the fame and success, all the awards and the money in the bank, I know that Maca would give it all back, give it all up in a heartbeat to have you by his side again."

I licked my dry lips before continuing. "Now don't go throwing one of your little hissy fits when I say this, but the amount of women we have throwing themselves at us nowadays is just insane. I mean it's great ... it's fucking superb. We could have a different bird to shag every hour of every day and we still wouldn't get through all of them that would be in the queue, but you know what? Maca, he don't see any of them. He's taken out models, actresses, royalty even, and he couldn't give a fuck about any of them and ya know why, G? You wanna know *why*? Because they're not *you,* and you're all he wants."

I let out a long breath and stared up at the ceiling. "I know after all the trouble I've caused you, you owe me nothing, but please, please would you give him a chance? Please just sit down and talk everything through with him. I know you're with someone else now, and even if there is no chance for you two, just give him the chance to explain what happened in that hotel room, would ya? Just hear him out and let him tell you exactly how he feels and if after that, you still don't wanna be with him, well, at least then you'll both have some closure."

I leaned over my sister and kissed her temple before making my way downstairs to my mum's kitchen, in search of a cup of tea and a chocolate biscuit.

I ended up raiding my mum's cupboards for all my old favourites, making myself a tinned corned beef and tomato sandwich. I layered each of the four slices of bread with salad cream and added a bag of Walkers cheese and onion crisps to the mix. I grabbed a bag of pickled onion monster munch, a breakaway, a blue riband, and a packet of McVities dark chocolate digestives. I carried my stash over to the dining table, moving endless vases of flowers out of the way so that I could sit down. When I got back to put milk in my tea, I spotted a packet of penguins in the fridge and grabbed one of them, just in case I was still hungry after my man-sized snack. I turned back to the table with my tea and almost jumped out of my skin when I saw my dad standing in the doorway, watching me.

"You hungry, boy?" he asked me in his gruff voice.

"Starving."

"Don't they feed you at these interviews you do? Looks like you ain't been fed for a week."

"Yeah, but it's not proper food like this. I feel like I'm six again when I open mum's cupboards. They're always full of my favourites. You wanna cup of tea? Kettles just boiled"

"Yeah, go on then," he replied while pulling out a chair and sitting himself down opposite where I'd set out my picnic on the table. He too rearranged the florist shop going on all over the house.

When I headed back to the table with his drink, he was shoving a half of one of my sandwiches into his mouth.

"What the fuck you got in there, crisps?" he asked through a mouthful of food.

"Yeah, cheese and onion."

He smiled and shook his head. "You're as bad as your sister. She always puts crisps in her sarnies."

"Yeah, I know. It was me that introduced her to that culinary delight." I admitted before taking a bite of my sandwich.

"How's she doing?" I asked him.

He lets out a long breath and shakes his head again. "She's not left her room all week, son. She scares me, I gotta tell ya. She needs to get over him and move the fuck on." He was quiet for a few seconds, so I offered him another half of my sandwich, which he took.

"It's not just her though, Dad. He hasn't moved on either, and he obviously wants to let her know how sorry he is." I gestured with my chin to all the flowers.

"It's getting on for four fucking years. They were kids. What the fuck is wrong with the pair of them?" my dad questioned, ignoring the fact that I'd just mentioned how sorry Maca was.

"I don't know, Dad. Apparently love can have all sorts of effects on people."

"Well, it's affected them two all right. I ought to bang their fucking heads together. Perhaps that would knock some sense into the pair of them, and then hopefully, we'll all get some peace."

I watched as he broke a chocolate biscuit in half and dunked it into his tea. "You not got a bird?" he asked.

"You're joking, right? After seeing how fucked up things are with my sister and best mate? No thanks. I'll keep on fucking then forgetting them for a few more years yet, if it's all the same to you?"

"As long as you're being careful, son."

"Always, Dad. My dick never gets wet, it's always wearing an overcoat," I assured him.

"That's good to hear … good to hear." He pushed up from the table and stood. "Clear up your mess, else your mother'll go mad in the morning. How long you here for?"

"I'm on a flight out of Gatwick first thing."

I stood and moved around the table, where my dad pulled me in for a blokey type of cuddle.

"You need to sort things out with your sister, and you need to come home and show your face around here a bit more often, son. I know you're a big star these days, but you're still our little boy and we miss you."

That was so unlike my dad. He never said shit like that and I fought to swallow down the big ol' lump that I had in my throat.

"I know, Dad, but it's been hard, ya know. What with work and Georgia not wanting to talk to me, and I feel bad—so fucking guilty for all the shit I've caused her and Maca— but I will sort it, I promise. It's why I've come home tonight. She's gonna have to talk to me before I leave. I'm not giving her a choice."

He nodded his head and patted me across the back with his big hand. "I understand, son, but just so you know, despite all the bullshit that's gone on with your sister and that dickhead thing you and your bushy-eyebrowed mate did in France, I'm proud of you, boy—very proud."

I fought to control the wobble of my chin and didn't even bother battling the two fat tears that rolled down my cheeks.

"You hear me? Me and your mother, we're both very proud of what you've achieved."

I nodded because talking around the tennis ball sized lump in my throat was proving to be impossible.

"Love you, boy. G'night."

"Night, Dad. I love you too."

I cleared away my mess and headed back upstairs to change into a pair of jogging bottoms and running shoes, thinking that I might have to go for a run before I could get any sleep that night. I splashed my face with water and cleaned my teeth before going to check on Georgia. I sat in the chair near her bed and watched her sleep for a little while. She talked in her sleep, but I couldn't quite make out what she was saying—something about Sean and a tiger? Well, as long as it was Maca she was dreaming of and not this new bloke, there was still hope, I thought to myself.

Her eyes opened and she shivered.

"Marley George Layton, would you please get in here and give me a cuddle? I'm freezing my fucking tits off."

I didn't even attempt to hide the smile from my face. It made my cheeks ache it was so big, but fuck it, my sister wanted a cuddle from her big brother and world-famous bad boy of rock or not, I was over the fucking moon.

"Fuck, it must be cold coz you've got some fuckin' tits to freeze off there girl."

She shook her head in my general direction, obviously not finding my joke about the size of her boobs funny. I toed off my trainers and climbed into bed beside her. She climbed under the duvet and pulled my back into her front so that she was spooning me.

I was assaulted from all directions by the smell that was so uniquely Georgia and once again, I felt like a six-year-old as I swallowed down the lump in my throat. I'd missed that, I'd missed *her*, so fucking much.

"Don't you dare fart on me," she warned.

"Oh please, George, don't make out. We all know that you're the farter of the family." I wondered if she could hear the smile in my voice as I spoke.

"Yeah right, Marls." She came back with a sarcastic tone. "Anyway, at least when I fart, it smells of roses. Yours smell like something crawled up your backside and died."

She gave me a dig in the ribs as she talked.

"Hark at you, fuckin Avon arse," I responded.

There was a long moment of silence. It hung heavy in the air. Despite the feeling of dread over the conversation we needed to have sitting on my chest, I couldn't wipe the shit-eating grin off my face.

I was there with my sister, and no matter how uncomfortable the next few minutes were about to become, I was just so fucking happy right then.

"Marls?" she said quietly, her breath making my hair move as she spoke.

"Porge?" I replied.

"I'm so glad you're here."

"I'm so glad you wanted me here," I told her honestly. I hated that there'd been this rift between us. I know I caused it, but fuck, I really thought that she would've forgiven me sooner.

"Let's never *not* talk again," she whispered.

"No problem ... Porge?"

"Marls?"

"I'm so sorry, for everything." I think that was the most honest thing I had ever said in my life at that point.

"I know you are, Marls. Let's go to sleep."

I listened to my sister's breathing even out, her heart beating into my back, and felt happier than I had in a long, long time.

Fuck the fame, fortune, and fake aspects of my life. Family was so much more important. Loving and being loved felt so much better than achieving a platinum selling album. I was acutely aware in that moment of just how miserable Maca must've been. I knew he loved my sister in a different way than me, obviously, else that would just be weird. But I thought, right then, that I could understand a little better what he had been going through.

I slid out of my sister's bed, grabbed my overnight bag and headed downstairs to wait for the car service to come and pick me up. I had a flight at seven thirty, so I was hoping they'd be there by five. I felt bad for leaving before everyone was up, so I left a note on the side, explaining my early flight and promising my mum that I'd be back soon.

SIXTEEN

1989

When I got back to Ireland, Maca was waiting to meet me at the airport with Milo and a car. He had a baseball cap on backwards over his long hair and a pair of aviator glasses.

"Rock star much?" I asked, totally taking the piss out of the quintessential band member outfit of the white T-shirt, jeans, leather jacket, and beads around his neck.

"Fuck you."

It was the first time he had spoken directly to me since the disastrous Sunday afternoon visit to my parents' place.

"Yeah, and I missed your smiling face too, brother, a whole lot," I said, holding my hand out to shake his as I did. He stared at my hand for a few moments, taking it, but then pulled me in so we bumped chests and he slapped me on the back a few times. You know, the way *real* men do.

"How is she? Did she get my flowers? Is she feeling better? Did she talk to you?" He fired his questions at me one after the other.

"Ladies." Milo called from the other side of the bonnet of the big four wheel drive he was leaning on. "You have to be at the television studios for this lunchtime chat show you're scheduled to appear on by eleven. Can you have your shag and make up session in the back of the vehicle while I drive, please? I have to get back to the hotel and pick up the rest of the girls."

We both flipped him the middle finger but climbed into the back of the SUV anyway.

"So?" Maca asked as soon as we were in. He took off his hat and glasses and raked his hand through his hair. I was instantly distracted by the new ink I could see below the V-neck of his T-shirt.

"You get a new tat?" I asked.

"Yeah." He pulled his T-shirt away from his skin to give me a better view.

"I've been thinking about it for ages and someone had recommended a bloke in Dublin, so I called him when we got here Monday and he fit me in yesterday afternoon."

I took in the lettering around his neck and recognised the words instantly.

'There's no one else. There never was. It's still only ever you.'

It was taken from our biggest selling single to date, *'With You,'* and he had written it for Georgia. Obviously he was still totally unaware that she was seeing someone else and there was no way I was gonna be the one to cause him any more heartache. My thoughtlessness had done plenty damage over the years, and I wasn't about to add to that.

"Cool. Looks good."

"Cheers. Now answer my questions. How's she doing?"

"You gonna cover your whole body in tats dedicated to my sister?"

He already had a G over his heart that matched the necklace he had given her one Christmas, years ago. I'd noticed last night that she still wore that necklace, but there was no way I was gonna tell him that and give him any kind of hope that she still cared.

"Maybe. What's it to you?"

"I couldn't give a fuck, but a future Mrs McCarthy might have a problem with it."

He turned and looked at me, biting down on the corner of his bottom lip as he did. "You just don't get it, do you? Read what's written on my neck, mate. The only Mrs Maca there will ever be is *her*. We *will* get back together. One of these days, it'll happen." He let out a long breath and shook his head.

"Now answer my questions. How the fuck is she?"

I let out a long breath of my own and looked out the window at the passing traffic for a few seconds.

"She's doing better. She's been a mess all week, but she was happy to see me and we had a bit of a talk and agreed to put an end to all the shit that's gone on."

His eyes widened at the news.

"Yeah?" he asked with a smile. "I'm pleased for ya, dude, I really am."

My stomach felt a little uneasy. I really didn't want to fill him with false hope. I knew that he would think that if George could bring herself to talk to me, then she might be on her way to talking to him.

"Did she say anything ... ya know? Did she mention me at all?" he asked quietly and I caught Milo's eyes looking at me through the rearview mirror. I shook my head slowly.

"Na, mate. I'm sorry, but she'd just had a bit of a breakdown after seeing you for the first time in almost four years. I wasn't about to bring up your name if she didn't." I told him honestly.

He put his hat back on. "Fair enough. I get it, dude, I really do." Despite his words, I could hear the disappointment in his voice and I couldn't miss the way his throat moved as he swallowed his emotions down.

"Baby steps, mate. Talking to me is a massive leap for her, and once she's back on her feet and feeling a little more stable, I promise—I swear to you that I will do all that I can to put everything right between the two of you."

He nodded his head slowly. "I'll give her a bit of time, but we need to get our shit sorted before the wedding."

Len and Jimmie's wedding was happening in June. When they'd first got engaged, a wedding in two years seemed forever away, but we were down to weeks. Bailey was best man. Myself, Maca, and the rest of the boys from the band were groomsmen, whatever that meant. My knowledge regarding wedding etiquette was as lacking then as it is now. All I knew was that Georgia and Maca would both be a part of the wedding and so like he had just said, they really needed to get their shit together before the big day.

"It'll get sorted, Mac. She's doing better and she's already told Jim that she doesn't want anything to spoil the day for her and Len, but this is George. Let her go at her own pace. You know what she's like if you push her."

The rest of our stay in Ireland went well, and Maca was definitely in a better place when we got home than when we left.

We had a quiet few months scheduled as Len had wanted time off both before and after the wedding.

Maca and I spent a few weeks writing before taking a week in Ibiza, and then we sailed with a couple of producer friends of ours on their boat around the Balearic Islands, off the coast of Spain.

We landed back in England on a rainy May Thursday, just around lunchtime. We had promised to call around to Len and Jimmie's place that night and so just stopped quickly at our place to shower and change our clothes. We were both tired after three weeks of partying and sailing in the sun, and our day of travelling. We almost called and cancelled, but the promise of a home cooked meal from Jimmie meant that wasn't an option, so we made the effort, both of us unaware that the decision to drag our tired arses over to my brothers that evening would ultimately change both our lives forever.

Dinner was great. Jimmie was an excellent cook and after the roast beef with all the trimmings, we had homemade apple crumble and custard for dessert.

I'd gotten over my issues with Jim and Len being together years ago. I viewed her as nothing more than a sister and I couldn't have been happier for her and my brother. They were so good together. The way they looked at each other even had me wondering if maybe, one day, I might want what they had.

We sat around the dinner table, enjoying a few wines and then more than a few bourbons as we told stories of our recent trip away.

This holiday had been a little subdued compared to our usual trips. We'd partied and clubbed the first week, but Maca hadn't done more than chat to a few girls and had no interest when a girl called Elanora from Italy or France, or wherever, had asked if she could come back to our hotel and fuck us both. Luckily, we had separate rooms and I'd gone back with her, along with a Swedish, Dutch, or wherever it was they made tall blonde girls that talk like the chef from the Muppets and are called Anna, Arrna or Hannah. They stayed for two days. By the third, I could barely walk and needed them to go.

The following couple of weeks, we'd spent fishing, snorkelling, and sunbathing while sailing on Max and Nicole's boat. They had just had their third baby so there was no partying on board. Most of the places we docked at night were quiet little fishing villages. Nic was happy to cook most evenings, as it was hard work taking three kids, including a newborn, out to dinner. A few times she sent Max out with us, telling us to go get drunk, which being the good boys that we were, we obviously obeyed. One night, we ended up staging an impromptu concert at a little bar in Palma on the island of Majorca. It was a place where the locals drank, but we had been instantly recognised and the singer from the band that was playing invited us up on stage to sing a few songs. We didn't get down for over two hours and it was the happiest I had seen Maca in what felt like forever.

We helped Jimmie load the dishwasher and clear up the kitchen before taking our drinks and sitting on the big comfy sofa's they'd just purchased. I was only half listening to Len go on about how they were custom made when the ring of the front doorbell came. Keen to get away from the riveting sofa conversation, Maca jumped up with an, "I'll get it," before I could get a breath out. He winked at me as he headed for the door, probably the first person ever to hope that he was gonna find a large religious cult on the doorstep, looking to spend hours trying to convert him.

"So yeah, if you're ever looking, I can put you onto this bloke in San Antonio, Texas." Len was telling me. I nodded and smiled, feigning interest before knocking back my drink. Imported cowhide? Shoot me now, cowboy.

I added ice from the bucket on the coffee table and started to top up both mine and Len's drinks when I thought I heard a woman cry.

"What was that?" Len asked.

"Dunno. Sounded like someone crying."

We were quiet for a minute, both of us trying to listen over the top of The Jam's *'Butterfly Collector.'* He looked around for the remote to the state of the art—for 1989—sound system that he'd had installed.

"Is that crying?" That was what I'd just said.

"I don't know, Len. Go and have a look," I suggested. He could do anything, as long as it wasn't talking to me about furniture.

"Where's Jim anyway?" I asked him, hoping that he would at least want to go in search of his wife to be.

Curiosity eventually got the better of him and he stood, walking out into the hallway.

"Fuck... Jimmie!" I heard him call out a few seconds later. I stood up and retrieved the remote from the dining table where we had left it earlier. Transvision Vamp's Wendy James started belting out *'Baby I Don't Care'* and my dick gave a little twitch of approval as

I remembered the video I'd seen of her singing it, wearing a basque, long gloves, and not a lot else.

"*Shit.*"

That was my sister's voice I heard as I stepped out into the hallway. Len was standing just ahead of me. I looked around him to see Maca sitting on the floor, his arms wrapped around my sister who was sitting in his lap and looking up at him. Jimmie was on her knees beside them.

"Who would want to hurt us like that? Who?"

George looked up at Maca and asked through her tears.

What the fuck had happened?

"What the fuck, George? What's wrong?" I started to move towards them, a million and one thoughts rushing through my brain. No one spoke. The only sounds were my sister's sniffs and sobs.

"Will somebody please tell me what the fuck is going on?"

Jimmie was crying too and goose bumps prickled my skin. Something bad happened … my mum, my dad, Bailey? I couldn't move. I opened my mouth to again ask for answers, but nothing came out.

All my mind was acknowledging was the fact that Maca was holding my sister in his lap. After all these years, all this time apart, they were finally here, together.

It was all gonna be okay. Life was gonna go back to the way it should have always been.

"The letters, Jim?" Maca questioned. "All the letters. You told me that she got them."

Jimmie looked past me to Lennon, then back to Maca. I'm totally lost as to what is going on.

"She did," she said to him, then turned her gaze to George. "You did." The tone of her voice made it sound like she was almost pleading with her to confirm what she was saying. "Your mum said that they upset you so much, that we weren't to talk about them."

Georgia's mouth opened and closed at least three times. It was almost comical to watch, except there was nothing at all funny about what was unfolding.

"No, no, Jim." My sister shook her head. "I never knew. I never saw a single letter."

"What?" Maca, Jimmie, and Len, all seemed to say at once.

George looked wide-eyed at all of us in turn. I'm not sure if she thought that we all thought she was lying, but she continued to confirm her story. "She told me that Sean phoned for a couple of weeks and that my dad threatened him; that he'd then stopped calling and that was it." Her eyes moved between each of us again. She looked small and fragile sitting in Maca's arms. He was bigger built than the last time they were together, and she was skinnier—a lot skinnier—and I was only just realising it then.

"Georgia, I swear to God, I called your house four or five times a day. I begged them to let me talk to you. I wrote letter after letter, begging you to see me." I was witness to his side of the story and knew for sure that everything he was telling her was the truth.

So what the fuck happened? Why did G not get any of his letters? There had to be a simple explanation to this because my mum and Dad would never lie about that shit. They knew what they were both going through, what they'd continued to go through.

I started to feel a little dizzy and light headed as fear unfurled in my belly. Something wasn't making sense.

Everyone was quiet for a while, all of them probably trying to work out how the fuck this had happened. None of us wanted to think the worst; that it could've been done deliberately.

"G?" Maca said quietly. "I love you, babe, but your arse is fuckin' bony and mine is going numb."

"Fuck, I need a drink. Shit's gonna go down if Mother's done this on purpose," Lennon said from beside me.

"No shit," I replied, following him back to where we had left our bourbons.

We sat down on the much talked about sofa's and each drained our glasses. Len topped them up this time. "I can't believe this," he stated.

"It's gotta be something simple. Mum's not a spiteful person. She was pissed off with Maca, but she'd never go out of her way to keep them apart," I said, unsure of who I was trying to convince more. My eyes met Len's and he looked as concerned as I felt. "Would she?" I questioned him.

"I have no fuckin clue, mate." He took a sip of his drink. "I feel like I don't know anything right now."

My mind started to race with thoughts of something strange that happened last year. My mum had asked me to keep the address of where we were living from Georgia, which was odd because she still wouldn't talk to me at the time anyway. Then she'd flipped out when Georgia had apparently found it out. She'd said at the time that my sister had been behaving a little erratically, and that she had been asking for our address. She was worried that Georgia was gonna turn up and cause a scene and it could all end up in the papers. I'd shrugged it off at the time. I assumed my mum was overreacting to something G may or may not have said, but what if it had just been another way of keeping Maca and G apart?

I had an uneasy feeling in my belly and my chest as I watched Maca carry my sister into the room and sit her in his lap when he sat down of the sofa. The sensation wasn't caused by watching those two together—that was great to see—it was the thought that my mum could've done something really horrible.

I moved to the armchair to give them some room as Len passed them both a drink.

I wanted to smile every time I looked at them together, but I was feeling sick with nerves that life might be about to come crashing down all around us again.

Georgia was rambling on about the fact that this must all be some kind of mistake, that our mum knew the mess they were both in and that there was no way that she'd deliberately keep them apart.

"You okay, big brother Marley?" George asked.

No, I'm not, really. I've finally got my family all back together and it was suddenly looking like it could fall apart again. I didn't want to tell George what else I knew, but I wasn't lying to her. I wasn't losing her again, especially if she and Maca were gonna work things out.

"Gotta say, little sister Georgia, that I'm with you. Mum just wouldn't do that … surely mum wouldn't do that?"

Please don't let my mum have done that.

I shook my head and continued. "I don't know if I'm overthinking things, but now that I'm thinking about it, she has gone out of her way over the years to stop you two from having any kind of contact."

There'd been a few occasions when she'd called me to make sure that I knew Maca wasn't invited to whatever family gathering or function we were attending if George was also gonna be there. I always assumed it was because she was worried about how George would react to seeing Maca, but now I was worried that there was something else going on.

"I just thought it was to protect you, George, and then after that Sunday the other month…" I trailed off as I watched Maca pull her tighter into him. I think on the memory of that shitty day, yet another one where I fucked up, big time.

I cleared my throat and carried on, "After the way you reacted that Sunday, I thought that she'd done the right thing."

My heart rate accelerated and my hands felt clammy. I'd stood on a stage in front of thousands of people. I'd performed live on television shows with audiences of millions, but I'd never felt as nervous as I did right then. However, my next sentence could've had the possibility of blowing my family apart. I felt sick and absolutely gutted at what I was about to do, but I didn't see that I had any other choice.

"I thought she was being a bit irrational when she told me not to give you our address, and then how pissed off she got when you found it out anyway. It makes me think now that she may have had her own agenda—that maybe there was more to it than protecting you? What if it was more about hiding what she'd done? I don't know, I'm just surmising…" I trailed off again when I took in the look on Georgia's face. She frowned, her mouth opening and closing again as she shook her head no.

"I don't understand, Marls?" I didn't hear much else for a few seconds after that, realisation crawling up my spine. Could I have unknowingly played an even bigger part in my sister and best friend's misery over the past four years than I thought?

"Ours, mine and Maca's. She told me not to give you our address. She said that she was worried that you'd start stalking him."

I feel like such a dick. I should've thought about it more at the time. I should've spoken to Jimmie. George may have been a little fucked up over their break up, but stalking? Yeah, that just wasn't her thing. Maca, yeah. Knowing how he felt about her, I could've seen him going there, but not George.

Georgia's expression had gone from shocked to angry as she looked around the room at each of us. "Marley, I have no fucking idea where your place is, and I had no idea that you and Sean lived together." She took a deep breath in through her nose, as if she was trying to calm herself down.

"Fucking hell," Len silently mouthed to me from beside where Maca was still sitting with my sister in his lap. His arms were wrapped around her like he had no plans of letting her go, ever.

The room was silent as we all tried to get our heads around what was going on.

"George, did you never go to the boys' place and try and get past the reception area?" Jimmie asked in a calm, even voice. "Did you not go there and scream abuse at the doorman and try and kick the doors in when they threw you outside?"

I'd actually forgotten my mum telling us about that. Obviously, the drugs and alcohol I'd consumed over the years had taken more of a toll on my memory than I thought. Perhaps my mum did have valid reasons for protecting George, and then I looked at my sister's face and I knew in an instant that she was telling the truth, and whatever

Jimmie had been told was a lie.

"Are you all deaf or just fucking mad? I have no idea where Marley lives, and I had no idea that Sean lived with him. No fucking idea."

Georgia's face crumbled for a minute and I thought she was about to cry. "Where is this coming from? Who told all of you that I had been there causing trouble?"

Her mouth was turned down and her bottom lip trembled a few times, but she held back the tears.

Jimmie looked around at each of us before shrugging her shoulders and saying, "Your mum, George. Your mum told us."

"Oh babe," Maca said as he kissed G's temple. She drew in a few deep breaths before letting out a loud sob.

"Why Sean?" She looked from him, to around the room at each of us. "Why would she do that to *me*? Why would she do that to *us*?"

I wish I knew. I wish I'd had an answer to give my little sister. She'd been hurt so much already. I was just thankful that Maca was there that night that they were together, and he was the one holding her and telling her that no matter what, they'd always have each other.

Over the next few hours, an elaborate story of lies and deceit unfolded in Jimmie and Len's house. My parents and eldest brother turned up and George had to be held back as she unleashed what she knew on my mum. I was torn, totally torn in half as I watched my mum shake while Georgia confronted her.

And when she held her head in her hands, I wanted to tell George to stop shouting at her. She was my mum. She may have made an almighty fuck up, but she was my mum and she shouldn't be spoken to like that.

I'd been in her shoes. I had a fucking good idea of how shitty she must've been feeling right then.

"Did you do it?" my sister screamed.

"What's going on, George?" My dad finally asked. I'm surprised he'd stayed so quiet for so long. "Bern?" He turned to my mum who still had her head in her hands.

My mum looked up and right at my sister. She knocked back the drink Len had just passed to her and said very quietly and with complete conviction, "I did what I thought was right."

Georgia flew from where she was sitting in Maca's lap, but he and Bailey caught her before she reached her.

"How could you? How fucking could you?" she screamed, still fighting to get away from Maca and my brother.

"That's enough, Georgia," my dad shouted, but it didn't slow her down.

Georgia must've been all of seven stone soaking wet, but the anger that propelled her forward scared the crap out of me. Bailey and Maca struggled to hold onto her.

My dad looked at my sister like she'd finally lost the plot and in that moment, I knew she wasn't far from it. The last time I'd seen her that angry was when she'd ripped a handful of Haley White's hair out at a concert we did at the back of a pub about five or six years ago.

"Will someone please tell me what the fuck is going on?" my dad asked again.

"Did you know? Were you part of it?" G turned her anger towards my dad, but I knew that he was clueless as to what had happened.

"No," my mum shouted in his defence.

"Part of what, George? I ain't got a Scooby what you're on about, love."

"Did you keep Sean's calls and letters hidden away from me? Did you pack them all in a box and send them back to him with a note, supposedly from me, saying to not contact me again?" Georgia took in a few shaky breaths. She wiped her tears and her nose on the back of her hand and it was on the tip of my tongue to tell her that she better not let mum catch her doing that.

"Did you tell everyone that I'd been to Marley's, and that I tried to smash my way in? Did you? Or was it just your lying, deceitful, spiteful wife?" George spat out.

"Bern?" My dad stared wide-eyed at my mum, as shocked as the rest of us at what he was hearing.

"It wasn't like that." My mum finally looked up at my sister. "At first I wanted you to get back with him … I wanted the two of you back together. But you were so broken, George, and you needed time. I couldn't let you talk to him. Whatever you may think now, you just weren't strong enough. And in the beginning, you refused point blank to have anything to do with him anyway."

Len topped up the glasses of everyone that was drinking bourbon. George took Maca's glass from him and downed the contents.

"I'm your mum, George, it's my job to keep you safe." She had a pleading edge to her voice. She wanted my sister to try and see things from her point of view. I knew my sister well enough to know that she wouldn't. *I* couldn't, so why would she?

"You'd only sent a few letters when I decided to let you talk to her on the phone. I was gonna wait until you were back on tour. I thought the distance would keep her safe," she told Maca.

Her shoulders sagged and she closed her eyes for a long moment, shaking her head no.

"Then one day, while George was at school doing the last of her exams, a girl knocked on the door. I had no idea who she was." She said it like she was ashamed, like she should've known who the girl was, before looking down into her lap again. The whole room was silent as we watched my mum stare at her perfectly manicured nails.

"Anyway, it was you she wanted to talk to, George. She said that she needed you to know that Sean had been two-timing you for years with her. She claimed that he had only stayed with you because he was worried about being kicked out of the band if it ever came out, but now that the band was making it big, he'd planned on leaving you anyway and that *they* were going to make a new life together."

Maca was shaking his head, and I was shaking mine.

"Na, no way," Len said.

"What girl? Who was she?" Maca questioned my mum.

"Sean," my mum said his name, using a sort of exasperated tone; the way she used to say our names when she was about done with our bad behaviour. I found it a bit condescending. Maca wasn't a kid. He was a grown arsed bloke who'd been treated like shit, by her.

"You'd just broken my daughter's heart into a million pieces. You weren't exactly my favourite person at that time. I didn't ... I just believed what she told me. I didn't check her story out with Marley, Len, or Jimmie because I was scared of causing trouble with the band. Everything was just taking off for you, so I simply stayed quiet."

Jimmie looked at me, her eyes wide. 'No way,' she mouthed while shaking her head, but I didn't know what it was she was getting at.

"You seemed to be getting a little better at handling the break up, George, and I didn't want Sean's letters setting you back, so I set up a post office box and had all your post delivered there. I thought that they'd stop coming eventually, or at least slow down, but they didn't. They just kept coming; letters, cards, parcels."

"That's because I fucking loved her. I missed her. I've never stopped, not for a single moment," Maca snapped out at her. She just looked back down into her lap again.

Georgia appeared to be in a trance, oblivious now to what was being said.

"In the end, I packed everything into a box and sent it all back to Sean with a note, supposedly from you, George, saying not to contact you again."

Georgia's eyes slowly looked up to meet my mums, and I thought for a moment that she was gonna launch herself at her again. Her stare was hard, angry, and cold. I felt more than a little guilty that I didn't actually feel bad that she was looking at her that way.

"I didn't hear from the girl again until you boys converted the old warehouse and moved in together."

I looked across to Maca, but his eyes were firmly on my mum.

"She phoned up and said that she'd heard through some friends that Georgia had been asking around for the address. She said that she was concerned that George had found out about them being together and was worried for her own safety."

"This is un-fucking-believable," Maca said quietly.

"You were doing so well, George. You'd got your confidence back and was smiling again. I just thought it would be easier to tell everyone not to tell you where the boys were living. I was just trying to do the right thing…" She trailed off once more.

My dad reached across and took my mum's hand, his actions causing yet another lump to form in my throat. When you're growing up, your parents are only ever that, 'Mum and Dad.' You don't think of them as husband and wife, a couple, and definitely not lovers, but as you got older, you appreciated what they were to each other—that once upon a time, they were young and in love.

I love my wife even more now than I did when I first admitted that fact to myself. I fancy her more too and know that no matter what, I would have her back. There's nothing she could ever do to make me doubt her. She's my lover, wife, and best friend, and there's no one that could ever replace her in my world, nor would I want there to be. I'm pretty sure that's how things were for my parents too. My dad would support my mum whether he thought she'd fucked up or not, and that was exactly how it should be.

"You should have said something … you should have said *something,* Bern."

"To who, Frank? If I'd told you and Bailey, you'd probably have gone after Sean. And if I'd said anything to Marley, Lennon, or Jimmie, it could've caused trouble for the band," she told him.

"What about me? Did you never consider talking to me?" George asked her.

"No, George. In all honesty, I didn't." She sounded adamant that she made the right call, but I wasn't so sure.

"You'd been fragile for so long. There was no way I'd chance setting you back. You'd been so badly broken by what you thought went on in that hotel, that I was terrified that if you found out Sean had been two-timing you for years, it might just kill you. I'm your mother. It's my job to protect you at all costs."

"Well, you fucked right up on that score, didn't you," Georgia bit out. "All you've managed to do is cause me untold misery these past four years." I watched as George took Bailey's glass from his hand and tipped the contents down her throat. She didn't even drink bourbon, but she was giving it a good go tonight.

"What I'm failing to understand is this story about George going to the boys' place, trying to get in and causing a scene. What's that all about?" Jimmie asked my mum.

"Well, that's when alarm bells should've started to ring," she replied.

"No shit, Sherlock," Bailey whispered loudly.

"Do you remember, Jim, when that magazine did that big feature on your wedding, and in the interview, the reporter asked if it was gonna be awkward having Georgia and Sean there together?" We all nodded. Jimmie had been a nervous wreck. She and Len were quite often photographed out with the band, but they were never stalked individually the way that Maca and I were. They were never front and centre of the attention the press paid us, and Jim was worried that by doing the interview and allowing photos of them to be used for the feature, that would all change.

"Well, this Mandy, the girl that claimed she was Maca's secret girlfriend, called me and said that Georgia had found out where the boys lived and had gone to their place and tried to get past security. They'd threatened to call the police, but she'd convinced them not to and explained that George was Marley's sister. She said that Georgia was obviously in need of psychiatric help, and that Sean wanted her kept away from him, including at the wedding."

Shit, I vaguely remember my mum calling me and banging on about that. I was severely hungover and had two birds—twins, if I recall—in bed with me. I actually couldn't get my mum off the phone quick enough and the call was instantly forgotten.

My brain was in overdrive ... Mandy? I know we've fucked around with a lot of birds over the years, but I don't remember a Mandy.

"I swear to God, this has nothing to do with me. I don't know any birds called Mandy," Maca stated, all the while looking at me for backup.

I think I mumbled something along the lines of, "No, no Mandy," all the while shaking my head and thinking, *'Do we know a Mandy?'*

My mum was talking, but the words weren't getting in as I tried to think of anyone we'd banged over the years that had stalkerish tendencies, but I came up blank. Well, apart from—

My mouth dropped open. My eyes caught Jimmie's, and much like mine, her mouth was hanging open.

Oh shit.

"When Marley and Sean came to the house with those girls, all you kept repeating, Georgia, was 'How could he? She looks just like her.' I eventually realised that it was the girl you had the problem with, not Sean."

I felt like I was drowning; choking and suffocating, all while suffering a coronary. I wanted my mum to shut up. I didn't want her to tell George who it was behind it. She'd blame me. I started the ball rolling by inviting the crazy bitch back to our hotel room. I'd just got my sister back in my life, now I was about to lose her again and possibly my best mate too.

"I made them for you, George," my mum's voice broke into my panicked thoughts. "Every piece of news on the boys, I kept and put it in a scrapbook in the hopes that one day, you'd be able to look at it."

My mum wiped a tear from under each of her eyes and I thought in that moment, we were all torn. Even George looked sorry for my mum, and then her expression changed. My sister was a clever girl, and her brain was beginning to put the pieces together. I knew in that instant that my sister had started to think exactly along the same lines as I was. I watched as she covered her mouth with her hand. Her wide eyes swung from mine to Jimmie's, and then back to my mum. I felt like all the oxygen had been sucked from the room, and we were all just barely managing to breathe.

"I kept the good stuff and the bad stuff," my mum continued with the words that I dreaded, that would potentially isolate me from my family once again.

"All of the newspaper pictures and articles, even old song lyrics. I kept them. I sat and went through them all until I found what I was looking for." My mum looked at my dad, tears rolling down her face as he held her hand tightly. "That's when I realised I'd made an almighty fuck up," she sobbed out.

"Oh no. No, no, no," George begged out loud, shaking her head as if it would stop my mum's words from being true.

Jimmie was shaking her head in much the same way as George was. She stared at Maca, but realisation hadn't hit him yet.

Len's eyes landed on mine as he whispered, "No fucking way."

My dad and Bailey just looked confused.

Jimmie and George locked eyes. "Whorely?" Jimmie half questioned, half stated.

"It was the girl from the rape charge," my mum said quietly.

Maca was up and on his feet before anyone could grab him. I lurched forward, fearing that he was gonna slap or shake my mum, but it was my sister he turned to.

"No, no fucking way. I have not clapped eyes on that girl since that day. There is *not,* and *never was,* anything between me and her, G, *never.* I swear on my life."

Fuck.

Maca was in meltdown mode. I was ready to jump in and back him up one hundred and ten percent when my sister shocked the shit out of me by saying, "I know, I know. I believe you."

The entire room went silent. Even Bailey looked stunned.

Maca sat back down next to George and took her hand. He

wrapped his arm around her shoulders and pulled her into his side as she wrapped her free arm across her front, like she was trying to hold herself together.

"*Fuck*," she said on an exhale, sounding like she still couldn't quite believe all the shit.

"That girl really does hate me. She's gone all out to ruin my life and keep us apart for all this time."

"Either that, or she's just a fucking nutter," Bailey finally spoke.

"I need a drink," Georgia said.

Drink? I needed that, and possibly every drug in town.

Haley White ... Haley fucking White.

What a conniving little bitch she was. I was stunned, I was angry, and so fucking relieved that nobody seemed to be blaming me for what she'd done.

SEVENTEEN

1989

The following night we went to one of our favourite Indian restaurants. We were regulars back in the day and had even held meetings there when things first started to take off for us.

Maca and George had stayed at Jimmie and Len's the night before. After my parents had left and things had calmed down a little bit, Bailey had mentioned in front of Maca that George had been seeing someone. We'd shut him down as quickly as we could, and then the lot of us had proceeded to get pleasantly stoned.

George had come over to our place that afternoon. She and Maca were all over each other, so I assumed Cameron King was no longer in the equation, and they had sorted their shit out and were back together.

Like the night before, after my parents had left that is, I felt this weird sense of ... I don't know what, exactly. I felt calm and content, happier than I had in a long time. I was sitting, eating dinner with four of the people I loved most in the world and it warmed the cockles, as my dad would say.

Despite Len booking a table towards the back and in the corner of the restaurant, we were still recognised and asked to sign autographs, but even those interruptions couldn't dampen my happy mood. In that moment, I didn't feel like a rock star. I didn't think about the places I'd been, the people I'd met, or the things I'd seen over the past few years. For the next few hours, I just kicked back and enjoyed my favourite food with my brother, sister, and two of my best friends.

Then we tried to leave the place and all hell broke loose.

Some fucker had tipped off the press and they were everywhere.

I'd just told George she needed to eat a few more curries and fatten herself up as we walked outside. She'd turned to me and said, "Fuck you, Marls. That's as insulting as telling a fat person they should eat less and lose weight."

"Ignore him, babe. You're fucking perfect," Maca had called out from behind me.

"You're such a brown nose, McCarthy," I told him.

"What?" he replied. "She is perfect. Too skinny, but always perfect in my eyes."

"You're such a wanker," I said.

Suddenly flashes were going off and Georgia was almost pushed over.

I heard a *"Fuck off,"* being yelled from Maca and an *"Oh shit,"* from Len, who had waited inside for Jim to use the bathroom.

I grabbed a hold of George and tucked her under my arm as the cameras flashed all around us as reporters screamed out questions.

"What's your name, sweetheart?"

"Are you going home with both the boys?"

"Are you the latest piece of meat in a Marley and Maca sandwich?"

Cheeky fuckers.

I wanted to knock the bitch that asked that last question flat on her arse, but I didn't hit women, even arseholes like her. I wanted to scream at all of them that she was my little sister, but there was no way I was giving up that piece of information.

"Keep your head down and don't say a word," I said into her temple, not sure if she could hear me above all of the commotion going on around us. I kissed the top of her head in reassurance as I could feel her entire body shaking as I held her.

Maca unlocked his car from behind me and I shoved my sister into the passenger seat.

"Keep your head down," I told her again before running back to help Maca, Len, and Jimmie out. They were surrounded by a bunch of screaming girls, as well as the journalists and photographers.

"Get the fuck outta here," I told Maca. "I'll go with these guys. You're probably better off staying at G's."

He moved away from Jimmie's side and I replaced him in protecting her from the pushing and shoving.

We'd given Milo the night off, convinced we'd be fine just nipping out to our local Indian restaurant with our family, but it was a lesson learned. It was no longer possible for us to nip anywhere and it dawned on me that Georgia had just had a rude awakening to what our lives were like these days, and I wondered how she'd deal with the press intrusion. Once they found out her and Maca were back together, her life would change considerably.

George rang me Saturday afternoon while I was still at my brother's place to invite me to a party at my dad's club that night. It was for a mate of hers and Jimmie's, and Len and Maca were both going. I said that I was up for it too. Everything felt right with my world, except I was still the odd one out, still the single one.

When Maca came to pick me up later, I knew something was up with him straight away. He was quiet the entire drive back to our place.

"What do you know about her and this bloke she's been seeing?" he asked, sitting down on the sofa as soon as we were in the door.

I took off my jacket and hung it on the back of a bar stool before sitting on the sofa opposite him.

"I don't know anything. Jim and Len mentioned that she was seeing someone a few months back, but that's all I know. She's never mentioned him to me," I told him honestly.

I didn't know anything about my sister's relationship, other than it was Cameron King that she was seeing. His family had a bit of a reputation around our way. They were the type that you didn't mess with. A bit like my family, I suppose, although I had never been a part of that life. I wasn't stupid. I knew that my dad, uncle, and brother had earned themselves a name as the type of businessmen you didn't ever want to upset, but that was all I would say on that subject.

That hadn't been Maca's question though. He'd asked about my sister's relationship, not who it was with. I should've stepped up and told him exactly who it was my sister was seeing, but I'd decided that I was staying the fuck out of their shit. If there were any revelations to be made, they could be the ones going '*Ta Da*,' not me. I was staying the fuck away from anything that might cause trouble in paradise. I'd learned my lesson, well and truly.

"She's been seeing him for a while then?"

"A few months, Mac. That's all I know."

"Is she fucking him?"

"What the fuck? I don't know. I don't wanna know and if you do, then you best have that conversation with my sister," I told him. She's twenty-years-old. They'd been seeing each other a while, so of course they were fucking. But like I said, I'm staying the fuck outta dodge.

He threw himself back against the sofa, letting out a long sigh and looking up at the ceiling.

"Maca, if this is gonna be an issue for you, then you need to either deal with it or move the fuck along. I'm not gonna sit back and let you break my sister's heart and then watch you fall apart with guilt all over again."

"I'm so fucking jealous and I've no clue how to handle it, Marls," he said with honesty. "This is all new for me. There'd been no one else before me ... I don't ... fuck, I don't know. I've just gotta get my head around the fact that she's lived a life while we've been apart," he said with a shrug of his shoulders.

"It's been four years, Mac. Have a little think about what you've been up to in that time. Like I said, you either need to move past it or move on." I'm pissed off with him now and feeling defensive of my sister. Whatever she may or may not have been doing with regards to her sex life, I'd bet she'd lived like a nun compared to the things we'd been up to, at least I fucking hoped she had.

I shuddered.

"Can we end this convo please? My sister's sex life is really not my favourite subject ... ever."

He gave me a small smile. "Ah, well, what's done is done. I love her and want her back regardless. I'm just a jealous fucker, but I'll get over it. She's meeting him Monday to breakup with him anyway."

He pushed up from where he was sitting. "I'm starving. We got any food here?"

"There's bread in the freezer and beans in the cupboard, if you fancy beans on toast." I tell him, grateful for the subject change.

We enter my dad's club for Georgia's mate's party, just after midnight. Len had arranged extra security and we were smuggled in a back door and straight up to the VIP area.

The only people I recognised were Bailey and Lennon. There was no sign of the girls.

"Gia not here yet?" Maca asked straight away.

"Downstairs dancing," Len said.

"For fuck's sake, Len, why'd you let her go down there?"

"She's a grown up, Mac. I can't tell her where to go. They wanted to dance, and it's not very busy up here yet."

"She'll be fine, mate," Bailey added. "She's here nearly every week and we never have any problems. You're the famous one, Maca, not her."

"I need a drink." Maca said.

We had a few bourbons and a couple of lines of coke before we left our place, and I could tell he was a bit edgy.

And before you judge about the drugs ... again, it was what it was. The area that we grew up in—the circles that we were mixed in—drugs were just a part of our lives. They were as normal for us on a Saturday night as a film and a takeaway were for others. I didn't indulge too much during those days, but I did still like a joint, and that would never change.

Maca went to the bar and got us both a drink, then went over to the balcony so he could look down at the dance floor below.

"You need to chill the fuck out, mate," I told him as he scanned the crowd for my sister.

"*Fucker*," was the reply I got. I followed his gaze and watched as my sister turned and gave it to some bloke that was trying to grind up against her. He held his hands up, as if surrendering, when George pointed her finger at him. He turned his charms on a girl in a silver dress whose face I couldn't see and I laughed along with Jimmie and George as the girl turned around and grabbed the bloke by the throat before calling over one of the bouncers. I still couldn't see the girl's face, but she had a nice arse. Jimmie held her hands up in an 'I give in' gesture, and the three of them carried on dancing.

"See, they can look after themselves. They're grown women, not thirteen-year-old girls anymore," Len said from where he was standing on the other side of Maca.

"They'll come up here when it gets too much down there. They just wanna have a dance. Come the fuck over here and stop torturing yourself," he told him.

We moved back over and stood at the end of the bar, where we were promptly surrounded by a group of women who my dad would describe as being dressed like 'Drury Lane Whores.'

They knew exactly who me and Maca were and couldn't keep their hands off us.

That type of behaviour from women had always puzzled me. Some, not many, but some would argue that Bailey and Len were better looking than us, but despite the pair of them standing right next to us, it was me and Maca they wouldn't leave alone. Why was that? Was it the money? The Fame? It was beyond me that people could be that shallow.

"So, I've heard you two like to share. How about the four of us get out of here and go have some fun?" One of the women suggested as she tried to unbutton Maca's shirt. I looked across at him and rolled my eyes. *Like we've never heard that chat up line before.* They were seriously letting the side down for you, ladies—slutty *and* unoriginal.

"How about you get your fucking hands off me, right now," Maca told her.

Before she could move or any of us could say anymore, George appeared, grabbed the woman's hand and bent it at the wrist, so far back, I thought it was actually gonna snap.

"Get your fuckin' hands off him," she said through gritted teeth.

I gave a little grin as I caught Maca smiling at George, a look of complete adoration in his eyes.

"Whoa, whoa, Georgia." Len jumped in and removed G's hand from the woman's.

"Georgia, baby. You are such a bad, bad girl," Maca said through his grin, while looking at my sister like she was the only other living thing on the planet.

Milo stepped out of nowhere, the way he always seemed to, and escorted the women away from where we all stood.

I grabbed a couple of glasses of Champagne from a passing waitress and passed one each to Jimmie and George. "Little sister Georgia, what are we gonna do with you and that temper of yours?" I tried to say with authority and not smile as I spoke, but I'd had a few bourbons and a line of class A so yeah, I failed.

"We're not gonna do anything with that temper of hers," Maca said while sliding his arm around my sister's waist, pulling her in so that he could kiss her neck, "because she makes me so fucking horny when she gets all green eyed. I love it." Maca made a snarling noise into G's ear and I think I threw up a little in my mouth.

"Fucking 'ell. I'm sure I must have some important paperwork to file, or security screens to monitor," Bailey said, giving a little shudder at Maca's words before turning and heading away from the bar.

I looked at Len and shook my head. "You two are a fucking nightmare," he told the lovebirds. "We had to practically sit on him just now when he saw some bloke trying to touch you up on the dance floor."

George wrapped her arms around Maca's neck and it felt so good to see the way that she smiled at him in that moment.

"Aw, did they, baby? Did you get all jealous?" she cooed at him.

He said something into her ear and she listened intently.

"Fifty quid says they have a barney and leave early," Len said. I shook my head because knowing those two, he was probably bang on the money.

"Oi, George. You gonna do the honours or what, babe?" A strong Essex accent came from behind my sister.

I turned to look in the direction of where the voice just came from and my heart felt like it plunged down to my balls, back up through my chest, and lodged somewhere in my throat.

Fuck. Me.

She was gorgeous. Not very tall, but she had curves in the exact places a woman should have curves. She was wearing a silver dress and black patent heels. Her hair was blonde, and her eyes were sort of a brownish blue, or bluish brown. I didn't know, that sounded stupid, but they were either brown with blue flecks or vice versa.

Yep. I got all that from just one look.

I caught George saying that her name was Ashley, and I just stared—not saying a fucking word—just stared.

Maca leaned across and lifted my chin, making me realise that my mouth must've been hanging open. What the fuck was wrong with me? I looked at my sister and then at Maca for some help, but they were looking at me like I wasn't all the ticket.

Speak, that's what I needed to do … say something.

"Happy Birthday, Ashley. *You. Are. Beautiful*," I told her.

I don't know where everyone disappeared to, but suddenly it was just me and her, standing and staring at each other.

"You're Marley Layton," she stated.

"I am."

"You said I was beautiful."

"I did."

"I'm not stupid. That sort of talk won't get you in my knickers."

I had to laugh at her bluntness.

"Who said anything about you being stupid?" I questioned.

"Well, *you* obviously assume that I'm stupid enough to believe that you think that I'm beautiful."

"I don't assume any such thing, sweetheart. I told you you're beautiful because you are. You're fucking gorgeous." Bloody woman. Most women lapped that shit up, not questioned it.

"Well, thanks. You're not so bad yourself, but I'm still not shagging ya." She flicked her blonde hair over her shoulder, moved her bag from one hand to the other, and took a glass of champagne from a passing waiter.

I lost the smile that was on my face as I watched her watching me from over the top of her glass as she took a sip of her drink.

"Why not?" I asked her. "What's wrong with me?"

She looked me up and down and shrugged her shoulders. "There's nothing wrong with you."

"But?"

"But you're Marley Layton."

"That's usually a help, not a hindrance. Birds usually wanna shag *because* I'm Marley Layton."

"Well, not this bird."

A group of people were headed in our direction and wished her a

Happy Birthday, so I turned and ordered myself another drink from the bar, hoping her mates fucked off and left us alone, sharpish. I needed to talk to this girl some more. I had no idea why, I just wanted to be near her ... I wanted to know her ... I wanted to know *about* her.

"So, how do you know my sister?" I asked when her mates had all gone off in search of drinks and their other friends. The party was now in full swing and the dance floor was packed. I steered her to the very end of the bar so that I could hear what she was saying.

"You're kidding me, right?" She asked. I shook my head no in confusion. "I went to school with your sister. I went to the same school as you," she said, obviously pissed off that I didn't remember her, judging by her tone.

"George was two years below me. I don't remember any of her mates," I told her honestly.

"You and Jimmie were always pretty tight." She reminded me.

"Yeah, well, Jim had been Georgia's best mate since she was about four. She used to sleep over at our house, come on holiday with us," I explained in a hurry.

"So you and Jim ... there was never anything between the two of you?" I shook my head no. I'm not gonna go into details about how I felt when I found out about Jim and Lennon. The past was the past and I'd been over that for years.

"Jimmie's been with my brother since she was fourteen. She's like a sister to me." She nodded her head in understanding. "Now will you shag me?" I asked jokingly, but actually, not joking at all.

"Nope," she said with a smile "I'll let you dance with me though, Rock Star." She grabbed my hand and started to lead me over to the dance floor.

"Oh, you'll *let* me dance with you, will ya?" I smiled as I asked, gripping hold of her small hand as I followed behind her, definitely not looking at her arse all the way. Not even once, or twice, or a few hundred times.

The Pointer Sisters *'Automatic'* was playing. Not too fast and not too slow. I pulled her front to mine, turned her around and grinded into her arse. I loved the fact that she grinded right back. The song changed and Frankie Beverly's voice rasped out the Maze hit, *'Joy and Pain,'* and the whole dance floor suddenly moved as one as they started this side stepping, line dance type of thing.

Now don't get me wrong, I can dance, but aside from on stage, I didn't get much opportunity. When we usually went to clubs, it was pretty much impossible for us to get out on the dance floor without being pestered, even in the VIP areas, so I just didn't bother too often.

So yeah, I was a little lost for a moment as everyone fell into step, seemingly knowing the moves by heart.

Ashley moved from beside me, and in front of me.

"Eyes on my feet, Rock Star. Just copy what I do." She winked at me and I did as I was told. As soon as I picked it up, she stepped back in beside me and we danced along, side by side, for the rest of the song. It was the most fun I'd had outside the bedroom in a long, long time, and I couldn't wipe the big fat cheesy grin off my face.

My cheeks ached because I was smiling so much. This girl was like a breath of fresh air.

The song finally ended and Ashley gave me a round of applause.

"Not bad, Rock Star. You're a fast learner."

"Oh, you have no idea, baby," I said at the same time I pulled her into me and moved us both to the sound of Womack and Womack's, *'Teardrops.'*

I kissed along the curve of her neck and whispered into her ear, "Come home with me?"

"No," she replied.

I kept us moving while trying to think of what I could say or do to get her back to my place. It wasn't just the fact that I really wanted to fuck her, even though she was the reason for the painful hard-on I'd had for most of the night. It was because I just didn't want the night to end.

What the fuck was happening. I sounded like a big fucking girl. I looked over Ashley's shoulder and around for my brothers, or Maca. I spotted them all together, but it looked like George and Maca were arguing. He stormed off, grabbed one of the women that was all over him earlier and started dancing with her.

"What's the matter? You lost interest coz I've knocked you back?" Ashley asked.

"No, baby. I'm just watching my sister and best mate argue." She turned her head in the direction I was looking.

"Shit, George will kill her," she stated as we watched the woman put her hands all over Maca, before going in for a kiss.

"Looks like she's about to," I said.

We watched as Georgia grabbed the woman by the hair.

"Oi, you're taking the piss now, love," Georgia shouted at the woman. I was surprised when she gave up without a fight. She called something out over her shoulder, but my sister and Maca seemed to be oblivious to it as they stared at each other like the pair of weirdo's that they were.

Gloria Estefan's, *'I don't wanna lose you'* started to play and Maca and G started to dance.

"Looks like they made up and no blood was spilt," Ashley said.

I looked down into her blue-brown eyes. I slid my palms over her hips and up to her armpits, back down and over her arse.

"Come home with me, Ashley. Not to fuck … well, not unless you force me, but just to talk." She gave me the sweetest smile, kissed my cheek and said into my ear, "Get me drunk, Rock Star, and I might think about it."

Two hours later, I was holding her hair back as she threw up in my toilet. I'd got her drunk, all right. So drunk, in fact, that I had to carry her from the club, out the emergency exit, and into the car that Dave, one of our drivers, was waiting outside for us in. About halfway home, Ash threw up all over me, herself, and the car.

Dave helped me get her up to my place, but I made him leave

before I stripped her out of the little silver dress she was wearing. I grabbed a T-shirt of mine and pulled it over her head as quickly as I'd pulled her dress off ... almost.

What? She was braless and only wearing a black thong underneath. I'm a bloke, for fuck's sake. Of course I had a little look ... twice ... or twelve times, but who's counting?

Once the T-shirt was in place, I'd taken off her thong, purely because as good as it looked, that thing had to be fucking uncomfortable. I pulled a pair of my boxers up her legs and managed to get them in place without copping an eyeful once, despite how hard I'd tried.

I laid her on my bathroom floor with her head resting on a towel while I stripped out of my clothes and jumped into the shower. I dried myself quickly when I got out and pulled on a T and boxers myself.

I was just done with loading all our clothes into the washing machine and turning it on when I heard her heaving. By the time I got back to my bathroom, she'd thrown up all over herself and my bathroom floor.

I ran my hand over my head and then over the stubble that was forming on my chin.

"What the fuck am I gonna do now?" I said to myself out loud. I didn't want to be in this position. I had an unconscious girl in my home and I'd already stripped her clothes off once, and now I was gonna have to do it again, but this time I was gonna have to shower her too, as it was in her hair and every fucking where.

I paced for a few seconds, then decided to call Jim. It might be four thirty in the morning, but I'd rather listen to Jimmie complain that I'd woken her than be accused of something I hadn't done ... again.

I got the phone off my bedside table and dialled their number while stepping back inside the bathroom. I folded a clean towel and put it under her head, wedging the phone between my ear and my shoulder as it rang.

I had this overwhelming feeling of panic creeping up my spine. I wasn't sure if I was worried about being accused of something, or if it was the fact that I wanted to look after her. No, fuck that, I didn't *want* to, I *needed* to; me, Marley Layton. I'd lived my life following the two F rule. I fucked 'em and forgot 'em, and as much as I wanted very much to fuck Ashley, the fact that I needed to make sure she was okay was overriding any horny thoughts I was having.

Len answered on the fifth ring with, "This better be a fucking emergency."

"Len, its Marls."

"Oh fuck, what've you done?"

"Fuck you, arsehole. I haven't done anything."

"What the fuck d'ya want then? The birds are fucking singing here and I've only just got to bed."

"I've got Ashley here at my place."

I heard him exhale, or inhale, I wasn't sure which, but it went on for an exaggerated length of time.

"Marls, I swear to God, if you've upset that girl, George, Jim, and Mother will have your balls."

"Mother? What the fuck has she got to do with anything?"

"Ash works for her and Georgia."

Well fuck, she hadn't mentioned that.

"I haven't upset her. She's out cold on my bathroom floor right now, covered in her own spew."

"For fuck's sake." Len uttered his favourite response to most things I told him. I could hear Jimmie asking who it was in the background.

"Len, put Jim on. I need to talk to her." The anxiety that was snaking its way up my spine was starting to bubble in my chest and I paced as I heard Len pass the phone over to Jim.

"Please don't fuck my friend, Marls. She's had a tough enough life as it is, she doesn't need you doing your usual fuck and run and breaking her heart."

"Jim, she's been sick and it's everywhere. I don't know what to do. What if she wakes up and she thinks I touched her? They won't believe me again, Jim. I'm not a rapist, but the papers won't care, they'll write shit about me again."

I felt like I'd been hit with a ton of bricks. The panic, hurt, and anger I'd felt at the comments made in the press and by others in our industry when Haley White made her accusations came clawing their way to the surface. I'd shrugged it all off at the time, had another drink, snorted another line, but it hurt. It fucking hurt and I didn't want to feel like that again, not ever.

"Marley, calm down, babe—"

"I'm not a fucking rapist, Jim. She spewed up over her party frock so I took it off her and put it in the machine. I put her in one of my T-shirts and a pair of boxers, but she's done it again and it's all in her hair this time. It's fucking everywhere, but I never touched her, Jim. I swear I never touched her."

I was crying like a fucking princess.

What the fuck was that all about?

"Marls, listen to me. You're not a rapist, and no one thinks that. She doesn't think that. Now calm the fuck down."

I took a few deep breaths. "I'm sorry," I whispered. I could actually feel my balls and dick shrivelling and being replaced with a vagina over my breakdown.

"I love you, Marley Layton. You're a good person, and don't you ever forget that. Now, go run a shower, get Ash in it and wash the puke out of my friend's hair. If you have to take her top off, try and do it in a non-pervi way."

"Jim, she's out fucking cold—dead to the world. I might like things a bit kinky, but I'm not into fucking girls who are passed out, I can assure you."

"That's good to hear, Marls. Now, go turn on the shower. I'll stay on the line in case she wakes up and freaks out."

After putting the phone down on the side of the sink, I turned on the shower and lifted Ashley up and sat her down again in the corner to let the water run over her. She tilted her face up into it and mumbled a few things that I couldn't understand. Leaving the boxers on, I pulled the T-shirt over her head and washed her hair, her arms, and her legs. Her tits were staring me in the face. My arm and even my hand brushed against them a couple of times. I had a hard-on the whole time and felt like the worst person on earth. She was fucking gorgeous. Even in this sorry state of hers, she did things to me.

I wrapped her in the biggest towel I could find and carried her out to my bed and laid her down.

"She's clean. She woke up a bit, but wasn't making any sense." I told Jimmie when I got back on the phone.

"Okay, well done. Put her in another one of your T-shirts. Give her hair a comb and tie it back if you can find an elastic band, and keep her lying on her side. She's gonna be mortified in the morning so go easy on her, Marls. She puts on a big brave front, but she's soft as shit and has a heart of gold under that mouthy bird she makes out to be."

"Jim?" I whispered quietly.

"What Marls?"

"I like her. I mean, like … I really like her."

My mouth felt as dry as a nuns mildred as I tried to get the words out. (Sorry God, nuns, and all you religious types, but you get what I'm saying here, right?)

"I know, Marls. I knew it as soon as I saw the way you looked at her in the club. Don't fuck this up. Now go sort her out and get some sleep. Love ya." She hung up before I said any more.

I went and found a comb and combed her long blonde hair as best I could, then dressed her once again in a T-shirt and boxers of mine.

I laid her on her side, facing me, and watched her sleep as my thoughts raced, my stomach churned, and my heart? My heart did not have a clue what had just hit it.

The little blonde thing had gotten to me. I'd looked after her, washed and dried her, made sure she was safe, and I wanted nothing more in return, other than to get to spend more time with her.

And that scared the shit outta me.

EIGHTEEN
1989

I was dragged back into consciousness by the sound of someone throwing up.

Where the fuck did we go last night for Maca to have drunk enough to be in this state?

I rolled over and pulled my pillow over my head, and realised in an instant that the sound was coming from *my* bathroom, not Maca's.

Shit.

Ashley.

I jumped out of bed and ran to my bathroom, stopping in the doorway as I watched her arch over my toilet as she sat on her knees in front of it. All the while, she was trying to hold her hair back and I remembered that Jimmie told me I should tie her hair in an elastic band.

I ran to the kitchen and pulled open the junk drawer. You know, that one that every house has, filled with elastic bands, Blu-Tack, paper clips, batteries, pens, and condoms? I rifled through it all until I found an elastic band big enough to hold all her hair, then I grabbed a bottle of water from the fridge before rushing back to my bathroom.

Her elbows were propped on the toilet seat, her arms crossed, and her head rested on top of them. Without saying a word, I pulled her hair back and attempted to wrap the elastic band around it. I didn't miss the fact that she stiffened as soon as I touched her. I rubbed her back a few times.

"There's a bottle of water there. Thought you might need it." She turned her head and looked at me kneeling next to her.

"Oh God," she groaned.

"Almost." I said as I winked and held my hand out, as if to shake hers. "Most call me Marley. They save the God title for when I'm making their toes curl."

She blinked those big blue-brown eyes at me before rolling them. "You're such a dick, Rock Star."

Yeah, I had to agree. Why the fuck did I just make that toe curl comment?

She unscrewed the cap on the water bottle, tilted her head back and swallowed. I couldn't take my eyes from her throat. The way it moved as she swallowed each mouthful, the way her lips wrapped around the neck of the bottle …

I'm kneeling in front of her, in just a pair of boxers, and I have a big fat chub going on and no way to hide it.

I'm fucked. Totally and utterly fucked.

"I'm probably one of the few people in the world that actually wished this was all a dream, and I hadn't really woken up in Marley Layton's bed."

Her voice brought me back from imagining all the ways I'd like to see her swallow and I thanked the God of hard-ons … Erectimus? I think that was his name, or was that a transformer? Erectimus Prime? Anyway, I thanked him, the God of hard-ons, that rather than making eye contact with me, she still had her head tilted back and was staring up at the ceiling.

"Well, cheers," I told her, feeling a little hurt. *Who the fuck doesn't wanna wake up in my bed? Is she still drunk? I wonder, does she know exactly who I am?*

She moved her head and her eyes and met mine. I'm not sure if they were glassy from her puke fest, or if she was actually about to cry and once again, I was hit with that unnerving need to make sure she was okay.

"Please tell me we didn't fuck?"

"Wow, are you for fucking real right now?" That hurt, and I hated that it was obvious in my tone. I fucking *hated* that what she just asked bothered me so much.

"You're Marley Layton. I'm not a part of your world. I work for your mum and your sister, who also happens to be one of my best friends, the other being Jimmie, your future sister-in-law. I don't want to be the dinner table conversation next time you all get together, and I don't want you all talking about how easy I was and what a slut I am. Despite what people think they know about me, I'm not that type of girl."

Tears rolled down her cheeks and I couldn't stay put. "C'mere," I whispered and pulled her into my lap. I rested my back against the bath and pulled her into my chest, stroking her back and her hair as she cried.

"Nothing happened last night, and even if it did, I would never talk about it with my family." Although that could've actually been a bit of a lie. We did tend to share in my family.

"So how come I'm wearing your clothes?"

Ah shit. And it was all going so well.

"Well, here's the thing. You sorta threw up everywhere, and I do mean everywhere; in the back of the car, over your posh party frock, over me—"

"Oh fuck," she cried, burying her face in my chest.

"Again, feel free to just call me Marley." That earned me a dig in the ribs from her dainty little fist.

"So, did you undress me? Please tell me you called Jimmie or George to do that."

"I called Jim." I reassured her and felt her relax against me instantly, but I know it's not gonna last.

"Thank fuck for that," she sighed out the words in relief.

"And she stayed on the line while I stripped you off, showered you, washed your hair, and dressed you again for the second time."

She made a loud, over-exaggerated sobbing noises. "Noooo, noooo. Why did I get in such a state? What happened? The last thing I remember is us dancing."

"Yeah, and then you told me to get you drunk and that you might think about letting me shag ya."

"Well whoo hoo, go you. You get top marks for getting me drunk, Rock Star." She said sarcastically, her face still buried against my chest.

"Thanks," I told her. She held up her hand for me to high five her and I did. Then I did something that I'd never, ever done with a girl before. I laced my fingers through hers and held her hand.

My dick stirred and I cringed. "Ash?"

"What?"

"My arse is going numb and my back hurts. You ready to go back to bed? I'll make you a cup of tea or coffee, and some toast if you feel up to it."

"The thought of making me breakfast is what's making your dick hard right now, Rock Star?"

Busted!

My mouth dried up again, and I decided to try an untested concept of total honesty with a girl.

"No, I've got a hard-on because you're sitting in my lap with your tits pushed against me and your arse pressing against my dick. And also because you're fucking gorgeous."

"I'm also not fucking stupid," she mumbled from my chest.

"What? I can't understand what you're saying with your face down there. Although, if you were to dip lower, I'd understand perfectly—every fucking word."

"Omit eth," is what I thought she'd said.

"Nd, er a king ervert."

"I've no idea what you're saying down there, baby, but if you're feeling a bit better, I'm gonna stand you on your feet. You should drink the rest of that water, and feel free to use my toothbrush. Then either come find me while I make us some breakfast, or wait in bed and I'll bring it up to you."

I stood her up on her feet, thanking that Erectimus bloke again that she just stared down at the tiled floor, her arms wrapped around her.

"Why the fuck won't you look at me?" I asked her.

"Vomit breath," she said more clearly.

"Ah, that's what you were saying. What was the second part that I didn't quite catch?" I asked, now fully aware of what it was she'd called me.

"I said, 'And you're a fucking pervert.'" I smiled, as I could imagine her blushing, and I really wanted to see that. Her skin looked so pale this morning that it'd be good to see some colour on her cheeks, like, really good ... and I was starting to get hard again. Fuck you, dick gods.

"Well, I think the fact that I showered you and changed you into clean clothes, twice, I might fucking add, without once touching you inappropriately, just goes to prove that I'm not a pervert."

She finally looked up at me, her blue-brown eyes still glassy.

"I'm sorry. Thank you for looking after me. I wasn't talking about any of that. In fact, I'm trying really hard to forget that Marley Layton has seen my tits right now."

"Then why am I a pervert? I don't understand?"

"Because you're you and I'm just me; a puke smelling, crazy haired lady, pasty faced nobody who obviously has no self-respect for herself because I came home with you last night, after only just meeting you."

Tears clung to her bottom lashes and my heart missed a beat, then seemed to rush around in my chest, trying to find its missing action.

"Well, you know what, sweetheart? If getting a fat on over the most beautiful, puke smelling, crazy haired, pasty faced nobody I've ever had the pleasure of knowing makes me a pervert, then I'm guilty as fucking charged."

A small smile pulled at the corner of her perfect mouth and I finally got to see that blush spread up her neck and over her cheeks. She swung her shoulders from side to side in the most girliest of gestures. I closed my eyes and thought of chords, notes, frets. I tried to write a tune in my head, anything to calm my boner down.

"I really wanna kiss the fuck outta you right now." The blood supply that usually inhabited my brain had obviously sunk south to my dick because I never, at any stage, intended to say that out loud.

"I stink of puke," she whispered.

"I don't give a fuck."

She looked over my face for a few seconds and I thought that she was gonna take a step forward, then something, I've no clue what, must've crossed her mind and her whole stance, even the look in her eyes, changed.

"I'll pass on the kiss, thanks. I'll just clean my teeth and meet you in the kitchen." She gave me a small smile, but I still felt the sting of her rejection. I nodded my head and left the bathroom, pulled on a pair of jogging bottoms and a T-shirt and headed to my kitchen.

Fuck this for a game of soldiers. That—that right there, women and their unpredictability—were the reasons I didn't do relationships. They were a complete mystery to me and that was exactly the way I wanted it to stay.

Fuck her and her blue-brown, brown-blue, or whatever the fuck eye colour she has.

Fuck her pink cheeks.

Fuck her perfect tits that I never looked at ... much. Maybe a little bit, or a few times, but whatever. Fuck them anyway.

Fuck everything about her and the way she made me feel so off balance.

I'd make her coffee and some toast, then call Dave to come pick her up, seeing as Maca seemed to have decided that Milo was for he and my sister's own personal use. So, fuck them too. They could all go fuck themselves.

"Why've you been so nice to me?"

I jumped at the sound of Ashley's voice as she leaned against the doorway, watching me pour hot water from the kettle into the coffee mugs I'd set out.

Yeah, *me*. I was making a girl coffee after a night of not even getting a shag, or a blowie, or even a hand job. You couldn't make this shit up. Un-fucking-believable!

"What?" My response came out a little harsher than I intended, and I hated that she flinched at my tone. She was still wearing my T-shirt and boxers, and had her hair up in what looked like a birds nest on top of her head. It was the sexiest fucking birds nest I'd ever seen.

I slid my hands into the pockets of my joggers and held onto my hardening dick so that she couldn't see it. "Ew, are you playing with your dick through your pocket?"

This girl seriously had no filter.

I blushed. I actually felt my cheeks burn as she stood there with a sexy as fuck smirk on her face. I'm Marley Layton. I *don't* fucking blush.

Ever.

"What? No. I was, I just ... my dick fucking likes you, all right. It has a mind of its own when you're around," I admitted while standing there, glowing like the Ready Brek kid.

"And playing with it helps?" she asked.

"I'm not playing with my fucking dick. I was trying to hold it down so that you wouldn't see that I've got a big fat boner going on."

I watched as she folded her arms across her chest.

Her perfect, perfect tits moved under my T-shirt and my disobedient dick twitched in my hand. I closed my eyes for a few seconds and tried not to think about how they looked when I showered her earlier this morning.

I failed. They were all I could picture.

"You didn't answer my question," she said quietly.

I opened my eyes and watched as she moved toward and then past me. She went to the fridge and pulled out the milk.

"What question?" I asked as she put the milk down on the work top and started opening cupboard doors. "What are you looking for?"

"The sugar," she replied in a tone that implied I should know that.

"Here." I opened the cupboard above the kettle and got it down for her.

"Tupperware? Oh, Rock Star, that bit of info would do your bad boy reputation no good if it were to get out. Did you go to a party yourself to buy it?" she asked while putting two heaped spoonful's of the golden granules into her cup, offering one up to me.

"One, please, and no, I didn't go to a Tupper-fucking-ware party. My mum came around and organised everything in here and brought us cutlery, plates, cups, and other shit. Anything else you wanna have a dig at me about?"

She stared down at our coffees as she stirred each one in turn.

"You gonna answer my question, or just keep avoiding it?" she asked without looking back up at me.

"What was the question?" I know full well what the question was, but I didn't have an answer that I was willing to admit to just yet—not to her or myself.

"Why've you been so nice to me—looked after me?" She turned and met my gaze head on.

"Because I like you, a lot." I didn't hesitate to answer, yet I couldn't believe I just said that. I was adamant that I was gonna say nothing, and then I just blurted it out.

This girl.

This fucking girl was tying me up in knots.

Me. This didn't happen to me.

"You don't even know me," she said bluntly with a defiant edge to her tone.

"We just spent a night together. I cleaned up your puke. I think I know you well enough."

"And despite that, you still reckon you like me?"

"No, Ashley." I didn't miss the fact that she flinched again, just slightly before I got a chance to continue. A little zing of pain hit my heart, like an electric shock, at the thought that I might've hurt her feelings.

"I don't reckon I like you. I know that I do. Despite the puke in my car, in my bathroom, and on my clothes. Despite you taking the piss out of my endless hard-on and my Tupper-fucking-ware, I like you. Fuck knows why, but I do and so does my dick."

Her response? She dragged her teeth backwards and forwards over her bottom lip and I almost came in my pants like a thirteen-year-old boy, right there in my kitchen.

"I'm still not shagging you." Was her only reply before taking a sip of her coffee, then smiling at me sweetly.

"Yeah, I heard you the first time, and all the other times you've told me," I sighed out, trying to sound defeated, hoping to garner some sympathy from her.

"What is it exactly you've got against me?" I questioned. I was actually curious now. I'd turned women down, occasionally. Well, no, that was a lie. I nearly always said yes, unless they were grabby. I don't like grabby, aggressive women. I've always worried they might go a bit psycho on me, but anyway, this? Having a girl blatantly knock me back? That was new ground for me, and I was a little unsure how to approach the situation.

On the one hand, I liked her, and I would like very much to sink my dick balls deep inside her. Just her mouth, would in fact, do at this point. But, on the other hand, I loved that she wasn't intimidated by who I was and didn't appear to be interested in shagging me just for the bragging rights. She didn't seem like she was expecting something permanent from me, convincing herself that she might be *'the one'* to tame me and make me settle down. She seemed too independent for that shit.

"I don't have anything against you. I just have a little bit more respect for myself than to shag someone on the night that I meet them, especially when they happen to be my boss' son."

I heard her belly rumble as she finished talking and moved to get some eggs out of the fridge. I was actually about to make this girl some breakfast. I shook my head at the prospect and felt like I should call Maca or my brothers to have them explain my actions because I had no clue what was going on with me.

"So, if you didn't work for my mum and sister, I might have been in with a chance?" I asked.

"I don't shag on the first night. Unfortunately for you, the fact that I work for your mum and sister means that I won't shag you on any night."

"What if I took you out tonight? Or next week? Do you shag on the second or third night?" I said jokingly.

Totally not joking.

Once again, something passed across her face and eyes.

"Marley," she said my name as though she was letting out a long breath or a sigh, and I felt all girly as my insides jumped about and my balls felt all tingly, in a most ungirly way.

"Ashley," I said in the same manner and a small smile played at the corner of her mouth.

"You should do that more often," I told her while reaching into the drawer for a frying pan.

"Say your name?"

"Saying my name is good, but you smiling is even better."

Fuck, I was even making myself cringe. Could I have sounded any more wankerish?

She smiled again and my charm sank to new depths. "See? That was beautiful."

"You're so full of shit."

I shook my head in frustration. I'm not winning with my words, so let's see what I could do with my culinary skills. "You want some breakfast?"

"You don't want me to leave?" she asked with raised eyebrows, obviously surprised that I wanted her to stay. I was bloody surprised I wanted her stay, but I did. She was hungry and that made me want to feed her. I didn't like the idea of her being hungry; hated it, in fact. Just like last night, I needed to look after her. I had no idea what any of it meant, I just knew that I was about to cook this girl breakfast for two reasons. One, so she'd no longer be hungry, and two, so that she'd stay a bit longer.

"If I wanted you to leave, I wouldn't be offering to cook you breakfast. I'm not a bullshitter, Ashley. I tend to say what I mean."

"Yeah, I tend to get into trouble for that," she said quietly while staring at her toes—her cute toes with purple nail varnish on them.

My eyes travelled from her toes and up her legs, from her legs to her body, that happened to be hidden away under my T-shirt. Eventually, my eyes hit her face and I was surprised to see her watching me. I abandoned the frying pan and stepped right into her space. She smelled of my shampoo and body wash. Thoughts of her naked as I washed her invaded every single space in my head and I took her face into my hands.

"You," I let out a long breathe. "You are so fucking gorgeous."

Her eyes instantly filled with tears.

What the fuck?

She shook her head slightly. "Don't, Marley. Please don't," she whispered, attempting to look down, but I gripped her face tighter, refusing to let her break eye contact with me.

"Don't what? What did I do?" I asked her, feeling totally confused.

"Don't say shit like that to me. Don't talk to me like I'm an idiot. I know I don't talk nice like your mum and your sister. I know that I sound common and I know what people say about my family." She swallowed and her jaw trembled. The sight of her struggling actually caused a physical pain in my chest.

"Ash, sweetheart, I seriously—"

"No, no. Let me finish, Marley. People can think what they'd like to about my family. Most of it's true anyway. They're not good people, and I'm fully aware of that. I also know that people tar me with the same brush, but I'll never be like them. No matter what happens to me, I'll never stoop to their level. People can think what they'd like, but here," she pointed at her head and then her heart, "and in here, I know the truth. Yeah, I like to go out and have a good time. I like a drink and I'll do the occasional line or smoke a joint, but I'm not a junkie and I'm not a slut. I don't sleep around."

She blinked and a lone tear rolled down her pretty little cheek. I knew nothing about her family situation, but I hated that she felt like that, that they'd made her feel like that.

"I'm also not as thick as I sound, and you can tell me that I'm gorgeous till the cows come home, but that won't get you inside my knickers. I'm not one of your supermodels who can pull a rock star any time she likes. I'm just a shop girl; I'm not in your league."

I didn't know what to do or say. I felt panic welling in my chest. I wanted to kiss her so bad—so fucking bad, but I didn't want her to think that I thought she was easy, or that I was just trying my luck.

My mouth forgets to engage my brain before it starts speaking, and words just start coming out of it.

"Ash, I honestly don't know anything about your family. I've no idea what their reputation is, and I most certainly would never, not in a million years, judge you on the way you talk. You're just a typical Essex bird to me; mouthy, funny, straight to the point, and in your case, sexy as fuck." She rolled her eyes, again.

"I'm not bullshitting you, babe, I've no need to. Believe what you'd like, but I'm telling you straight up, you are a pretty girl and I would really, really like to kiss you right now."

I bent my knees slightly so that I could look into her eyes, which were once again cast downward.

"Whatever you may think, Ash, at the end of the day, we're just you and me; an Essex boy who really wants to kiss an Essex girl. Just because I do what I do for a living, it doesn't make me any better than you and I hate, fucking hate you putting yourself down. You working in a shop is what you do for a living. Well, me playing in a band is what I do. They're just jobs. They don't make either of us better or worse than the other, and I don't ever want to hear you say something like that again, you hear me?" I brushed the tears from her cheeks. I was gonna call Jimmie or my sister later to find out what the fuck had gone on in this girl's life that caused her to have such low self-esteem, despite the 'full of confidence' bullshit and bravado she liked to put on.

I gently kissed the corner of her mouth, then pulled away to gauge her reaction. She slid her arms around my neck, so I slid one of mine around her waist, and one around her neck so that I could hold onto the back of her head. I held her still and moved in to kiss her again.

I placed my mouth gently on hers, barely moving my lips at first. I ran my tongue along the seam of her lips and savoured the combination of coffee, toothpaste and salty tears, which made up the taste of Ashley. My tongue probed harder and eventually she allowed it access to her mouth. There was the sound of a groan and I had no idea if it came from me, her, or if it was a joint effort, but it prompted me to slide my hand down to her arse and pull her in tight against me. My dick was hard and I knew she was able to feel it against her belly. But I really didn't give a fuck. I wanted her to know what she did to me. I needed her to know that I really did think that she was sexy as fuck.

She shocked the shit out of me by lifting her leg and hooking it around my hip. I didn't hesitate in cupping her arse and lifting her so that she was forced to hook her other leg around me to hold on.

I moved with her wrapped around me and sat her down on the kitchen work top, not breaking our kiss the whole time. As soon as her bum touched the granite, or marble, or whatever shit it was made from, I slid her forward so that I could continue pressing my dick right between her legs. I could feel her hot little cunt against the tip of my dick, and didn't even attempt to stop the "*fuck*" that slipped out of my mouth against hers.

I moved my hips so that I was rubbing myself against her. The heels of her feet were pressing into my arse cheeks, forcing me harder against her.

"Fuck, Ash. I wanna be inside you. I wanna be inside you so bad, baby." I spoke without moving my mouth from hers.

"I know, but we can't. I'm not like that, I don't do this. I'm not like that, Marley."

I stopped kissing her and rested my forehead against hers. I didn't want to pressure her, and I didn't want to make her feel guilty, so I drew in a few deep breaths.

"I understand, but we need to stop, baby. If I kiss you, then I'm gonna wanna be inside you. You're too fucking sexy for me not to want you. I've got no fucking control around you, Ash."

I felt her chuckle as I kissed her neck.

"You and me both, Rock Star. You and me both."

No idea how I managed to do it, but somehow I pried myself from between that little temptresses legs and instead of poking at *her* eggs with my dick, I scrambled some with a whisk for breakfast, along with toast and more coffee. By the time we were done and cleaned up, it was after three. I found her a hoodie and we laid under a blanket, curled up on the sofa, watching videos.

I'd never done this. I'd walked the red carpet with a model, an actress and once, even a princess on my arm, but I'd never laid on the sofa, with a girl's back pressed into my front and watched a film. If I'd have had any clue as to how good it felt, I would've spent most afternoons this way.

We took turns choosing films. Obviously, being the gentleman that I was, I let Ashley choose first and was relieved when she chose Willow and not Beaches out of the choices available. It remained, to this day, 'our' film, along with 'Big,' and 'The Land Before Time,' which we also watched.

Yup, Yup, Yup, we did.

We didn't talk much. I wasn't the sharpest tool in the box back in those days, but I'd already worked out that Ashley didn't like to talk about her family, or the fact that she worked for mine, so for the most part, I stayed quiet, just answering any questions she asked me.

Sometime during the evening, my hand had found its way under the T-shirt and hoodie of mine that she wore, and my fingers stroked over her waist and the curve of her hip continuously. I desperately wanted to move my hand higher and cup hold of her tits, or slide my hand below the waistband of the joggers she wore and feel the heat between her legs.

I'd done a lot of things with a lot of different women in my life, but that, lying on my sofa with her little body pushed against mine and the sensation of her silky skin beneath my fingers was by far one of the most pleasurable moments of my life.

I kissed her neck, which was fast becoming a favourite thing of mine to do to her, loving the way her skin erupted in goose bumps when I did it. I whispered into her ear.

"Please stay here with me tonight?"

She was quiet for a few seconds. I'd felt her breathing halt and then noticed the long breath that she let out.

"No, Marley. I have work in the morning. I need to go home."

So just after midnight, I packed her off in a taxi. She'd refused point blank to let me drive her home and was too mortified about throwing up in my car last night to let me call Dave, so in the end, I called her a cab.

I gave the driver eighty quid and told him to make sure that he dropped her at her door.

Ash had refused to even give me a phone number to contact her on and told me to just call the shop if I wanted to see her again.

Did I want to see her again?

Yes … No …I had no fucking clue.

My bed smelt of her and I loved it. I held onto the pillow that she'd laid on, but that didn't help me sleep. Eventually, I watched a porno that I'd picked up in Amsterdam and had a wank into a condom.

It was all about the rock star life for me!

My hand job the night before did nothing to reduce the size of the hard-on I woke up with the following morning. After giving myself another little tug in the shower, I got dressed and drove myself to my brother's office.

Although Len was still our manager, he no longer worked for the record label. He'd successfully branched out as a manager and agent for other bands, singers, actors, and models. He was a shrewd businessman, and had also invested his, mine, and Maca's money into executively producing a couple of films, and even the albums of a few up-and-coming bands. It basically meant that we financed the projects and shared in the profits of their success. So far, Len hadn't let us down and we had made money on all of our investments.

Jimmie worked alongside Len and they had recently moved into new offices in Canary Wharf, not too far from where Maca and I now lived.

Jim had called yesterday to check that I'd gotten Ashley home safe; to say that she was shocked that Ash was still at my place at seven Sunday night was an understatement, and I actually had to put her on the phone with Jim to prove it.

I tapped my fingers against my legs as I rode up in the lift to speak to my future sister-in-law and tried to think of a way of getting the info that I needed, without Jimmie jumping to conclusions.

The lift opened on the eighth floor and two secretarial looking types stepped in. I pulled the cap I was wearing down a little lower and pushed my sunglasses up my nose.

"Going up?" The redhead in the skin tight skirt asked.

"Yep," I replied.

"Would you go down for him?" The brunette whispered, way too loudly to her friend as she pushed the button for the twelfth floor.

I couldn't help but give a little smile, but my dick didn't even open his slitty little eye.

A redhead and a brunette. Apparently, my dick was favouring blondes at that moment.

The girls stepped out at their floor, both of them looking over their shoulders at me as they did. The redhead even gave me a wink. I waved as the door closed, but that was just to maintain the image.

I opened the doors and stepped into my brother's suite of offices. He'd done well, my big brother, and would probably end up richer than all of us. I couldn't have been happier for him.

"Mr. Layton, I don't think we were expecting you today." Gina, the receptionist greeted me.

"Morning, Gina, it's actually Jimmie I'm here to see, not Len. If she's got a minute, that is." I took my glasses off and gave her my very best smile.

"I'll just check that Ms. Emmanuel is free."

She put a call through to Jim's office and her door flew open a few seconds later. Jim stepped out looking every inch the highflying executive assistant that she now was.

Jim had been a part of our management team for a lot of years, and always looked good in her business wear.

"Looking sharp, Ms. Emmanuel … looking very sharp for a Monday morning," I told her while leaning in to kiss her cheek.

She frowned as she looked me over.

"Mr. Layton, this is a pleasant surprise. I didn't realise that you rock stars knew that this time of day even existed."

"Oh, you'd be surprised at what us rock stars know."

"Hmm, doubt that," she said with a smile. "What are you after?"

"A quick word, if that's all right?"

"Of course, come in. Len's got someone with him, but he'll be done in a bit," she stated.

"Tell Len to come into my office when his eleven o'clock leaves, please, Gina. He's got no one else due till after lunch."

"Sure thing," Gina replied.

I followed Jimmie into her office and I couldn't wipe the smile off my face as she sat behind her desk and I sat opposite her.

"What you grinning at?" she asked, her brown eyes sparkling.

"You. Us. All of this." I gestured around the room. "We've come a long fucking way since our summerhouse and the transit van."

She sits back in her chair and lets out a little laugh. "From smelly backrooms in pubs with half a cider, to Wembley Stadium and a chilled bottle of Bolli. It was all down to the hard work put in by you boys. I'm just the assistant."

"Fuck off, Jim. You're as much a part of our success as me, Maca, Bill, Tommy, or Len. Even George is responsible for part of it. We're a family, connected by the band, not just blood or marriage, and I hope it always stays that way," I told her, hoping she truly believed the sincerity I tried to express in my voice.

"Me too, Marls, me too." She swiped under her eye. "You're gonna make me cry and ruin my make-up, you fucker. Is that all you came here for?"

Now, this was the part where I needed to be stealth like and ask my questions in such a way that Jim, who let's face it, could probably have gotten a job with MI5 if she didn't work for us, wouldn't work out what I was up to.

"You heard from George or Maca since Saturday night?" I asked.

"Yep, spoke to them this morning. They're going house hunting. Can you believe it?"

"Seriously?"

"Yeah. Maca told Len, then I called and spoke to George. She said that Sean wants them to move in together. Enough time's been wasted so he doesn't want to hang around." She tapped her pen on the desk as she watched my reaction. "Sorry, Marls. You should be hearing this from Maca, not from me."

"Na, it's fine, Jim—honest. I thought they might just fuck off somewhere on the quiet and get married, so it's not like it's come as a shock that they wanna move in together. I just hope it all works out for them."

"Yeah, me too," she said with a smile. "Me too."

We were silent for a few seconds before Jimmie jumped in.

"So, you and Ash. How'd that go?" I knew she wouldn't last long. Jimmie was the one person I could rely on to know everything about everything. If you wanted gossip, go to Jim. Nothing got past her. This also meant that I was playing with a double-edged sword. I wanted info on Ash, but I didn't want Jim clocking onto the fact that I liked her, a lot.

"She's a nice girl. We had a laugh together." I tried to sound casual as I lifted my right ankle to rest on my left knee.

"Must have been hilarious if you kept her hanging around until Sunday evening."

I shrugged my shoulders, whilst trying not to shrink back into the chair and hide from Jimmie's scrutiny.

"We watched a few films, lost track of time."

"What time did she leave?"

Shit!

"What time did she leave your place?"

I scratched my eyebrow. "Ah, not sure. It wasn't that late."

She nodded her head and looked me right in the eye. "Marls, I've never interfered in the way you live your life. None of us are angels, we never have been. Now, I'm not the judgy type, but I just wanna put this out there. Ash hasn't had the greatest of upbringings. She comes from a rough family. Her dad and her brother have both been in prison and her mum has been on the…" She trailed off and tapped her pen harder on her desk. "Ashley's story isn't mine to tell. I don't think George even knows the whole truth. She was going through the whole Maca breakup and dealing with the press during our exams when I found Ash crying in the girls' toilets one day at school. She told me some shit about her home life and I had her come stay with me for a while." She kept her eyes on me as she chewed on the inside of her bottom lip, as though contemplating what to say next.

My heart was hitting my ribs. It was pounding so hard I could feel my pulse in my ears. I was scared of what she would tell me. Just the thought of Ashley crying in the school toilets made me want to break something, or someone. I'd really like to know who, or what, made her cry that day, but at the same time, I was worried what my reaction might be. I'm not a violent person by nature. Bailey and George are the fiery pair of our family, but just the idea of someone hurting or upsetting Ash had me feeling a little bit out of control.

"Luckily, her brother had just come out of prison so she was able to go and live with him," Jim continued.

"You sent her to live with her brother? What was he banged up for?" My voice sounded too high, giving away my panic.

"Her brother's Ryan Morrison. You remember him from school, don't you Marls?"

Fuck!

"The dealer? Her brother's Ryan Morrison, who we used to get our gear from?"

Jimmie nodded.

"I thought you knew that. I can't believe you don't remember Ash from school."

I couldn't fucking believe it either.

"So, what about now? She still live with her brother?" My voice was once again rising with panic.

"Na. She lives on her own somewhere now. I'm not sure where, though. Can't be too far from the shop, as I think she walks to work."

A thousand and one thoughts rushed through my brain. I needed to find out where she lived. I needed to make sure it was safe. I needed to find out what went on with her family, and I needed to keep her brother the fuck away from her.

"All I'm trying to say here, Marls, is that that girl has been through a lot of shit so please, please don't mess her around. Did you shag her?"

Fuck this cloak and dagger shit. I was just gonna put it out there. "No, I didn't, Jim, and ya know what? It was one of the best times I've had with a girl in like, forever. I really like her, Jim. I wanna see her again, but she wouldn't give me a number. She told me to call the shop if I was serious about seeing her again."

Jimmie had stopped tapping her pen and was just staring at me with her mouth slightly opened.

"Say something, Jim." My cheeks burned.

I don't blush, ever. At least, not since yesterday.

"I don't ... Marley, I can't."

The door adjoining Len's office opened and he walked in.

"Little brother Marley, how's it hanging?" Len asked. He moved to kiss Jimmie on the cheek but stopped, looked at her, then at me.

"What'd ya do?" He asked.

Jimmie and I remained silent.

"Marls? What the fuck have you done?"

"Nothing. He's done nothing," Jimmie assured him.

He leaned on her desk beside her, facing me, wearing a frown and a look of concern.

"What's going on then?" he asked.

"We were just discussing Georgia and Maca, and I was asking how things went with Ashley," Jim stated, giving me a wink that my brother missed.

"Ah, yeah. How did that all work out in the end? Heard she was still at your place last night, didn't leave till after midnight."

Jimmie's mouth dropped open at Len's revelation. *My* mouth dropped open, in fact.

"How the fuck d'ya know that?" I asked.

"I just spoke to Maca. The doorman at your building told him this morning. Maca was checking you were alone before he took G up. Ya know, didn't wanna catch you in the act."

Unbelievable. Every fucker now knew my business. "I, uh, yeah, it went good. I-I really like her," I admitted, sorta.

"D'ya bang her?"

"*Lennon*," Jimmie admonished him. I gave Jim a frown and a 'what the fuck' face. Didn't she just ask me the exact same question? In return, I get an affronted glare, meaning, 'Yeah, but I'm Jimmie. I'm allowed to ask those kinds of questions.'

Len looked between the two of us and started to laugh. "Seriously? You didn't bang her?" he asked again.

"I never said that. I never said anything, dickwad." I folded my arms across my chest and shot my brother a death stare.

"Oh my God, you like her. You actually like her." The fucker threw his head back and laughed. "You actually care about this girl."

I stood up to leave.

"Ya know what, Len? If you ever actually took the time to get to know me, you'd realise that I care about all the birds I take home. I'm always respectful and I always make it clear that it'll mean nothing more than a shag to me, so that their feelings don't get hurt when I don't remember their name, or that we've even met the next time I might bump into them."

My face was burning and my neck, back, and palms felt sweaty. I don't know why his comments pissed me off, but they did, big time.

"Marls, he didn't mean..." Jimmie started to speak, but I shut her down.

"Na, it's all right, Jim. I'm aware of what you all think. Len's the brains, Bailey's the brawn, and then there's good ol' Marley, merrily shagging his way through life without a care in the world. Not too sharp, but the girls, they just can't get enough." I licked my lips and nodded my head as I looked between the pair of them. "Well, just so we're clear, I care. I care a lot more than any of you give me credit for."

I turned and left. They didn't call out, they didn't attempt to follow me, and I was glad. I'd no idea why I was struggling to keep my emotions under control today, but right at that moment, I actually felt like I could cry.

NINETEEN
1989

I didn't want to park right outside my sister's shop and draw attention to myself. Maca was holed up in the flat above with Georgia, so I parked in a car park up the road and pulled my hat down low as I walked along Brentwood High Street. I was planning on going around the back and through the tradesman's entrance, but as soon as I turned into the alleyway at the rear of the shops, I could see a couple of photographers lurking.

The press had no hard evidence at that point that Maca and G were back together, but the rumour mill was undoubtedly in full flow.

I ducked between some vans and then through a narrow walkway that led me back to the front of the shops and headed straight through the door of 'Posh Frocks,' my mum and sister's little empire.

Everything about the place screamed high-end, and I felt a surge of pride at what Georgia and my mum had managed to achieve in our little corner of Essex. Their shop would have looked good on 5th

Avenue, Knightsbridge, or Rodeo Drive.

The place was all creams and golds. A couple of French looking sofa things sat facing each other with a marble coffee table in between. On that sat a huge vase of cream coloured roses and some other flower—lily's I think, the type George liked. Above that hung a large crystal chandelier, and against the wall, a huge gold framed mirror rested. It wasn't hanging, just leaning back against the wall. 'Cool' I'd thought and nodded to myself. Again, feeling impressed with what my mum and sister had done with the place.

"Can I help you, sir?" I jumped as a woman of about thirty asked me.

As I looked up to meet her gaze, I spotted Ash over her shoulder. She was standing with another woman in front of a full-length mirror and was helping her try on hats.

Looking at her made both my heart, and my belly, feel weird, but not in a good way. In a way, that made me feel panicky. I didn't like it.

The girls who worked here were obviously expected to dress in a certain way. Everything about their outfits screamed money and class. Ashley was wearing a pair of navy, wide legged trousers, a silky cream top type of thing, and a pair of heels. Her hair was pulled back off her face and as she turned to adjust the hat on the woman's head. I could see that it was sort of folded in on itself at the back of her head. Her make-up was a bit too heavy for my liking. She looked stunning when she woke up at my place Sunday morning, and she wasn't wearing any then.

I'd been staring at Ash for just a few seconds, but was acutely aware of the fact that I'd taken in everything about her.

I was either about to grow a vagina, or I was getting twisted up in knots by the girl. Neither option really appealed to me. I'd never considered myself a control freak, that was Len's job, but I was hating how out of control of my feelings were around Ashley.

"Sir?" The woman asked me again.

"Oh, yeah. No, no. I'm good, thanks." I stumbled over my words.

She stared at me with big brown eyes, as if I were a little odd, and then I caught sight of myself in the huge mirror. I was wearing jeans, a pair of high top Chucks, and a Rolling Stones T-shirt, the one with the tongue. Also, a Boston Red Sox cap and a pair of mirrored aviator sunglasses. I probably wasn't their usual kind of customer.

I cleared my throat. "Yeah, sorry. I mean, I'm just waiting to have a word with Ashley."

She looked over to where Ash was at the till, ringing up her customer's purchase.

"I'll let her know you're here," she said and went to step away.

"No, no, that's fine. I'll just wait till she's free."

I liked watching her. Was that creepy? Oh well, fuck it. Creepy, not creepy. I was still watching her.

"Can I get you anything while you wait, sir? Tea, coffee, water?" The woman interrupted my creepy watching.

"No, thanks. I'm good."

I looked back to Ash as she closed the sale and said goodbye to her customer. As she held the door open for her, her eyes swung across to look over my face. Her mouth dropped open as recognition hit. Even through all that make-up, I could see first her cheeks, then her chest turn pink. And then she was there, my Ash, with her sexy smile and that sparkle in her eyes, which were definitely blue that day.

She moved from the door and walked towards me. I couldn't move. My entire blood supply had left my brain and diverted its way down to my dick, causing the signal to move one leg in front of the other and towards the sexiest thing I'd ever seen, to get lost somewhere in my chest cavity and instead, caused my heart to feel like it was pogoing around.

"Rock Star, you came," she said with a smile on her face.

"Not yet I didn't, baby, but I think there's still hope for us." She closed her eyes for a few seconds, as if that thought turned her on as much as it did me.

"What can I do for you?" she asked before realising the many comebacks her question could present. Se blushed, licked her lips, and again closed her eyes for a second, but this time it was because she was waiting on, possibly dreading the response she would receive.

I think I came in my boxers a little bit and had to actually control the shudder that rocked my body at her words.

"So much, baby. Where should we start?" I couldn't resist.

She tilted her head, still smiling. "What do you want, Marley?"

"You, Ashley. I want you," I told her honestly.

"Well, I'm working right now. It's this thing that poor people have to do so that they have a bed to sleep in at night and don't starve to death."

That pissed me off a little bit. Was she implying that what I did wasn't work?

"Oh, I know what work is. I've done plenty of it in my time."

She studied my face for a few seconds, but because I was still wearing sunglasses, she obviously couldn't see my eyes. She seemed a little unsure of what to say next, which was most unlike her.

"I didn't mean … I meant …" She trailed off and looked down at her feet. I felt like an arsehole.

I lifted her chin with two of my fingers and took off my glasses with my free hand. "I came to see if I could take you for lunch today."

"Me?" Her eyes widened as she asked.

"No, the bird that works in the hairdresser's next door. Yes, you. Are you free?"

She looked around to where the other woman was unpacking scarves and hanging them up and called out, "Hey Lorna, mind if I take first lunch and go now?"

"Go for it," Lorna called out without looking up.

"Give me a minute to grab my bag," Ashley said before dashing off towards a door.

I met Ash for lunch on Tuesday, and Wednesday too. I also took her for dinner each of those nights. Each time she insisted that I pick her up from the shop and that she got a taxi home, alone. I'd had a few theories as to why that was, but I didn't want to embarrass her by bringing them up.

When I took her out on Wednesday night, she complained of a headache and sore throat, so she left early. I turned up at the shop to meet her for lunch on Thursday anyway, but Lorna told me that she called in sick and left a message for me to say she'd be in touch.

I didn't think she was blowing me off, at least I'd hoped not. We'd been having a good time. I'd done something I'd never done before—I was dating a girl. Every time I'd tried to convince her to come back to my place, she'd refused, so we'd had dinner and done a lot of talking. Well, I'd done most of the talking, she asked a lot of questions.

She had admitted to having no contact with her parents, but not the reasons why. And she also told me that her brother was a drug addict and was constantly in and out of prison. She told me that she lived with him while she was at college, but he was always stealing from her, so as soon as she was able to get a full-time job, she'd found her own place to stay.

I wasn't sure what kind of wages my family paid her, but I knew how expensive rent was in the area we grew up in, and if she was living near the shop, she wouldn't have been leaving herself a lot to live on once she'd paid out rent money.

This worried me. I hated the thought that she might have so little when I had so much, and I was only too happy to share it with her. She didn't have a car either, and I wanted to change that. I'd known Ash less than a week, but I knew for a fact that if I was to turn up with a car for her one day, she'd probably run me over with it.

I slipped out the back doors of the shop and up the stairs to Georgia's flat. I've not seen Maca since last Saturday night, and had only spoken briefly to either of them on the phone.

I pressed the intercom and stood and waited like a lemon for someone to answer.

It was George. "Yeah?"

"It's Marls, let me in," I replied self-consciously into the machine. I hadn't noticed any photographers outside, but you never knew where those slippery little fuckers could be lurking.

The door opened and I walked along a short corridor. As the front door opened, Maca was standing there, grinning at me. He was shirtless and wearing a pair of jeans that were undone. His hair was a long, ratty mess, and his beard needed a sort out, but it was the happiest I'd seen him looking in years. I couldn't help but smile back at the wanker.

"Dude." He pulled me in as I held my hand out to shake his and slapped me on the back.

"How's it going, bro? You moving in here permanent or what?"

He sat himself down on the sofa, still smiling. "Na. We've been out looking for a new place of our own, but haven't found anything yet."

"What, you're leaving me? I'm heartbroken, seriously heartbroken," I told him.

"Yeah, well, it had to happen one day, mate. I hear you're gonna be moving Ash in soon anyway." He winked.

I took off my cap and raked my hand through my hair. "Chance'd be a fine fucking thing right now. I can't even get her to come back for a coffee," I admitted. "Where's George?" I wasn't sure of how much I should confess to in front of my sister. I know I can tell Jimmie anything, but I'm not sure about Georgia. She and Ashley were pretty close, and I didn't want her running back with all my secrets, yet.

"She just jumped in the shower. We were still in bed when you buzzed," Maca explained.

"Yeah, I didn't really need to know that, dude, like ever." I shuddered to express my point.

"Get used to it, Marls. The Georgia and Sean show is back on in full blown colour." He was smiling his big, cheesy smile again.

"I'm pleased for you, mate, really pleased, but I don't need to hear about the sleeping arrangements."

"You want a drink? Tea, coffee, beer?" he asked as he moved over to the kitchen area. The place wasn't huge, but because the kitchen, dining, and living area were all one big space, it felt bigger than it was. I followed Maca and sat myself down on a stool at the work top.

"I'll have a beer if there's one going."

He leaned against the kitchen work top, sipping on his beer before asking, "So, Ashley. What's the go there?"

I took a long swig of my own beer before letting out a long sigh. "I like her, Mac. She's a great girl. We've had lunch every day this week, and dinner every night."

"So what, you've been going back to hers?"

"No, mate. *I've* been going back to mine ... *Alone.*"

His shoulders moved as he gave a little laugh. He studied my face for a few seconds before he worked out that I was serious.

"Seriously? You've been ... you've not?" He just stood there with his bottle raised to his mouth, but neither took a swig, nor said any more, just stared.

"Just lunch and dinner, dude, nothing else," I admitted.

He finally took a mouthful of his beer and leaned his elbows down on the work top.

"I actually don't know what to say. I mean..." He shrugs and looks around, then runs his fingers through his hair.

"Well shit, I'm really pleased for ya, mate. Really pleased," he told me and I knew that he meant every word. One of the reasons I loved that bloke so much was because he was straight up. He didn't lie or bullshit about anything. He was lost and heartbroken when he was away from my sister, and he didn't care who knew it. He wore his heart on his sleeve and told the world. Now that they were back together, I was sure he would be shouting it from the rooftops about how in love they were.

I gave my shoulders a little roll. "Well, we're not a couple or anything yet. It's still early days, but I like her a lot."

He simply nodded his head.

"Big brother Marley." I heard from behind and turned to see

Georgia approaching. She was wearing a Nirvana T-shirt and a pair of black skin tight trouser things. Her hair was up in one of those messy birds nest things like Ashley's was over the weekend, but G's didn't look sexy coz that would just be weird, right?

She wrapped her arms around my neck from behind me and kissed my cheek.

"Little sister Georgia, you smell lovely," I told her. She laughed and walked around and into the kitchen to kiss Maca on the cheek, then leant her elbows on the work top next to him. They grinned and stared at each other, giggling like a couple of kids.

"What are you two so smiley about?" I asked.

"Nothing," Georgia said, but still smiled big, looking guilty as sin.

"See, I'm on the outside here. You used to let me in on your jokes. How times have changed. I'm gonna end up with abandonment issues." I shook my head and feigned sadness.

"Dude, seriously. You would not want to know. Trust me on this one," Maca said, but I was curious then and wanted to know what they were finding so amusing.

"Please ya selves." I told them with a shrug, obviously sulking.

"If you really wanna know, I told her to go shower because she smelt like fresh fuck. You saying she smelt good was funny because you wouldn't have said that if she still smelt—"

"Yeah, yeah. I get it, Mac, thanks. Sorry I fucking asked," I interrupted him.

"I did warn you, dude."

"Whatever." I sounded even sulkier.

"So, what are you doing here, Marls? How's things with Ash? Hope you're looking after her."

I studied my sister for a few seconds before I answered. Her eyes were clear, bright, and blue, and I couldn't help but notice how good they looked together. Her and Maca I meant, not her eyes. No wonder the magazines were all after the first photos of the two of them as a couple.

"You'll have to ask her about that, George, but I'm doing my best. Its Ash I came 'round to see you about, actually. I'm after a favour."

"What's that?" George asked.

"Apparently, she's sick. She wasn't feeling well last night and she's called in sick at work today. I was just wondering if you had her address so I could send her some flowers."

George bit down on her bottom lip before asking, "Has she never given you her address? Have you never dropped her home there?"

"Na, she usually gets a taxi home. I always pay, but she always insists she doesn't wanna put me to any trouble."

"I'd actually be breaking the law if I gave her address out to you, Marls. Confidentiality and all that."

"But I don't want you doing it as her boss. I want you to be doing it as her mate. What about her phone number? Surely you can give me that?"

"All right, I'll get you her address, but I'll have to call down to the shop and get it. I actually have no idea where she lives."

"What? How long have you been mates?" I asked. How could she not know where she lived?

"Since school," she said. "I knew where she lived then, but I never went around there. Then she was in a flat over on the council estate with her brother. I lost track after that. I know she's in her own place now, but I've no idea where. We usually go out straight from work so she gets ready here. I'm a bad friend, ain't I?" George asked.

"I just can't believe you don't know where she lives," I replied.

Georgia made the call and ten minutes later, I'd said my goodbyes. I was in my car, trying to work out where the fuck I was going. In the end, I pulled over at a florist, bought some flowers, nipped next door to the supermarket and bought Lucozade, cold and flu medicine, sore throat drops, sweets, chocolate, and crisps. I left my car parked up in the car park and after signing a couple of autographs, I got the nice lady from the florist to call me a cab.

The house the cabbie dropped me at was a big ol' place that looked like it should be pulled down. I felt a little confused as I walked up the driveway, then I realised that the place had obviously been turned into flats at some stage, and Ash must've been renting one.

I pressed the buzzer for her number, but got no response. I pressed again, and just as I did, two boys of about fourteen come barrelling out the door. I caught it just before it closed and made my way up the stairs.

Brentwood was, still to this day, a really nice area, but that place? That was bloody horrible, and not somewhere anyone would *choose* to live. There was no lift, and as I walked up the stairs, the smell of rubbish, weed, cigarette smoke, and piss, got right up my nose.

I eventually found Ashley's door tucked into the corner of the second floor. The front doors on either side of hers were both boarded up, as were eighty-five percent of the rest of them in the building.

I knocked hard on the door, but got no answer. I went to knock again when I heard someone sneeze. I'd been worried at first that she was sleeping off her sickness, and that I would wake her, but then I was worried that she deliberately wasn't answering. I banged again, harder and called out, "Delivery for Ashley Morrison. I need a signature."

I heard shuffling and more sneezing, then the door opened as wide as the security chain would allow.

Ash blinked at me through watery eyes a couple of times before sneezing, then started to cough.

"Ash, open the door, babe. I've brought you some shit to make you feel better," I called out as she shut the door in my face. "Ash?"

"What the fuck are you doing here, Marley? How did you get this address?" she called through the door, her voice sounding croaky.

"Ash, babe. Don't be mad. Just open the door and let me in. I've got medicine and flowers."

"Fuck off, Marley. You shouldn't have come here. I'm gonna kill Lorna when I see her." She started to cough again.

"It wasn't Lorna, now open the fucking door. You sound like shit and I've got stuff to make you feel better."

"No, just go away. Go away and forget about me."

What the fuck?

"Not gonna happen, Ash. You either open this door, or I start knocking it down," I said while looking at the door and thinking that there was no way I'd even be able to rattle that thing, it was so solid.

"Yeah, good luck with that. I've got a security chain and three bolts on the inside. You could be a while." She was probably right.

"Fair enough. I'll just make some calls and get someone 'round here to take it off."

"You wouldn't dare."

"Babe, you should know me well enough by now to know that I most certainly would." Her reply was another coughing fit, followed by three sneezes.

"Come on, baby. Open the door, else I'm gonna have to go make some calls," I pleaded.

"Fuck off and make your calls. I ain't letting you in here."

"Please yourself, but don't say I didn't warn ya." I contemplate leaving the flowers and the things I've brought with me outside the door, but when I spotted a mouse running along the edge of the skirting, I decided against putting anything down on the floor.

It took me ten minutes to find a phone box, and another five to convince Lennon that he needed to call me a locksmith, or someone that could help me get Ashley's door open.

Thirty minutes later, it was Milo that turned up with his tool kit. I swear that bloke was a safe cracker, or something equally dodgy in the past.

"Nice place." Milo stated sarcastically as he walked to the bottom of the stairs. "Jesus, Marls. Did someone take a shit on the landing or what?" He screwed up his face as he talked.

"Probably mate, probably." It certainly smelt like it.

I knocked once more on Ashley's door and told her that I had someone with me that was about to take her door off its hinges. I was once again met with a 'fuck off,' and threats of legal action if I dared touch her door.

While waiting for Milo, I kept the entry door wedged open with my bag of goodies and had a look around the place. Most of the windows were boarded up; the guttering was hanging off, and there were roof tiles missing. I was pretty sure the place should've been condemned at least thirty years ago, leaving me convinced that no one would be suing me for taking a door off.

Milo started to pick at the lock and it sprung open in an instant. Next we used brute force, but it turned out that Ashley, was in fact, a little liar. The only other security she had in place was the chain, which Milo broke with one shove of his shoulder.

Milo stood back and I stepped inside the door before coming to a complete standstill.

What. The. Fuck?

There was a mattress on the floor, which Ash was sitting on, her back to the wall. Her eyes were red and watery as she watched me take in the room. Next to the bed was a small wooden table with a saucer on it. Resting on the saucer and flickering wildly was a large candle. There were three others burning around the room, and those were the only source of light. There was a clothes rail, and the clothes hanging from it, along with the shoes lined up underneath, looked totally out of place in those surroundings. There was a doorway off to the left, and I could see through it to a room that contained a small sink and toilet, but the saddest part of all, the bit that really hurt my heart, was the childlike suns that had been painted or chalked in bright yellow on the boarded up windows.

I looked from them, back down to where she was sitting on top of her purple and silver bedding. Her knees were pulled up to her chest and her arms were wrapped around them with a tissue in her hand.

"Ash," I said quietly. "I bought some cold and flu tablets, stuff for your sore throat, and pain killers. I know you said last night it was hurting."

"Why are you here?" she croaked.

"I was worried about you, baby. You said you didn't feel well last night, and then today when I went to the shop…"

She shook her head and I trailed off.

"Well, now you can leave."

"What? Why would I leave? I thought I could come play at being doctor Marley, or nurse Marley if you'd prefer. Whatever floats your boat, baby." I wiggled my eyebrows and gave her my best rock star on the front of a magazine smile.

"Don't make out, Marley. Don't pretend that you want to spend another second in this place." She held her hands out as if she was presenting her home to me, her pride and joy, instead of a room that was really not even fit for the rats she probably shared it with.

"I wanna be wherever you are, Ash."

"Yeah?" She tilted her chin in the way she did when she was feeling challenged.

"Yeah." I nodded my head and hoped that she could see that I meant it.

"Well, the last place I wanna be is here." She started to cry. "How could you, Marley? How could you come here? I'm so ashamed, I'm so embarrassed."

I fight to stop my bottom lip from trembling. "The last place you wanna be is here? You don't wanna be here?" I asked.

She wiped her tears on the sleeve of her hoodie and shook her head no.

"Milo," I called out.

"Boss?" He popped his head in around the door.

"Pull the car up to the front doors and I'll take Ash down to it. Can you come back up and gather all of her clothes, shoes, anything personal, and bring it down for me please?"

"No problemo, Marls." He disappeared out of view and I walked towards Ashley.

"What are you doing?'

"You're coming home with me. I'm calling you a doctor and

while you get yourself better at my place, we'll find you somewhere else to live."

"Somewhere with lights and glass in the windows and everything?"

"And everything." I promised her.

She looked up at me through watery blue eyes. My heart pounded in my chest, echoing in my throat and ears. I'd hoped she wouldn't fight me on this because there was no fucking way I was leaving her there.

She let out a long sigh.

"I'm not sure Marls, I'm just not sure."

"Ash, look, whatever you might think of me and my reputation, all I wanna do is help you out right now."

"Why?" Her chin wobbled as she asked and I hated that she just didn't get that I was genuinely interested.

"Like I keep trying to tell you, I like you, a lot. I like being with you. I don't know Ash, I don't have the words. I just know that I've never felt like this before. I need to know you're safe and that ain't gonna happen if I leave you here, so either you come to mine, or I'm staying here with you."

"I might not want you here with me."

"Tough fucking shit. Them's your options, baby."

She looked around the room before she looked back at me, saying so quietly, I could only just make it out, "I'll come with you."

She wrapped her arms around my neck as I lifted her up. "I still ain't shagging ya," she said in my ear.

"We'll see about that, sweetheart … we'll see."

TWENTY
1989

It took a week for Ash to fully recover. I had a doctor out to see her as soon as I got her to my place and tucked up in my bed. He declared she had laryngitis, as well as a chest and sinus infection. He prescribed a five day course of antibiotics and paracetamol for the pain. After taking her tablets and eating a bowl of tomato soup, she slept for almost fourteen hours.

In that time, I got myself setup in Maca's room and moved all her clothes and girlie shit from her place, into my room.

I left her to rest the first couple of days, just bringing her food and making her drink plenty. She was up and about by the following Thursday, and watching telly on the sofa, curled up next to me under a blanket.

It'd been a week, and I already didn't want to imagine her not being there every day. It was killing me to lay in bed at night, knowing that she was in the other room.

We'd done nothing more than curl up next to each other, or kiss each other's cheeks goodnight. I desperately wanted more, but I knew that I had to prove to her that I didn't just want her there for sex. I had to make her understand that I wanted her there because I couldn't stand the thought of her not being there.

I got out for a run on Friday morning, then headed into our home gym and lifted some weights, anything to take my mind off sex, specifically sex with Ashley.

I'd just showered and was making Ash and myself a sandwich when my phone rang.

"Madam Vaginas Brothel, how can we help you today?" I answered.

"Please tell me George is with you?" It was Maca.

"Na, mate. Not seen her."

"Fuck." I got instant goose bumps.

"Mac, what's wrong?"

"Dave fucking sat back and did nothing when she left with Cameron King's minder."

What?

"What the fuck, Mac? When?"

"Six fucking hours ago."

"Where are you?"

"At the flat."

"I'm coming over."

"Okay. Your dad's on it and on his way over too." He was quiet for a few seconds. "You don't reckon she's gone back to him, do ya Marls?"

"No, mate, I don't." I had no fucking clue.

He hung up.

"What's wrong?" Ashley asked from behind me.

She looked a lot better. She'd actually dressed in clothes rather than her PJ's. Her hair was all clean and shiny, and she had some colour in her cheeks. She looked beautiful—*perfect*.

"George left the flat with Cameron King's minder six hours ago and no one's seen her since."

"Oh shit."

"Yeah. I'm gonna head over there."

"I'll come."

We literally walked through the front door of my sister's to an entire Layton family reunion.

My dad was on the phone, shouting out orders to someone and my mum was on the sofa, looking worried.

Bailey was trying to shout over my dad to whoever it was he was talking to on the phone.

"If he touches a hair on her fucking head, I'll have him and his bald fucking sidekick. They'll both end up at the bottom of the Thames wearing concrete boots."

Jimmie was making tea and Len was talking quietly in the kitchen to Maca.

All eyes turned to us.

"You know anything?" Maca directed his question to Ash. He was obviously unaware that she was with me when he'd called.

She shook her head no, but then called out to Bailey, "He won't hurt her."

Everyone once again turned in her direction.

"Hang on a minute … Fin, hang on," my dad said as he sat down the phone.

"What?" Bailey and Maca both said at once.

She looked up at me, terrified, and I watched her throat move as she swallowed. Then she pulled her classic Ash pose; shoulders back and chin out, that was my girl. She walked farther into the room.

"He won't hurt her. I spoke to him at the wine bar last week." She turned and looked in my direction as she said it, probably because she knew that it was news to me. "I popped over there after work with Lorna before going out one night and he was there."

"And?" Bailey snapped, and that was exactly what his neck would be doing if he talked to her like that again.

"He was half cut and told me that he was in love with George, that he'd planned a future for them together, but if Sean was what she wanted then he would stand aside and let her be happy." She looked around at everyone, looking them in the eyes, but I could see her fingers and thumbs rubbing together. I knew she was nervous. "He loves her. He'd never hurt her."

Maca ran his hand through his hair, then over his beard. His shoulders slumped and I knew what he was thinking in an instant.

"She'll be back," I told him, but he shook his head no.

"What about Georgia? Has she said anything about him to you?" he asked.

"Na, I've hardly seen her the last coupla weeks. She's been with you all the time."

"What about you, Jim?"

"Na, same as Ash. I've hardly seen her."

I'll call you back in a sec, Fin." My dad ended his call, just as a wide-eyed Georgia came through the door. She stopped in her tracks and looked at all of us. It was a classic 'deer in headlights' moment as she took us all in.

"Where the *fuck* have you been, George?" Bailey jumped in first.

My dad moved towards her and wrapped her in his arms. "Princess, you scared the fuckin' life outta me. Don't ever, and I mean *ever,* do that again!"

Princess? Fucking Princess? My sister seriously got away with murder.

I watched Maca, watching 'Princess George,' with a look of … I don't know what, on his face. He looked relieved, but still worried. She was back, unharmed by the looks of things, but he was obviously as curious as me to know where it was exactly that she'd been all day.

I tune Bailey out as he bollocked my sister and told her what a selfish little bitch she was, and I had to say, I agreed with him on that score.

Georgia made her apologies to everyone, which I was surprised at. Usually she'd just storm off and slam doors, but she took it on the chin and said sorry. I actually thought she meant it.

I gestured to Ash that it was time for us to go. Now that I knew G was safe, I wasn't hanging around to listen to her get a Frank special. He could go on for hours, my dad, when you displeased him, to the point where your ears would bleed.

By the time we got back to my place, Ash was tired and I was starving, so we called out for pizza and got back on the sofa to watch 'The Untouchables.'

Mrs. Cooper, our cleaning lady, came over and helped me make a Shepherd's pie on Saturday, and wrote me a list of what I needed to buy for a Sunday roast.

Milo was out with Georgia and Maca while they looked at houses. Everything seemed to be sweet with them when I called to check that morning. I read the shopping list out to Dave over the phone and sent him to the shops to get everything that I needed.

Working for rock stars can be seriously dangerous work at times, I kid you not. Just ask Dave.

Ashley had hardly said a word since she got here. Yesterday was the most I'd heard her speak, and the majority of what she had to say was aimed at other people. I wasn't sure if she still had the hump with me Saturday afternoon when I leaned against the bedroom door and asked her if she'd like to get out of bed and eat, or if she wanted me to bring her food in on a tray.

The antibiotics had taken full affect at that stage. Her voice wasn't as croaky, and she wasn't coughing as much. She'd had some colour in her cheeks for the past few days, and I couldn't help but notice how pretty she looked as she contemplated my question, quietly.

"I'll have a bath and then I'll get up, if that's all right?" Her reply finally came.

"Of course it's all right. I told you to treat this place like your own while you're here. There's some muscle soak bubble bath shit under the sink if you wanna throw that in."

"Thank you."

"You need help washing your back ... or your front?"

"Do you ever give in?"

"Never. So, do you?"

"No, Marley, I think I can manage."

"Just shout if you change your mind, baby."

I couldn't tell if her eyes were watery because of her condition, or if she was about to cry. "Why are you doing this for me, Marley? Why are you looking after me?" Shit, she was about to cry.

I walked into the room and sat down on the edge of the bed next to her. I got Milo to buy her some girlie bedding yesterday, and Mrs. Cooper washed, dried, and put it on the bed for her earlier. I told him to get purple, as she seemed to like it.

She looked so young sitting there, surrounded by purple pillows and sheets. I tucked a wayward strand of blonde hair behind her ear before I spoke. "Why won't you believe that I really like you, Ash?"

"Because boys like you don't waste their time on girls like me."

"So boys like me have no interest in smart, funny, mouthy, sexy girls like you?" I asked. She shook her head no.

"That's got fuck all to do with it. That shit's all just for show. I'm talking about me, the real me; where I come from, who my parents are, where I was living."

Now it's my turn to shake my head. "Where you come from, who your family are, and where I found you living, have all gone into making you the person that you are, and I happen to like that person, Ash. I don't know why you keep banging on about blokes like me. I come from the same place as you. We went to the same school, for fuck's sake."

I wasn't a snob, and I'd never looked down my nose at anyone—that's not the way we were raised—and it was pissing me off that she kept implying that I somehow thought that I was better than her. Yeah,

I described the place she was living as a shithole because it fucking was, but I wasn't judging her for it.

"We hardly had the same upbringing though."

"What the fuck has that got to do with anything?" I asked, my voice sounding high-pitched in disbelief. "I like you, Ash, a lot, and if you like me, then there's no reason why we can't give this a go, that is unless you *don't* like me, and you're just coming up with bullshit excuses as to why we can't be together. And if that's the case, well then, that's fine. I'll help you out anyway because I like you. Just say the word and I'll back the fuck off and leave you to get yourself well, then I'll help you find a new place to stay."

Please don't say the word. Please, please don't.

"I'm not a charity case. I'm not a little project for you and your family to work on."

What?

"What the fuck has my family got to do with this?"

"Well, there's you feeding me bullshit so you can get into my knickers. There's Georgia being my mate, just because she doesn't have too many to choose from, and there's your mum, giving me a job and treating me like the rain in Spain bird, out of the Doctor Doolittle film, trying to make me talk and dress all proper."

That's what she thinks of us?

I watched in silence as she wiped her nose on the back of her hand. That was why I didn't do relationships. That was why I didn't do that caring bollocks. It just made your chest hurt.

It took me a few seconds to calm the emotions bubbling inside of me, trying to think of what to say. She could bitch about me all she wanted, but bringing my family into it, I was gonna get pissed off.

"Well, I'm glad you've clued me up on how you really feel. I won't waste any more of your time, but just so you know, the only thing I was planning on feeding you today was the Shepherd's pie I've spent the last two hours making us for dinner. Georgia is just choosey about who she lets into her life, and you should feel fucking honoured that my sister has let *you* in and given *you* the title of friend. As for my mum ... from what I hear, my mum gave you that job because apparently you're an excellent sales woman. She gives you an allowance to spend on clothes because it's a perk of the job, and good advertising for the shop. And as for the bird from the film? You're even wrong on that score, sweetheart. Her names Eliza Doolittle, and the play's called *Pygmalion,* the film is *My Fair Lady*. Doctor Doolittle has got fuck all to do with it. Even I know that much."

We stared at each other for a few seconds before Ash started to climb out of bed. "I'm off. I don't need this bullshit, and I don't need to be lectured by you." She headed into my wardrobe and started pulling her clothes off the hangers.

"Where the fuck are *you* gonna go?" I snapped. I shouldn't have used that tone, implying that I was her only option. I knew it as soon as I said it.

She spun around and stared at me with an armful of her designer dresses, held against her chest. "You think I don't have places to go? People that I can stay with? People that care and don't just see me as a charity case?"

Whoa, that fucking hurt.

"When the fuck have I ever made you feel like a charity case?" I asked, astounded.

"Oh, I dunno." She shrugged her shoulders. "Only since I met you, and especially since you turned up to my flat, uninvited."

She tilted her chin in that way that she did, and my heart rate increased. Why? I didn't have an answer to that.

She moved to try and put her hands on her hips, but they were still filled with her clothes. She didn't even have a suitcase to put them in. Pretty much everything she owned was what she held in her arms. I couldn't imagine how that must've made her feel, but I didn't want it to be inadequate, unworthy, or beneath me, or anyone else. She was a better person than I could ever hope to be. I just needed her to understand that.

"I came to your flat because I was worried about you. I had no fucking clue you were living in those conditions. Does my sister know? My mum?" That probably wasn't the best way to go about making her feel better about herself.

Go me.

Her nostrils flared, just before she threw her clothes at me. "Where I live has fuck all to do with your family, and fuck all to do with you or anyone else."

Okay, perhaps I didn't care how she felt. As she screamed at me, she picked up the pile of clothes a few more times and repeatedly threw them at me before collapsing on top of them in a coughing fit.

I watched her for a few seconds, trying to decide whether I wanted to get her some water, or smack her arse for behaving like such a bitch. This type of behaviour was what I'd expect from George, but I'd never had thought Ash capable of it.

I turned and got a bottle of water off the night stand and threw it so it landed in her lap.

"Thank you," she said through her sniffs and her tears.

"You're welcome."

I stood and watched her as she sat on her pile of clothes, crying quietly. My fists clenched and unclenched. I wanted to sit on the floor with her and pull her into my lap. I wanted to kiss her fucking senseless and make everything right in her world, but I shouldn't want to feel any of those things. What she said about my family was nasty and spiteful, and I shouldn't want anything to do with her.

She finally looked up at me. "I'm sorry." She got out before her face crumbled and she pulled that full on ugly face you do when you cry hard.

I was done.

Within a split second, I was on the floor with her, holding her in my lap and stroking her back, kissing the top of her head.

"I'm so sorry, Marley. I really don't think that. I don't think any of those things. I love your sister and your mum ... sh-she..." She let out a few sobs before continuing, "She's the only one I've got."

I pulled her into me and held her tight.

"I ain't got no one, Marley. No people that care, and I've got nowhere to go. My life's a fucking mess." She started to cough. I lifted her up and carried her back to bed. I sat with my back to the headboard and kept a hold of her in my lap.

"Ash, just so you know, whatever happens between us, you'll always have me. And don't say that you've got no one coz you have my mum, George, and Jimmie. They *all* care."

She looked up at me through teary eyes, blinked a couple of times and opened her mouth to speak.

"If you ask me again why I'm doing this, I'll fucking strangle you," I told her.

She smiled, despite the tears clinging to her lashes, then started to cry again.

I held on to her until eventually, we both fell asleep.

We ate reheated Shepherd's pie later that evening, and on Sunday, we cooked a roast dinner together.

She fell asleep later on the sofa with her head in my lap. I ran my fingers through her hair as I stared down at her.

Ever since we met, I've felt like my heart had beat too fast, too hard, and too erratic. My stomach felt like it had been tied in knots and my head—my head was all over the show. I thought one thing, then did or said another.

I'm not entirely sure how I felt about any of it. Terrified, mostly. The fact that I had no control over what I was feeling scared the crap outta me, and it was that fear that ultimately lead me to fuck everything up and make yet another one of the biggest mistakes of my life.

I turned the telly off by the remote control and carried Ashley to bed. As I laid her down, she pulled me towards her.

"Where are you going?" she asked.

"The other room."

"Don't go. Stay, please?" She sat up and put the lamp on at the side of the bed. "I'd really like you to stay, Marls." My belly flipped at the abbreviation of my name. I wasn't sure if I'd heard her use it before, and I liked it, almost as much as Rock Star, in fact.

We'd both been a bit quiet since our little fallout yesterday, but she'd barely left my side and had been very touchy feely when she'd been near. I had no idea what it meant. I was hoping that she was finally 'getting' that I liked her for her. I'd held back, *sorta*, on all the flirty stuff that came so naturel to me and just tried to keep things on a *sorta* platonic level.

"Ash, if I stay ... I can't. I'm not sure that..." For fuck's sake, Layton, just tell her if you stay, you'll likely bang her brains out.

"Rock Star, do I have to spell it out for you? I want you to stay. I know what that means, and I want you to stay."

My mouth went dry, to the point where my tongue stuck to the roof of my mouth and my lips to my teeth.

She climbed out of bed and headed towards the bathroom. I grabbed her hand as she passed me. "Where you going?"

"I want a quick shower and to clean my teeth. My breath smells like Brussel sprouts."

"I like Brussel sprouts." It was possibly the most pathetic thing I'd ever said in my life, like, ever.

"Yeah, on your dinner, maybe, but do you really wanna snog one?"

I didn't answer her question, mainly because I'd say something that would make me sound like even more of a pussy, or a complete twat, so I let go of her hand and let her carry on into the bathroom. I went and collected my toothbrush and then came back, unsure of what to do next.

Me, unsure? That was a fucking joke, but that was what she did to me.

I took off my clothes and stepped into the shower with her. She had her back to me, face tilted upwards, letting the water bounce off her chin and down her chest. Her hair was piled up in one of those sexy birds nest things. I leaned in and kissed the curve of her neck and slid my arms around her from behind. She stilled for a split second, and then pressed her back into my front.

"You are so fucking gorgeous," I told her.

We had the showers designed with a built-in sound system and *'Mystify'* by INXS was playing.

Leaving one hand on her belly, I slid the other up and cupped one of her tits. It fit my hand perfectly. Squeezing her nipple, I dragged my teeth up her neck and over her ear.

"Baby, we need to get washed and get out of here before I embarrass myself and come before you even touch me," I whispered.

She shuddered, fucking shuddered, and goose bumps spread across her skin. I bent my knees slightly and grinded my hips into hers.

She bent over to get the shower gel and I nearly came all over her arse.

"Fuck me, Ash, seriously. Don't be bending over near me like that, babe, else this'll be over before it even gets started."

She turned to face me and rolled her eyes. The water from the shower head beat down between us. I slipped my arms around her hips, gripped onto her arse cheeks and pulled her towards me.

"I want to climb inside that head of yours and carve into your brain how fucking perfect you are so that you'll finally believe what I'm saying to you." I hate that she doubts that I'm telling the truth.

"It's just…" She tilted her head to the side before shrugging her shoulders, then looked down at my chest. Her tits were squashed up against my bare chest, but I'd not even been aware of that fact because I was too busy worrying about what she was thinking.

"Look at me, Ash," I ordered. I expected a big *'fuck you,'* but instead, she brought her eyes up to meet mine.

"Trust me when I say this, baby. You are perfect." She slowly nodded her head.

"If I trust you, Marley, please promise that you won't let me down?" she whispered. Her voice was still a little bit croaky, but I could hear the plea, the desperation in her words regardless, and then I did something I should never have done.

"You can trust me, Ash. I'll never let you down."

We kissed under the flow of the water before slowly washing each other's bodies. After turning off the shower and cleaning our teeth, we crawled into bed.

I spent the longest time I'd ever spent, exploring and worshiping a woman's body. I kissed, licked, sucked, and bit my way from the tips of her toes to the top of her head.

When my mouth got back down to the top of her thighs, I lifted her knees and pushed her legs as wide apart as I could. She was spread bare for me. I ran my fingertips over the small patch of fair hair that sat above her perfect, perfect pussy.

Her hips bucked off the bed and she let out a moan as I spread her open with my thumbs and licked where she was wet.

"Marley, please." I loved the begging tone to her voice—fucking loved it.

"You like that, baby?" I looked up at her and asked. She had one hand in my hair, her nails raking at my scalp, and the other was bent back behind her, gripping the pillow. Her cheeks, neck, and chest were flushed pink and I swear, I had never seen anything more beautiful in my life.

"Yes. Yes, I've never … no one's ever—"

"No one's ever what, baby? Kissed you here?" I kissed her clit. "Licked you there?" I swiped my tongue through her cunt, then pushed it inside her as she ground her hips into my face.

Her taste, her moans, the way she smelled, everything about her was so fucking perfect.

"You like that?" I asked after I blew over her wet skin.

"Yes," she stated, still grinding her hips up towards my mouth.

"You want me to make you come? You wanna come all over my face?"

She nodded her head as her hands clawed at the sheets on either side of her hips.

"Use your words, baby. I need to hear you tell me what you want." Her eyes widened as she worked out that she was gonna have to beg, or at least ask me nicely for an orgasm.

"Please Marley, please. I wanna come. I want you to make me come."

Did I mention that I fucking loved the way she pleaded with me? *Loved. It.*

I could've come myself just from listening to her beg. I kissed her belly before sliding my hands underneath her arse cheeks and tilting her hips towards my face.

"I'm gonna use my mouth, baby. I'm gonna use my mouth and my fingers, and I'm gonna blow your fucking mind." I flicked my tongue over her clit, sliding two fingers inside her, and curled them forward. She was so tight.

Tight, wet, and so fucking perfect.

I pumped my fingers in and out of her, curling them and stroking her from the inside, slowly. My opposite hand was resting against the silky soft skin of the inside of her thigh. I wanted to keep tasting her, but I also wanted to watch her come. After a few more flicks, I replaced my tongue with my thumb and kept working her clit as I sat up on my knees so I could watch her face.

Both her arms were over her head, holding onto the pillow. Her shoulders were pulled back, her tits moving as she rode my hand. I slid my hand up her body and squeezed one of her nipples as I looked at both her eyes, and her parted lips.

"Perfect. *You* are fucking *perfect*," I said, because it was the truth.

"Ahh," was the first sign I got of her impending orgasm, and then everything happened at once.

Her internal muscles tightened around my fingers and her legs trembled as she let out a loud moan. I gave my cock a couple of strokes and shot off all over her belly. All the while, Ash continued to convulse all around me. Her legs, her stomach, internal muscles and her clit, all squeezed, twitched, and shook, and the whole time, she never once broke eye contact with me.

Sexiest thing ever.

When her insides stopped pulsating, I slid my fingers out of her and licked them clean as she watched. Then I reached for the towel I left on the floor after our shower together.

I wiped off the mess I made on her belly, then laid on top of her, kissing her mouth gently. She opened her legs, welcoming me in between them. I slid my tongue across the seam of her lips until eventually, she opened her mouth and allowed my assault. I couldn't get deep enough as I tangled my tongue with hers. I swiped it over her teeth, her mouth, and her lips. It didn't take long for me to grow hard again.

After kissing her senseless for a while, I gave her nipples the attention they deserved, which seemed to drive her fucking nuts. Her nails dug into my arse cheeks and I had to laugh out loud at her enthusiasm as she pulled me against her.

When neither of us could take it anymore, I slid inside her. This time it was quiet and gentle. This time I lasted. This time I laced my fingers through hers and stared into her eyes. This time was beyond perfect—beyond anything I had ever experienced in my life.

I knew before I even said the words that it was wrong of me, that I was lying. I promised I wouldn't let her down, but I knew that one day I would.

She'd been let down before, I could see it in her eyes. I heard it in her insecurities, her self-doubt, and I never wanted to be the reason behind any of that, so later that night, when we'd showered together, fucked once more, and she'd fallen asleep in my arms, in my bed, in my heart, and my dirty, tarnished soul, I watched her. I watched the rise and fall of her chest, memorising her long eyelashes as they fanned out across her cheeks that were still flushed pink with the sex and the showers we'd shared. Then I gently kissed her perfect mouth, slid out of my bed, packed a case with my clothes and left her a short note. I called a car service to collect and take me to the airport.

It was five in the morning, but from the phone in the security office of my building, I called Andrea, mine and Maca's PA. I told her I needed a flight to anywhere, ASAP, and she called back within fifteen minutes. Three hours later, I was touching down in Paris.

I stayed drunk in my hotel room for two days. I was still too close, too tempted to go back and claim her, to make her mine, at least until I would do what I did best and fuck things up again, until I broke her.

I called Andrea again and booked a flight to the States.

I checked in with Len and told him I just needed some time to myself. We had nothing on anyway. With only a month till his wedding, we had nothing scheduled until later in the year when we'd start the new album.

I needed to be back in England in three weeks for my final suit fitting, which gave me plenty of time to be seen and photographed with a different woman on my arm every night. I went to every place in LA we usually avoided. Every club, bar, and restaurant I knew the press hung about outside, I was there. I made sure I gave them plenty of opportunity to get their shots of me leaving, and I made sure I was with a different woman each time.

It wasn't that I wanted to hurt Ash, I didn't, not at all, but I knew if I went where I was sure our feelings were taking us, I'd eventually let her down. I'm Marley Layton, fucking things up is what I did.

With just a couple of days left in LA, I spoke with Maca on the phone and he told me that he and George had found a place in Hampstead, and had been able to move straight in. Ashley had taken over G's flat, which she had left fully furnished for her.

"I take it things didn't work out between you, what with the way you just took off?" Maca asked me down the phone.

"Why, what's she said?" I asked, waiting for Georgia to jump in and give me a bollocking. I was actually surprised I hadn't heard from her or Jimmie by then.

"Nothing much. Gia has only seen her a couple of times. G's tried going back to work, but the press are up her arse so she's promoted Ash to area manager. The flat and a car come with the job."

Well, that made me feel a little better and a lot worse.

In the note that I'd left for Ash, I'd told her to stay at my place for as long as she liked. Despite the shitty thing that I'd done, I was hoping that she might still be there when I went back for the wedding.

"I think she told G that she'd gotten back with her ex, and that's why things hadn't worked out between you two. I assumed that's why you took off. I know you said you liked her."

"Her ex? What fucking ex?" I paced the floor of my hotel room as I shouted down the phone. What ex? There was no ex? She never told me about any fucking ex. Probably because I didn't hang around long enough for her to tell me much about anything.

Images of Ashley, small, vulnerable, curled up all warm beside me, hot and sweaty from sex, water dripping from her in the shower, flashed like snapshots through my brain. The thought of someone else seeing her like that, sharing moments like I had with her, touching, tasting and smelling her, made my head feel like it was about to explode.

Whoever the fucker was, he had to go.

Even kidnap and murder seemed like reasonable possibilities in that moment.

"Oi, hold your fucking horses. I don't know what ex, she's your bird."

"She's not my bird." I bit back.

"Well, not if she's back with her ex, she ain't, no." We were both quiet for a few seconds. "Sorry mate. I thought you knew. I thought that's why you left."

I let out a long sigh. My head was now pounding and my brain was in overdrive. I needed to get back to England and put things right.

I'd fucked up. Yeah, yeah, I know, it was what I did, but this time

I'd fucked up massively, and possibly lost the best thing that had ever happened to me.

"Mac, I need to go. I'll be home tomorrow and give ya a bell then. Give my love to George." I never gave him a chance to say goodbye before I cut him off.

I called Len and asked him to get me on the next flight back to London, and to have a car waiting for me when I landed.

By ten the next morning, I was pulling up outside Posh Frocks. I pulled my cap down low and ran into the shop.

"Morning, Lorna. Ashley about?" I kept it casual and talked to the girl like I'd known her forever. We'd chatted a few times when I'd been waiting for Ash and I'd signed some stuff for her.

"No, she's out on the road today. She might come back here later, but not until around four. I can call one of the stores she's visiting today and let her know you're looking for her?" she said with a smile.

I liked Lorna. She was a bit older than me, and wasn't fazed by who I was.

"Na, that's all right. I was hoping to surprise her," I told her with a wink.

"Oh, so she's not expecting you?" she asked and something in her tone had me questioning her.

"No, why's that?"

She tilted her head sideways and folded her arms across her chest.

"I've no idea what's gone on between the two of you, but I don't think you're her favourite person right now, Marley."

"Lorna, I *know* I'm not her favourite person right now. That's why I need to speak to her, and if she knows that I'm looking for her, she won't see me so please, would you give me the chance to put things right? I fucked up and I *need* to speak to her."

"Yeah, well, good luck with that. I won't say I've seen you, but you better put things right. She's a good girl, Ashley is, and I've hated seeing her upset these past few weeks."

"She's been upset?" I asked, feeling bad for sounding so hopeful.

"Yeah, she's been upset, especially when she sees that." She nods her head towards the coffee table where there's a copy of Hello Magazine. My ugly mug was smiling from the front cover, Alexis Kanchelski, some model I met in a club a few weeks back, wrapped around me.

"Fuck." Is all I could say. I actually planned on her seeing it. I'd hoped that she'd see it and hate my fucking guts. That in turn would make it easier for her to move on and forget about me.

Well, job well done, Marley. Job well-fucking-done.

"Right, yeah. Well, like I said, I've fucked up and I need to put things right, so I'd really appreciate you not saying that I've been here."

"She won't hear it from me. Now piss off and put a smile back on that girls dial," she ordered. I stepped in and kissed her cheek.

"I'll do my best, Lorna. I'll do my very best." I promised.

I got Dave, who picked me up from the airport, to drop me off at home. My plan was to take a shower and drive back to Ashley's flat and wait for her arrival.

The first I realise that there was a problem was when I couldn't get my key in the lock. I called Ronnie, one of the doormen up to take a look. He called out a locksmith when he couldn't do anything with it. The locksmith arrived and promptly told me that a key had been snapped off inside the lock.

He drilled it out, but ended up having to replace the whole barrel. I couldn't stand the damage that it did to my front door, so ended up telling Ronnie to tell maintenance to order me a new one.

As soon as the door was opened, it was apparent that the place stunk.

"Bloody hell, mate. You forget to empty your fridge before you went away?" Bert the locksmith asked.

I was already pissed off at that point, so I bunged him a twenty quid tip and told him to invoice me for the bill.

Once I stepped all the way inside, I could see where the smell was coming from.

Sitting on my kitchen work top was the contents of my freezer. Two chickens, a whole salmon, a loaf of bread, a box of ice poles, and a tub of ice cream. I assumed that the freezer had broken, but why the stuff wasn't thrown out, I had no idea. To make things worse, the place was like a sauna. The heating had obviously been left on the whole time I was away.

I go to call Maca to find out what the fuck had gone on when I realised I had no way of contacting him. I didn't know his new number.

I grabbed a black sack and threw everything in it, then ran it down to the bins. When I got back up, I sprayed the place with what I thought was air freshener, but turned out to be furniture polish. Still, lemony pledge smelled a whole lot better than rotten chicken and fish.

When I walked into my bedroom, I was hit by another strange smell.

"What the fuck?"

I looked down to see what was causing the strange squelch under my feet and realised at once the cause.

My bed had been stripped back to the bare mattress, and the carpet had a two inch layer of water cress growing over it. The carpet was wet, and when I pushed down on my mattress, so was it. On the night stand next to the bed was the note that I left Ashley, along with the front door key I left for her, half of it snapped off.

Underneath what I had written, Ash, I assumed, had added…

WELCOME HOME
FUCKER!!!

I laughed. I didn't actually know what else to do, so I stood on my water cress carpet and laughed.

Fuck. If I didn't love that girl before, I definitely did then.

Yes, so fucking what. I admitted it. I loved her. I knew it a month ago and I sure as shit knew it now.

I took off my cap and scratched my head.

"Ah, Ashley Morrison. What are we gonna do with you?"

TWENTY-ONE

1989

I contacted Andrea and asked her to send a cleaning crew to my place.

It only took the supervisor one look at my bedroom to tell me that I needed new carpet and a new bed. I decided to play it safe and opt to leave the original timber floor exposed instead of having new carpet laid.

Chances were, this wouldn't be the only time I'd piss Ashley Morrison off and she'd pull another stunt like that.

I eventually showered and changed and left my house to a team of cleaners, who had also, for an undisclosed amount of cash, agreed to rip up and dump both my carpet and mattress.

I arrived back at Ashley's just after five. There was a brand new silver Ford Fiesta sitting in the parking spot assigned to the flat at the back of the shop.

The problem I had now was that I didn't know if Ash was in the shop or at home. I really didn't fancy arguing with her in the shop, so I walked to the nearest pay phone and called Georgia's old number, assuming Ash has kept it. It picked up after the third ring.

Like the complete coward that I was, I hung up. I walked back to her flat and went up the stairs and pressed the buzzer.

"Hello?" A bloke answered.

Fuck, a bloke. I wasn't counting on that. Fuck my luck. Oh well, I'd come this far, I wasn't backing down now.

"Delivery for Ms. Morrison." I held my nose and said.

Fuck knows why I held my nose, but I did.

"Yeah, come through." The bloke, fuckhead, told me.

I cracked my knuckles, unsure of what I was about to encounter as I headed through the first set of doors and along the short hallway to the front door.

What I wasn't expecting was a bloke of about a hundred, holding a screwdriver.

"All right, mate. She's just popped downstairs to the shop for minute. I'll take…" He trailed off, pushed his glasses up his nose and looked a bit closer at me.

"'Err, ain't you one of Frank's boys? The rock star one?"

Ha, result. I knew this bloke. He'd worked for my dad for years.

"Yes, mate. Bloody hell, Joe, ain't it?" I held my hand out to shake his.

"Sammy, actually, but close enough, son." I'm so shit with names.

"Sammy, of course. Sorry mate." He shook my hand anyway.

"I'm here putting a new bed together that that young Ashley had delivered. She shouldn't be long. I was just hanging about till she came back, but if you're here, I can shoot off," he said.

"Yeah, yeah, you go, mate. Get off home." I pulled a twenty out of my pocket. "Thanks for helping my girl out. I've been away, else I would've done it myself. Get yourself a beer on the way."

"Well, that's very nice of you, boy. Cheers, I'll do just that." He gave me a salute and headed off out the door.

And that was how you dealt with fuckheads, or in that case, really nice eighty-year-old handy men.

I knew it was wrong, like really wrong, but I nipped into Ashley's bedroom and bathroom and checked for any blokey stuff. There was only one toothbrush, which was a good sign—no aftershave, deodorant, or hair gel in any of the bathroom cabinets, and nothing hanging in her wardrobe.

Back with the ex, my arse. She's full of shit.

But then I felt bad. She probably only made that story up to save face. What an arsehole I was. She worked for my sister and my mum. How the fuck must she feel facing them at work, knowing all the things we did the night before I left her?

I went back to the living room, sat on the sofa and waited. I went over what I was gonna say in my head. I decided that honesty was gonna be the best policy. Ash would see straight through any bullshit excuses I came up with.

I stood up and went into the kitchen, leaning my elbows on the work top and faced the front door, then I paced, wiped my sweaty palms on my jeans, and then leaned back down on my elbows.

I'd played sell-out concerts at Wembley, for fuck's suck, I could do this.

Could I do it? Was I really what she actually *needed* in her life?

I started to consider leaving when I heard the first security door close. For a split second I thought about climbing out of a window, but then the front door swung open and there she was.

You remember that kids game Buckaroo? Well, that's how my heart was feeling right then, like the horse had bucked, throwing bits of it in every direction. It was hitting my ribs, my belly, and my throat.

It took her a few seconds to notice me, then she screamed, dropped her bag and moved one hand to her chest.

"Fuck," she said breathlessly, sexily. Her face changed in an instant.

"What the fuck are you doing here?"

"Didn't my mum call you?" I asked.

She frowned and shook her head. "No, why?"

"Hmm, sorry about that. I thought you knew I was gonna be staying here." I tried to sound like I was sorry.

Obviously I wasn't, not in the least.

"Wh-What? Staying here? Why?" She stuttered out, all colour now drained from her face.

I should've felt bad, but I didn't.

"Well, you wouldn't believe what's happened at my place. Some *"fucker,"* I used finger air quote thingy's when I said it, "has broken into my place and left rotting food everywhere. And a thick, green mould growing all over my bedroom. Could take weeks to put right." I held my hands out, shaking my head and trying to look as if I was in despair, which I kinda was.

"So yeah, anyway. What with the wedding being just next week, I needed to be in town, so my mum said that since you have a spare room, I should stay here, at least until after the wedding."

She was shaking her head before I even finished talking.

"No. I can't have you … I won't have you here. Get out. Get the fuck out right this fucking minute. How dare you even come here?" She picked up her bag and stepped closer as she spoke.

I stepped closer as I listened, but ignored what she was saying.

"Ash, look, I'm so fucking... Argghhhh. What the—" I couldn't see … I couldn't fucking breathe. Fuck, I was on fire. My skin was fucking dissolving, along with my eyeballs.

"Get out of my fucking flat."

"Oghaghfuuuck," was the sorta sound I made as my legs gave way and I crumbled to the floor. A kick in the balls would do that to ya.

I rolled onto my back and held onto my balls, which were now hiding somewhere near my ears. I coughed and spluttered as my eyes burned and streamed with tears. I reached up to rub them.

My eyes … not my balls.

"Don't rub them, you'll make it worse," Ash said from above as she dug, what I assumed was her shoe, into my ribs.

"What the… What the fuck?"

"Pepper spray. Your mum supplies all of us girls with it. She likes to know we're safe when we walk out to our cars, or into our flats. Never know what weirdo's could be lurking."

I couldn't believe what I was hearing. She fucking pepper sprayed me, then kicked me in the balls when I couldn't see it coming.

"Stop complaining. I aimed it over your shoulder. You didn't even get a full blast, else you wouldn't be able to breathe right now."

I laid there, rocking from side to side on my back, still cupping where my balls used to be; eyes bleeding and foaming at the mouth as my skin burned away, and ya know what she said? Go on, guess.

"Can you see your way to the front door yet? I wanna take a shower. I'm going out in a bit."

I threw up. I didn't do it on purpose, it just came up out of nowhere.

"Great, now you're throwing up on my floor," she complained.

She complained about *me* throwing up?

"Don't you even dare fucking complain. I spent a whole night dealing with your spew." I coughed and spluttered out.

"You only did that so that you could see my tits."

"Believe me, babe, I don't need to clear up spew to get a bird to flash me her tits."

"Well, from what I can tell, Ankles Legitrowski's ain't worth flashing."

"Who the fuck's Ankles Legi—" I didn't get to finish.

"The long legged, flat chested Russian you've been fucking." She dug me in the ribs with her shoe again as she spoke.

I tried to open my eyes to glare at her, but it was too painful. "Fuck, this burns."

"Yeah, that's kinda the point," she sarcastically replied. I heard her move around and the fridge door opening and closing. Surely she wasn't gonna leave me here while she made a cup of tea?

"Arghhh," I shouted as something cold and wet hit my face.

"What the fuck have you done to me now?"

"Milk. S'posed to help with the burn." It actually did, but I wasn't gonna tell her that.

I laid there quietly for a while, too scared to move in case I got poked in the ribs by a pointy shoe, or roll over into my own up chuck or a puddle of milk.

"I'm sorry for running out on you the way I did, Ash," I started to explain.

"Save it for someone that cares, Rock Star. I don't wanna hear your bullshit excuses."

"But I just wanna—"

"What part of 'I don't wanna hear it' do you not understand?" I knew she was pacing the floor. I could hear her footsteps. I just wished I could open my fucking eyes. At least I didn't feel like my throat was closing up anymore.

"I don't care what you've got to say, Marley. As soon as you can see, I want you to get the fuck outta here, and then I want you to stay the fuck away from me."

I remained silent. It was pointless trying to argue with her in my condition. I'd lost this battle, but the war was far from over.

I'd left Ashley's the night before without getting a chance to say anything that I wanted to. I ended up driving to Len and Jimmie's to stay the night, not wanting to face the mess or be alone at my place.

Luckily, Jim was already in bed and Len was about to head up when I got there, so I didn't get asked too many questions.

I spent the following week calling Ash, buzzing at her front door, and generally making a nuisance of myself, but she wasn't having a bar of it, and I got nowhere.

Jim told me that she'd be at the wedding so at least I'd get to see her then.

When the day finally arrived, Len looked the part in his velvet collared suit and boot lace tie. Jimmie looked stunning in her fifties-style wedding dress, as did all the bridesmaids. The church service went off without a problem, apart from the fact that Ash turned up with a bloke. I was at the front of the church, showing people where to sit when she walked in.

She looked stunning in a blue dress and silver heels—no purple in sight. Her gaze met mine and I watched as she squared her shoulders, tilted her chin and reached for the hand of the fuckhead standing next to her.

"Fuck," I said under my breath. I instantly felt my mother's eyes burning into me. She was twenty fucking feet away. The woman had bionic hearing when it came to swear words.

"*Sorry*," I mouthed to her. She narrowed her eyes and shook her head like I was four-years-old.

The service was lovely and romantic and blah, blah blah bullshit. Jim gagged at even the whiff of shit or puke, so there went the in sickness bit, and there was no way she'd ever obey Len, so that was out the window too. I seriously didn't see the point of all that bollocks, except I did, and she was sitting four rows from the back with a Desperate Dan lookalike. He was four feet wide and nine feet tall. I just knew that he'd eaten a whole cow in a pie for breakfast that morning. In fact, I swear he had part of the tail caught in the designer stubble on his chin and a hoof stuck between his front teeth.

I looked at her a total of seventeen times in the church and desperately tried to get near her as the photos were being taken.

"Will you get the fuck over here and stop wandering off," Bailey growled through gritted teeth. He was taking the best man bullshit far too seriously if you asked me.

"You're behaving like a fucking bored toddler the way you keep wandering off." I dug my hands in my pockets and kicked at the gravel, probably looking a lot like a bored toddler.

When the photos were finally done, Ash was nowhere in sight. When we got to the function hall, she was sitting nowhere near me.

I spent the next few hours eating, drinking, and smiling my way through the speeches. Kissing aunties and cousins and being chatted up by no fewer than nine women, most of whom I was related to.

Finally, when the tables began to be cleared, I stood and made my way past where she was sitting and out to the bar.

It didn't take long for her to follow. She had her arm looped through Georgia's and she totally ignored me as they both headed towards the ladies toilets.

A minute later, Maca appears next to me with the Neanderthal in tow. He cleared his throat and looked a little uncomfortable. "All right, mate? This is Ashley's fella, Dan." I spat my bourbon. I kid you not, the fuckhead's name was Dan.

I nod my head in his direction.

"All right. Ashley's boyfriend, eh? She moves fast, that girl."

I shouldn't have, I really shouldn't have.

"We've only just broken up. I can't believe she's moved on so quickly. We only decided a few days ago that we were gonna try and work through our problems."

But I did.

His mouth opened and closed a few times before he said, "I'm not ... I'm not her boyfriend. I'm just her date for the night. We don't really know each other that well. This is our first date, really."

And your last.

Ash and Georgia came back from their bathroom break and there were a few seconds of awkward silence.

"Ashley, you look absolutely beautiful—stunning, in fact," I told her.

She narrowed her eyes on me then opened, looked inside, and then closed the bag she had with her. We all watched, mystified as she patted herself down, as if checking her pockets. She then looked all around her.

"What are you looking for?" I asked.

"The fuck I'm supposed to give about what you think of how I look."

Oh, she's such a comedienne.

"Nup, can't find it. I reckon that means it don't exist." She turned her attentions to Dan the cow killer.

I should've just said fuck this for a game of soldiers and walked away, but I wasn't done yet.

"Ash, can we go somewhere and talk for a minute please?" I reached out and put my hand on her arm. She looked down at where I was touching her before meeting my gaze, her eyes filled with tears.

"No, now take your fucking hands off me." She spoke to me through gritted teeth and I didn't hesitate to remove my hand.

"I'm sorry. I just wanna—"

"Just wanna what, Rock Star? You just wanna what? Fuck with my head some more? Fuck *me* some more? Or just fuck *off* and leave me, *again*? What, tell me?"

'Desperate to be anywhere but here' Dan said nothing. He pretty much stood with his back to us as he tried to get served at the bar.

I wasn't doing this now. It was Jimmie and Len's wedding. I wouldn't do what everyone expected and cause a scene.

"Nothing, Ash, nothing. You look beautiful, that's all. I just thought you should know."

I watched as a tear rolled down her perfect cheek, then I did what I did best; I turned and walked away to the sound of Georgia calling out my name.

I spent the next couple of hours chatting with family members and drinking far too much. Maca found me sitting at the bar at the opposite end of the room to where I left him.

"I had no idea she was bringing him, else I would've warned you. What the fuck is going on with you two anyway? I had no clue things had gotten serious."

"Well, if you'd have been the fuck around, you might know a bit more," I said without looking at him.

He sat down on the bar stool next to me. "Fair enough, but I've had some bridges to build with your sister. We needed some time on our own to get back on track."

I felt like an arsehole. What had gone on with Ashley was in no way Maca's fault. I was just pissed off at the world.

"How are things with my sister?" I asked, whilst destroying a cardboard beer coaster. "You get to the bottom of the Cameron King thing?"

"We're okay. I'm not sure that she's all in yet. There's gonna be trust issues for a while, I've gotta expect that, and he's messed with her head, big time. Told her that he loves her and went on a drink and drug binge."

"Fuck. Seems hard to imagine, a big hard bloke like that falling apart over my little sister."

"Yeah, she's good at getting blokes to do that," he said with a shake of his head.

"She's feeling guilty over what she's done to him and still struggling to totally trust me. I think she's already worrying about next year's world tour."

I nodded my head, knowing a little of how he felt and being only too aware that I'd fucked up any chance of Ashley ever trusting me.

"So, you two gonna get married?" It seemed like the logical move to me. He surprised me by shaking his head no.

"We're not gonna rush into anything. We've got four years of catching up to do. If we get married, people are gonna expect babies, and we just want some time for us right now. We've both grown up and changed a lot in the time we've been apart. We need to get to know each other again. We'll get around to it when it suits us, not everyone else."

He gestured to the barman for more drinks. Someone came up and made small talk, a cousin of Jim's, he said. When he left, Maca asked, "So come on, then. What's the go with Ash? She's really pissed off with you, dude. She was almost in tears when you walked away."

"We had something good." I turned and looked him in the eyes. I wanted him to know that for once, I was serious. For the first time ever, I, me, this bloke right here, had feelings for a girl that went beyond sex—way, way beyond. "We had something good and then I did what I do best and fucked it all up."

"How?"

"I had her move in with me because she was sick and I wanted to look after her. She was with me for over a week and I never touched her," I admitted.

His bushy eyebrows raised up into his hairline. "All this time, and you haven't slept with her?"

"I slept with her plenty of times, but we didn't have sex, not until the night before I left."

"You fucked and ran," he stated.

"I panicked. She's perfect ... too fucking perfect and I'm..." I shrugged my shoulders at him. "I'm just me, and I knew that eventually I'd balls it all up and let her down somehow, so I thought it'd be better to get out sooner rather than later." It felt good getting it off my chest, even if it didn't change anything.

"So you jogged off and banged the Russian?"

"I didn't bang anyone. I made sure I had my picture taken with plenty of birds so that she would hate me and move on, but I didn't bang a single one of them. I couldn't. I could only ... all I can think of is her. I want her back, Mac, but she won't listen to a word I say."

"Have you tried talking to her in private? Like, not at a bar at a celebrity wedding?"

Oh, I tried, and ended up traumatised for life and probably unable to father children. "I went to her flat."

"And?"

"She pepper sprayed me and kicked me in the balls. I went down like a sack of shit."

He spits his bourbon all over the bar. "She did ... what the fuck, Marls?" He actually had to hold his sides as he laughed.

"Yeah, yeah, laugh all you like. Don't forget I've seen the state you've been in over my sister."

He cleared his throat and took another sip of his drink before speaking. "That's a classic, mate. I tell ya what, you two are made for each other. You've met your match with that girl, and that's exactly what you need."

"Yeah, she is, but am I what she needs?"

He leaned away from me and opened his mouth a couple of times before any words came out. "Why the fuck wouldn't you be?"

"Come on, Mac. This is me we're talking about … Marley? When I'm not busy fucking up my own life, I'm busy fucking up other people's."

"Marls, listen, mate. You need to get your head around the fact that what happened between me and G wasn't your fault. Yeah, you were there and yeah, you did nothing to stop me … encouraged me, in fact. But at the end of the day, it was down to me. Me and no other fucker. *I* had a girlfriend waiting at home. *I* had the option to say no. *I* knew that what we were doing was wrong but *I* did it anyway, so stop being a martyr and beating yourself up over it."

I sipped my bourbon in the hopes that it would push down the lump in my throat that Maca's words had caused.

"Dude, you're the founding member and guitarist of one of the most successful bands this country has ever seen, and you're what, twenty-three? You, my friend, are so *not* a fuck up. You're like a brother to me, so as one brother to another, take it from someone that knows. If you want a future with that girl, then you don't stop telling her until she listens. Scream it from the rooftops. Fuck, you're a musician, write it in a song."

"You're the songwriter, Mac, not me." I reminded him.

"Well there's nothing wrong with your voice. Yours is every bit as good as mine, so sing her a song, do what you gotta do to make her listen."

I drained my drink, thinking about what he'd said. It was all right for him, he had no issue with expressing his feelings. He'd loved my sister since they were kids. Outside of him and my family, I'd never loved anyone. I'd never been in love.

"What sort of song am I gonna sing to her?" I asked him, feeling clueless, feeling like ... I don't know what. I can't believe a girl had gotten me so twisted up in knots.

"You're sweating, mate. You feeling all right?" Maca asked with a grin.

"No. Just the thought of singing something to her is making me wanna throw up."

His eyes dart all over my face. "You really like her, don't ya?" He draped his arm over my shoulder as he asked.

"Like you wouldn't believe. Like *I* don't believe."

"Happens to the best of us, mate," he tells me. "You gonna come back to the other bar and have a drink with us or stay down here? I need to get back to Georgia."

We both turned around to look in the direction of where my sister was but instead, I spotted her, Ashley, and Jimmie's sister on the dance floor, where the three of them were strutting their stuff to Chaka Khan's *'Ain't Nobody.'* I couldn't take my eyes from Ashley's arse as she raised her arms above her head and moved her hips.

My hard-on was instant

Georgia moved in behind her, Keeley, Jimmie's sister in front, and the three of them grinded and moved against each other.

"Fuck me," Maca said from beside me.

"Please tell me you're not getting a boner watching my sister while you're sitting next to me?" I pleaded, despite the fact I was sporting one myself.

"Na, I'm getting a boner watching your bird and your sister while sitting next to you," he laughed.

"Yeah, me too."

"We're going to hell," he said with a smile.

"Hope they have guitars."

The next few seconds happened in slow motion and fast forward at the same time.

Desperate Dan appeared from nowhere and pulled George forcefully away from Ash, then pulled Ash towards him, grabbing her arse so that she was pressed right up against him.

I don't know who moved first, me or Maca, but before we were even halfway to the dance floor, George had grabbed Dan by the hair and Ash had thrown a punch that caught him on the right side of his jaw.

I almost jumped through the air as I saw him raise his arm to hit either George or Ash. Luckily, Bailey got there and grabbed it, twisting it behind his back.

I swung as soon as I was within shot and my fist connected with his jaw. And as much as it hurt, it felt so fucking good so I did it again, and again. The only noise I could hear was my own blood rushing through my ears. The only sensation was my fists burning as the skin split when it connected with his teeth and the stubble on his chin. I didn't even see his face in front of me, just the way he pulled my sister out of the way and his hands on Ashley's arse.

I'm grabbed under the arms and hauled backwards. When I finally focused, my dad and Len were on either side of me, holding an arm each. Ash stood a few feet away, Bailey at her side as she sobbed. I tried to shrug off my dad and brother and reach out to her, but she stepped back, recoiling almost, and shook her head no.

"Stay away from me. Just stay away from my life," she screamed before turning and leaving. I was held in place, going nowhere until fuckhead was thrown out.

I went into the toilet with Len and washed the blood from my hands, whilst apologising continuously.

"Marls, chill. He had it coming. He'd already abused the bar staff and threatened to knock Uncle Ted out. You put your hands on a woman, then you have to expect comebacks. He's just lucky that you jumped in before Bailey got a chance to. He almost ripped his arm from his socket as it was."

I was shaking badly and I had nowhere to channel the adrenalin.

"I need a drink," I told Len.

"You and me both, brother, you and me both."

Once we're back at the bar, I found out that George and Maca had taken Ashley home. The venue was only around the corner from her flat, but I was worried 'Soon To Be Dead Dan' might follow her home.

I knocked back a double scotch, and then another before I spotted Georgia barrelling across the room towards me.

"What the fuck has gone on between you two?" She was right in my face as she asked.

"Georgia," Maca warned when he finally caught up.

"Why, what's she said?" I asked, getting a sense of déjà vu. I'm sure I'd asked that question before, or was the single malt fogging my brain?

I catch Maca shaking his head over George's shoulder to let me know she was just digging. Ash hadn't told her anything.

"It's what she didn't say, Marls. She's so upset and angry with you and I don't understand why. Ash don't get that way over blokes. She never lets anyone close enough, so what's gone on?"

Now I wanted to cry again. First Maca, and now my sister, setting me off like I'm on my period.

"You all right?" Genuine concern was in her voice as she reached forward and kissed my knuckles. I pulled her in and gave her a cuddle.

"I think I'm in love with your mate, Porge," I confessed.

She stared up at me, looking a little confused.

"Wh-You mean Ash? You're in love with Ashley?"

I nodded and smiled at her. She burst into tears and turned and looked at Maca. "My brothers love my two best friends. You love me, and we're all gonna be a family."

I kissed the top of her head.

"How much she had to drink?" I asked Maca.

"A lot," he replied.

By the end of the night, I've had a bollocking from my mum

before impressing her on the dance floor with my waltz. I'd gotten kisses, cuddles, and propositions from women aged between fifteen and rigor mortis. I'd had a slow dance with my sister and my new sister-in-law, the most beautiful bride I'd ever, at that point in my life, seen.

I'd taught a bunch of seven and eight-year-old cousins how to moonwalk. I'd told my dad, brothers, and Maca that I loved them at least a dozen times, and I'd drank far, far too much whiskey, bourbon, and champagne. I'd done everything except sing to my girl.

Despite being warned not to by just about everyone, I left the wedding and walked/staggered around the corner to Ashley's flat and leaned on the buzzer until she answered.

"Fuck off, Marley."

"S'not me. Him, s'not him, I mean. Open the door, Ash. I need to sing to you."

"Go home, it's late."

"No, I can't. I've bed no—I've got no bed. It green grew mouldy you memberer?" In my head, I knew exactly what I wanted to say, but my mouth had other ideas.

"Ash?"

"Rock Star?"

"Fuck, Ash, tha-that makes my balls tingle when you call me that. Say it again, baby, please, please, please."

"Shall I tell you a secret, Rock Star?"

"Yeshssss. Yessss. Yes baby, tell me. Tell. Me." I was seriously thinking about having a wank right there on her doorstep while I listened to her voice because for some reason, right at that moment, it seemed like a good idea.

"When you call me baby, it makes my fanny flutter."

"Oh fuck. Oh *Ash*. Fuck me, baby." I tried sliding my hand down the front of my trousers, but they were too tight. I'm up a flight of stairs, in a back alley. Surely no one would see if I just flopped my todger out and gave it a lil' tug? No one would see.

"I like that, baby. I like that a lot, that I make your fanny flutter makes me happy. Hard and happy. You gonna let me in?"

"I might."

"G'on. You know you wanna."

"It's nothing to do with whether I wanna, it's whether I should."

Ha, todger. That was a funny word. I wondered how someone came up with that one.

"If I let you in, are you gonna behave?"

I nod my head yes. "Absolutely not."

"I shouldn't even be considering this. I've had too much wine."

"You should. You so should, Ash, and shall I tell you why, shall I baby? My baby, baby, baby love?"

I heard her laugh, but I couldn't see down the intercom, so I didn't know what was funny.

"Tell me, Rock Star … why?"

"Coz, baby. Coz if you met le… met, fuck's sake. If you let me in, not only will I make your fanny flutter, but I'll make—" I suddenly get the giggles and can't get my words out.

"What, Rock Star? You'll make what?"

"Ahhh. Oh dear. Yeah, sorry." I cleared my throat. "I'll not only make your fanny flutter, but I'll make your minge twinge."

Funniest. Joke. Ever.

I laugh so much I throw up.

"Marls?"

I stand from my bent double position to find Ash standing in the open doorway of her flat.

"Ash, I'm sry. I'm so, so sry. I'm am sorory I ran. I'm think… I think love you an… and I think I just crapped myself…"

"Whoa. Whoa. Whoa. Back up, Rock Star. You think you love me? You mean you don't know yet?"

I laughed coz when she went all 'Whoa Whoa Whoay' on me, I thought I was gonna get another bollocking, but I didn't, so I was gonna laugh.

"Ha, of course. Of course I know. I knew at your party, baby. It's your party, baby, and you'll cry…" I sing to her, coz I was a good singer, right? I was in a band and all that. Then I panicked.

"No, no, don't cry. I'm sorory I made you do that cry. I am so surry."

"I'm not crying, Marls. What the fuck you on about?"

"I dent… I. I dunno. Ash, baby, I think I might be a dit brunk. Drunk. A bit drunk."

"Ya think, Rock Star?"

"Yeah, yeah. I think so."

"And did you just say that you crapped yourself?"

"Yeah, yeah. I think I did."

"What, like literally?"

"No. No, that would stink, you'd smell it if I did that. I like meant scared. When I ran away. I'm sry I did it but I was … I was scared, baby."

"A scared Rock Star, eh?"

"Tefferied."

"You better come in then."

And that's the last thing I remembered about the night I convinced my wife to marry me.

We flew to Vegas the next day and never told a soul. We kept our secret wedding a secret for twenty-five years. So much of our life was public knowledge, so much of our time was spent dealing with my family that we kept that little piece of info just for ourselves, just for us. We threw a party for our Silver wedding anniversary and didn't tell anyone what it was for until they got there. I thought my mum was gonna kill me, but it was George that landed the first blow, then Jim, but they forgave us and I'd like to say that from that point on, we all lived happily ever after, but some of us didn't.

TWENTY-TWO

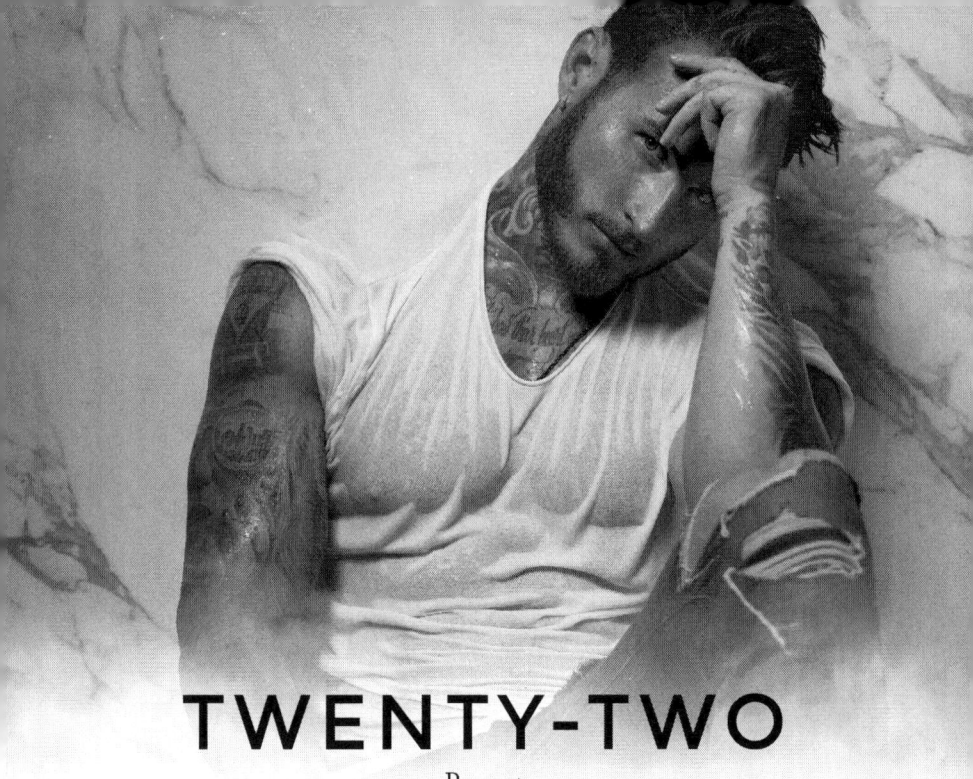

Present

I wake to the sensation of a weight being lifted from my chest and being replaced by a pair of warm thighs straddling me.

I open my eyes to see my wife looking down at me. "I was just dreaming about you," I tell her with a smile.

"Yeah? Was it a hot dream?" she asks before leaning in and kissing me, her breath tasting of mint, coffee, and Ashley.

Sexiest breath ever.

"You were in it baby, so of course it was hot." She reaches behind her and slides her hands inside my boxers, giving my morning wood a tug.

"Hmmm. Well, if you would've come to bed last night, I could've dealt with this for you," she says while giving me a delicious little stroke.

"You were out cold and I need to get this book read and make a decision." That ends her attention to my dick.

"How's it looking?" She turns back to face me and asks.

I slide my hand up her T-shirt and give her tits a squeeze.

"Not as good as these," I tell her honestly. We'd had a massive argument about these after she had George and Cam's twins.

Cam had paid for her to have a tummy tuck, which I wasn't entirely happy about, but as she'd done something so life changing for them, I kept my mouth shut and went along with it. But then once that was done, she started going on about a boob job and there was no fucking way that was happening.

"Your tits fit my hands so fucking perfectly."

"Don't change the subject. What's going on with the book?" She slides her hands up my T-shirt now and rakes her nails over my nipples.

"Ouch," I whine.

"Book, Rock Star. Talk to me."

"Ow," I screech as she does it again.

"All right, all right. Yeah, it's … I don't know. Some of it's too personal and needs to be taken out, but I wanted it all in there to start with so I was clear in my head what should or shouldn't stay."

She looks at me with a frown.

"If you know what I mean?"

"Not really," she replies honestly.

"Na, me neither," I admit. "I'll just read it till I'm done, take out what I think should be taken out, and then let you have a look."

"Why don't *you* read it, then let me and *I'll* tell you what *I* think needs to come out. Wouldn't that be a more objective way of doing it?"

"Maybe."

"When will you be done?"

"By tonight if I spend today on it."

"You not rehearsing?"

"Na. Tomorrow and the rest of the week, but today I'm free."

"Wanna start it with a bang, Rock Star?"

My dick gets harder when she calls me this, and as ever, my heart and insides do strange things. "That sounds like a plan."

"I need to go have a quick wash first. I didn't shower last night."

"No ya don't. Apart from the fact that you're wearing too many clothes, you're perfect as you are." I tell her, whilst trying to lift her T-shirt over her head.

"I don't feel fresh," she complains.

"You feel fucking fine to me, baby," I tell her while sucking on a mouthful of tit. "How many times do I have to tell ya, I like your fanny smelling like a fanny, not like gooseberry and dandelion, or whatever other shit you shower with."

"Patchouli and saffron," she says on a groan as I rub my thumb over her clit.

"Whatever. None of it smells as good as Ash fanny au natural. If only we could bottle that, I'd be wearing it on my fingers, tongue, and around my neck all fucking day."

I slide her down my body, lift her by her hips and slip inside her.

"Fucking perfect," I tell her.

"Make me come, Rock Star."

"It'll be my pleasure, baby. My absolute fucking pleasure."

Being the dutiful husband that I am, I make my wife come more than once, and then we shower together and I make her come again.

We enjoy a lazy Sunday, reading the papers, answering emails, and I spend a bit of time on a conference call with my sister and brother, discussing the upcoming Triple M charity concert.

G has liaised with Josh from Dig It Promotions, who would be running the event for us. All the staff were now hired. Cam gave us as many of his staff as we needed, free of charge, but we always needed more.

Len had confirmed with the management of every act performing or hosting, as well as all the television companies that would be televising the event. We didn't have a single slot left to fill. In fact, we were using some A-listers just to present as we just couldn't fit them into the show.

The event had gone from strength to strength and now raised money the entire year, but the concert was still our biggest fundraiser.

The donations that came in went to the charities that were closest to our hearts. Len, Jimmie, Cam, George, Ash, and myself, all picked charities linked to things that had impacted our lives, and which we thought Maca would be proud to be associated with.

Georgia and Cam were passionate about helping low income families obtain fertility treatments, helping young drug users rehabilitate, and bereavement counselling aimed specifically at sole survivors of accidents or trauma.

Len and Jim had started their own charity that built recording studios in inner city and rural areas, which were available, free of charge, to anyone that wanted to come in and lay down tracks. CC music, mine and Len's label, had now signed five acts that had made demo's using these facilities, and it was something that I too had become equally passionate about. We were lucky when we were starting out. My dad believed and invested in us, helping to get our first demo out there.

Ash and I were patrons of a lot of the charities the foundation supported, but the closest to our heart was one that ran respite care, provided emergency accommodation, counselling, and anything else that was needed for the children of substance abusers.

I had eventually found out from Ash, the reason she had no contact with her parents, and her story was truly horrifying, and sadly, not uncommon.

It was the night that we'd brought Joe home from the hospital. She stood watching over him as he slept in his Moses basket in our front room. I was enjoying the sight when I realised Ashley's shoulders were shaking.

"Ash? Baby?" She turned to look at me, tears streaming down her face.

"What if I'm no good at this? What if I turn out to be just like my parents?"

"No, baby, no. You'll be great—fucking amazing. We'll learn together. We've got this, baby, we've got this."

I wrapped my arms around her and held her tight. When her tears slowed down, I moved us over to the sofa and sat with her in my lap.

She'd still never told me much about her home life. I knew she would when she was ready so I'd left it alone. That night she was ready and I couldn't believe what she told me.

"My parents weren't nice people, Marley. My dad's a junkie, my mum an alcoholic, who's been on the game my entire life to support both of their addictions. They had my brother serving up for them from the time he was eleven to help bring in more money to feed their own habits. He was jacking up heroin by the time he turned thirteen. He did it to try and forget what he was, what they'd turned him into." She cried hard and pushed the heels of her hands into her eyes and my heart just broke for her.

"A dealer?" I asked.

She shook her head and cried even harder. "No." She almost choked as she struggled to get the words out. "They had him working the streets with my mum. He was eleven years old the first time they sold his arse."

"Oh fuck, Ash, fuck, baby. You never said. Why'd you never tell me?"

Her whole body was shaking from her sobs, and as much as I wanted to hold her, I needed to hold my son. I sat her on the sofa, fetched Joe from where he was sleeping and placed him in Ashley's arms, then I wrapped them both in mine.

"He was a great brother, Marls. I know what everyone thinks because of his habit, and the fact that he's always in and out of prison, but he did what he could for me. They would've had me go the same way as him, but he put a stop to it. He was already sixteen when I turned thirteen, and they tried to get me on the streets. Ryan went mad and threatened to call the police and social services. He was making good money from dealing and was able to go rent a one bedroom flat from a mate. I went and lived with him, the problem was he was always going missing, going on benders, and getting himself locked up. Just before I left school, we'd had to go back and stay with them, my parents, for a week as we'd been kicked out of his flat and had nowhere to go. I came home from school to find a strange bloke in my bedroom. He was someone they owed money to, and they'd sold him my virginity to settle the debt.

I was just so unbelievably lucky that Ryan heard me scream as I tried to fight the bloke off. He had to fight both my mum and my dad to get into my bedroom, but he did it. Then he stabbed the bloke in the shoulder, who at that stage had me pinned underneath him on the floor as he tried to rip my school uniform off."

I felt like I was gonna pass out as she told me her story. I stroked the soft dark hair on my little boys head and kissed Ashley's temple, breathing her in, both actions calming me down.

"We got out that night and slept in someone's shed that we broke into. I had to go to school the next day to do an exam. I was still in the clothes I'd worn the day before. I looked a fucking mess. Jimmie found me crying in the toilets." That memory brings a smile to her face. "She lent me some make-up and I felt a bit better. I went and stayed with her for a few days and then Ry managed to get somewhere else for us, so I went with him."

She brings Joe up to her chest and we both breathed him in. "He tried, Marls, he really tried, but they'd ruined him." She cried again as she looked up at me. "The drink and the drugs were the only way he could cope with his demons. He just kept getting banged up and he was always nicking money off of me, so in the end I moved out. That place you found me was all I could afford."

"Fucking hell. I'm so sorry baby. So sorry."

Joe made a little noise and we both studied him for a while. It was all we seemed to do since he'd been born, just looked at him in wonder.

"Ash, I swear to you that we'll give this little boy everything that you never had. We'll give him so much love, we'll all be falling over it. He will never spend a day of his life not feeling loved, safe, and protected."

"Will you help me be a good mum?"

"No, baby, I won't need to. I already know that you're gonna be the best mum there ever was."

"Can we call him Joseph Ryan?" She asked quietly … hopeful.

"Yes, we can."

"Thank you."

"I love you, baby."

"I love you too, Rock Star."

We both looked down at Joe, who was then wide-eyed and staring up at us.

"We love you, baby rock star," we both tell him.

Did I mention that Marley and Ash love Joe?

She was one of the lucky ones. She'd gotten out and stayed first with Jim, then her brother.

We'd tried our best to help Ryan over the years. We'd payed for rehab and even had him living with us, but he still managed to get himself into trouble, despite us paying for the best lawyers to get him out of it.

Ryan died in prison on his thirty-second birthday. He committed suicide in the most horrific of ways, which I won't go into.

"I'll set up a rehearsal timetable for everyone else, but Cam's people have said you can have access any time this week." Len states, interrupting my thoughts.

"Yeah, I've spoken to Reed. He has shit to do tomorrow, but we'll be there every day from Tuesday." I tell him. "We just need all the staff sworn to secrecy. I really don't want this getting out. The event is already a sell-out, so we can't increase sales and I think it'll be a show stopper if we can just get up on stage, unannounced, and play songs from both bands."

"It's gonna be epic," Georgia states.

"Epic? Fucking epic? You've been hanging with Paige and Harley too much, Porge. That's their word of the moment," Len said.

I can't help but laugh as he takes the piss out of her.

"Fuck off, Len. There's nothing wrong with epic," she tells him.

"There is when you're forty-six, dude."

"I'm a dudette, and still eighteen in my head."

"Ah, God no. Not eighteen-year-old George. I wouldn't wish her on anyone. Even Paige and Harley are better behaved than she ever was."

"I wasn't *that* bad. Big brother Marley, back me up here," she demands.

"Drop me out of this one, Porge. Let's just say dad's right on this one and you got the daughter you deserved with Lula."

"I was never as bad as Lu. I blame Ash. I swear her genes filtered through the placenta and corrupted my perfect child's DNA."

"Then how come Kiks is such a good girl?" Len asks.

"Coz she's only got mine and Cams genes. Ashley's crazy DNA was all absorbed by Lu, making her extra naughty."

"I can hear you." Ash sticks her head into my office door and shouts.

"Hey, Fag," Jimmie calls out from Len's end, "I'm with you on this one, boys," she adds.

"Tallulah is all George. You seem to have a very selective memory of what a diva you were," Jimmie tells her.

"What d'ya mean *was*? She's still a fucking diva," I add.

"Shut up, Butt. I thought I could at least rely on you for backup. T, my brothers are picking on me," she calls out to Cam in her best whiny voice.

"Don't call me Butt," I tell her through gritted teeth.

George and Jimmie thought they were hilarious one drunken Christmas when they called Ash, Fag … Fag Ash, geddit? Yeah, I didn't laugh either, and because of my lack of humour, they christened me Butt ... Fag Butt. The three of them ended up on the floor laughing at their own very unfunny joke.

We were now entered into everyone's contacts list as Fag & Butt.

The following Christmas, Jimmie had gone to a local retirement home and asked the old dears to knit us a couple of jumpers with our names on them, then offered to donate one thousand pounds to a charity of our choice if we wore them all day. Len and Cam also adding a thousand if we went through with it, leaving us with little option but to agree.

Hilarious ... *Not.*

The amount of times we'd been in the company of Americans and had to explain that Fag Ash and Fag Butt had nothing to do with neither very burnt, or the backsides of homosexuals.

"Children, children, back to the matter in hand. I'll email you a rehearsal schedule as soon as it's done, that way you'll at least know when to expect others to be turning up. The riggers and electricians will be in and out all week, so they may need the power switched on and off at various times too. Anything else?" We all remain silent.

"This year's event is bigger and better than any other. We'll be able to add at least ten more charities to our books next year. Goes without saying that whoever we choose, we'll bear in mind where Maca would've liked the money channelled."

Ashley comes and curls into my lap as Len talks.

"He'd be so proud of what you've achieved with this, so fucking proud," Ash states, loud enough for the others to hear on their ends of the phone.

I hear Len clear his throat, but George remains silent.

"Porge?"

"Don't, Marls, don't."

"All right. Well, that's it for now then, boys and girls. I'll be at the offices all day tomorrow. I'll see ya there if you're about." He hangs up. I hear George sniff and then she's gone so I disconnect from my end.

"Wanna watch a film or SamCro with me?" Ashley asks.

I slide my hand under her vest and love that she's braless. So much so, that I have to give her nipple a little suck.

"What, so you can sit and get all wet and excited over Jax?" I ask.

"Well, come on. Even you get a hard-on over Jax."

I throw my head back and laugh as if she's being ridiculous.

"Seriously, you know full well that it's Bobby that my heart belongs to."

"Whatever. You watching or not? I have the whole of season six to get through. I'm sick of avoiding spoilers everywhere."

"Put it on, but d'ya mind if I read?" I question. I feel guilty that I've done nothing but read these last few days.

"Go for it," she tells me before kissing my mouth, sliding off my lap and heading out the door.

TWENTY-THREE

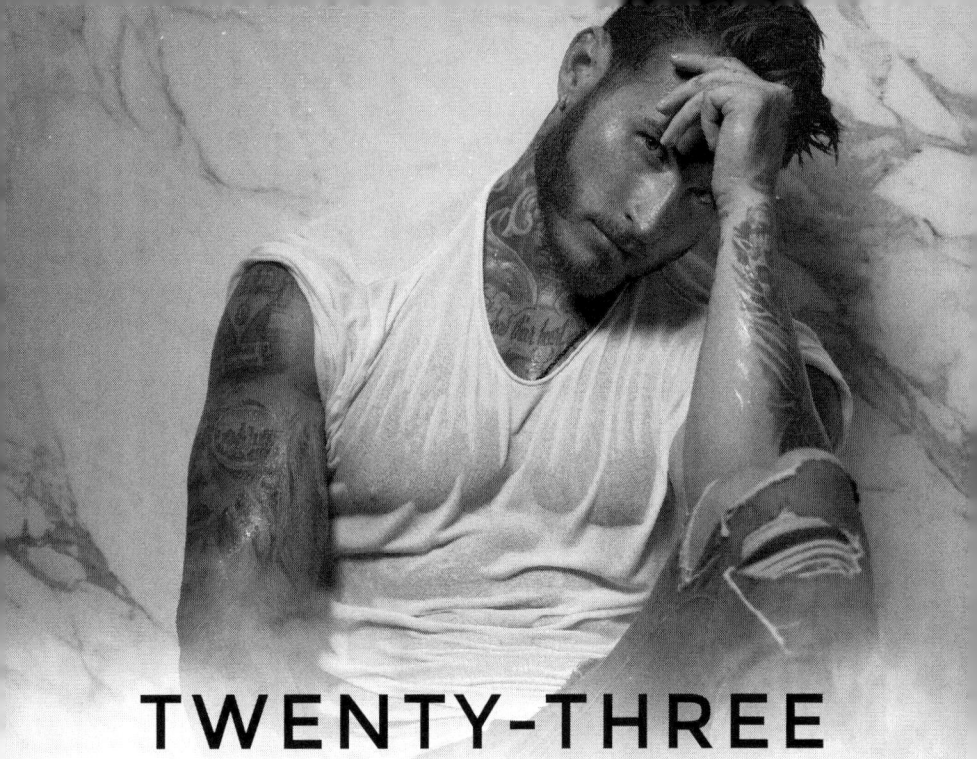

1989/2014

The following years saw Carnage go on to bigger and better things. Our tours were worldwide and we played at the biggest stadiums in the biggest cities. Our albums were multi-platinum selling, and our singles always went to number one.

In our personal lives, all of us, but Maca, became fathers. Some of us a lot sooner than expected. It turns out I knocked up Ash the very first time we had sex.

What a champ.

In March 1990, Ash gave birth to our son. Watching what she went through to give me a gift I'd never be able to thank her enough for, was the most moving experience of my life.

I'd like to say that Ash was amazing and coped brilliantly with the labour, but I'd be lying. She was a fucking nightmare.

She screamed at me, the midwives, and doctors, and when a team of student obstetricians came into the room to ask some questions, she threw her jug of water at them.

Finally, when none of us could take any more, the anaesthetist arrived to set her up with an epidural. I requested he put it in her jaw, but apparently that's not standard practice, so I got a no.

The rest of the labour was a piece of piss. No idea why women bang on about that shit.

Joe was delivered safely after just twenty-eight hours of unnecessary ranting and raving from my wife.

Calm yourselves, women of the world! I'm joking. I will never, ever understand why any woman would choose to go back and do that more than once. I was in pain just from watching the pain she was going through and it's something that will stay with me forever.

When Joe was put into my arms and wrapped all of his little fingers around one of mine, the world fell from under my feet. I quite literally fell onto the bed next to Ash, and as the doctors cleaned and stitched her up, we both stared at him in wonder. He was totally and utterly perfect.

I would give up everything that I'd ever achieved in my life for this one success. In my head, I prayed to a God I've never been quite sure existed, and asked him to help make me the dad that this little boy deserved, and as I did, Joe opened up his eyes and looked right at me and I knew that I would do anything, lay down my life, sell my corrupt soul to the devil if necessary, to love and protect him for the rest of my days.

Within the space of five years, we'd added two little girls to our tribe, and within six, Len and Jimmie had two of each. When you added Billy and Tom's five to the mix, touring sometimes became crazy.

I wanted Ash and the kids with me when I was away, but waking up a five and three-year-old at three in morning to get off a plane when it's below freezing outside, is not fun. Add a newborn to the mix and it actually becomes a nightmare.

My kids woke up starving at two am and were ready for bed at eleven in the morning by the time they were on their fourth time zone in ten days. They were miserable, Ash was miserable, and I just felt guilty.

On the few occasions they did stay home, I'd end up exhausted due to flying back to them on our days off.

On top of that was the press. The fucking press and their ridiculous, made up stories. We were nowhere near as wild as we were in the early days, but we still liked to party and you could always guarantee that if there were women in the room, a photograph would somehow be leaked of them standing within a twenty foot radius of myself or Maca.

Georgia was never very far from Maca's side, but for Ash, being the one sitting at home with three kids, sometimes the rumours were hard on her. Picking up the paper every day to read who your husband was apparently fucking was no fun.

Luckily, we were tight. I missed her and the kids like fuck when we were apart, and Georgia always backed me up when the stories got too much for her.

I've never strayed. Not ever. Ash and I had a threesome once with another woman, but even then, she was all about Ash and didn't touch me.

I could go into detail about that experience, but my wife will have my balls and my kids might read this so yeah, not happening. You'll all just have to use your dirty minds.

I totally understood why George and Maca held off on having kids. Touring with them put a massive strain on our marriage, and we'd have some huge blow-ups because we were both so tired and stressed. Studio time was the best time for us. It meant I could be home for dinner most nights and able to bathe and tuck my kids into bed. That's all I wanted from life, my family. The rock and roll lifestyle held no appeal for me anymore. Like I said, we still liked to party, but I did it with my wife beside me nowadays. Ash and I have always had a fiery relationship, we're both passionate people, so that will never change.

George and Maca finally decided to tie the knot in October of 1998, the stars finally aligning to put us all together in the same place at the same time.

We had just finished a short tour of the States and were taking a break in Florida before flying home.

Maca brought my mum, Dad, Bailey, and Sam over and the happy couple said their 'I do's' in front of us all on a beach in St Petersburg at sunset. The day was perfect; chilled, laid back, and without a single member of the press in sight.

The happy couple delayed their honeymoon until the following year and then took off on a world tour of their own, spending most of their time in Australia.

I did very little in 1999, except kick back and enjoy time with my family. We'd stayed on in Florida, loving it so much that we'd bought a house there before we left.

We had been booked to play at the opening game of a European football competition in September and George and Maca returned from their travels just before then.

The album we had released the year before had been recorded in the South of France, and the bloke that owned the studio was also part owner of one of the teams that were playing. He'd invited the whole production team to watch the game from a private box.

Carla was in attendance. It was the first time we'd been in her company since Maca's wedding and I could tell straight away she wasn't happy. She'd started the evening ignoring us, but as she got slowly pissed up, she got brave.

"Dude, you seriously have to get her away from me, otherwise I'm leaving," Maca told me quietly over his beer. It was the third time Carla had tried to engage him in conversation and he'd brushed her off.

"I don't understand what her problem is. You've been back with G for years. She must've known that you'd get married at some stage."

He let out a long sigh before looking me in the eyes. "She didn't. She's always thought that G and I were bad for each other, and that she and I should be together."

I fucking knew I didn't like the girl.

"And how the fuck do you know that?" I asked, sliding from best mate to big brother mode in an instant.

"Because she's told me, more than once," he admitted.

"And you've said what? Told her to fuck off, I hope."

"Yeah, pretty much. I love my wife, Marls, you and I both know that. I'm not interested in Carla. She was a diversion. Even when I was seeing her, it was nothing more than sex and a bit of company. I told her from the start that it wouldn't lead anywhere."

"Don't think she got the memo, mate," I told him as I watched Carla sway toward us.

"Maca, can we talk? Can we go somewhere in private and talk please?" She stood in front of him and asked.

His eyes swung to me, looking for help.

"We're here to watch the game, Carla. Call on Monday to talk business," I told her.

"I want to have a private conversation with Sean, if that's all right with you, *Marley*," she spat back.

"No, Carla, we can't go anywhere and talk. Anything you've gotta say, you can say it here." Maca finally spoke up for himself and told her.

"You sure?" she asked, and I got a horrible feeling in my belly.

"Absolutely," He assured her.

"Why'd you marry her, Mac? You know how much I love you, so why would you just take off and marry her like that?"

Maca's eyes dart all around the room as Carla stands in front of him and cries. Luckily there was a ban on the press in private boxes, so we were amongst friends.

"Are you fucking delusional?" I asked her. "They've been

together since she was eleven years old. Whatever made you think they wouldn't get married?"

She glared at me for a few seconds. "You have no clue about me and him—no fucking clue—so why don't you stay the fuck out of our business."

"So come on, enlighten me? He's married to my sister so no, I won't stay the fuck out of your business when it involves my family."

The little bitch was pissing me off and Maca was pissing me off for not shutting her down.

"Carla, what we had was ten years ago. I don't know what you—"

"What we had was a fucking baby, Maca. That's what we had."

Oh fuck!

"Wh-What d'ya mean, a baby? When? What are you talking about?" Maca's eyebrows were drawn together in confusion.

"You fucked me, just before you went off on your holiday to Ibiza. You fucked me and you got me pregnant."

My heart beat so loud, I swear it could be heard over the crowd cheering.

"Well, what happened? Where's ... I don't understand?" Maca stuttered out. He had beads of sweat forming on his forehead, and I had them running down my back.

"You wouldn't take my calls," she said through gritted teeth.

"I was back with Gia," he replied, using the same tone.

"Yeah, and didn't I know it. Well, good for you and your happy new life, and tough fucking luck for me and the mess you'd left me in."

"I didn't fucking know," Maca shouted, bringing the room to a standstill.

"Well, if you'd replied to any of the messages I left you, then you would have."

"So what? What happened? What did you do?" I could hear the panic rising in Maca's voice as he asked.

A secret kid is so not what he and George needed thrown into the mix right now—not at any time, really.

"I murdered it. I went to an abortion clinic and had all traces of you sucked right out of me."

Maca's eyes closed for an instant before opening, filled with tears.

"Why? Why would you do that?" he asked quietly.

"Why not? You didn't want me. I wasn't gonna be stuck with a kid on my own."

"You wouldn't have been on your own." He wiped a tear from under his eye as he spoke.

"No? You would've left her and come back to me, would ya?"

He shakes his head no. "I'll never leave her, not in this lifetime, and not in the next."

"And that's why I did it. If I couldn't have you, then why should I have your kid?"

She is seriously a piece of fucking work, this girl.

"I would've helped, I would've been there… I would—"

"I wanted you." It was her turn to shout now. "I wanted all of you, not just a part-time dad for my baby. I wanted you, us, together as a family."

Maca just stood there, shaking his head no.

"Mac, come on, mate. Let's get out of here." I reached out and touched the top of his arm.

His brown eyes looked across to mine. "I didn't know, Marls. I didn't fucking know."

"I believe ya, mate. Come on, let's get out of here. We'll see if Len can change our flight and get us home to the girls earlier."

"Oh, that's right, drag him back to wifey."

I've never hit a girl, but I swear to God I came close that night. I spun around to face her.

"You little bitch. Just shut your fucking mouth and fuck off out of my sight. You've had plenty of chances to tell him all this over the years, plenty of ways you could've contacted him and explained. Why the fuck would you do it like this, here tonight, in front of everyone?"

"Because he should've married me, not her, me," she roared.

"You are off your fucking head if you think that was ever gonna happen." I pointed at Macca's neck.

"You've seen the words! It's only her, it'll *always only* ever be her. Get your fucking head around that, else you can kiss your career goodbye and never work for us again."

I grab Maca's arm and lead him out the doors.

Milo was waiting for us outside and he called Len, who didn't come to the game, but lined up a couple of meetings for that evening instead. Len contacted the private plane company, but they couldn't get us a pilot straight away, so we went back to our hotel where Len met back up with us.

"What the fuck's happened." Was Len's first response as I let him into Maca's room.

We'd had a bottle of Jim Beam sent up to the room and had sat in silence for the ten minutes we'd had alone before Lennon arrived.

He looked at both of us, and noting our sombre mood, he changed his tone. "What happened ... is something wrong?"

My chest felt tight, so I let out a long sigh before speaking. "Maca had a bit of a run in with Carla," I started.

"Carla, producer Carla?"

I nodded my head, prepared to continue, but Maca interceded.

"I was seeing her on and off right up until I got back with G," he admitted.

"Well, I think we all knew that, Mac. You never said it but I think we all knew something was going on between the two of you. What's the problem then?" He asked while pouring himself a drink.

Maca looked up, his eyes moving from Len, to me, and back again.

"Apparently, the last time we were together, I got her pregnant and she had an abortion. She's held onto some misplaced belief that me and her would get back together. Tonight's the first time I've seen her since the wedding. She's pissed off and decided to tell me and the rest of the room her pregnancy story."

"Fuck," Len stated as he sat down on the sofa next to Maca.

"I've never liked that girl. Now I know why," I told them both as I sat down in the wingback chair facing them.

"Yeah, you've said before," Len confirmed what I'd told him a few times.

"How you feeling, Mac? That couldn't have been good to hear, or the best way to find out?" Len asked.

"Like a complete cunt."

"You didn't know, mate. What were you supposed to do?" He looked at me for a few seconds before answering.

"How would you feel if that was your baby?"

I got goose bumps. If he'd asked me that when I was younger, I'd have just been relieved it had been taken care of, but now, since Ash? Since becoming a father? I filled up at his question. I could only nod my head, unable to speak past the lump in my throat.

"Exactly."

"I'm sorry, dude, I really am," Len said.

We were all quiet for a few moments, none of us wanting to address the elephant in the room. Thankfully, it was Maca that spoke first. "I don't want Gia knowing about this. I'll tell her, but just not right now. We're trying for a baby at the moment and I'd hate for her to doubt my commitment. And I don't want her flying off the handle either. You know what she's like."

I looked across to my brother and we both shrugged.

"Your call, mate, but you sure she won't go public with this?" Len asked.

"Not if she wants to keep her job," I told him.

"Well, they're signed for the next two albums. We start recording in January. Hope this isn't gonna be a problem?"

Maca shook his head no. "I'm pissed off with the way she told me, but I understand why she's so angry. I'll talk to her, we'll keep it professional."

I shrugged and shook my head. I personally thought he should stay the fuck away from her, but if he thought he could handle her shit, then on his head be it.

On New Year's Eve of 1999, we played in New York's Time Square. Georgia surprised the shit out of us all when she walked out on stage and told Maca that she was pregnant.

The celebrations that followed were of epic proportions. The babies were all at home in England with my parents, so even Len and Jimmie partied like it was 1999. (You see what I did there?)

By the time we landed back in England though, things took a frightening turn for the worst, and Georgia was rushed into the hospital.

Her pregnancy was ectopic and she lost her baby, and nearly lost her life. Maca nearly lost them both, as well as his mind.

Jim, Len and myself were waiting outside the room they'd taken George into when suddenly all hell broke loose. An alarm sounded, doctors and nurses came running from every direction, and when the shout went out for the crash team, I threw up in the rubbish bin.

George was wheeled past us on a trolley, a team of medical professionals working on her. I stepped into the room to find Maca in a chair, sobbing.

"Mac, what happened?"

He looked up at me, his eyes almost vacant. His face was a mess of snotty tears.

"The pregnancy is ectopic and they think it's ruptured. She has internal bleeding." He couldn't hold back the sobs anymore. "She went into shock, then cardiac arrest, where they couldn't get the blood pumped into her fast enough."

Jimmie walked past me and wrapped her arms around Maca, holding him as he cried.

The next few weeks were hard. George moved back to my parents' place so that my mum could look after her. We were busy working on a new album in the studios Maca had had built on the grounds of their home in Hampstead. That's where we were most days. We had the usual team working with us, which included the delightful Carla.

George and Maca had bought an old farmhouse just up the road from us and now that George was up and about, she was working with the builders and designers to modernise the place. She still looked pale and was very quiet, but at least she was focused on something, although she still hadn't moved back home and was still staying out at my parents' place.

I'd worked out that things were a little strained. I could understand George going to my mum's for a week maybe, but this had been almost two months.

I'd stayed over at Maca's one night after a late recording session and we'd smoked a little weed and enjoyed a few glasses of Glenmorangie when he said to me, "I think I'm losing her."

"Who?" I knew who, I was just trying to gather my thoughts before I spoke.

"Gia. I've asked her to come home but she's said no. She's not ... we... when I go over and stay at your mum's, she barely says a word. It's been over six weeks, Marls. I know that this isn't something that we'll ever forget happened, but it's like she's just holding onto it, like she's punishing herself." He knocked back what was in his glass while I remained silent, letting him talk.

"She was like this for a while the other year, just after we got back from Australia—distant. I put it down to the fact that she hadn't fallen pregnant straight away, but then we bought the new house and she seemed happier." He took in a deep breath, then let it out slowly. "I was worried then that there was something going on between her and Cameron King."

Whoa.

"You remember when the girls went to the opening of his new club and ran into Haley White?"

I shifted in my seat, memories of that weekend making me feel uncomfortable.

It was the weekend Carla had come out with her little secret. We'd eventually hired a pilot to get us home early that night. The girls had called us numerous times to let us know that there'd been a bit of an incident between Haley White and George. Because of Carla's revelations, we'd all chosen not to answer our phones, too worried to speak to them in case they picked up on the fact that something was wrong.

Jimmie was like an intelligence officer in the way she didn't miss a trick. Ash was like the Spanish Inquisition when she knew she wasn't getting a straight answer. George … George just had Maca wrapped around her little finger and she'd soon have him spilling his guts. Perhaps that would've been a good thing, getting it all out in the open, but that wasn't what he wanted and so I'd committed to the lie, never speaking again about it to anyone, including my wife.

"The day after, on the Sunday when we got home, there were all sorts of pictures of them together. I thought that maybe something had happened that night."

"Georgia was with the girls all night." I tried to reassure him. There had been a lot of rumours about those photos and the way Cam was looking at her.

"And you don't think they'd back her one hundred percent and lie for her if they had to?" That thought pissed me off.

"Ash wouldn't lie to me," I told him.

"Na? You told Ash about what Carla said that night?"

Oh. I let out a long breath and shake my head no.

"We all have secrets, mate. Even the best of marriages have secrets."

It actually caused a pain in my chest to think that. I hated the idea that Ash kept secrets from me. Double standards, I know, but yeah, I'm a bloke. It's how we operate.

"She'd told me years before that when we first got together that she was in love with him, but she'd never realised it when they were together. When she left him for me, he told her, and he told Ash if you remember, that he loved her, but would step aside if that's what made her happy."

I think back to the day George had disappeared with someone from Cam's staff and no one could find her for six hours. I remember Ash saying that day that Cam had told her he was in love with my sister.

"You only had to look at the way he looked at her in those photos to know he still felt the same way, and I've got a feeling it's mutual."

He sipped his drink and waited for my reaction.

"But that was only last year. Those photos were only a year ago."

"It was the year before, but close enough. Anyway, after those pictures came out, she was a bit weird. I can't put my finger on what kind of weird, just ... I dunno? Nervy, jumpy. Then when we found the new house, she went from loving it to not being sure overnight. One minute it was perfect, the next it was wrong. I thought she was just making excuses, and that she didn't want to buy something new with me because she was planning on leaving me for him."

"Fuck, you never said anything. Why didn't you say? I would've had Ash ask her?"

He looked right at me, "Coz if she was gonna go, I didn't wanna know about it."

Poor fucking bloke. I felt so bad for him in that moment. Between my sister and Carla, I was surprised he had any faith in women at all.

"Anyway, this, how she's behaving this time, is worse—much worse. I feel like she's completely shut me out, Marls, like this has only happened to her. It was my baby too. I thought I was gonna lose them both. While she was having surgery, I actually sat and thought about how I would kill myself if she didn't make it."

I let out a long breath at that. I had no words because I totally understood where he was coming from. If anything had happened to Ash before we had kids, I wouldn't have wanted to live either. Now, it was different. I wouldn't want to, but I'd carry on for the sake of our babies. I shuddered because the thought alone was too horrible to contemplate.

"I know this is easy for me to say, Mac, but you just gotta give her time. You know what George is like. She deals with things a bit different than the rest of us. She shuts everyone out until she's ready to face things again. It's how she was when you two broke up. Just give her time, but keep reminding her that you're there for her as soon as she's ready to move forward."

He's poured us both another drink. "I just ... I miss her. I miss her company. I miss our chats when we go to bed, I miss waking up with her. I miss her shit all over the bathroom and listening to her sing in the shower. I even miss her crap cooking."

"Na, I'm not having that. George is the only person I know that can burn a salad." I tried some humour. My sister could hold a tune, no problem, but could not cook for shit.

"I just miss human contact."

I talk to Ash the next day and she tells me that she'll have a chat with Jimmie and arrange a girl's night out and try and work out what's going on with George.

When Maca and G split up when we were younger, I was clueless to what he was going through. I had no concept of love and the emotions involved. Back then, I could see no further than the next orifice to fill. Now it was different. Now I totally understood. Ash was my world and I fully understood where he was coming from.

Two nights later, I went from wanting to help my brother-in-law out, to wanting to throttle the fucker.

We had a break from recording so I'd spent the day with Ash and the kids, just doing normal things. I'd taken them to school and because it had snowed, we'd built a snowman after I'd picked them up. I'd let them toast marshmallows in front of our open fire and they'd eaten them as they drank their Ovaltine before I tucked them into bed.

Ash had gone over to Jim's for dinner with George the night

before, but had nothing to report. George had repeatedly stated that she was fine, and remained pretty much silent other than that. I decided to drive over to Maca's to see how he was doing, picking up a bottle of whiskey on the way.

Because the house was behind key coded security gates, despite being in London, the front door was never locked, which is a shame, really.

I stood in silence for a few seconds, my brain trying to process what was going on.

Maca was leaning with his back against the marble work top, arms spread wide, his knuckles white as he gripped the edges. His head was tilted towards the ceiling with his eyes squeezed shut.

His shirt was unbuttoned, as were the top button of his jeans.

Carla was kissing down his chest as she stroked her fingers over his abs.

If I'd had a gun, I would've shot them both. Extreme, I know, but that's how pissed off I was with the pair of them—him for being such a fucking idiot, her for being so devious as to attack while he was weak and vulnerable.

Yeah, I know it takes two and all that, but they were in *his* house. She'd obviously come to him. Not that that made him any less to blame, but she should've stayed the fuck away.

I watched in silence as Carla attempted to slide her hand inside Maca's trousers. I held my breath. I swear, even my heart stopped beating as I hoped and prayed that he would do the right thing.

Without even looking down, he grabbed her wrist and stopped her hand from moving any lower. Carla stared down at his hand around her wrist for a few moments and I decided then would be a good time to make my presence known.

To this day I can't believe how calm I managed to make my voice sound when I spoke.

"I'm just gonna leave this bottle on the table here. I think it'll help with the guilt later, Mac, when you wake the fuck up to yourself and realise that you've just made the second biggest mistake of your life."

I stood and waited for their reactions.

Carla turned and smiled at me. Maca started to cry.

"Get out," I told her. "Get the fuck out and do not *ever* set foot near him, us, or our band again."

She stood up straight and walked towards me.

"Your sister's a cunt. She won him back once, but I'm fighting to keep him this time."

"My sister might be a cunt, but don't ever underestimate what those two have between them, sweetheart," I gritted my teeth as I spoke.

"If what they have is so fucking special, then what's this? What was that we were just doing?" she snarled like a rabid fucking dog.

"*That*, like I said, was the second biggest mistake of his life." I nodded my head to where Maca was still standing. His shoulders shook as he cried, his jeans and shirt still open.

"See, you're so inconsequential, sweetheart, that you don't even take the top spot for fuck ups. If the number one spot didn't finish them, then you sure as shit won't. Now move along."

She stared at me for a few seconds. "Oh," I added, "if word of this is ever repeated, I'll know, and I'll make sure that you *never* find work in this industry again. Now FUCK.OFF!"

She left. When I looked back at Maca, I noticed the coke lined up on the kitchen work top.

"I wanna kick the living fucking shit outta you right now, but that'll have my sister asking questions. Do up your jeans and sort yourself the fuck out."

He did as he was told and turned to look at me.

"What the fuck have I done ... what the fuck have I done?" He bent himself in half and threw up all over his kitchen tile.

"Fuck's sake." I grabbed him by the arm and marched him upstairs to his bedroom.

"Get yourself showered and sort your shit out. You're going over to my mum's, and you're gonna be the husband that my sister needs. That—what you did down there—will never, ever be talked about again. Are we clear?"

He blinked a few times, but remained silent. I slapped him. I actually slapped him like a little bitch. I wanted to punch his fucking lights out, but that would leave bruises and cause questions, so instead, I cracked him right around the face.

"Are we fucking clear?"

"Yes."

"Good. Anything you've got going on with her ends right now. You will never see her again."

"There's not … it wasn't … she turned up with weed and coke and she was just … there's nothing going on. Nothing has ever happened since I've been back with G, I swear, Marls. Tonight was a mistake, a giant fucking mistake." He started to cry again. "I'm lonely, so fucking lonely. She won't let me touch her. I just wanna love my wife. I want us to be able to grieve together and I wanna make her better." He pulled an ugly face as he sobbed and blew snot bubbles out of his nose, which just made me wanna crack him again.

"Well banging the staff ain't gonna achieve that, is it, Einstein? Now stop fucking snivelling, grow some balls, get in the shower and go and get your wife back."

I was shaking from head to toe. The urge to go and hoover the rest of the marching powder up my nose was almost overwhelming, but me and Ash, we had a pact. We only did that shit together nowadays, that way neither of us did anything stupid without the other. Perhaps I should pass that tip on to Maca, the stupid prick.

A week later, Maca and George were sunning themselves in the Caribbean. Things were a little tense between him and me for a while, but we moved on. Yeah, I was pissed off with him, but as a bloke, I sort of got it. It wasn't right and I should've been loyal to my sister, but I'd seen those two apart and I knew that the world didn't work properly when that happened. Neither of them were perfect, but they were perfect together.

I was just leaving the sports hall at Joe's school when my mobile phone rang. His football training had been moved inside because of the snow that had fallen on and off all week.

It had hit England early this year. February was usually our coldest month, but today was only the first of December and it was bitter.

"Big brother Lennon." I pressed the key fob to unlock the car and let Joe in as I answered the call.

"You need to get to the Royal Free as soon as you can."

My blood stopped pumping and my insides instantly became as cold as the snow under my feet.

"What, why?"

"George and Maca have been in an accident. It's bad, Marls. Really bad."

I got in my car and suddenly I was driving along. My phone was on speaker and Len was telling me that Bailey and my parents were on their way. My brain slowed. I couldn't think. I had to get Joe home. Ash would want to come with me. The girls were at dance. What was I gonna do with Joe? The girls?

"Marls, are you listening to me?"

I was listening, but I didn't hear a word.

"Dave is on his way to your house. He'll stay with the kids so that you and Ash can come to the hospital. You need to drive carefully, but you need to hurry. Do you understand what I'm saying, Marls? They might not make it. You need to hurry."

The traffic and sounds blurred. My heart had stopped and failed to restart properly.

"Dad, what's wrong?" Joe asked from the back of the car.

Everything.

"Nothing, mate, all good. I just need to get you home. Dave's gonna come over and play FIFA with you for a bit."

"Aw, sweet."

I'm at my house without knowing how I got there. Dave pulled up as I did, Ash already waiting at the front door. I send Joe inside.

"What happened?" I asked anyone that might have an answer.

Ashley looked at Dave, then they both turned and looked at me. Dave shook his head no, and Ashley cried.

I didn't want this. I didn't want this to be happening. I wanted to go inside my nice warm house. I wanted Joe to beat me at FIFA. I wanted to see my daughters in their tutu's, showing me the moves they learnt this week.

"We have to go," Ash stated. "Can you drive, Marls, or d'ya want me to?" I stared at her in silence for a few seconds. "Marley, we have to go."

I held my arm out in a sweeping gesture, offering her my car. I don't know why I did it, I just did. I didn't even say goodbye to my kids, or Dave. I just got in the car and drove. I wasn't even sure of the exact location of the hospital, I just knew that it wasn't far from George and Maca's house in Hampstead, so I headed in that direction.

The radio was playing Carnage songs. Ashley switched the system to play CDs, and Creeds *'With Arms Wide Open,'* started to play.

I turned it up loud as Ash reached across to take my hand.

I listened to the words of a song about a man finding out he's about to become a father.

My sister was due to give birth to a son in four weeks' time. She was looking the healthiest she'd ever looked in her life. She'd not put on a lot of weight, but she was glowing. Maca was the happiest I'd ever known him to be. They'd been through so much, this was finally *their* time. They were about to finally have *their* moment; become parents, become a family, become complete. They'd lived a lifetime together, and yet their lives were only just about to begin.

The song ended and *'Praise You'* by Fat boy Slim started to play. My car's CD system had a function that allowed it to choose a track from each of the fifteen CDs that were loaded. I drove, unseeing, just listening to the music and trying my hardest not to think.

The Cardigans, *'Love Fool'* played and I laughed because it reminded me of Maca—not the words, but the title of the song.

'Red Alert' by The Basement Jax was up next and I cranked the sound system louder.

Eminem, *'Stan.'*

Moloko, *'Sing it Back.'*

Armend Van Helden, *'U Don't Know Me.'*

Oasis, *'Wonderwall.'*

Nirvana, *'Smells Like Teen Spirit.'*

Massive Attack, *'Unfinished Sympathy.'*

Bones Thugs N Harmony, *'Tha Crossroads.'*

There were others, I'm sure. Those though, were the ones that would forever remind me of the silent drive my wife and I made to the hospital.

When we arrived there was chaos; reporters, television crews, photographers, and fans. They were everywhere.

Fuck 'em all.

I pulled up right outside. "Wait here," I told Ash.

I walked around to her side and opened my door. Taking her under my arm, I started to walk us inside. I had no idea where I was going, but I needed to get there soon.

"Sir, you can't leave your car there … Sir." I turned to see a copper talking to me. I threw him the keys.

"Move it, tow it, keep it, burn it. I *don't* fucking care."

As we walked towards the hospital entrance, I spotted one of the PR people that worked for our label. She was instantly joined by four policemen and a half dozen minders. We were surrounded. I went where they led and when we got there, I saw Len.

We were in a private room when Len told Ash and I to sit down. He was shaking. Not just his hands, but his entire body. He had no colour in his usually olive complexion. His skin looked almost see through.

My eyes wanted to close. My brain wanted to shut down. I wanted to disappear.

"George and Maca were on the pavement outside a baby shop on Brentwood High Street," he started. "I don't know the exact details, Milo's still with the police, but a car came up onto the pavement and hit them."

He started to cry. I squeezed Ashley's hand as she started to cry too. I don't know if I started or if I was already crying. I don't know. I don't know. I *don't* fucking know.

"Marls, it's not good. It's so not fucking good."

"Oh God, oh God, oh God, oh God," Ashley chanted from beside me.

"He's gone, Marls. Maca's gone. They're keeping—" He cried and cried and cried. We all cried. I hurt. Everything hurt. My insides, my outsides, my breath and my soul. It all hurt.

I wanted my babies. I just wanted to go home and hold my babies. I wanted to go to my house, hold my wife and kids, and lock out the world.

"They're keeping Maca alive on life support until George is out of surgery. She has massive internal bleeding. She's lost the baby. She's lost the baby and they're just trying to save her now."

"No," It just came out of my mouth. "No, tell them no. Don't save her. They mustn't save her, Len. She won't want that. They need to let her go. They need to be together."

Before he replied or I said any more, my parents arrived with Bailey and Jim. Everyone was crying. Everyone was hurting but it didn't change anything. All the tears, all the pain, all the love in the world. None of it changed anything.

When Georgia was brought out of surgery, I volunteered to be the one to tell her what happened. I brought Maca into her life that sunny August day back in 1980, and I'd be the one to take him away on that bitterly cold December day in 2000. *Twenty years.* They'd lived, laughed, loved and cried more than most do in a lifetime, but they'd only known each other for twenty years.

My mum insisted that we were all there when George woke up, but I should be the one to tell her.

She opened her eyes and looked straight at me. I gave her a chance to get her bearings, remaining silent until she was fully conscious.

"A car hit us, Marls. A fucking car came up on the pavement and hit us." Tears rolled down the side of her face and into her ears as she spoke. She was hooked up to blood and fluids and had wires on her chest, as well as a blood pressure monitor that kept tightening automatically. The bed she was on was huge, and she looked so tiny.

"Porge—"

"Where's Sean, Marls? Is he with Beau? Did they have to do a C section? Can they get me a wheelchair so I can see him?" Her jaw and lip trembled. She knew … she must know.

"Porge, they had to operate."

"To get Beau out?"

"Yes, Porge. They had to operate to get Beau out, but he didn't make it, baby girl. He didn't make it."

She let out a sob. It came from her throat, her chest, her DNA. It came from every part of her being and it echoed through every part of me.

All I could hear around us were tears; tears rolling down cheeks, tears being held back, tears that would never stop.

"Where is he, Marls? Is Sean with him?"

"No, no, no." I knew that was my mum without even looking around.

"It's okay, Mum. Sean'll keep him warm till I see him. We'll get through this. There'll be more babies."

I heard the door to the room open and close and I assumed that it was all too much for my mum. Instead, a nurse and a doctor approached the bed, the nurse took Georgia's hand.

"Mrs McCarthy, are you aware of what's happened with your

baby? Has everything been explained to you?" The doctor asked.

The nurse let go of her hand and put a tissue in it. George wiped her nose and nodded at the doctor.

"Very good. Well, we have a policy at this hospital of giving the parents time to grieve and the opportunity to spend time with their child. Is that something you would like to do?"

She nodded. "Yes. Yes, I'd like to see him."

"Well, we'll get that arranged for you then."

The nurse and Doctor leave and we're all left to destroy what's left of Georgia's heart.

"Where's Sean, Marls? Is he okay?"

I can't lie to her. She's my little sister, it's been my job for most of my life to protect her, but I can't save her from this. I can't even soften the blow.

I can't get my words out and when she noticed me struggling, she knew.

"Marls... no, Marls, no, no. Don't make it bad. Please don't make it bad. Daddy!" She looked over my shoulder to where my dad was standing. "Tell him, Daddy, tell him... please."

"He hit his head, George. He hit his head really bad. He's never gonna recover from it. They've got a machine breathing for him, but he's never gonna wake up."

I expected crying and sobbing. What I didn't expect was silence and the vice-like grip she had on my hand. The door to the room opened and the nurse walked in, carrying Beau. My mum collapsed, my dad holding her up the best he could.

My nephew, my best mate's baby boy was wrapped in a blanket, but I could see his dark hair on the top of his head.

"Can you all leave please? I want to be alone with my son," George asked.

I wasn't going anywhere.

"Go, now. Please, everyone."

The room emptied.

"Marls?" I heard Ash say my name from behind me. I shook my head no.

"I'm not leaving her," I tell Ash. "I'm not leaving George," I tell my sister.

Ashley left the room.

Georgia laid her son on the bed in front of her and unwrapped the blanket. He was perfect, and he looked like Maca.

"Oh Marley, why, why? He's just a little baby. Why him, why not take me?"

"I don't know, George. I don't have the answers tonight, I'm sorry."

I poured water in the bowl that the nurse brought in. I made sure it was warm—not hot, not cold, but warm—the way that babies like it. I grabbed some of the cotton wool that was sitting next to it and took it to my sister. I stood and watched as Georgia washed her son. She asked me to pass her the bag that was sitting on the shelf in her room. Milo had dropped it off earlier, once he'd finished giving his statement to the police.

From the bag, George pulled a nappy, a vest, a babygrow, and a blanket that had guitars over it. She dressed Beau, then wrapped him in the blanket.

I sat on the bed next to her and held her son. I told him all about his Dad and what a great musician he was. I told him, much like I did my own son, how much his Dad and all of us loved him. I tried to think of everything that Maca would say. I tried to make him feel safe and loved.

Sometime later, the nurse that was in earlier, brought a wheelchair in and told us that it was time to take Beau to meet his Dad.

When we got to his room, the rest of our family was there, along with Maca's parents and half-brother and sister. That pissed me off. He'd seen a bit of his Dad over the years, but not his Mum, and he'd only ever met his brother and sister a few times.

Bailey and Len lift George onto Maca's bed. It's the most

heartbreaking sight I'd ever witnessed.

George moved Maca's arm so that it was around her and she undid the blanket a little and introduced Beau to his Daddy.

"Look what we made, Sean. Just look at how perfect he is. He looks so much like you. Just look at all that hair, all curly, just like yours used to be."

She wiped the tears from under her eyes. "They're not letting me keep him though Sean. They're taking both of you away from me. He has to go to heaven and they've decided that you need to go to heaven with him so that he doesn't get scared and lonely."

She kisses Beau, then she puts him to Maca's lips so that they press against his son's head. Then she kisses Maca.

"I love you both, my beautiful boys. I love you both so much and I'll see you very soon."

She closed her eyes with her husband's arm around her, their son held in her arms.

Maca's life support was switched off and he passed away quietly at 11.43pm.

Georgia had to be sedated before the nurses could take Beau from her arms or remove her from Maca's bed.

Georgia was kept sedated for a further forty-eight hours and was evaluated by a psych team before she was allowed home to my parents' place five days after her surgery.

Life for the rest of us was hard. We were all in shock, all grieving for Maca, for Beau, and for what Georgia had lost.

Ash and I made love constantly in those first few days. We'd cling to each other and cry, during and after. We just needed that connection.

We tried our best to explain to the kids in an age-appropriate way what had happened, but Annie had nightmares for weeks afterwards. And for the whole of December and part of January, we slept with all three of our kids in bed with us.

On the afternoon before the funeral, the bodies of Maca and Beau were brought to my parents' house. Georgia insisted that the coffin go out in the soundproofed room that we'd all hung out in so much.

Now that she was up and about, she'd been sleeping in there. She was taking tablets to help her do it, and she was on a low dose of Valium and antianxiety medication. My parents seemed to think that she was over the worst, but I knew my sister better than most, and insisted that someone was with her at all times, so we all took it in turns. She wasn't there mentally during that time, her mind gone, or just shut down till she could cope again.

We were each given time to spend alone with Maca and Beau. I asked Ash if she wanted to go together but she said no, that she felt I needed to say goodbye alone.

Beau was lying face down on his daddy's chest, Maca's hands placed protectively over his sons back. I kissed the top of my nephew's head and I kissed my best mates forehead before sitting in the chair next to the coffin.

"I don't know how to do this," I told him honestly. "I always thought it'd be me. I thought I'd fuck up, crash my bike, or my car. Go on a bender and have a heart attack … I dunno, summit. I just always thought I'd be the one to die young, not you, Mac, never you."

I pulled one of the man-sized tissues from the box that someone had thoughtfully left on the coffee table, probably my mum, and blew my nose. Then I started to laugh.

"Remember when we were on the bus going to Detroit and I had a cold and asked if anyone had a tissue?" I smiled and shook my head thinking about it.

"And you, you dirty fucker, passed the one you'd wiped your cum stains up with when you'd had a wank earlier. I had your fucking Jizz all over my nose, you fucker. Billy was really hungover and threw up after gagging a few times … Ah, funny times, Mac, funny fucking times."

I sat and spent the next hour reminiscing and promising my mate that we'd all look after George, and we'd always keep him and Beau in our thoughts when Georgia walked in. I stood and wrapped her in my arms and just held her.

"I brought this for Beau to wear. I wanted a piece of me to be with him. Sean has my name tattooed on his heart, so I want Beau to have this."

She held up the necklace with the 'G,' held in the angel wings that Maca had bought her one Christmas many, many years before.

"It's perfect," I tell her.

She didn't have to undo the clasp, she was able to just slip it over Beau's dark little head.

We all gathered together in that room later. My parents eventually went to bed, but myself, my brothers, our wives and Georgia, we drank. We raised our glasses and told stories of our memories of Maca.

I caught George smiling on the odd occasion, but I knew it was just a mask. I knew the whole scene was a farce. Each and every one of us were terrified about what tomorrow would bring.

The outpouring of grief from around the world was mind-blowing. I had visited the scene of the accident with Ash and laid flowers amongst the hundreds and hundreds of others that had been placed there. The place was a shrine.

Despite the funeral taking place at midday, the cars started arriving at my parents' at around ten thirty. The funeral directors had already informed us that the roads leading from just beyond the gates at the end of the drive, all the way through town to the church, were packed.

My sister's body was the only part of her in attendance that day. Her mind had gone, totally checked out. She stood alone in my mum's kitchen, staring out the back patio doors at the cold December morning. Her arms were wrapped around herself, the way they often were since she'd left the hospital. Even from the back, I could see how thin she was looking.

I moved to stand beside her but didn't speak for a while.

"I know what you're planning and I totally understand, Porge, but

I just need you to know that despite what you're thinking, what you're feeling now, we all want you with us. We all want to help you come to terms with this and move forward." I dug my hands deeper into my suit pockets and tried to compose myself. I didn't want to cry while I was talking to her; there'd be enough tears later, so for now, at least, I wanted to remain composed.

"I know that this is … this loss is something that none of us will ever get over, least of all you, but we all need to help each other find a way to live again. I've lost my nephew, my best mate, my bandmate, and my brother-in-law. I can't lose you too. I need ya, George, I need ya so much right now. So, I'm begging ya, for me, please don't do anything stupid."

Georgia overdosed the first time, just nine hours later.

She'd told my mum she was taking a bath. It was an hour later that I noticed her missing. Everyone had had a lot to drink after one of the worst days of our lives.

I won't go into the details of Maca's funeral here. If George ever decides to write a book, then I'll leave that as her story to tell, so for now, that day will remain private.

I walked along the galleried landing of my parents' house and the first thing I heard was the song, *'Fade to Black'* by Metallica, and I knew in an instant what she'd done.

I ran. I ran as fast as I could, but it felt like I wasn't moving. I reached Georgia's bedroom door and pushed it open. Apparently, I'd already called out for help as I was running because as I stood staring down at my sister's small body, curled up on her bed. I heard the commotion of my family arriving behind me.

The note she'd left beside her summed up what we were all feeling.

I'm sorry, I just can't do this. It hurts too much. The pain is more than I can bear. If you love me, then please just let me go.

G

At the end of January, she did it again, and that time, they only just managed to bring her back. So, we took the hard decision to have her committed to a private mental health facility once she was well enough to leave the hospital.

It was a few weeks after her release that I had an idea that I thought might just help pull my sister from the depths of hell, where she was currently residing.

I went and got her old car, Hilda, out of storage.

George was in her usual spot, on the old leather Chesterfield, when I found her.

"Up ya get, George. I've got something out here for you to see."

I thought she'd stare at me blankly, that far off vacant look still in her eyes from all the medication they'd had her on in the hospital. She'd been home almost a month then, and they were gradually weening her off them.

So I was surprised when she just wiped tears from under her eyes and followed me outside.

She stopped in her tracks, one hand flying to her chest, the other to cover her mouth. Her tears were instant.

Might make me sound like a shitty person, but even her tears made me happy. That reaction, it let me know she was still there. My little sister, our Porge, she was still fucking in there. I almost choked on the great big lump lodged in my throat as Georgia sobbed.

"Oh, Marley. Where did you get her from? Have you been to my house?"

I draped my arm over her shoulder, pulled her in, and kissed the top of her head. "I have. Hope you don't mind? I thought you might like to take her for a drive?"

She looked up and for the first time in a very long time, not only did she smile, but I knew that she saw me. My sister saw beyond her grief, and she actually saw *me*.

"I don't want to go out on the road, Marls, but I'll drive her around out here."

I can't put into words the happiness I felt right then. Raw, pure fucking delight made my heart feel like it was about to burst out of my chest.

"Yeah?" I couldn't wipe the fucking smile off my face as I spoke.

"Yeah," she smiled back up at me.

"Well, it's a fucking start, I s'pose." I kissed the top of her head again, before grabbing her hand and pulling her towards the car.

EPILOGUE
2014

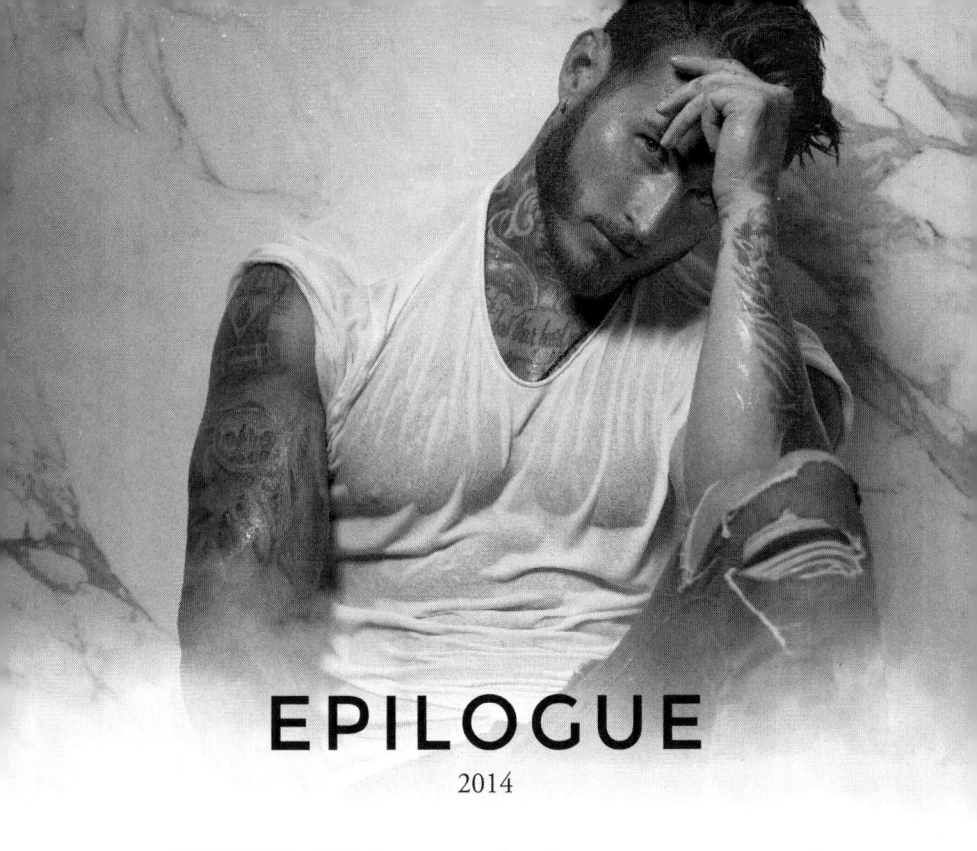

We've managed to keep our appearance at the Triple M fundraiser secret; not even a hint of what we're up to has appeared in the papers or on any social media sites. I'm nervous as fuck. I usually make a short appearance on stage each year, and I've played on my own plenty since we lost Maca, but this is different. I'll be fronting Shift, replacing their lead singer Jet Harrison, who had recently taken his own life. I would be singing a few songs by Carnage, then Conner Reed would take up the mic and we would perform a couple of Shift songs.

The lights go down and the place is in relative silence, considering it's packed to capacity.

I hit the first notes of *'With You.'* Reed follows me in on bass and the crowd goes wild. The curtain lifts and I swear the fucking building shakes.

I can barely see through the stage lights, but I know roughly where my family is standing, and I try to pick George out on the balcony.

This is just one, of so very many songs Maca wrote for her and I always worry, even after all these years, how she copes with hearing them.

When I'm done, I address the crowd with a lump in my throat and thank them all for coming. Reed then takes the mic and dedicates the next song to his girl. Rock stars, we're all a bunch of pussies.

I'm pumped when we come offstage.

"You fucking rocked it, Reed. You slayed them," I tell Conner. I really like working with this boy. He's full of great ideas and we have very similar tastes in what we like to listen to. He's looking to get out of the spotlight and I think he's someone I could easily work with, either producing or writing music with in the future.

It's his first time up on stage since he's lost his mate, so I make a point of telling him that it'll get easier—never better, just easier.

Ash is waiting backstage with a bottle of Cristal and I'm feeling so wired that I know that the only thing that'll bring me down from my rush is a special bit of Ash loving, so I drag her off to where I happen to know a rather spacious storage cupboard is situated.

All about the romance me—broom cupboard sex, and Cristal. I take my wife on the best dates.

Just thirty minutes later, we join the rest of our family up in the VIP bar, even all of our kids are with us this year.

I get a round of applause as we approach and lots of pats on the back.

"Did you phone ahead and tell them how good my performance in the cupboard just was?" I whisper into Ashley's ear.

"You're shagging was shit, but you play great guitar, Rock Star," she whispers back.

Cheeky cow.

We spend the next few hours drinking and enjoying the company of the people we love most in the world.

Only one person is missing, but he's never far from my thoughts. Our lives have continued along without Maca. Our kids have grown, and music has continued to be made. For us, nothing much has changed. For Georgia? Her world is one that none of us thought would ever happen.

When Cam came into her life, or should I say, back into her life, none of us were best pleased and by none of us, I mean myself and my brothers. Ash, Jimmie, and my mum seemed to be over the moon. Ash admitted to me then that she always felt that if she and Maca hadn't reconnected that night at Jimmie and Lens, then George would've ended up married to Cam. I had never seen them together, so I had no clue about their relationship back then. All I knew was that bloke worshipped the ground my sister walked on, and would do anything for her and their kids.

Georgia had been unbelievably lucky when first Jimmie, then Ash, offered to become surrogates when it was found that her eggs had been frozen.

I was shocked when Ash asked me if I would mind if she carried George and Cam's child for them, and I honestly didn't think she would actually see the whole process through.

She didn't mind being pregnant, but she hated that she always gained so much weight.

Me, I fucking loved her curves, but this would be different, it wouldn't be our baby growing inside her.

I agreed, thinking that when it came down to it, she'd back out. She didn't, and then *I* sort of had a wobble. I felt guilty. Maca was my best mate, my bro, and here I was letting *my* wife carry the child *his* wife had created with another man.

Len was in the same boat as me, so it was him I went and spoke to about how I felt, and all he said was, "Just think about how happy Maca would be to see her finally become a mother."

I was sold and we were all over the moon when both of the girls fell pregnant.

When Ash found out she was carrying their twin girls, she wasn't quite so ecstatic. She actually didn't put on as much weight as she did with our own kids, but her belly still seemed to grow daily.

I thought that it might be a little weird making love to my wife, knowing that she had another man's babies growing inside her, but it wasn't. In fact, she just looked more beautiful to me because of the amazing gift she was giving to my sister.

Despite the fuck awful tragedy that had decimated our family for a while, we were now a happy and contented bunch. Despite the glare of publicity, our kids were all growing up great and were all as close to each other as I had remained to my brothers and sister.

Life was good for the Layton family, life was fucking good.

Oh, and that book? I hit delete and never showed it to a soul. Some stories are just best left untold.

The End

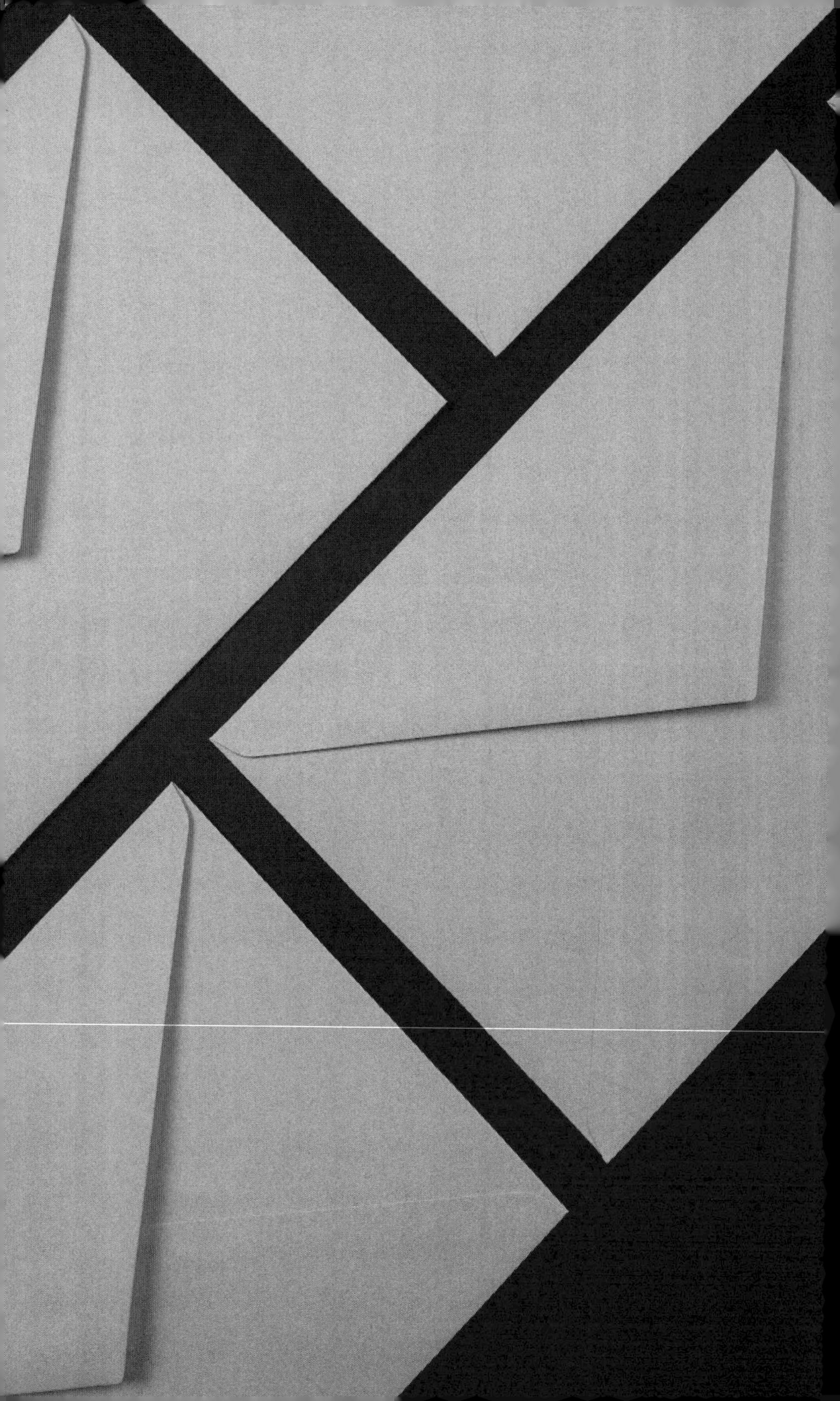

THE
LETTERS

carnage
book four

LESLEY JONES

DEDICATION

For my readers.
You asked.
I hope I delivered.

ONE
Cameron

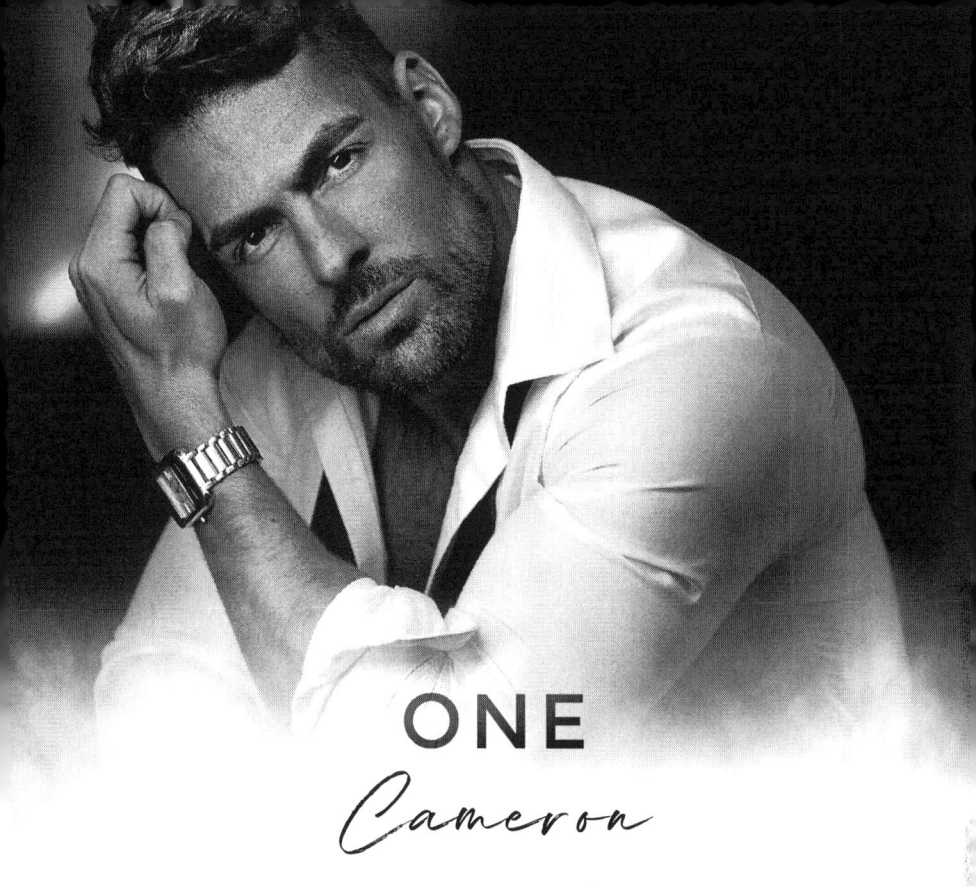

I clear customs in record time. The upside of landing at two in the morning I suppose. I'm tired, miserable and just want to get home. As I enter the arrivals hall, I scan the space for my driver, who should be holding up a card with my name on it. I could've called Benny but thought I'd spare him the task. He hasn't been well lately, blood pressure and a dodgy knee are both causing him problems. I'd paid for him to start working out with a personal trainer three times a week, and as much as he moaned about it, he has lost over three stone this last six months, and even though he won't admit it, I know he's feeling better for it.

I spot a a card with my name on it and a bloke looking right at me.

I do my best to keep my name out of the papers as much as possible, but he's obviously recognised my face. Giving him a small tilt of my chin in acknowledgment, I head around the barrier, dragging my suitcase behind me.

I could use the company's private jet to travel, but it seems like such a waste for just one person, so I fly first class instead. No hardship there.

"Mr King, let me take that for you, sir," my driver says as I reach him. "My name's Parker, sir. I'll be your driver tonight." I give him another nod and let him take my case as I contemplate cracking a joke and asking him to call me Lady Penelope, seeing as his name is Parker. Like I said, though, it's two in the morning, and I'm not particularly cheerful right now.

"If you'd like to follow me, sir, we'll get you settled in the car and home in no time."

I remain silent and follow him to the Jag that's gonna get me home. Home to my Kitten and my kids. I hate being away and rarely make trips without Georgia, but this one was too important for me not to attend. We have one club in Australia, one in Asia, and four clubs throughout Europe now, and these past couple of weeks I had to meet with the heads of security for each one. Gone are the days of trying to stop underage kids with fake IDs, hidden miniature bottles of alcohol, or drugs in shoes. Now, the staff are searching for guns and suicide bombers. The world is a scary place and nightclubs are not immune to terrorists or rampaging idiots with guns. Our clubs are all upmarket and frequented by celebrities, as well as your average clubber looking for a good night, and I want each and every one of them to feel safe. The meetings over the last two weeks were about upgrading all of our systems and brainstorming best practices. It was far from exciting but very necessary. On any given weekend, my clubs are filled with other people's children, and I have a duty of care to each and every one of them. One day, my kids would be off out clubbing, well, not until they are at least thirty, of course, for my daughters it may be never! But anyway, when that time comes, I want the standards of club security to be at a lot higher level than they were when I first started out.

My kids.

I couldn't even think the words without smiling.

Two boys and two girls.

Those four little people and their mum are my world. A world I never thought would exist for me, and definitely not one would happen with their mother.

My Kitten. The absolute love of my life.

We'd taken a long and winding road, with unimaginable loss and heartbreak along the way, to get to each other, but we got here. Middle-aged and the happiest and most content we'd ever been in our lives.

We have been beyond fortunate to have brought four beautiful babies into this world as a bonus. Four little people that grow every day into young adults. Harry, who's fifteen now, is all legs, exactly the way I was when I was his age. We got lucky with that kid. As sad as it is to say, I'm relieved he has none of Tamara's personality traits. H is generally the mediator amongst the kids. He's pretty calm and easy going and no one would guess he's only a few months older than the rest, because he acts like an adult already. He's in the year above them at school and made sure everyone knew not to even think about breathing in the direction of his sisters, let alone looking at them when they joined him at the secondary school they all attend.

He steps in between their fights, which are frequent, and he helps them with their homework. He rarely argues with his brother or gives us any lip. He knows his background and that Georgia isn't his birth mother. She's the only mum he's ever known, and since the day he could talk that's all he's ever called her, because that's exactly what she is to him. I'll admit that I was a little worried that her feelings might change towards Harry when George and the twins arrived. That never happened, and the older he gets, the closer they seem to become. He goes to his mum for everything, and I mean everything. Hair product, girl advice, what T-shirt to wear to the shopping centre, all Georgia. The little shit never asks my advice on anything, his usual response to anything I say, is, "Get with it, old man". He even sends her pictures of things before he buys them. I mean seriously, if you can't dress yourself by the age of fifteen, then what fucking hope is there for world?

I watch the lights of the A13 pass by as we head away from City Airport and back towards Essex, to my home, my wife, my children, my world.

By the time I walk through my front door, it's almost four in the morning, and I need to be inside my wife. One week is far too long to go without feeling her skin against mine.

I've surpassed tiredness at this stage, my body clock totally confused as to what time zone we're now in, so I head straight through the house towards the kitchen. I'll have a coffee and some toast and then go wake my wife up with coffee with my extra special cream and a kiss … from my dick.

I take my shoes off so they don't make noise on the hardwood floor. I'm home a day and a half early, and I don't wanna be scaring the crap outta Georgia.

Walking down the hallway towards our family room, I pass my office first and then Georgia's. We tried sharing, but I find her too untidy and distracting. Every time she leant forward or bent over, I'd end up fucking her and neither of us ever got any work done, so I relocated the gym out to the pool house and turned the extra room into a separate office for Georgia. I had it soundproofed, too. Georgia likes to listen to music when she works, I like silence.

I stop in my tracks and take a step back as I see a light shining from the slightly open door to my wife's office. Still holding my shoes in my hand, I push the door open slowly and take a look inside.

Georgia's office is the complete opposite of mine. Where I have a huge wooden desk facing the door, Georgia has a deep ledge against the window that she works from with her back *to* the door. My walls have a couple of pieces of art I've collected over the years by Peter Granville Edmunds and my bookshelves have pictures of Georgia, myself, and the kids on them.

Georgia's office furniture is made from what looks like drift wood, she has one wall painted with a pop art looking piece. It's black and white and divided into squares. Each square is a continuation of the picture in the adjoining square. In the centre is a re-joined image of us kissing, around the edges are pictures of the kids. It sounds like a complicated mess, but the impact knocks my breath away every time I step into the room. On the opposite wall, she has the kids' heights marked out, starting from the time they could stand. The rest of the wall is covered in ours and the kid's handprints, and each one has something written in the palm: Love. Trust. Live. Family. Laugh. Be kind. Be honest to yourself. I love you all, are just some of the words and phrases that jump out at me. Every time I look at this wall it gives me a lump in my throat. On the walls on either side of the door are the gold, silver, and platinum awards Carnage has won over the years, and on the shelves on either side of the window where her desk sits are the awards she's won for all of her charity work, framed photos of us and the kids, and drawings the kids have made for her. Her office is all family, mine more professional-looking, which sometimes makes me feel like a bit of an old fart.

Georgia's office is never tidy, but right now, the mess is off the charts. There's what looks like an old tea chest, or packing crate sitting in the corner and piles of documents and books on every surface. I look at the floor, and my heart rate speeds up when I see her.

Kitten.

She's lying flat on the floor in a pair of shorts and an old Carnage T-shirt. Her hair is piled on top of her head, and she has her pink Beats covering her ears.

She has a piece of paper pressed against her chest, and although her eyes are closed, I can see she's crying. She makes no sound, there are no facial expressions, just tears. They track from the corners of her eyes, into her ears, around her neck, and into her hairline.

I fight the urge to go to her, to sweep her up and hold her tightly in my arms. To rock her and tell her to hush, that everything will be all right, because it won't.

She's crying for him. Her lost love.

She's crying for them. Her lost babies.

And there's nothing I can do or say to make it better.

There was a time when I would have gladly taken their places. When I would've given my life for theirs just to bring the light back into her eyes, but not now. Now, I'm a dad. Sacrificing myself for them would mean my, *our* children, wouldn't exist. So, now I say nothing when she has her bad days. I just reassure her it's okay to feel the way she does.

Does it hurt? Of course it fucking does. I'm only human.

I'm all too aware there's a part of her that will forever mourn Sean and the babies they lost. But I know my girl inside and out, and feel right down to the marrow in my bones, that even when she cries for them, she loves me with everything she has.

I'd be a fucking liar if I say I don't feel just a little stab of jealousy when she has her meltdown moments and cries for the loss of another man—a man she also loved with all her heart until she met me and gave me a piece of it too. A man she once left me for, and went on to marry. A man she cheated on with me when she let me fuck her senseless against my office door. A man she refused to leave so we could be together. But I learnt a long time ago that being jealous of a dead bloke is futile and a complete waste of energy… But still, I feel it.

I know Georgia struggles with her guilt, and I understood that. Yet, neither of us could change the tragic events that afflict our pasts; twisted, bent, and moulded our futures; and then ultimately led us back to each other. What I can do is hold her when she cries and reassure her it's okay to let the tears flow. She loved him for most of her life and it's okay to still love him now, to cry for her loss.

I knew when I married her there would always be a piece of her heart I could never mend. A piece that will always belong to them, but it's part of what makes her Georgia, and I wouldn't change her for the world. We both had to kick, bite, and claw our ways from the deepest depths of hell to find what we have now. It was hard, but we did it—against the odds, we fucking did it.

My wife turns onto her side and pulls her knees up to her chest as she gives out a sob. I don't know what she's listening to, as the music is being Bluetoothed from her laptop to her ear phones, but I would bet my arse it's either one of his songs or something that reminds her of him.

I contemplate just leaving her to it and not interrupting what should have been a private moment. She's not expecting me until tomorrow lunch time and will be mortified to know I saw her like this.

I hear a door creek upstairs and turn my attention towards it. The last thing I want is for one of the kids to come down and find her in this state. Prioritising my kids, I leave my wife to the moment she obviously needs to have, and take the stairs two at a time, spotting Kiki heading into my room as I reach the landing.

"Kiks?" I call her name quietly, not wanting to wake the other three.

She turns and looks at me over her shoulder and her face lights up.

"You all right, Treacle?" I ask her as she steps into my open arms.

"I thought you weren't coming home till tomorrow? We missed you," she tells me, whilst wrapping her arms around my waist.

I breathe in the scent of her hair, long and deep. She smells like home. I kiss the top of her head and then tilt it so she's looking at me.

"What you doing up?"

"I had a bad dream," she tells me, not meeting my eyes.

"The same one?"

She nods her head.

Before Harry started at secondary school, we sat him down and told him what happened to his mum. He was eleven and had access to the internet, so we thought we needed to do it before some little arsehole at school got in before we did. There was a fair bit of publicity around Tamara's suicide, mainly because she tried to take me out with her and that only made the news because of my relationship with Georgia. To this day, the press and the public seem to have a fascination with my wife. We've managed to protect the kids from it, but they're fully aware I was shot and that their mum was married to someone famous before me. They know the circumstances of his death and about the two babies Georgia lost.

If it were my call, I would've waited until they were older, but as my kids keep telling me, this is the twenty-first century. One click and the kids would've found out the truth, or a version of it, so we decided to be upfront and honest with them. We told H about his mum first and then we told the other three about Tamara and about Sean.

They took it okay, well, sorta. Kiks cried because it was so sad Tamara chose to leave Harry in that way. Lu mumbled something about it being a good thing she had died, otherwise *she* would be hunting her down and shooting Tamara herself. George just asked me if it hurt.

Unfortunately, since then, Kiki has had nightmares. They don't happen often, but they're always about the same thing: either someone is chasing her with a gun, or she's involved in a car accident.

We both feel guilty about this and still wonder if we'd made a bad call telling them all too soon. Then, when Lu got in a fight because some little darling said her mum told her that Georgia was in the papers for having a threesome with some rock stars when she was just thirteen, we knew we had made the right decision.

Being a parent is tough, toughest job I've ever had. I do what I can to protect them, but at the same time I have to prepare them for the outside world. For our kids, it's always gonna be a little bit harder out there, both their mum and their uncle have lived their lives making headlines from a very young age. They have one cousin in an up-and-coming band and another whose face is plastered on billboards, the front of magazines, and sometimes on the telly. Even I've made the front pages a few times. Because of all this, there are some little fuckers out there who just want to have a go. Our kids aren't brats, we've gone out of our way to raise them not to be, but still, they're targeted purely for coming from a famous family, and it pisses me the fuck off.

All of this has meant we've had to arm them with as much age appropriate information about our past lives before they find it out on line, or through some gobby little shit at school.

They have laptops and smart phones. We didn't allow them to have Facebook accounts until they got to secondary school, but now they have it all—Facebook, Twitter, Snapchat, and Instagram. There are probably others I don't even know about; the whole thing is beyond me. What ever happened to just knocking on your mate's door and asking if they want to come out?

We have a strict no phones at the dinner table rule, and the only time it gets broken is when they all start taking photos of their food before they start to eat. What the fuck is that all about? I'm glad Georgia is the one in charge of watching their online shit and not me because I seriously don't get it.

Georgia is all over the social media shit and she regularly checks the kids accounts to see what they're looking at, but she's warned me that it's gonna have to stop soon, especially with Harry. She trusts him and says he's entitled to his privacy. Yeah, we'll see.

I walk Kiks back to her bed and lie down with her for a little while. She's the sensitive one out of all my kids. She always used to rescue lady birds and any other creature she found in the garden when she was younger. She cries if a sad story comes on the news, and she donates part of her allowance every month to the local animal shelter.

"So, you missed me, did ya, Treacle?"

She nods her head and yawns at the same time.

"We all missed you. Mum's been sad all week. We watched your wedding video the other night, and she cried all the way through."

My heart bangs so hard against my chest, it echoes in my ears. Most people don't see the gentler side of Georgia. They see the smart business woman that runs a successful chain of fashion stores and an even more successful charity. They see a woman who overcame the very public loss of her first baby and then her husband and a second child. Georgia's public persona is that of a tough-as-nails, smart-mouthed Essex girl. Me, our children, and her family know different. The kids laughed when she cried when Harry scored his first goal and when Kiki was an angel in the school's Christmas play. They have no clue why she cries when she hears the national anthem sung before a football match or when certain songs come on the radio. They don't understand why she cries when someone gets voted off X Factor, or why she bursts into tears when I come home with flowers for her, just because.

But I know.

I know Georgia inside out. From the twenty-year-old girl with sad eyes who walked into my wine bar almost thirty years ago, to the stunningly beautiful, mostly vibrant woman she is now, I know her like no other. Every tear, gasp, and sigh. Every curve, bump, and crease. Every twitch of her lips and thought that crosses her mind, I know and can read them. We talk without words. I can look at her and know when someone is making her uncomfortable, when she's had too much to drink and it's time to go, or when someone's pissing her off and it's time to step in. I know all of this because we're a team, united. There is so much more to her than the public could ever conceive.

"Mum looked so beautiful in her wedding to you. I like that dress better than the one she wore to her other wedding."

"Me too, Treacle, me too."

"Hope I'm as beautiful as her when I grow up." She yawns her way through her sentence. I kiss the top of her head again.

"You already are. Don't you worry about that. You, your sister, and your mum are the best looking girls in the world."

She nods her head, her eyes now closed.

"Ollie Chalmers said that me and Lu were the fittest twins he's ever known, but it's not surprising coz our mum's a MILF."

What the actual fuck?

I'm paying six grand a term, per kid, to send my girls to a school where they get told shit like this? I'll be on the phone with that stuck-up headmistress first thing Monday morning, and who the fuck is this Ollie kid anyway?

"How old is this Ollie kid, Kiks? Do the boys know him?" I choke out because I've forgotten to breathe. She doesn't answer, so I give her a nudge.

"Whaaaat?" she whines.

"This Ollie, how old?"

"Same age as us, fourteen he's in the same tutor group as George, and they play on the same football team."

He's only fourteen, but I still wanna punch the little fucker.

I listen to my daughter's breathing change as she drifts back to sleep.

"I love you," she mumbles

I kiss her forehead this time.

"Love you, too."

I climb from her bed, and as I reach the door, she calls my name.

"Daddy?"

My heart feels like it grows too big for my chest. That shit never gets old. No matter how big of a man I think I am, when my little girl calls me daddy, game over.

"Yes?"

"You looked very handsome in your wedding video ... Mum said so, too."

"Thanks, Kiks," I tell her with a smile.

TWO
Cameron

I make my way downstairs quietly, the sun is coming up and the birds are starting their dawn chorus. I wanna shoot them.

I was a fourteen-year-old boy once, I know exactly how their filthy little minds work. I need to get Harry on board with this, and make sure he tells that little toerag Ollie to stay the fuck away from my girls—all of them. What the fuck is he doing eyeing up my wife anyway? He's fourteen for fuck's sake.

I take a few deep breaths and stick my head inside Georgia's office door. Her earphones are off and she's curled on her side facing me now, obviously asleep. Her mouth is slightly open, and I'm instantly hard as I watch her.

I go to the kitchen and make us both a coffee. Taking them back to her office, I put them down on her desk next to the two empty bottles of wine I failed to spot earlier. No wonder she was such a mess. Georgia, wine, and memories of Sean are really not a good combination and nearly always end in tears.

There's a stack of letters sitting next to the empty bottles, and I pick the top one up. It's addressed to Georgia when she still lived at home with her parents. I lean over her to make sure she's still sleeping and slide the letter from the envelope.

Oh shut up, like you wouldn't have a look!

It's handwritten on a plain piece of paper.

> Let Me Know...
> Should I wait for you?
> Or let you go
> Shall I hang on to our love
> I need to know.
>
> My heart, it's yours
> For as long as we live
> It beats fierce and strong
> And has so much to give.
> Just let me know...

Fuck!

I know what this is. Georgia has had a crate of stuff sitting out in the garage for years. It had all of Sean's stuff in there, including a load of shit she never looked at. Letters, tapes, diaries. She has always put off going through it, obviously, she's decided now would be a good time to make a start.

I slide the first note back into its envelope and pull out another.

> I fucked someone else tonight, George. I hope you're happy with that! Hope you're pleased, hope it's what you wanted, coz I just feel like shit. It didn't have to be like this. It shouldn't have been her who woke up in my bed this morning, it should've been you.

It should be you every morning, but you chose this. You chose to behave like a spoiled selfish little cunt, and now I've gone and done exactly what you accused me of in the beginning. Well fuck you, Georgia. Fuck you!

Shit! It should make me happy that Archangel Sean wasn't quite as perfect as Georgia seems to think he was, but this will break her heart. No wonder she was such a mess earlier.

I go into my study and get a throw from the wingback chair I have in there. She's gonna have a stiff neck and a sore head when she wakes up, so the least I can do is keep her warm.

I drink my coffee, as well as the one I made her, and decide to keep reading. I don't care if she's gonna be pissed off with me later. If she's been through all of these and they've upset her, then I wanna know about it. If they're full of poncy words and bullshit, I wanna know that too. What can I say, I'm a nosey fucker, and if it involves my wife, I wanna know it all.

I slide down on the floor next to Georgia and start with the pile that's next to her.

So what now, G? I just give up? You think by ignoring my calls and letters that's it, the end of us? Coz that will never fucking happen. Ignore me all you like, marry someone else, have ten kids with him, it won't matter. There'll still be an us. There'll always be an us.

That looks like anus haha and don't marry anyone else. Fuck, don't even go out with anyone else, and definitely don't have any kids. Beau and Lilly remember? Our babies, G. The babies we're gonna have. We still have to think of a name for our other boy. I was thinking about it the other night, what about Frankie? I think your dad would like that. Beau, Frankie, and Lilly, our kids. Mine and yours.

Fuck, I miss you so fucking much. I don't know what I can

say to fix this. I fucked up, I know I fucked up massively, but this is us, we're talking about, Sean and Georgia. Georgia and Sean. We're meant to be, baby, wherever you are, whatever you're doing, there'll always be an us, and you know it. You fucking know it, G.

Why won't you just talk to me?

Ok, don't even do that, just answer the phone when I call and let me talk, just let me tell you how much I love and miss you. Your smell, your touch, your soft skin, and those beautiful blue eyes. Your mouthy Essex attitude, even your temper, G, and your tits—fuck, I miss your tits, your perfect, perfect tits. Every part of me aches. My heart, my soul, and my bones, they all ache for you, baby, so much, so, so much.

I have to go now. We're in Birmingham, Jimmie's here with Len. You should be here with me, and you fucking know it.

I love you, I miss you. I'll call you tomorrow morning around 8 after your dad's gone. Pick up the phone, G. Please, please pick up the phone.

I love you Gia, with everything I am, I love and miss you. Just pick up the phone and talk to me baby. Let me put this right.

Sean xxx

Georgia, Georgia give us a kiss
Georgia, Georgia show us ya tits.
That's all I've got.
Just wanted ya to know that I'm thinking of you.
Love and miss you baby xxx

Georgia, today has been really hard. We're in our new shared house near the studios in West London. We had a day off today, and everyone has gone out, except me. I had nowhere to go. This is where I live, but it's not my home. It's the place where I eat and sleep. Where I shower and wash my clothes. It's where I exist, barely, but it's not my home. My only home is wherever you are. Home is you, the taste of you, the feel of you, the smell of you.

Today, I spent alone. Today, like all the others lately, I spent homeless, because without you, that's what I'll always be.

I love you, Gia. You know that, it never changes, not even when I think I hate you. Even then, I know deep, deep down that it's just another way of loving you. I hope you read this one day. I hope you read this and finally understand, finally get it. Xxx

I wrote a new song, but your brothers, yeah, two of them and your best friend weren't impressed, and I got a punch in the mouth off all of them. I might just make it anyway. I might just go solo on this one and put it out there by myself, what d'ya reckon?

What should I call it? I was thinking "A Song for G", or how about "Fuck You, Baby". How's that sound?

You called this on.
Now you've got your way.
Time for me to move along.
Tomorrow's another day.
Fuck you, baby, I did my best
Fuck you, baby, now I'll go fuck the rest.

I tried to reason, to make you see sense
But you walked away ... No recompense.
You gave me no chance to talk or say my sad goodbyes
You ignored my pleas, ignored my cries.
So fuck you, baby, now I'll go fuck the rest.
I fucked you baby ... You weren't the best.

When you meet another, which I'm sure you will.
Just remember me and the way I can make you feel.

*When he slides inside you, and when he holds you tight,
I hope you think and dream of me, all through the night.
When he pushes deep and looks into your cold hard eyes.
When he says and does those things only I know you like,
Don't you forget that I was your first, the first to hear your moans, the first to hear your sighs.*

*So, fuck you, baby. My time here is done.
I'm through crying, time for me to have some fun.
Fuck you, baby, maybe see you around some time.
Then you can join all the others and wait your turn in line.
You like that? Hurts doesn't it? Well good. At least if it hurts, it means you still have a heart. If it weren't for this permanent pain, this continuous ache I have in my chest, I'd be numb. I've got nothing else right now, G. I'm done.*

My heart races as I read. I switch from totally understanding the bloke's heartbreak to wanting to smash his face in. Then I remember that he's dead and getting pissed off with him is pointless. I don't understand why she's putting herself through this. It's been fifteen years, why would she want to drag up all of these memories now?

I look down and watch Georgia sleep. As much as I like to think I know what makes her tick, I'd still love to get inside her head sometimes. Like now, just so I can understand the thought process that led to her believing this could be a good idea.

My eyes are starting to sting, and I decided to wrap myself around my wife and rest them for a little while.

THREE
Cameron

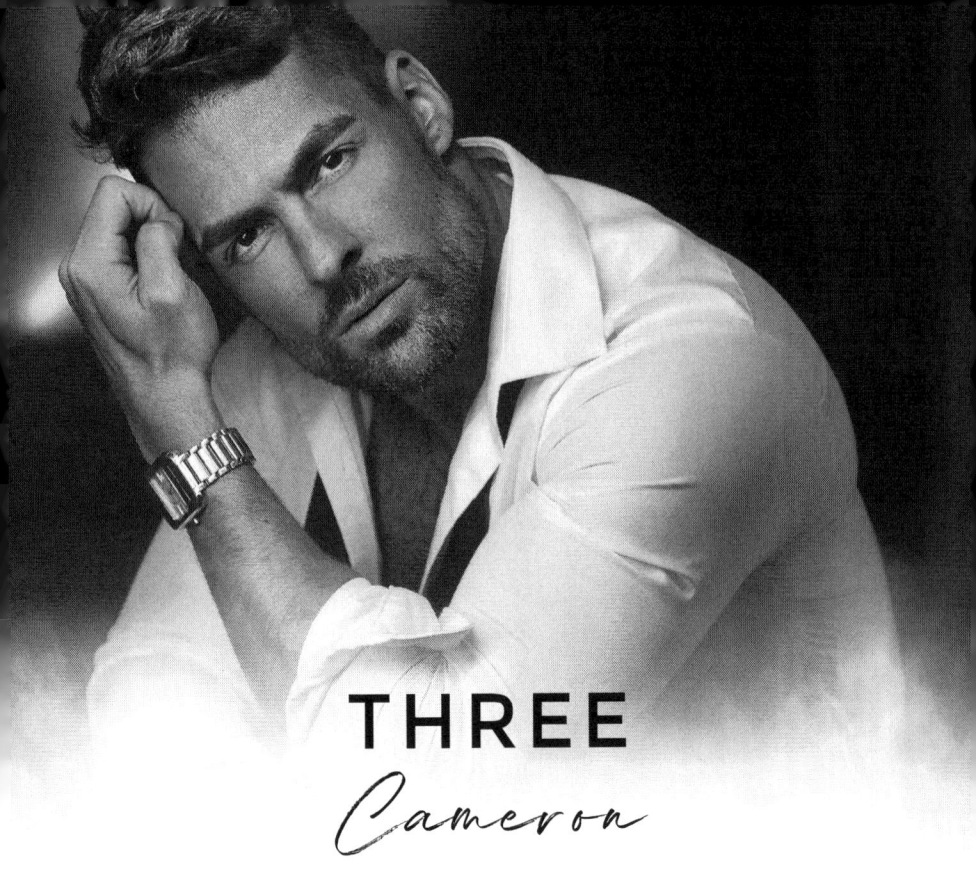

After what feels like just five minutes of sleep, I wake with a start. I open my eyes and see Georgia lying in the recovery position next to me. Her side pressed into mine as I lie on my back. I hear quiet footsteps walk past the study and on into the kitchen. I assume it's one of the kids but get up anyway to check.

At some stage, I must have taken off my jeans, as I'm now just wearing a T-shirt and a pair of boxers. Georgia stirs and so does my dick as I hear her little sigh. I adjust what's happening inside my Calvin's, collect the glass things Georgia insists we drink our coffee out of, and head up the hallway.

Tallulah is standing at the coffee machine with her head resting on her arms, which are resting on the kitchen worktop. Her long dark hair, which is the exact same shade as her mother's hair, is hanging down her back, and she's watching the hot dark liquid fill her cup.

When the fuck did my daughter start drinking coffee?

Tallulah is probably going to be our problem child. She has a short fuse and a quick wit. She can cut with a glare from her blue eyes or a single word from her sharp tongue. She's also loyal, possessive, and protective of those she loves. Lu has no fear, and her strong will and defiance have already gotten her into trouble. She takes no shit from anyone—not even her teachers, and I've had to go up to the school on more than one occasion. She's not naughty, per se, just outspoken, fearless, and headstrong. She's a passionate kid. I don't wanna sound like I'm making excuses for her, but I don't want the system to knock her spirit out of her. Despite what life has thrown at Georgia, she still maintains hers to this day. In fact, it's what I think got her through everything. I want Lu to grow up to be as resilient as her mum. I want that for all of my kids.

The problem at home is that Lu and Georgia are a fucking nightmare when they start going at each other. Their personalities are identical, and when they clash, most of Essex hears about it. Georgia always thinks she knows best, and Tallulah can't, or won't, be told she's wrong. Like I said, she's a carbon copy of her mother, right down to her striking blue eyes.

That's the other reason I worry. The girls turned fourteen in February, Georgia was just twenty when I first met her. In six years' time, they could potentially have men like me sniffing around them. I clench my hand into a fist and push it against my chest where it suddenly feels like I'm having a heart attack.

Lu must catch my movement, because she spins around and her hand flies to her own chest.

"Shit, Daddy. You scared the crap outta me!"

"Language, Syrup," I say in my best warning voice. That's the other thing Lu has in common with her mother, her foul mouth. She swears more than her brothers, and I blame that on her mother.

She rolls her eyes and folds her arms across her chest, and I already know what's coming.

"Don't call me Syrup."

Lu hates the nicknames I've called the twins since they were babies. She's always been Syrup, Kiki has always been Treacle.

She walks towards me, wrapping her skinny arms around my chest.

"Sorry for swearing, you made me jump. I thought you weren't coming home till later."

"I missed you all and managed to get a flight home last night." I kiss the top of Lu's head as I speak. Her hair smells of mint.

"You been nicking your mother's shampoo again?" Another cause for conflict between Georgia and Lu, they have the same taste in a lot of things. Lu likes to borrow without asking, Georgia throws a fit, and Lu tells her to take a chill pill and be flattered that at her age, her fourteen-year-old even likes her taste. That's when I generally step in to prevent my wife from throttling our daughter.

I feel her shake her head against my chest. "Nah, Mum treated me to the shampoo and conditioner while you were away. If she'd have just done that in the first place, it would've saved a lot of arguments."

I can't help but laugh at my daughter's reasoning. "I hope you also said thank you?"

"Do you think she woulda let me keep it if I hadn't? You know what Mum's like with her manners."

"Manners cost nothing and will get you a long way in life, Lu, believe me."

She doesn't reply, but I can hear her brain thinking that one through.

"What you doing up so early anyway?" I ask her.

"I didn't muck out last night. I need to get over to the stables and get it done."

"What about Kiks and Mum?"

She shrugs her shoulders and huffs. "No, they did theirs. I went to Lakeside with Harley and Jimmie. We went for pizza after. Mum said it was fine as long as I did the horse stable this morning."

She steps away from me and pours milk into her coffee cup.

"Fair enough, but take your phone." I tell her.

"Dad!" She rolls her eyes as she says my name. "You can see the stables from the back patio if you're that worried."

This is true. It had made sense to have them rebuilt reasonably close to the house. Georgia has kept a horse ever since we bought and renovated the place, and the girls have had ponies since they could walk. Kiki still rode with Georgia regularly, but Lu is starting to lose interest, preferring to spend her time at the shopping centre with her mates. I'd threatened to sell Bella, her horse, on more than one occasion, but Lu's only response was to ask if she got to keep the money, seeing as the horse *was* a Christmas present and it was only *fair*!

Lu drinks her coffee while I make one for myself and Georgia, and then she heads upstairs to change.

I step back into the office and note that apart from kicking off the throw I put over her, my wife hasn't moved. She's not a big fan of mornings and she's probably gonna have a hangover if she drank the contents of the two empty wine bottles sitting on her desk.

I park my arse on the floor next to where Georgia sleeps and sip my coffee. We have more bedrooms than the Hilton in this house and my wife chooses to sleep on her office floor.

I watch her sleep for a few more minutes. Her T-shirt has risen, and I fight the urge to run my fingers along the strip of skin showing at the small of her back.

I lose the battle, and very gently trace a line along the top of her barely-there shorts with my fingertips. She has the best arse and legs and the most amazing tits. My dick's hard again, and I close my eyes, debating whether or not I should just slip myself right inside her and fuck her and the consequences.

I open my eyes and she's looking right at me. She blinks, once, twice, and then a smile lights up *her* face and *my* entire existence. I love the fuck outta this woman.

"You're home," she states, still smiling as she speaks, her eyes sparkling with mischief. I know that look and exactly what it means, I can't help but smile back at her.

"I couldn't keep away."

"I missed you."

"I know."

"I'm so fucking horny," she tells me, whilst moving to straddle my lap.

"I know."

"How?"

"Kitten, I'm your husband, it's my job to know what my wife wants, and besides, I need to be inside you right fucking now."

I tap her arse cheek. "Get these shorts off." She stands, whips them off, and lowers herself back down onto my lap, as she does, I release my dick from where Mr Klein has been smothering him and slide right inside her.

"Fuck, T," she groans, whilst wrapping her arms around my neck. I slide my fingers into her hair and pull her face towards me. She resists.

"Morning breath."

"I don't give a fuck. Kiss me."

She does.

My dick throbs, my heart soars, and all is right in the world.

I slide my hands over her skin, up under her T-shirt, and brush my thumbs over her nipples, all while moving my hips underneath her.

"Fuck, Kitten, I've missed you."

Before she gets the chance to reply, the office door flies open.

"Dad, have you seen— What the fuck? Oh my god!" Tallulah shrieks.

"Shit!" Georgia shouts.

"Lu, language!" I shout.

There are a few seconds of silence as Lu just stands in the doorway and casts her gaze around the room. Georgia buries her face in my chest, and I wrap my arms protectively around her. Luckily, the T-shirt she's wearing is long and covers everything important. Just as I think Lu is going to step out of the room, the door is pushed further open and our two dogs, Rooney and Becks, come bounding in, closely followed by George.

Georgia screams, and I jump as Rooney sticks his nose right where I imagine her arse crack must be.

"Oh god," Georgia groans, trying to bury herself further into my chest.

"Get the fucking dog's outta here!" I shout.

"Rooney, Becks—" George's mouth snaps closed, and he stares for a few seconds, taking in Georgia's shorts lying on the floor and the fact that she's straddling my lap. "Oh my god, are you two actually having sex?" he chokes out.

"This is so gross. Who does that?" Lu is still shrieking.

Rooney barks, and Becks tries to squeeze his way between Georgia and me so he can sit in her lap.

"Get out. Get the fuck out," I bellow. "And take the dogs with you."

Lu turns to step out just as a bleary eyed Kiki appears.

"What's going on?" she asks through a yawn.

"Don't go in there, Kiks. Mum and Dad are having sex," Lu warns her.

"Ewww, gross," Kiks replies before turning and leaving with Lu close behind her.

George is still standing and staring at us. "I didn't even know you could still do it at your age," he states.

"What?" As soon as the words left my lips I wonder why I would even ask.

"Sex stuff. I thought you were too old."

I feel Georgia's shoulders shake as she laughs silently against my chest. I look into eyes the exact same shade as mine and, as calmly as

I can, say to my son, "Take the dogs, George. Take the dogs and close the door on your way out."

He calls Rooney and Becks, and they trot out of the room at his side, the door closing quietly behind them.

I pull Georgia's hair gently so her face tilts up to mine.

"And what exactly has tickled your fancy, Kitten?" I ask, feigning seriousness.

"Rooney's wet nose, and it wasn't my fancy he tickled, it was my bum hole."

"Lucky dog."

"Never gonna happen, T. Besides, you're too old for that kind of thing."

"Like fuck I am. I'll show you …" My voice trails off as I notice Georgia's eyes fill with tears.

"Kitten?"

"Thank you," she whispers as tears spill onto her cheeks.

"For what, baby?"

She holds her arms out palms up and moves them around her.

"For all of this. This life, our home, the chaos, our children. Bum-sniffing dogs. For all of it. Thank you for this second chance." She smiles and sobs at the same time as more tears overfill from her pretty blue eyes. I shake my head.

"Georgia, this, our home, our kids. You never have to thank me for any of it. We built this together. Us baby, me and you. We're each other's second chance. Don't ever thank me."

I pull her in closer. My dick, which is still inside her despite the commotion that just went on around us, starts to stir, and I proceed to show my wife just how old I ain't.

FOUR
Georgia

I turn off the shower and reach for a towel, singing to Chet Faker's "The trouble with us", as I do. I wasn't a big fan of his earlier stuff, but I love this song.

I walk out of the en suite and into my bedroom as I wrap the towel around myself. Cam's lying on our bed with his back pressed against the headboard, his big arms folded across his broad chest, and his long legs stretched out in front of him, crossed at the ankles.

I know he's waiting for an explanation as to why he found me sleeping on my office floor, surrounded by empty wine bottles, and the contents of the packing crate labelled "Sean's stuff".

I know he won't ask me about it. I know he'll just wait until I'm ready to talk, and I know full well he knows I know all of this.

"That was an interesting homecoming, Kitten." He both winks and smiles as he speaks, making my insides and toes curl simultaneously.

"Well, the orgasm was unexpected but most definitely welcome. Becks' wet nose in my arse crack and our audience, *hmmmm,* not so much."

"Never before in my life have I been jealous of a dog." His eyes shine as he talks.

"Oh yeah, always wanted a cold wet nose, have you, Tiger?"

"If it gains me access to that tight little arse of yours, then fuck yeah, I can do cold and wet."

There's a moment of silence as we stare at each other. My heart hammering hard in my chest as I contemplate the conversation we need to have and the explanation I should offer.

Our relationship is based on total honesty, it always has been. Cameron King has never made me feel guilty for the thoughts, feelings, grief, or guilt I still carry for the death of my first husband.

He's jealous and possessive, but he's never ever done anything other than hold me tight and tell me to let it all out whenever I have a meltdown, which thankfully happens rarely these days.

I chew on the inside of my lip as his eyes rake over me from my head to my Racy Red shellac-coated toenails.

I try to organise my words before speaking. The last thing in the world I would ever want to do to this man is hurt him or make him feel as if he is anything less than the centre of my world.

The life we have, our children, the chaos that surrounds our hectic home life, the love we share, are all things I would sell my soul to keep. The man lying on our bed in front of me is responsible for it all, and I love him beyond any kind of measure. And yet, there's Sean. There always has been Sean, and there always will be Sean.

I lick my dry lips and draw in a breath, preparing to offer my explanation, but he shocks the shit outta me by saying, "Come over here and talk to me, baby," while patting the mattress next to him.

"Let me just put some clothes on," I request.

"I prefer you naked."

I stop in my tracks and tilt my head to the side and smile at him before starting up again and disappearing into our walk-in wardrobe. "Yeah, but we don't get much talking done when clothes don't factor into the equation and naked bodies do."

My husband's been gone for two weeks, so I'm more than ready to jump his bones again. First we need to talk, and then I need to organise the kids. I pull on a pair of shorts and a T-shirt, not bothering with underwear.

Instead of sitting beside him, I straddle his lap so I can look him in the eyes. Which I do, while he pulls my hair out of the messy bun I had it in for my shower and lets it fall down my back.

He pulls me towards him and drags his nose up my neck and through my hair, before tucking it behind my ears.

"Fuck, I've missed you."

"We've missed you too." I rest my forehead against his as I speak.

"So, you bought Lulah some of your shampoo? Her hair smelled just like yours when I got a cuddle off her this morning."

"Yeah, rather than keep arguing with her, I called Conner's wife, Nina, and she got me some wholesale. It meant I had to buy twelve bottles but—"

"But anything to stop the screaming matches that go on between you two?" he interrupts.

"I scream because she takes it out of the shower. I wet my hair, and then I realise it's missing. I don't mind her using my stuff, as long as she puts it back where she finds it." I let out a small huff before continuing. "We really need to have a word with her about her language, too. She's a fourteen-year-old school girl, not a twenty-five-year-old brickie on a building site."

He throws his head back and gives me one of his big Cameron King laughs.

It still does things to me, and my belly squirms.

"Oh my god, that's funny! All these years, Kitten, all these years I've picked you up about your language, and now, your complaining that our daughter sounds just like you."

"But I don't swear around the kids, you dropped the F bomb more than once this morning when you were shouting at them."

"We were shagging, they wouldn't leave the room. Then the dogs tried to join the party. Of course I bloody swore."

We're both quiet for a few seconds. I assume, that like me, he's reliving this morning's embarrassing events in his head, which I know are going to lead him back to what he really wants to know.

"I opened that old crate, the one that's labelled 'Sean's Stuff'."

"I know, I saw."

I nod my head and chew on my lip again for a few seconds.

"He would've been fifty this year, and Tom and Billy have agreed to play at the Triple M event to mark the occasion. Conner Reed is gonna play lead, like he did the other year, and Marley is gonna front the band."

He brushes the back of his knuckles over my left cheek and lets out a long sigh.

"Why'd you need to open the box?"

"Marley's been trying to write a new song for the band to perform. I thought maybe there might be something amongst all of the stuff in there that might help him out. Marley's great with the music, but it was nearly always Sean that wrote the lyrics."

He puffs his cheeks and purses his lips, they roll together as he blows out air. He looks over my shoulder, either unable or unwilling to meet my gaze. My belly twists and turns in on itself. He's not happy about this.

"Kitten ..." he sighs out my name, and I get goose bumps across my skin. "I've always supported you. Every year, I've done whatever I can to help out with this event, and I will always do that. You've achieved great things and helped untold charities and I couldn't be more proud of you, I really couldn't." I hold my breath as I wait for the "but".

"But ..." And here it comes. "You, are my priority. When I

come home early from a business trip and find you curled in the fetal position on a cold hard floor, surrounded by empty wine bottles, alone and sobbing, well, that's when I can't help but think you need to take a step back."

I close my eyes when I realise he had come home and seen me crying. I'd had my Beats on, Bluetoothing my music through them so I didn't wake the kids, and obviously missed his arrival. I feel a combination of guilt and shame as I consider how he must have felt walking in on that scene.

"I'm sorry you came home to that," I whisper, but he just shakes his head.

"Don't be sorry, I've told you a million times never to be sorry for feeling what you do, that's not the issue, Kitten, it never has been."

He rubs the tips of his fingers up and down my bare arms, once again causing goose bumps to spread down my spine to my toes, despite the fact that I suddenly feel too hot.

"The issue is with you deliberately seeking out something that you know is going to upset you so badly. That, and the fact that I'm not overly impressed with you knocking back two bottles of wine when you're here on your own with the kids."

I remain silent as I fight the urge to jump in guns blazing to defend myself. I try to remain quiet and calm when I do speak.

"I didn't drink two bottles, it was one and a bit, the first one was open and only had about a half glass worth in it. And I'm not deliberately seeking out things that are gonna upset me. I was looking for lyrics to pass on to Marley, and I decided that while I did that, I might as well go through everything that was in there. That bloody box has sat there long enough, it needs sorting through."

"Why, why now?"

"Because it's sat there taunting me for long enough. I should've done it years ago, I shouldn't have left it this long."

"Well, it's because you've always known how fucking upset it would make you." I shrug my shoulders.

"Regardless, it needs doing. It's going to upset me no matter how long I wait, so I might as well just get it done. There could be something useful in there, something that Marls can work his magic on and raise money with."

He slides one hand around the back of my neck and pulls me in for a long lazy kiss. He lets out another long sigh as he breaks away.

"All right, I understand all that. But you do it now while I'm around and not when you're here all on your own. What the fuck would the kids think if they saw you in that state?"

I nod my head in agreement. As usual, I'm wrong and he's right. "I'm sorry, I shouldn't have done it while I was here by myself. I had a few wines for courage, but they just ended up making me feel even more emotional."

"You all right now?" he asks, and for some reason, his concern touches me deeply and tears sting my eyes. He's so good to me, so unbelievably good *for* me. The emotion of the moment suddenly overwhelms me. My face crumbles as I let out a sob, wailing, "I love you," as I launch myself against his chest.

He holds me tight for a few long moments, running his big hands over my back, arms, and scalp.

"Thanks for putting up with all my shit, Cam. Don't you ever get sick of it? You must. I get sick of myself sometimes." I eventually look up at him and ask, "Don't you ever think about trading me in for someone without a shit load of issues?"

His eyes dart all over my face. "You don't have issues, babe. You just have a past. We all have one. Ours, yours and mine, is just a little more traumatic than most." He gives a small smile and then a quick peck on the lips. "That's why we work. That, and the fact that I love you. No one will ever love *you* like I do, and I'd never want *anyone* to love *me* like *you* do."

He pulls his knees up, and I lean back on them and look over his face.

"I read a few of them," he says matter-of-factly.

Shit!

"The letters?" I know what he's on about, I'm just trying to work out how I feel about that. He nods his head slowly, eyes darting all over my face, assessing my reaction.

"Are you pissed off with me?"

I'm not, not at all. I'm just not sure how I feel about it.

"Cam, shaving and leaving your whiskers everywhere, leaving the milk out of the fridge, or not putting your seat belt on before you pull away are things that piss me off. You reading those letters doesn't. It makes me feel a little bit uncomfortable though."

That's the only way I can think to explain how I feel on the subject, *uncomfortable*.

Cam has a small box of memories from his first marriage: wedding photos, birthday and Christmas cards he and Chantelle sent each other, her wedding and engagement rings. I'm a woman, so of course I've been through it. I've looked at the photos of the pair of them. She was beautiful. I know she's dead and no threat to me, but I still had to look. I'm not sure if it's a woman thing or just my warped little mind, but when I saw it in amongst his things when we first moved in together, I couldn't help myself.

"Yeah, they made me a bit uncomfortable, too," he admits.

"Then why'd you read more than one?" He shrugs his big shoulders.

"Morbid curiosity I suppose." Ah, so it's a human thing then, or is it just us two?

"Yeah, I get that. I've looked at the photos of you and Chantelle more than once." His eyebrows shot up to his hairline. Oops, I assumed he knew this.

"It's just human nature, babe. We're wired to be curious," he says after a moment.

We once again both quietly contemplate each other's admissions.

"So?" I ask.

"So?" he repeats.

"You're okay with it then? For me to keep going through this box?"

"Would there be any point in telling you no, Kitten?" I give him a big cheesy grin.

"Absolutely none, but I'll only do it while you're around, I promise."

FIVE
Georgia

I've got this thing about looking at the moon lately. It makes me feel connected to you. Because I know, with one hundred percent certainty, that during your lifetime, you've looked at that same moon. It's all I've got right now, G. The moon, the stars, and the sun. Even the air that I breathe, I take in great gulps and wonder if there's even a remote chance that it's maybe air, that at some stage, you've breathed. Is that even scientifically possible I wonder?

I know I don't bother to post these letters to you anymore, but still, I continue to write them. They help me sort shit out in my head. You could always help me sort shit out, you always gave me a different perspective, a different way of looking at things. I'm an over thinker, and I analyse everything. But you, G, just go with your gut. You react on your first instinct, all guns blazing. I hope that hasn't *changed. I hope you're still the Gia that loved me so passionately. Is it loved or love? Do you think of me at all? I could ask your brothers and Jimmie but it still hurts so much G. I've tried to move on but there's nothing there, there's no connection, not like we had. It makes me panic sometimes, makes me doubt that the way I remember things is just my imagination prettying it up. Did we really love each other that intensely? We were so young, was it even possible to feel the way I think we did at such a young age?*

I wish you were here to answer all of these questions. Perhaps if I had answers, it would give me some closure. It's been almost three years. Are we different people now? Has too much time passed, has too much life happened to make what we had ever work again for us? Coz I do believe that, G. It will happen. I don't know when or how, but I just know that our time will come. We will talk, we will work things out, and we will live, laugh, and love the way we used to. So, whatever tense you might be using, I'll stick with the present. I love you, Gia, and until the day you come back to me, until then, I'll keep looking at our moon and breathing in our air.

Sean and Georgia. Georgia and Sean. The way it's meant to be.

I'm sitting on the floor of my office with a cup of tea in one hand and this letter from Sean in my other. I spent all of Saturday afternoon trying to organise everything into piles. I've worked out which are songs and poems, and I've messaged my brother to come over and look through them with me. There's a pile of VCR tapes, but I've no clue what's on them; some have labels and some don't. It doesn't matter because I don't have anything to play them on anyway. There are some notebooks and diaries, a few photos, and then there are the letters.

When I had this crate shipped to me in Australia, I put what I could in sequential order according to the post office date stamps. Somehow, they got messed up, so I had to just go through them as I got to them. Because most were never posted, there weren't any date stamps, and if Sean hadn't written the date, then I tried to work it out by the things he wrote about.

I've read five letters today, but this is the first to make me cry—the first to break me. I think the thing that did it was the similarities in our thought process. I would often look at the moon and think along the same lines. Were we ever looking into the sky at the same time and thinking of each other?

Cam puts his head around my office door, which I've kept closed as I don't want the kids seeing me upset, especially over a man that's not their dad. His warm smile is gone the instant he sees the tears on my face. He comes in and closes the door behind him.

"What happened?" he asks, while squatting down in front of where I'm sitting, legs crossed, Indian style.

"Words," I reply.

He smooths some stray hair that's escaped from my messy bun and tucks it behind my ear.

"Well, words were his thing, babe. He wrote songs for a living, bloody good ones."

I sniff and nod my head. "I know. I know that …" I trail off and blow my nose on the tissue that Cam passes to me.

It's all suddenly too overwhelming. Why the fuck am I doing this to myself? To us?

"I'm so sorry, Cam. I can't imagine how this is making you feel." He leans his back against my pop art wall, stretches his long legs out in front of him, and then pulls me into his lap. He remains silent as he does this.

"Does it bother you? Be honest with me, does it bother you that I still cry for him after all these years?"

I turn and sit myself so I can see his face, his eyes dart all over mine and he lets out a long breath.

"Georgia, I'm only human, of course it bothers me to a certain extent, but at the same time, I'm one hundred percent certain of your love for me—"

"Good," I interrupt him.

"What we have ... Shit, I don't know how to explain this. Our relationship is unique. It probably wouldn't work for a lot of people, but it works for us, and it's worked for us for a lot of years now, baby. You were married to someone you loved deeply, that you'll always love. He died, and well, here I am. I've every confidence that you love me just as much as you loved or love him. That's just the way it is. I knew this when we got back together, and I've been fully aware of it throughout our marriage. It is what it is, Kitten. He's dead, I'm here. What's the point in me getting pissed off over your tears?"

I don't really know how to respond to his answer. He actually sounds a little bit angry.

"So is that a yes or a no?"

"For fuck's sake, Georgia, you're my wife and I love you. Of course it fucking bothers me. He's been dead for sixteen years, build a bridge and get the fuck over it. Is that what you wanna hear from me?"

I'm stunned into silence for a few seconds. Then I try to scramble to get out of his lap and away from him, but he holds me in place by my waist.

"You asked me a question; now listen to the answer." I stare at him, wide eyed and still too shocked to speak or attempt to move again.

"Part of what makes you the person you are, the woman I've loved for so long, is your passion. If you didn't still feel the way you do, or if you didn't react to his words the way you are now, then it wouldn't be you, not the version of you I love. I love you, and part of loving you is accepting that you still hurt deeply over the death of your first husband and the loss of your babies. I try not to feel jealous. I try really fucking hard, but I'm only human. So yeah, to some degree, it does bother me, but do you know what bothers me more?"

I shake my head, terrified of attempting speech in case I choke on the tears silently running down my cheeks.

"What bothers me more is seeing you so conflicted, watching you being eaten alive by the guilt you feel *because* you cry, *because* of how you feel. He was your husband, Kitten, and this is the first time you've seen these letters. Just like I'm human and feel jealous of a dead bloke, you're human and can't help but still be in love with that dead bloke. I accepted it and came to terms with it a very long time ago. You really do need to do the same, babe."

Wow.

I have no words. Everything he said is true. I've been in love with two men for around thirty years. I was in love with Sean while I was with Cam and then I got back with Sean, but either unknowingly or unwillingly, I remained in love with Cam. Sean died and just a year later, I was back with Cam, and now, here we are, years after Sean's death and I'm still in love with both of them.

I rest my forehead on Cam's chest and sob. "But it hurts so much. It hurts that he's dead and it hurts that I'm crying for him and hurting you." I gulp in air and end up giving myself the hiccups.

"Why does it have to be so painful? I don't want him to be dead, and I don't want you to hurt. I don't wanna cry. I love him, I love you, and I love the kids. If he hadn't died, they wouldn't even exist, maybe, or would they? Would we have still happened? I don't know. I don't know how I'm supposed to feel. I'm a grown up, I'm supposed know this shit, and I don't."

He kisses the top of my head and my tear-streaked face, while holding me close. My heart and my thoughts racing.

"Oh, Georgia. My biggest worry was that you'd react like this to what you'd find in that box."

"I'm sorry, Cam. I'm so, so sorry."

I feel him stand with me still in his arms and walk through my office door. I thank Dr. Dre and his Beats for the fact that my children will hopefully remain unaware of their mother's monumental meltdown and burry my face in Cam's chest as he carries me upstairs to our bedroom.

These letters and the emotions that they've stirred up have hit me hard. So much harder than I was expecting them to.

He lies down with me on our bed and spoons in behind me. I feel drained. Mentally, physically, and emotionally wrung out, and it takes no time at all for my eyes to feel as heavy as my heart and for sleep to claim me.

SIX
Cameron

I turn and look over my shoulder as the church quietens.

"You ready for this?" Robbie asks from beside me.

"No," I reply through gritted teeth, trying not to move my lips.

I watch as Chantelle, wearing a big white puffy dress and holding onto a frail looking Colin's arm, walks up the aisle. Her eyes are on me, and they shine. She loves me, she's in love with me, and I feel ... nothing. Not a thing.

"If you don't wanna do this, bro, then you need to pull the plug now. Put a stop to this and just both move on."

"It's too late," I whisper as an overwhelming sense of panic rises from my toes to my chest.

"It's never too late, Cam. Run. Run now. I'll make up some bullshit excuse for you."

I look my brother squarely in the eyes.

"Run, Cameron. Run now while you still can."

I turn my head, looking from my bride-to-be and her dad, who are rapidly approaching, and then to my brother, who's pointing at the doorway behind us that the vicar came through a few minutes before.

I give my brother a quick nod and move to make my escape through the small arched exit, but my legs feel like lead weights. I actually grab my left thigh in both my hands and lift it, I do the same with my right, but it's no good, not fast enough.

"I love you so much, Cameron. We're going to be so happy together." I can hear Chantelle calling from behind me.

I throw myself on the floor and attempt to crawl towards the door, but there are hands everywhere, grabbing at me.

"Come back, Cam! You promised." I hear Chantelle's voice above all of the others that are calling my name.

"Cam, baby, wake up."

I sit up, nearly headbutting Georgia as I do.

"Jesus. Shit. Fuck," I get out between gasps of air.

Georgia comes into focus, kneeling beside me and holding my right hand between both of hers. I drag the fingers of my left hand through my hair. Her eyes are wide and her mouth's slightly open as she watches.

"You all right?" she asks quietly.

"I was dreaming."

She rolls her eyes.

"I gathered that much, babe. Was it bad?"

I slide my hand from between hers and scratch my head whilst yawning. Georgia remains staring at where I just removed my hand from her hold.

Her head slowly rises, and her eyes meet mine. They're still wide, but now, they're also shining with unshed tears.

What the fuck is she getting upset for?

"Was it bad, your dream? A nightmare?"

She watches my throat as I swallow, and despite still feeling a little shaky and disoriented, my dick stirs to life when she licks her lips.

"C'mere." I gesture with my head and hold out my arms. Now, it's my turn to watch as *her* throat moves when *she* swallows. My erection not giving a shit about the inappropriateness of his appearance.

"Are you pissed off with me?" she asks quietly without making an attempt to move towards my open arms and waiting lap. Which doesn't make me in the least bit happy.

"Why the fuck am I pissed off with you, Kitten?" My voice sounds croaky from sleep. I watch as she laces her fingers together and sets them on top of her knees, rolling her thumbs around and around each other.

Georgia looks nervous. Georgia doesn't do nervous. I've no clue what could be going through that complicatedly beautiful mind of hers.

"My meltdown at lunch time. You've stayed up here all day. You've not even seen much of the kids."

I feel like I'm living in a parallel universe. I must still be foggy from sleep because I feel like I'm missing something.

"What the fuck are you talking about?" My question comes out harsher than I intend, but I'm baffled.

"You were pissed off with me earlier when I had my meltdown of Georgia proportions. You carried me up here, and we must've fallen asleep. Harry came in and woke me up because he was starving. We promised the kids TGI's tonight, remember? I woke you up, and you said you were coming, but you went back to sleep. I ended up taking them on my own."

"Wha, wait, wait, wait. What time is it?"

"Just after twelve."

"At night?"

"Yeah."

"Fuck. I'm so sorry. I don't even remember saying that I was getting up." She's still kneeling next to me, looking all wide eyed and sorry for herself.

"Come the fuck over here, Kitten. I won't tell you again." She silently slides herself into my waiting lap, and her scent is all it takes to calm my racing heart. I kiss the top of her head.

"I thought I'd finally fucked things right up this time," she says into my neck. I feel like a complete prick.

"The jetlag must've hit me and then kicked my arse. I'd never stand you and the kids up, babe. I'm surprised you would even think for a minute that I would."

I move her legs to either side of my hips and pull her in close so I can look into her face.

"You really think I'd do that?" I ask her. She shrugs her shoulders and lets out a long breath.

"I thought I'd driven you to do that." She blinks repeatedly, but it doesn't keep her tears at bay. They hang from her dark lashes, and my gut twists at the thought of her feeling shitty the whole night.

"I'm so sorry about earlier, Cam. It was so unfair of me to behave like that. You'd just come home and I laid all that shit on ya."

I don't think I can remember a time when I've seen Georgia so emotional. Opening this bloody box has had a bigger impact on her emotions than I think even she was expecting.

I've never known her to be insecure, especially about us. Not that she's ever let on to me and I'm pretty good at reading my wife.

"Baby, please don't cry. Of course I didn't stay up here on purpose. There's nothing you could say or do that would keep me away from you. Not even a meltdown of Georgia proportions."

She finally smiles and her blue eyes sparkle. She rakes her fingers through my messy bed hair, which is badly in need of a cut.

"I don't deserve you," she says while kissing my neck.

"Well, you've got me regardless. I need to shower and clean my teeth, baby. I want those little shorts and that vest gone by the time I get back. I need to taste you, and then I need to fuck you." I've already lifted her out of my lap and am headed to the bathroom like a man on a mission as I speak.

"Then will you tell me what your dream was about?" she calls out, stopping me dead in my tracks. I turn back to look at her. She's sitting in the middle of the bed with her legs crossed, looking as young as she did on the night I met her.

I love the fuck out of this woman. Have done it for almost thirty years. Will till the day I die. And if there's any way for it to be possible, I will keep on loving her after that.

"Yes, Kitten. Then I'll tell you about my dream."

We don't really ever talk about Chantelle. I don't think it's a deliberate thing, it's just the way that it is. I have a small box in my safe with a few keepsakes from our relationship in it, including our wedding rings. I haven't kept them for any sentimental reasons, I just don't really know what to do with them.

After Chantelle died, I asked her sister if she'd like her jewellery. She told me to poke it up my arse. That wasn't an option, so I put it in my safe and that's where it's stayed, mostly forgotten.

Simone Price was Chantelle's half-sister; same mum, but different dads. I've no idea who her biological father is, but Colin, Chantelle's dad, always looked after her right. Colin and I were joint owners of a club. When he died, Elle inherited her dad's share. I assumed after Elle's death, it would go to me, but she left it to her sister. I can only assume she did it because it was the only thing she had that was solely in her name. I also don't suppose for a minute she expected to die so young.

I let the heat from the jets of water penetrate my skin and sooth my muscles as I think about how ironic it was that Simone eventually sold Elle's share of the club to the Layton's. Entwining mine and Georgia's lives before we even realised it.

I would never forget the first time I noticed her walk into my wine bar. I'd spent the hot August day on the golf course, getting my arse whipped by Robbie. After, I'd gone back to my flat to shower and change, and as I came down the stairs and into the bar, I saw her.

She was tall, taller than the two girls she was with, and my eyes were drawn to her as she flicked her long dark hair over her shoulder. I moved through the bar without taking my eyes off her, desperate for a good look at her face.

I reached my brother and a couple of mates he was standing with at the bar, and he passed me a bourbon. I nodded a thank you and took my eyes from her, to meet his for a split second. When I looked over to where she was standing, she'd turned her back to me, but I positioned myself at the bar so I could watch her. I didn't have a clue what the draw was; I just needed to see that face.

I chatted mindless shit with Rob, Tony, and Gary at the bar, but all the while, I took in her long legs and the fitted black dress she was wearing. She was skinny, a lot skinnier than most birds I'd been with … well, the ones I could remember anyway. I got this weird uncomfortable feeling in my gut at that moment, like, I don't know. It just felt wrong to be thinking about other birds while I was looking at her.

My life was just getting back on track after the chaos that ensued after the death of my wife. If I were being totally honest, things had been spiralling out of control for some time before that. The drink, the coke, the women—I sampled them all to excess, and then after my marriage, the excesses became something of an addiction.

I'd married Elle out of a sense of duty and for the good of the family. Robbie was already engaged to Teresa, Josh just too young and irresponsible, and so it was left to me. I had felt the pressure to do right by the family business and marry Colin Turner's only surviving heir and strengthen the King name by tying all of his businesses to ours.

Robbie was happy, we had strength in numbers and money coming in from all over the country. We kept our noses clean and our pockets lined. We didn't step on anyone's toes and didn't encroach on anyone else's manor. We didn't need to. Life was sweet. But I was miserable. Chantelle had been around for most of my life. Our parents were friends, and so she was just there. Holidays, daytrips, family gatherings, she was there. She was pale and blonde and never wanted to join in any of our rough "boy" games when we were kids.

I didn't like or dislike her as we were growing up. I just didn't think much about her to have an opinion either way. As we got older and hormones started to play a part, things changed a little. She got boobs, so yeah, I noticed her more. She was still quiet and never wanted to sneak outside for a cigarette when we were together at parties and the grownups were drunk. She never wanted to get involved when we stuffed potatoes into the exhaust pipes of all the cars in her dad's driveway during Sunday afternoon BBQs. She would never swim in the ocean when our families went to Spain together for holidays, opting to lie back on the beach alone and watch the rest of us from a distance instead.

She was a nice enough girl, but she just had nothing about her. No spark. No sense of adventure. Nothing. And yet, I still married her.

I regret that decision every single day of my life. If I had stood my ground and said no, she'd probably still be alive today. And this guilt I feel is exactly the reason why I understand the anguish in Georgia's eyes when she cries over Sean. I totally get it.

I love my life. I love my wife and my kids and everything we've built together. I wouldn't change it for the world. Does that mean I'm glad that Elle died? If she hadn't, the life I have now wouldn't exist. I couldn't have this life without the death of another, and although I don't wear my emotions on the outside like Georgia does, the guilt is still something I struggle with on a daily basis.

I didn't love Chantelle, but I still think about her death and the death of my son every single day, so I can only imagine what Georgia goes through while battling her demons over losing Sean.

They died, we didn't. It's pointless beating ourselves up over it. It won't change anything. I love her, and she loves me. We've been blessed with four amazing children, and since I'm not a religious person, I thank modern science, the wank bank, and my sisters-in-law for that.

While I've learned to accept all of this and move on, Georgia still struggles.

Georgia.

That first night I saw her at Kings, I'd watched and I'd watched, and then finally, she turned around. She'd moved to the other side of her friend that was sitting on a stool to let someone pass, and she hadn't moved back.

She was stunning. Olive skin and the most amazing blue eyes.

The saddest eyes I'd ever seen.

I wanted to go to her and find out why she looked so sad so I could put it all right.

The two girls she was with were also both very pretty, but they had nothing on her …

"S'cuse me please, mate. Can I just squeeze in there so I can get served?" a voice asked from beside me in a strong Essex accent. When I turned my head, the blonde girl that was with Little Miss Sad Eyes was standing behind me.

"You can squeeze right in here if you wanna, sweetheart," Gary told her. She looked at the space he'd made for her and then at his hands.

"You touch my arse, and I'll knock you the fuck out, Grandad." Robbie spat his beer, Tony threw his head back and laughed, and even I smiled. Gary just stared at her open-mouthed.

"Who the fuck you calling Grandad, you cheeky little cow?"

Gary was close to forty but told everyone he was thirty-two. He was a good-looking bloke and had no trouble whatsoever pulling the birds, so why he lied, I have no clue.

"You. You gonna move and let me get served or d'ya need your Zimmer frame first?"

"I'll give you fucking Zimmer frame …"

"Gaz!" I interrupted him. "Give the lady some space," I ordered.

"What lady? There's no lady around here," he said, probably

thinking he was clever.

I never even saw her hand move, but I heard the crack as her palm made contact with his cheek. I stepped between them before he could react.

Great, just what I needed. For the first time since getting out of rehab, I finally see a bird that stirs my interest, and Gaz goes and insults her mate.

"You, fuck off with the insults," I told him over my shoulder. "And you, blondie, keep your hands to yourself." She opened her mouth to speak, but I kept going. "Now, what would you like to drink? It's on me." Her mouth closed and her face softened.

"Thanks, good to see one of you has got some manners. We'll have a bottle of wine please. White, make it decent, none of that Liebfraumilch shit." That comment left me standing there with my mouth hanging open. That girl had more front than Tesco and nothing had changed in all the years I've known Ash.

I gestured to Keith, my barman, and ordered a bottle of wine and a bottle of Moët. I placed the bottle of wine in blondies hand.

"You got an ice bucket on your table?" She narrowed her eyes and looked at me.

"I might be from Essex, mate, but I've got some class. I do not drink my white wine warm."

"That's good to know," was all I could think to say. This girl was like a mini tornado blowing through.

"Take this to your table, too. I'll send someone over with some glasses and have them cork and pour it for you."

She looked from the bottle of bubbly to me before taking it. "Cheers, mate, you're a diamond," she said with a wink, sounding just like something from a Dickens' novel.

"And you, mate, are a complete tosser," she called out to Gary, who I assumed was glaring over my shoulder at her.

She headed off back to her table and her mates, while I asked Keith to go over with some champagne glasses. I ordered myself another drink and turned back around just in time to see Rob, Tony, and Gaz raise their glasses towards the girls.

I looked in the direction the boys were, and my eyes met her blue eyes, and fuck me if her stare didn't do things to my dick.

At that moment, something—I have no clue what, but something—passed between us. I knew, in that instant, I knew I had to have that girl. I had to know her, and I had to have her. Not in my bar. Not in my bed. I had to have her in my life and by my side. For good.

Oh, if only it had been that easy.

SEVEN
Cameron

I walk out of our bathroom and towards our bed, where my wife is now lying naked and sleeping soundly. I watch her for a while, debating on whether to wake her, to slip inside her from behind while she sleeps, or to leave her be. Neither of us slept well Friday or Saturday night but it would seem I've managed to catch up by sleeping all of Sunday away.

Georgia's lying in her usual recovery position, on her stomach, left leg bent out to the side, both her arms crossed under her pillow. Her long hair is spread everywhere, and I take a few seconds to brush it back from her flawless face.

We argued about her getting Botox the week before I went away. She thinks she needs it. I don't. Jimmie and Ash have both had a little help over the last few years, I even paid for Ash to get a tummy tuck after she carried our twins for us, but now Georgia is feeling left out and wants to get crap pumped into her pretty face when there is absolutely no fucking need for it.

I've learned over the years that saying no to Georgia is a pointless exercise. So, rather than arguing with her and worrying that she would go off and do something drastic to herself while I was away, we cut a deal. She wouldn't have any work done until she was at least fifty, and I would grow my hair back to how it was when we first met. And as easy as that, it was all sorted. Happy days.

I pull the quilt over my wife's naked back and leave her to sleep. She'll keep till morning and my hard-on definitely isn't going anywhere.

I head downstairs in search of food. Since my body clock is shot to bits and my belly has no clue what time zone it's on, my stomach is growling loudly at me.

I hunt through the fridge for food, steering well clear of anything Georgia might have made. I love my wife to distraction but she can't cook for shit. She tries. She's spent endless hours with her mum and Marian, watching and taking notes, but nah, none of it helped.

I think Georgia just has too many things going on in her head at once. She bakes a cake and forgets if she put sugar in. She puts something in the oven and forgets that it's there. I've come home before to find the timer on the oven will be bleeping. When I ask George, "What ya cooking?" her response will be, "Nothing, why? ... Shit, I wondered what that noise was." As if the house filling with smoke and the burning smell weren't clue enough.

Fried egg sandwich, that's the only thing she doesn't mess up, but that don't help me or the kids out because she won't let us eat fried food at home.

We had a few months of misery when Marian hung up her apron, living on burnt offerings and takeaways before Georgia finally conceded and we got a new housekeeper. Her name's Christine and she comes in Monday thru Thursday. She cooks the dinner, vacuums, mops, irons, and cleans all of the bathrooms except the kid's.

The kids are in charge of their own bathrooms and have worked out their own little routine for clearing the table, loading and unloading the dishwasher, and getting in the washing if it's been hung out on the line to dry.

Our kids have grown up privileged, but we've made sure they aren't spoilt in anything other than love and attention.

I make myself a cheese and tuna toasted sandwich and open a beer. Heading into my office, I open my laptop and read through my e-mails, reply to a few, and then decide to go watch some telly.

All the time I'm doing this, I'm acutely aware that all I really want to do is go into Georgia's office and read some more of those letters.

Those fucking letters that are causing so much tension between us.

I don't care if she reads them and they make her cry … much.

I just wish she'd hurry up and get it over with.

I just care about how upset it's making her. My telling her not to feel guilty is pointless. Nothing I say will change how she feels, so the sooner she gets them read, the sooner we can move on with our lives.

In the meantime, I just wanna have a little read through them, so if there is anything in them that's too upsetting for her, at least I'm prepared. That's what I tell myself anyway as I head out of *my* office and into my *wife's*, grabbing another beer from the fridge on my way.

I sit at her desk with just a lamp on for light. It looks like two bits of rusty metal with a bare light bulb hanging from it, "industrial" Georgia calls it, scrap metal is more like it.

The first stack of letters I come to are in envelopes but have no stamps or address written across the front. They just say "Gia" in what I now know to be Sean McCarthy's handwriting.

I open the first one, lean back in the leather chair, and take a swig of my beer.

Gia,
I'm watching you sleep as I write this. D'ya think that's creepy?

I don't care if you do. I've been away from you for two whole weeks while I worked. I wanted you with me, but I understand your reasons for not wanting to go back to the States. Everyone there remembered us announcing the pregnancy on New Year's Eve, and everyone was offering me their condolences and sending you their love and best wishes. It was painful, and it was hard to hear on my own. I wanted you with me, but at the same time, I was glad you stayed home and didn't have to listen to it all.

We'll never forget Baby M. We'll always make sure he's a part of our lives. I know we don't know for sure, but I'm pretty positive he's a boy.

I can't begin to tell you how fuckin happy I am right now, you coming to the airport to surprise me and the fact you waited for me to get home before you took the pregnancy test.

Pregnancy.

Pregnant.

We're pregnant, G. We're gonna have a fuckin' baby.

My cheeks ache because I've smiled so much over the past few hours. Things will be good this time. I just know it.

We'll see the doctor Monday and make sure you get the best of care.

You can moan all you want at me, woman, but I will be waiting on you hand and foot. Hand and fucking foot. No lifting, stretching, and definitely no horse riding.

A baby, G. I'm so fucking happy (did I say that already?) and so proud of you. I'm so glad this year has turned around for us. It started off so fucked. I was so scared, G. So fucking scared I was losing you. So many thoughts were going through my head, you've no clue, babe. No fuckin clue about the dark place I was in. I was thinking all sorts. Convinced you were leaving me.

And now, here we are, out the other side, still going strong. Sean and Georgia. Georgia and Sean. The way it's meant to be, except now it's gonna be Sean and Georgia and baby Beau.

I know you're gonna shake your head when you read this, but mark my words, gorgeous wife of mine, that's another boy I've put in your belly, and we will be calling him Beau. No girls for us until she has at least two or three big brothers to look after her.

I love you. Please don't forget that. You're not just my wife and lover, you're my best friend as well, so just remember that and please don't shut me out.

I know you're gonna be nervous after what happened last time, believe me, I know. I'm fucking shitting myself, but I want you to talk to me, please? If you're worried about anything, share it with me. He's my baby too, remember? Which means I now have the both of you to worry about. That's my job, though. It's my role in all of this. You keep our little man tucked up safe and warm in your belly till he's big enough to meet us, and I'll do all the worrying for the both of us. Deal?

Right, my eyes are getting heavy. This is my fourth time zone in three days. I love ya, G. I think I'm the happiest bloke on the planet right now, but I need to sleep. Night, G. Night, Beau. Love ya both xxx

P.S. Just in case I'm wrong and you're a Lilly not a Beau, don't worry, I'm your daddy and it'll be my job to protect you till we get you some brothers x

My head pounds as I finish my second beer. No wonder she loved him so much. Fuck, if I were a woman, even I'd— Nah, let's not go there.

I could never compete with that. I love Georgia and my kids just as much as he loved her and their kids. I would just never be able to put it into words as eloquently as he does … did.

I don't have an artistic bone in my body. A doodle of a cock and balls is a about my limit, I might add pubes and spunk squirting out the end if I'm feeling particularly arts and craftsy, but that's where my artistic flair ends.

Georgia, on the other hand, has her own fashion line that's sold exclusively through Posh Frocks, and she's been hands on with every design. She refuses just to put her name and face to it and now draws and sketches her own ideas and is on board throughout the entire production, even modelling some of them for magazines herself.

She can sing and play guitar and she has designed a couple of custom-made pieces of furniture for our home when she couldn't find what she wanted in the shops. Even this office, she knew exactly how she wanted it to look and feel and worked with the decorators to get it to how she wanted it. No wonder she left me and went back to him.

My chest feels tight when I think about one of the worst moments of my life. So much so that I know I need something stronger than beer. I go into my office and grab my Laphroaig and a whisky tumbler.

I set them down on Georgia's desk, pour the whisky from the decanter and into the glass, and take a sip.

When Georgia left me and went back to Sean, I really never saw it coming. I honestly thought we were on the same page. We were spending a lot of our days and most of our nights together, and I really believed we were ready to move in and start to make a life together. Never in my life have I gotten something so wrong. I'd lost my wife and unborn son but nothing hurt like losing Georgia when she left me for Sean McCarthy …

Our argument that Thursday night at dinner had been over something so petty I can't even remember what it was. I know I was in a shitty mood. I said something, she said something back, I replied, and she got up and left.

I should've followed her. Instead, I ordered another drink, sat, and drank it, thinking I was giving my angry Kitten time to calm down. I knew Benny was outside in the Jag, and I fully expected to find her sitting out there waiting for me when I finally paid the bill and stepped outside. Biggest. Mistake. Of. My. Fucking. Life.

"Where the fuck is she, Ben?" I asked him as I opened the car door and found the back seat empty.

"She stormed off up the alley, boss. The motor won't fit down there so I couldn't follow. I didn't wanna go around the block to the road in case you came out and wondered where the fuck we were."

I climbed into the front seat next to him. "Go to her place, she probably jumped in a cab and went home."

I sent Benny home and let myself into Georgia's place, using the key she had given me.

It was empty.

I was both pissed off and worried and even more angry that I cared enough to worry. I couldn't call anyone. Bailey and Lennon had threatened me with a slow painful death if I ever upset her, so I wasn't about to go there, and I had no contact details for her other brother, Marley. He'd probably just tell the other two anyway, or worse still, their dad. I most definitely didn't want Frank Layton on my case on top of everything else.

I had been having a spot of bother with a couple brothels and coffee houses we owned in Amsterdam. It was all legal and above board, but the Russians recently moved into the area and were pushing their luck. Trying to make me pay for protection. Me? I didn't fucking think so. They obviously had no clue who they were dealing with, so I sent a dozen blokes over there to introduce themselves. I thought they'd gotten the message. Then two nights ago, one of the coffee shops burnt down and three of our girls were roughed up. A point needed to be made, and it had to be made in person. We were gonna have to fly to Amsterdam sometime soon and sort this out ourselves, which was the last thing I needed. I was in the middle of negotiating the purchase of a house for myself and Georgia. I had thought it was a done deal. I had thought my offer had been accepted. Apparently, I had been wrong. I got a lot of things wrong that week.

I eventually crawled into Georgia's bed, and like the sad fuck I was, I fell asleep with my face buried in her pillow.

There was no sign of her at her flat the next morning. I went down to the shop and asked down there. I didn't know the girl who was working, but she made some calls and then told me Georgia was taking a few days off.

I went back to my flat and checked my answerphone, nothing except a message from Benny telling me I needed to get in touch with him ASAP regarding our "Russian problem". I showered and went down to my office at the back of the wine bar.

Robbie was waiting for me.

"Rob?"

"You need to fly over to Amsterdam this afternoon. The rest of the boys are on the ferry on their way over there now. I've set up a meet with you and Nikolay Kadnikov for tomorrow."

Fuck, I thought I'd at least have the weekend to smooth things over with Georgia and get this house deal done.

"Why the rush?"

"The rush, little brother, is because they slapped another one of our girls last night. Sending the boys on their own didn't work, so one of us needs to go. Josh is still in Marbella, Teresa is due to have the baby any day and needs me close, so that, sunshine, just leaves you. Flight's booked, and you need to be at City Airport by three. You fly out at four thirty."

"For fuck's sake, can't this wait till Monday?"

"No, it can't. I promised Krystal we'd get this sorted. We've always looked after our girls, and right now, they're all too terrified to take a trip to the supermarket or to pick their kids up from school in case another warning gets delivered. Krystal said Marika's nose was broken last night. These Russian's are taking the piss. I want it sorted, today. Whatever piece of fanny you've got lined up can keep till next week."

I was so pissed off by all of this, I was pacing. I didn't pace. Not until I'd met Georgia, anyway.

"Georgia is not a piece of fanny. Don't fucking talk about her like that," I warned him before sitting myself down in my office chair—the "twirling" chair.

"Georgia? Frank Layton's daughter? You still tapping that? Playing with fire there, bruv. When big bad Frank finds out, you won't just get burned, you'll get fucking cremated."

"Fuck off, Rob. He's the least of my worries."

"Oh really? Since when did your balls get so big, Bertie Big Bollocks? Coz I've never met anyone that wasn't at least a little bit scared of Frank or his psycho brother Fin, not to mention crazy fucking Bailey. You must want your brains testing."

My foot was tapping and my jaw was twitching. I was also giving myself a headache from grinding my teeth together. I wanted to knock my brother the fuck out.

"I'm buying a house, I'm gonna ask her to move in with me. We'll talk to her dad before then. Of course, whether I get his blessing or not, it's gonna happen."

"Whoa, whoa, whoa, you're buying a house but you haven't asked her to move in yet? What if she says no?"

"She won't."

"Don't you think she might wanna say in what type of house she lives in if she does say yes then? Does she not get to choose it with you?"

Fuck. I hadn't thought of that.

"It's got stables and it's near her mum, she'll love it."

"I fucking hope so, mate." He clicked the nib of the pen he was holding continuously as he spoke, something else that pissed me off. I snatched it out of his hand, snapped it in half, and threw it across the room.

My phone rang.

"Speak," I ordered.

"Cam?"

My heart bounced about inside my chest and my stomach went into free fall at the sound of her voice.

"Kitten?" I watched as my brother's eyebrows shot up to his hairline when I said her name, so I raised mine and gave him a look that said, "Not one word, dick head, not one fucking word." He picked up another pen from the pot on my desk and started clicking it. I wanted to snap off his thumb.

"Fuck. Where the fuck are you? Don't you ever do something like that to me again, you fuckin hear me? I've been worried sick. Where are you?"

I cracked my jaw to relieve some tension while I waited for her answer.

"I'm sorry. I'm fine. I should've called you last night. I didn't mean to make you worry."

Worry? Fucking worry? The three times I'd woken during the night, I'd worn holes in her bedroom carpet as I paced and tried to think where I should start to look for her.

Apparently, I did pace.

I wanted to shout at her, but I didn't want her hanging up on me.

This skinny little girl had me so twisted up in knots, I didn't know which way was up any more.

"Where are you? I'll come and get you," I said calmly. I knew she didn't have her car. It was still parked outside her flat when I'd left there that morning.

"No, no. it's fine. I don't need collecting." She sounded panicked. Warning bells sort of went off, but I chose to ignore them.

I turned the chair around and faced the wall in my office so I didn't have to look at my brother's obvious pleasure over finding out this girl had me by the balls.

"You okay? I missed you," I told her quietly. She said nothing. More alarm bells. I stamped on them till they shut the fuck up. Shoulda gone with my gut.

"I stayed at yours last night. I needed to be able to smell you. I fuckin' hated sleeping in your bed and waking up alone."

Robbie made a gaging noise from behind me. I spun the chair around, picked up the pot containing the pens, and launched it at him. My stapler followed.

She was silent. Nothing but the sound of her breathing was coming through the phone, but I could barely hear it over the sound of my own heart beating loudly in my ears.

"Georgia, you still there?"

"Yeah, yeah, I'm still here. Look, Cam, we need to talk."

No, no we do not need to talk.

"But not on the phone. I need to see you in person."

Fuck. I closed my eyes and tried not to voice the panic rising in my chest.

"Well, I just said I'd come and get you, but I only have an hour. I have a flight to catch at four thirty. I won't be back until Monday."

"Well, I'll just wait and see you Monday then."

Monday? Monday was forever away.

"I'd really like to see you now, Kitten." I spun in the chair back away from my brother, who was still rubbing his forehead where the stapler had hit him. Serves the wanker right.

"Monday's a long way off, and I want to show you how sorry I am for being such a prick last night."

"Fuck Me!" my brother whisper shouted. "I'm gonna take a piss, I can't listen to any more of this." He got up and went into my bathroom.

"I can't, Cam. You don't have to keep apologising. You shouldn't have behaved like a prick, and I shouldn't have stormed off like a diva. Go catch your flight and give me a call on Monday once you're home."

Fuck my luck and fuck those Russians. I raked my hand through my hair and let out a long sigh.

"If I could get out of it, George, I would, but something's come up with some business I have going on in Amsterdam, and I need to fly over and sort it out. I only just found out myself I had to go."

"It's okay, you go and sort out your business and we'll talk on Monday."

Tell her you love her, tell her how you feel …

"I miss you, Kitten. Have a good weekend."

Tell her for fuck's sake!

"You too, Cam. Bye."

Fucking tell her. My own voice roared in my head.

"George, I ..." The door to my bathroom swung open and my brother stepped back into my office.

"Nothing, I'll see you Monday."

I flew to Amsterdam rearranged the meeting with Kadnikov and saw him Friday night. I was thoroughly fucked off with the situation and the inconvenience it had caused me. I took my fucked offness out on his face and made him see the error of his ways. It was NOT okay to hit women, and it was NOT okay to burn down buildings we owned. We would NOT be paying him for protection. He would NOT mess with us again. He got my point, along with a broken nose.

I got a flight home Saturday lunch time.

Before we took off, I called Georgia, she'd slept in and I'd woken her up. Her voice was all croaky and as sexy as fuck. I turned my back to the airport crowds and tried to readjust my hard-on as I spoke to her on the phone.

She was even less talkative than she'd been when she called me Friday morning. All I learned was that she'd gone out to an Indian restaurant with Jimmie Friday night, but she didn't drink much because she was saving herself for Ashley's party. In that split second, I decided not to tell her I was coming home and just to turn up at her place to surprise her later.

Once we landed, I went home to shower before going over to Georgia's and found a message waiting from the estate agent on my answerphone. The offer on the house I'd spent the last two weeks trying to buy had finally been accepted.

I didn't call Georgia or go to her place that afternoon, deciding to turn up at Ashley's birthday party that night and surprise her instead.

She was fucking surprised all right.

The first thing I noticed when I pulled into my reserved spot was the extra security in place, even at the back of the building. I walked around to the front, where there were not only more of my staff than usual but also faces I didn't recognise.

"What's going on?" I asked Steve, one of my head doorman.

"Private party, boss. Frank's boy, the one that's in the band? He's up there with another bloke from the band."

I looked around at the queue as he spoke and spotted a few photographers hanging about. Oh well, it'd be good publicity for the club and would most definitely raise our profile having them here.

"Who's paying for all the extra security?" I asked him.

"Nothing to do with us, boss. They came with the band. Bailey's inside, have a chat with him."

I nodded my head but I was only half listening. Georgia was inside, and after two lonely nights without her in my bed, I planned to drag her out of there just as soon as she'd let me.

I had a key with me. It wasn't the actual key to the house I'd bought, but she wouldn't know that. I was gonna put it into a glass of champagne and pass it to her.

The club was packed to capacity, and the bars were four deep with people waiting to be served. I made my way through the crowds and up the stairs to the VIP area.

Bailey stepped in front of me, blocking my path from the bar to the dance floor in the sectioned off area.

"I thought you were away till next week?" he questioned. His eyebrows were drawn down and he blinked rapidly as a look of complete panic washed over his face. It was only there for a few seconds before he composed himself. Bailey Layton looked worried, what the fuck was that all about?

"I got things sorted sooner than expected and thought I'd fly straight home to surprise your sister."

He swallowed hard and nodded his head slowly. He wasn't happy that we were together, but he'd been pretty good about things so far. I wasn't sure how he was gonna feel about Georgia moving in with me, though. Fuck, I missed her. I needed to see those pretty blue eyes that finally had some light back in them.

"Where is she?"

He shrugged his shoulders and sat himself down on a bar stool. "Not sure, but if I know Georgia, she's probably dancing. Have a drink."

He caught the attention of Kelly, one of our barmaids, and motioned with his finger between us. She brought over a bottle of bourbon and two glasses, moving the ice bucket along the bar so it was within our reach.

"So, your brother's here, the one that's in Carnage?"

"Er, yeah. Yeah he is. Both my brothers are here." He looked all around himself as he spoke. He looked like he was either in pain, or he was terrified.

What the fuck was going on?

My office door opened.

"I think George said she was gonna go to the dance floor downstairs, perhaps you'd be better off looking for her there," Bailey said, wiping the sweat that was shining on his forehead.

"Why the fuck would she go down there?"

A bloke that seemed vaguely familiar appeared over Bailey's shoulder, dangling a bunch of keys.

"Cheers, mate. We owe you big time."

I looked from the bloke, to the keys, to Bailey.

He closed his eyes and seemed to hold his breath before turning around on the stool he was sitting on. I followed his gaze.

Kitten.

"You wanna drink, baby?" the bloke, the key-dangling fucker, kissed her temple and asked.

I was torn between telling him to take his hands off my woman and smiling at her. I opened my mouth to speak when realisation of who he was started to seep into my poor, stupid, love-fucked brain.

The singer from the band.

Mac?

Maca?

Something like that.

I looked from her to him, he'd kissed her and he was holding her hand. I looked at her face. Her mouth was slightly open, as if she were about to speak, and her eyes were wide. My gaze swung back to him to find him looking at her as if she were the most beautiful, amazing creature to have ever graced the earth.

He'd kissed her.

He was holding her hand.

I couldn't fucking breathe.

"Gia, what's wrong?" he asked her gently. Love, devotion, concern, and worship all too obvious in his voice. My heart stopped beating. For a few split seconds, I thought I was going to choke on it as it crawled from my chest and lodged itself in my throat.

Two days.

I'd been gone for two fucking days.

I needed to get out of there.

I needed to … I had no clue what I needed, but it needed to make me numb.

I turned to walk away.

"Cam?"

That voice. Her voice. She was calling my name, talking to me. Hope began to infiltrate the empty spot my heart had just left vacant, and stupidly, for a few seconds, I allowed it to affect my way of thinking. I'd got it all wrong, they were friends, just her brother's band mate. She'd probably known him for years. I had nothing to worry about. She wouldn't do that to me, not my Kitten.

I swung back around, and the control I had over my own fists was hanging tenuously by a thread.

Bailey jerked in his stool. He could read me like a book. Him and I were the same, it was in our genes. We could read a person's body language from ten feet away and sniff out trouble from twenty.

Because I needed to do something—anything other than stand

there, dying—I held out my hand.

"Cameron King, joint owner of the place."

"Sean McCarthy."

My world ended. I nodded in acknowledgment of this fact.

"You're Sean? The lead singer of Carnage. Of course." I had no clue how I managed to string that sentence together.

He looked from me to her.

"Do you need a minute to talk?"

He knew. That fucker knew about me.

I sure as shit knew about him. Sean. Her Sean.

She gave her head a slight nod in answer to his question.

I wasn't sure whose head I wanted to rip off the most—hers, his, or my own.

He said something in her ear and then turned to me, "I'm gonna go get a drink from the other bar."

Good. Fuck off and don't come back. I wanted to wrap my hands around his throat and squeeze.

"I'll leave you two to talk," Bailey stated in his rough voice.

"Cam." She reached out to touch my arm, hesitated, and then put it back down to her side.

Touch me. Please touch me and tell me that I've got this all wrong. I need that. I need you, Kitten.

"I'm so sorry. I didn't want to tell you over the phone."

No. No. No. This wasn't the way things were supposed to go.

I'd bought a house.

For us.

A fucking house with stables.

She was killing me. Every word she spoke killed me a little more.

"I thought you were away till Monday. I wanted to tell you then, face to face."

I thought she felt the same as I did. I thought what we had meant something to both of us. I flew home early. I bought a house. I bought a house with fucking stables. For her. It was all for her. I needed to make her see. I should've gone after her Thursday night. I should've told her on the phone how I felt. I should've done things differently.

"I came home early to surprise you. I wanted to see you, to tell you, to show you how sorry I am for my behaviour on Thursday night. Kitten, you remember that? Thursday. Two fucking days ago?" I was losing it.

I had never hated and loved someone so much in my life, would never have thought it was possible.

"Two nights ago, Kitten, when I stupidly thought you were in a relationship with me." I punched my fist into my own chest, but it did nothing to subdue the anger building inside me.

Georgia flinched. "I was. We was ..."

I glared at her whilst battling to control the rage burning in every part of me.

I picked up my drink from the bar and downed it in one go. I needed more—more than bourbon, more than beer. There was only one thing that would give me what I needed. One thing that would make me feel like I was invincible and not dying a slow, painful, excruciating death with every word that came out of her lying, cheating, whoreish mouth.

"Sean McCarthy, now why didn't I work that one out?" I asked her through gritted teeth, barely holding back the need to throw up at the mention of his name. "I knew all about Sean. I just didn't realise it was *that* Sean."

Why didn't I? How had I never worked that one out? Because I was a love-fucked cunt that was why.

"I didn't stand a chance did I? Me or a twenty-two-year-old fucking rock god?"

"Cam, please. It's not like that. I've known him since I was eleven years old. He was my boyfriend from the age of thirteen."

She looked at the ground before looking back at me with those beautiful and oh so blue eyes.

"He's the only boy I've ever loved."

Boom. There it was, the very last of my will to live leaving my body.

"Thanks, Kitten, thanks for that."

I turned and walked away, leaving my love and my life at Georgia's feet.

I grabbed a couple of bottles of bourbon from the bar downstairs and took them home with me. I'd almost finished the first one by the time I'd pulled up outside the wine bar.

When I got to my flat, I went straight to my bedside chest of drawers and found an old contacts book.

All it took was one call. One call, and all of my hard work to get and stay straight the last few years went to shit. What did it matter? I had nothing to live for anyway. If I died, I died. Anything was better than thinking, than remembering her.

EIGHT
Georgia

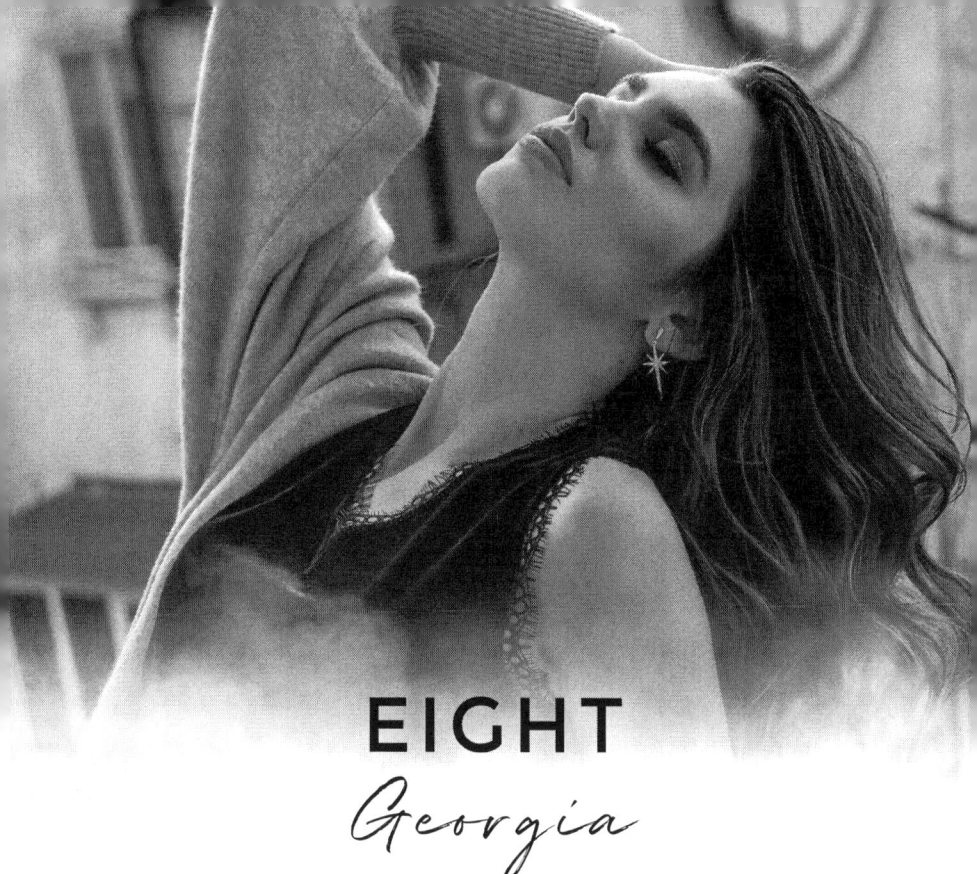

I'm not sure what wakes me, probably the turmoil that I've got going on in my head right now.

This weekend has been horrible and it is all my fault. I thought I was ready to finally have a read through all of Sean's old letters. I was wrong. It isn't just about the words they contain, it's a combination of hurt, anger, and guilt. It would've all been so different if one of us had just reached out to the other. Our lives would have taken such different paths if we hadn't remained apart for those four years.

But then what?

Where would Cam have fit in the picture if Sean and I had married and started a family at eighteen like we had planned? Would I have had him in my life? Would we have still somehow ended up together? Would our children even exist if Sean hadn't died? I always thought I would have given anything for Sean to still be alive, but I would never give up my family and what I have with Cam.

So what does that mean? What does it say about me as a person? A wife and mother?

I am so sick of it all going around in my head. I am driving myself nuts, so I've no clue how Cam must be feeling having to watch me struggle with all of this. Again.

I had never doubted us or the strength of our relationship until yesterday. When he didn't get up to take the kids to dinner with me, I really thought he'd finally had enough of me and my meltdowns. I made excuses to the kids about him being tired and forced my food down when we got to the restaurant. I smiled and joked with the kids the entire time we were out, but on the inside, I was falling apart.

On the drive home, One Direction's "History" came on the radio. I am just grateful that the car is dark and the kids are too engrossed in their phones to notice my tears.

I couldn't lose him. I wouldn't survive without his love. I went over a hundred scenarios in my head, considering different ways to convince him not to leave me.

I'd drunk a bottle of wine once I got home and the kids had gone to their rooms. When I finally plucked up the courage to go upstairs and face him, I found him still in our bed and in the middle of a nightmare.

He'd told me it was jetlag. He tried to reassure me that he was fine and that we were good, but I wasn't convinced.

I slide my leg across to Cams side of the bed to find it cold and empty. The surge of adrenalin that happens when the self-doubt I'd been suffering from makes a rapid reappearance, makes my stomach churn. I get up and go to the bathroom, before grabbing a T-shirt that Cam left hanging over the back of the chair and put it on. God, I love the way he smells. He has a half dozen different aftershaves in his bathroom cupboard, but the Givenchy he's been wearing since we first met is still my favourite.

I pad down the stairs barefoot and along the hallway to our family room.

Empty.

I make my way back down the hall to Cam's office, which is also empty. It's as I'm backing out that I notice a thin sliver of light coming from under the door to *my* office.

Fuck!

There's only one reason he would be in there, and its not so that he can add himself to the kid's growth charts pencilled on the wall.

My husband is an inherently nosey person. He, Marley, and Lennon often have conference calls about juicy bits of gossip they may have heard about someone we know. I kid you not, Ash, Jimmie, and I have nicknamed them T. M. and Z. They are as up on the gossip as my girls. For someone who doesn't "do" social media, Cam still manages to know the names of every one of those Kardashian kids.

I push at the door with my fingertips and it opens silently.

He's sitting at my desk with his back to the room, a stack of Sean's letters to the side of him, two sheets of paper in one hand, and a crystal whiskey tumbler in the other.

It's three in the morning. My husband is sitting in my office, reading the words of love, Sean, my now dead husband had written for me, whilst sipping on whiskey.

For me? Is that really the right term? He'd written them *to* me, but I'm not sure he ever planned for me to see all of them. Some, maybe. But there were a few I think he may have removed before letting me have a read.

I guess I'll never know.

Cam takes a sip of his drink and lets out a long sigh.

"What are you doing?" I ask him quietly.

The glass he has in his hand jerks in surprise at the sound of my voice, and I watch as the amber liquid sloshes from side to side. As the light from my desk lamp catches it, I can't help but to compare the colour to Sean's eyes. His were brown, with little flecks of gold, whiskey coloured. Cam's are a rich, warm brown, looking almost black when he's turned on or angry.

Tallulah is the only one of our children to get my blue eyes. The other three have dark eyes like their dad.

I wonder what colour eyes Baby M and Beau would've had?

"*Shit,* Kitten you made me jump."

And it's those kinds of thoughts that are tearing me apart. Two of my children had to die in order for the other three to exist. Is that how it works? I am not a believer in God, but surely if he did exist, he wouldn't force us to make choices like that?

"Georgia?" Cam interrupts my theological musings.

"Wha?"

"I said get your arse over here, woman."

I blink a few times before stepping fully into the room and making my way over to him.

I climb sideways into his lap. He wraps one big arm around my back and one across my hips, sliding his hand up my T-shirt so he can cup my bare arse and pull me into him.

He rubs his nose into my hair, over my ear, and down my neck. I tilt my head to the side, allowing him better access. Enjoying the sensation of goose bumps spreading across my skin from each point of contact his nose and warm breath make.

Wrapping my arms around his neck, I turn myself to face him. He's biting down on his bottom lip and his eyes are searching my face, looking sexy as fuck while he does it.

"Georgia, would you tell me if I ever weren't enough for you?"

What. The. Actual. Fuck?

I open my mouth, but he speaks again before I can.

"I know I don't get the whole music thing and your love of it. I can't paint, or draw, or design clothes and furniture. I'm not always good with words. I can't write songs for or about you like he did, but that doesn't mean I don't love you any less than he did. I just ..."

My eyes fill with tears, and I don't even attempt to stop them from falling as I interrupt him.

"No. No, Cam. Please stop. Of course you're enough. You're everything. Too much sometimes."

I hold his face in both my hands and kiss him repeatedly, speaking through my tears.

"I love you, Cam. You're my whole world. You and the kids are the reason I exist. You're my everything. Every-fucking-thing. Please don't ever doubt that. These last few days, yesterday especially, have been horrible. I really thought I'd pushed you away. That you were finally sick enough of my bullshit to leave me."

"I'd never leave you, Kitten. Never, and it pisses me the fuck off that you'd think for a moment that I would."

"Well, that's how I feel about you thinking you're not enough. Why would you ever think that? You're more man than most women could ever handle."

Cameron King is the most confident—almost to the point of being arrogant—man I've ever met, and I absolutely hate that I've made him doubt himself.

He tilts his hips up and makes small circular movements, grinding his dick into my arse.

"I'm not talking about the size of my dick and the ability I have to fuck you into multiple orgasms with it."

There he is. That right there is my Cam. My TDH.

"Then what, Tiger?"

"I can't write you love songs or send you love letters telling you the way I feel."

So, that's what this is all about? I might just set a torch to those bloody letters and never read another word.

"But *he* didn't have a nine-and-a-half-inch dick." My attempt at humour fails miserably.

His face remains blank as he blinks his eyes whilst staring at me for a few seconds.

"What the fuck has that got to do with anything? My dicks bigger than most blokes."

"And most blokes can't write songs or a love letter like Sean McCarthy."

"I'm well aware of that; I'm one of them."

"But I don't need you to, Cam. That was *his* thing. That's what I had with *him,* and it's irrelevant to you and me. That's not what I have with *you.*"

"No, all you get with me is a big dick and multiple orgasms."

"And four beautiful children and the confidence to know that I'm loved, worshiped, and adored every single day of my life."

"I didn't give you that yesterday. Yesterday you thought I was leaving you."

I drop my head back and stare at the ceiling in frustration. I can just make out the mural of a unicorn standing on a cloud and farting a stardust-sprinkled rainbow out of its arse that's on my ceiling.

I had it painted to remind me that life isn't always perfect. My life most certainly hasn't been and wasn't now but it was perfect for me, for us.

Sometimes in life, bad things happen just *because*. It's not "meant to be" and it's not "God's will". It just is. My life isn't about fluffy clouds, stardust, and rainbow-farting unicorns. It's about everything that's on the walls beneath the hand-painted sky above our heads. It's family photos of kisses, cuddles, and laughing smiling faces, pure happiness and joy. It's hand prints filled with our family rules and inspirational quotes, the pencil-marked walls showing the kids' heights since the day they could stand. It's love, warmth, temper tantrums, loud music, and chaos. Barking, bum-sniffing dogs, muddy football boots, and shit-covered riding boots left in the hallway. It's Harry, George, Lula, and Kiks. It's Cam and his rules and lack of technological know-how. It's me and my terrible cooking. It's everything that I thought I'd never have and everything he gave to me.

Him. Cameron King.

"That's because of my own stupid insecurities, not because of anything you did."

"If I were doing my job properly, you wouldn't have any insecurities."

I raise my eyebrows and look at him, giving him my best "You've got to be shitting me" look.

He rolls his eyes, knowing full well I have him. We both know nothing will put a stop to my insecurities. I'm a woman, they come with the job description. I give him my best smile, telling him, "You look like Lula when you do that."

"Lu's my daughter, it's her that looks like me."

"Whatever."

"Now you sound like Harry. Anyway, Lu's all you. I swear she's a combination of you and Ash. I don't think there's anything of me in there."

He looks into my eyes without saying a word for a few long moments.

"Our babies," he says very quietly.

I nod my head, unable to speak around the big knotty ball of emotion that's lodged in my throat.

"We're so fucking lucky. I've got daughters, George. You gave me girls." He says it like he's realising this for the very first time.

"Never in my life did I imagine myself with girls. Boys, yeah, I always expected boys, but never girls." I can't help but laugh at the astonishment in his voice.

"For a while, I never thought I'd have either," I confess. He holds my face in his big right hand and brushes the tears from my cheeks with his thumb.

"And here we are with four," he whispers.

"And all because of you."

He shakes his head, leans in, and kisses me oh so gently on the mouth.

"Because of us."

"And that's what you've given me. That's why you'll always be enough. When you're not busy being too much that is. You gave me *back* my life, and then you *gave* me a life. One that I could never have imagined, hoped, or dreamed of ever living."

He stands up, holding me tight in his arms. I feel safe and secure as he carries me upstairs to our bedroom. I make sure to lock the door behind us.

As soon as he lays me down on the bed, I pull my T-shirt off. Cam manages to get naked in the few seconds that it's taken me to undress.

I lean back on my elbows and watch him as he watches me from the end of our bed.

"Bend your knees and open your legs. I wanna see you," he orders.

I do as I'm told, never taking my eyes from his.

"Are you wet?" He stares between my legs as he asks.

Is he serious right now?

He's Cameron King. Of course I'm fucking wet, but I won't be telling him that. I nod my head.

"Rub your clit for me, baby. Lemme watch."

I slide my middle finger into my mouth and suck on it, hard. Pulling it out, I twirl my tongue around the tip before dragging it down my throat and through my cleavage.

"Fuck, Kitten," he whispers, taking his cock in his hand and stroking.

"Dim," Cam orders, and like most other things in this world, our voice controlled lights obey him, leaving the perfect amount of lighting for us to be able to see each other but not the room around us.

He winks at me.

And I melt.

Fuck, my husband is hot.

I watch *him* bite his lip as he watches *me* drag my finger down my belly and past my belly button, until I reach my clit.

I let out a breathy *uhh* sound as I press on the little button of nerves.

"Wider, George. Open your legs wider. I wanna see how wet you are. Slide your fingers down lower, I wanna hear your juices."

I do as he orders. The noise that action makes would leave even the hard of hearing with no doubt as to how turned on I am.

"Fuck," he groans before climbing onto the bed and burying his head between my legs.

He assaults me with that big, wide tongue of his and I love it. He bites the inside of the top of first one thigh and then the other as I moan. I haven't even come yet, and I already feel boneless.

Then he pulls what we call his "master stroke" on me, scissoring his fingers, he presses his thumb onto my clit and flicks his tongue around it. His index and middle fingers slide inside where I'm wet and so desperately waiting for him and his ring and little finger sink slowly into my arse. When he works the whole lot together, I see stars.

The groan that escapes me is so much louder than I intend and I cringe in case it wakes any of the kids. Cameron chuckles.

"You like that, baby?"

"*Yes*, fuck yes."

He kisses up my belly, making me shudder as he sucks my right nipple into his mouth. My fingers rake through and grip his hair, pushing his head down into my chest harder.

He kisses a path across to my left nipple. Capturing it between his teeth, he looks up at me with soulful, dark eyes. I witness my whole world reflected back at me.

"I love you Tige—" His mouth is on mine before I even finish getting the 'r' sound out of it.

His lips are soft but so demanding, forcing my mouth to open for him. His tongue darts inside, and I gladly welcome the assault, giving back as good as I get the whole time. He rains kisses down on my face and then moves his lips to my neck and behind my ear, where he licks, sucks, and drags his teeth, making me groan and rake my nails down his back.

I tilt my hips, trying to gain friction, or better still, access to that big dick of his so I can guide it inside me.

"You want me, Kitten?"

"Yeah." Is all that I have.

"Tell me. Tell me what you want, baby."

"You, T. I want you."

"Where, baby. Where'd ya want me?"

"Inside. I want you inside me, over me, on me. I want you everywhere, Cam. Fuck me, please."

He slides inside me, joining us together. United.

He stops moving his hips and pushes himself onto his elbows so he can look at me.

"I love the fuck outta you, Kitten."

Overwhelmed by the moment, the emotions, our conversation, and admissions, I can't stop the tears that roll from my eyes and down towards my ears.

He moves his soft lips to mine, but this time, he's gentle. His tongue flicks along the seam of my mouth as he moves his hips, pushing himself deeper inside of me. It isn't enough. I dig my fingers into his tight arse cheeks and pull him, closer, harder, tighter towards me.

He's buried to the hilt, and I'm only too beautifully aware of it.

Cam does this thing. He has this way of moving that I love. He rolls his hips, pulling his dick out of me, dragging it first up and then down over my clit before burying himself back inside of me. Over and over he repeats the move. I can't even make a sound. I just lie there and take what he gives me until he switches it up and continuously grinds himself inside and against me. I move to meet his movements, and soon, I'm seeing solar systems, not just stars.

"Ahh," The only communication I am now apparently capable of.

"Fuck, baby. *Fuck,*" he whisper shouts into my ear.

The room spins. Dots dance in front of my eyes. My legs twitch as I try to back away from the orgasm that's sending tremors through my entire body. It's too much but not enough. I need to get away, but I crawl towards it, begging for more. I give up the fight and let it claim. Then I let it own me.

I can't even hold on to Cam as he comes. I feel him throb, pulse, and explode inside me, but I can't move my arms to hold him to me like I want to.

He eventually still his movements. The only sound in the room is our heavy breathing as he rests his forehead against mine.

"I love you, Kitten. Please, don't ever be in any doubt about that. Not even for a second."

He holds onto my arse cheeks and rolls over onto his back, bringing me to lie on top of him.

Without another word, we go to sleep.

NINE
Georgia

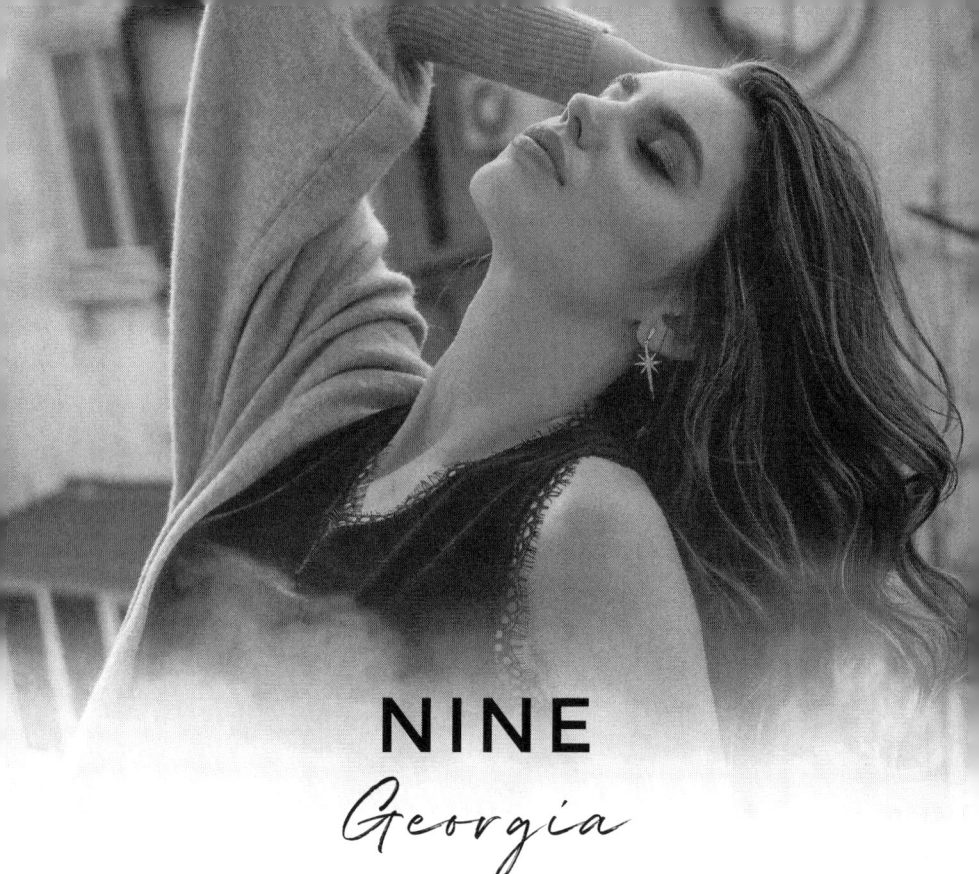

The week that followed the best make-up sex ever had by anyone in the history of the world was a pretty good one.

The kids are busy but behaving. Now that Cam has all of his security issues sorted out at the clubs, he is happier and not on the phone as much. This means that he has time to help me with a few of the arrangements for this year's Triple M concert. The event has grown too big for his London club and now, we now hold it in a football stadium instead. KLUB still hosts the Sydney event, and Cam supplies the venue and all of the staff to us free of charge.

I really do have the best husband.

Who, coincidentally, just left this morning for a golfing weekend with my brothers, so Jimmie and Ash were coming over to stay. My twins are away on a four-day residential in the New Forest with the school and both the boys have sleepovers tonight.

I've managed to separate a pile of lyrics from all of Sean's stuff for my brother to go through when the boys got back on Sunday afternoon. Some are whole songs, some a few verses, some just a line but there could be something amongst it all that Marley can use.

I've put Sean's diaries into a separate box to look at another time. I just don't have it in me right now to read them. Maybe I never will. His letters are hard enough, the thoughts and feelings that he *wanted* me to know. I'm not sure that I'll *ever* want to know or read the ones that are private and were never meant for me or anyone else to see. His private thoughts should probably remain that, private.

On my desk sits the last pile of letters addressed to me, a pile of miscellaneous stuff that I've yet to sort through and a few video tapes, one of which I was now about to start watching.

Marian has loaned us an ancient portable television that must've been about twenty years old. It has a video player built into it and I've just pressed play when Harry knocks, then walks into the room.

He leans over my shoulder and looks at the screen, which is still just displaying white noise.

"What is *that*?"

I pause the tape. I have no clue what's on it and don't want anything inappropriate popping up and surprising me.

"It's a video clip of Carnage."

"No, I meant that, the telly. Why's it so big?"

I laugh. Harry's generation only know flat screens, curved screens, 3D, LCD and plasma. They would have no concept of the huge back part televisions used to have on them or of having to actually get up and turn it over.

"That's a little one, a portable that you would have in the bedroom or kitchen," I explain.

"Why's it blue?"

I look over the very nineties bluey silver colour of the telly.

"I've no clue. You could get them in all colours to suit your room, back in the day."

I watch him as he walks across the room to get the spare chair that's sitting in the corner. He moves exactly like his dad. Long confident strides. He pushes the front of his dark hair back before lifting the chair with ease and putting it down next to mine. He picks up a Polaroid photo that I'd found amongst everything else. It was of a hot and sweaty Sean and Marley. Their guitar straps pulled tight across their chests, their guitars resting across their backs. They each have a beer in their hands and Marley's arm is slung over Sean's shoulders. They'd obviously just finished a show somewhere.

They look so young. Twenty at the most. So it was probably at a time that we weren't together. I'd kept it out to give to Marley. I have a couple of photos of the pair of them in my office, and I even keep a photo of me and Sean in here. It was my favourite one of the two of us that was taken on my birthday. I'm around five or six months pregnant with Beau, Sean has his hand on my pregnant belly, my hand is on top of his. Both of us were looking down at our hands at the moment the image was captured.

I fail to blink back tears and swipe at them discreetly from under my eyes.

"Do you miss him?" Harry asks from beside me.

I take a deep breath while I think about how to word my answer.

Our kids are aware of the basics when it comes to the story of Sean and me.

There's lots of information, some true, some complete bullshit, out there on the internet to be found, so we've raised them with a policy of, if they ask, we won't lie, we'll give them an answer that's as age appropriate and as near to the truth as we can.

"Yeah, I miss him. He was my best friend as well as my husband. We grew up together. I'd known him since I was eleven years old."

"How did you meet, at school?" Harry asks, still looking at the photo.

"No, Marley brought him to our house. He'd just moved to our area and been recruited by the band. It was the summer holidays. Jimmie and I were hanging upside down on the monkey bars when they walked up the garden at Nan and Pops old house."

He turns his attention from the photo to my face as I talk. I wonder how much I should tell him. I wonder what's appropriate for a fifteen-year-old having a conversation like this with his mum. Are there even guidelines for a conversation like this?

"Then what?"

"Marley told me to stop flashing my knickers."

Harry laughs. "Sounds like Marls."

I won't mention that Sean asked me to show him my tits.

"And then what?"

I let out a long breath and decide to be totally honest with my son.

"I fell in love. I was eleven years old, but I knew without a shadow of a doubt that I loved him."

His brown eyes, Cam's eyes, look over my face.

"So how old was you when you met Dad?"

"Nineteen, almost twenty I think."

"But he was still alive then, Maca?"

"Yeah, we split up when I was sixteen, got back together again when I was twenty ..." I trail off. Would he ask?

"But you were with Dad then?"

Of course he asks, he is Cam's son.

"We split up. Sean and I got back together, eventually got married, and were together for fifteen years before he was killed."

"And then what? You got back with Dad? I never knew that. I thought you met Dad at his club in Sydney."

I nod my head. "We met *back* up in Sydney. I was there to escape the press and the public on the first anniversary of Sean's death. I had no clue your dad owned the club. We bumped into each other and started seeing each other when we got back to England. We've been together ever since."

He picks the photo up and looks at it again.

"So, if he hadn't died, you and Dad wouldn't be together and my brother and sisters wouldn't have been born." It's a statement, not a question. I don't even attempt an answer.

"I don't wanna be glad he died, Mum, because I've seen how upset you still get about things, but I'm glad you and Dad met and got back together."

I have to wait a few seconds before I can speak, and even then, my voice wobbles.

"You don't wish things had worked out differently with your ..." I can't call her his mum, she's not his mum. I am.

"Tamara?" he offers up. I love this kid so bloody much.

He tilts his head to the side and smiles at me, knowing full well I'm struggling. "With Tamara?" I continue.

He shakes his head no. "If they'd have sorted their shi— Themselves out, then where would that leave you? What about the twins and George? Without Dad, they wouldn't be who they are. They might not even exist."

He's expressing all of my own inner turmoils, and I'm kinda glad. It makes me feel like my thoughts are normal. It also makes me wonder about Cam and Chantelle. Before me, and even before Tamara, there was Chantelle, Cam's first wife.

My stomach lurches. It's as if H is reading my thoughts.

"Strange really, that Dad's first wife died, then your husband, then Tamara killed herself, and you two end up together after both going through all of that."

I nod my head, agreeing with him.

"Life's strange sometimes, mate, that's just the way it is. Sometimes it can be very wicked, too."

"And lucky. You both had bad luck, but then you had good luck when you bumped into each other in Australia. You had good luck again when Jimmie and Ash had the twins and George for you. We were all lucky Dad didn't die when Tamara shot him. That is all *good* luck and none of that is wicked."

This kid is so bloody perceptive. I reach out to ruffle his hair, but he ducks out of the way.

"What ya doing? Don't touch the hair, I'm going out in a minute."

"Where you going?"

"Westfield's with George and Ollie."

As if on cue, George comes through the door.

"Here you are. Don't you answer your messages?"

H sends me a sideways look. George's voice has broken over the past few months and is deeper than both his and Cam's right now.

I nudge Harry, silently telling him not to make fun of his brother, but George catches it.

"What?" He looks between the both of us, wiping his hand over his face, paranoid that he has something on his chin.

"Nothing," we both laugh and say at the same time.

"Does this look all right?" George asks us.

He's wearing a short-sleeved shirt, which is buttoned up to the neck, and a pair of skinny jeans that have an extra low crotch so they don't split when he tries to walk in them. Cam hates the things and is constantly telling the boys to pull their trousers up when they slide down and expose their boxers underneath.

"Yeah, you look nice. You both do."

Harry is wearing a similar outfit, except with shorts in the same style as George's jeans.

They are handsome boys, and I am noticing more and more that girl's heads turn when we are all out together.

I sort of got used to it with Sean. He was public property and it went with the job. I didn't like it, but I got used to it, to a degree. I don't like it when it happens with Cam, and it does, often. When it does, I politely explain to women in bars and restaurants that it's highly disrespectful to look at my husband like they want to ride home, on his face. But when it happens with my boys, whoa. I will glare back at the little slutetts that stare like they want to eat them with a look that says, "You're fourteen, sweetheart. Fuck off home and do some colouring, play with Barbie, put on your My Little Pony jarmies, wipe those big black scary eyebrows off your face, and go to bed."

Then Cam reminds me what I was doing at fourteen.

I tell him to shut up and mind his own business.

He laughs.

I don't.

"You got money?" I ask them.

"Yeah, Dad transferred my allowance a week early. I saw a pair of football boots I wanna get, and he said he'd go half with me," George replies.

"Dad transferred you money? How?"

"Online," they reply in unison.

"How? Dad don't know how to do online banking."

"Yeah he does. H put the app on his phone, and we showed him how to use it yesterday. His practice go was sending me my allowance."

Well, wonders would never cease. My husband is finally getting with it.

"I showed him how to send photos in a text as well. I told him he should get Facey coz it's cheaper, but he just said fu— No. He said no, he didn't need it."

Yeah, I could well imagine what Cam would have to say about getting a Facebook account. It would've been far more than no.

George looks at his phone. "Ollie's outside," he announces.

"You gonna be all right here on your own tonight?" Harry asks.

"I won't be on my own. I can call the dogs inside and Jimmie and Ash are coming over to stay. Paige might come over too if she's not too jet-lagged."

"Paige?" they both enquire at once.

"Is she bringing any of her mates?"

Like father like sons. Paige had come over for a family BBQ when she was home one time last year and she'd brought a friend. A very pretty friend. As young as my boys were, they knew what they liked, and that day, it was Kitty Calder, the young Australian model that Paige had with her. Unfortunately for them, Kitty was twenty-three and didn't even know they existed.

"Unlucky boys, she's on her own."

They shake their heads and slouch their shoulders in mock disappointment before kissing me goodbye and heading out the door.

Harry was right, I was lucky, in so many ways.

A few minutes later, I receive a text from Cam.

TIGER: Wanna see a dick pic?

ME: Depends whose dick the pic's of?

TIGER: My fuckin dick. Why, who the fuck else sends you dick pics?

I don't reply, and my phone rings thirty seconds later, and just for fun, I silence it, sending the call to my message bank.

I laugh as I think about how much trouble I'm gonna be in later.

Last night was the scariest of my life. Even now, knowing that you're safe, my hands still shake and my throat and chest still ache.

Our baby's gone, G. I only knew about him for a few short hours and then he was gone.

I'll never forgive myself for staying down at the bar, G. I should've gone up to bed with you. You're my wife, you were carrying our child, and I stayed at the bar drinking and celebrating while you was alone and in pain in our room.

I was so hungover yesterday morning, I didn't even realise how quiet and pale you were.

As soon as Jimmie mentioned it, as soon as I finally paid you some attention, I knew in an instant something was wrong.

And then everything happened so fast. You were sick, and then when I held you in my arms you were so cold and clammy. You just laid there, limp like a rag doll. I can't begin to put into words the level of fear I felt during the few minutes it took us to get to the hospital.

I knew it was bad when they gave you a bed straight away.

I held you, Georgia. I held you so tight in my arms, but I couldn't stop you from shaking. I didn't wanna let you go, G. I was so fucking terrified that I would never get another chance, that it would be the last time I ever got to hold your soft warm body against mine, that I didn't wanna let you go.

But then the convulsions started. George, I lost it. I fucking lost it. Marley was holding me back when they wheeled you away. Fuck George, I knew the baby was gone. There was blood all over your jeans, and I knew what that meant, and my brain was sorta accepting that. But you, George? No, I couldn't lose you. I wouldn't survive, George. I wouldn't fuckin' want to.

And then it was quiet. After all the noise and chaos, they showed us to a waiting room and it was just nothing, silence.

Two hours I spent, contemplating how I was going to end my life if they didn't come back soon and tell me you were ok.

You know I'm not religious, but I begged and I prayed to anyone that was out there listening, even the devil himself. Me for you George. That's what I offered. My life for yours, but at the same time, I had to work out what I was gonna do if no one listened. I had two hours to work out exactly how things would go if you didn't make it. I'd have to make sure you had a proper funeral, George. I'd be dying inside, but I'd get through it, knowing that soon enough, I'd be joining you too.

So, I would give you the perfect funeral, and then I would join you and our baby, George.

Then the doctor came and explained everything. Ectopic, fallopian tubes, rupture. Apparently, we were lucky, we lost our baby, but we got to the hospital in time to save you. I don't feel too lucky right now, but I'm so fucking grateful I still have you.

I love you, Gia, my beautiful girl. I love you so fucking much. This next few months are gonna be hard. We're gonna be sad, and we're probably gonna fight and cry and blame each other. We just need to remember that when it all feels like it's too hard or when *it's all too much, we're Georgia and Sean. Sean and Georgia, and we're meant to fucking be.*

Sleep soundly now. Tomorrow is a new day, and I will do my absolute best to make it a little brighter for you, because if your heart is as broken as mine right now, then I know just how much pain you will be feeling.

I love you, Gia, my brave and beautiful girl. I love you Baby McCarthy, I'm so sorry that we never got to meet you, but rest assured, you will be remembered with every beat of my heart. xxx

My head hurts and my face stings with the salt from my tears.

He hurt so bad after we lost baby M, and I was so selfishly wrapped up in my own grief that I never saw it. It was all about me. Never once in those first few weeks did I think about the fact that he had thought that he'd lost us both.

Aside from the anguish he conveys in this letter, I can't help but notice the irony in the similarity of the way we thought.

He planned on getting through my funeral and then killing himself if I died. When he died, I attempted exactly that.

"Oh, Sean, life was so unfair to us, babe. Can you see me now? Are you watching me? I hope you're happy for me. I hope I've made you proud."

I pull a handful of tissues out of the box I have next to me and blow my nose.

Back in the early days, after Sean died, I was convinced I could feel him around me, but that's not happened in a long time now.

Occasionally, when I'm in the car or the house by myself, I'll be thinking of him and a song will come on that reminds me of him, but other than that, nothing. I wonder if it's because he's stepped aside. That would be such a Sean thing to do, to just step away and leave me to live my life, knowing that I have Cam and the kids to take care of me.

Zara Larson's "Never Forget You" starts to play, and I laugh through my tears.

"Is that you? Are you talking to me through the songs?" I look around the room while I ask, but I get nothing. I don't know what I was expecting but I can't help but feel a little disappointed.

I throw myself down on the beanbag I've dragged in from the game room and start reading the next letter in the pile.

> Why, why does it still have to hurt so bad?
> When, when will it stop?
> This hurt.
> This ache.
> I need it to go away.
> I need it to never leave.
> Do you feel it? This longing, the sense that something's missing.
> Or are you just numb? Numb and cold.
> I hope you feel it too.
> I hope we share this misery.
> Just one more bond to forever tie us together.

I let out a long sigh. I feel like we had so many "If Only's" in our relationship, and as much as I regret the time we spent apart, it was all such a long time ago that having regrets over both our actions back then seems pretty pointless now.

Lukus Graham's "7 Years" filters through the sound system, serving as a little reminder of how quick life passes us by.

Three more. I'm going to read three more and then I'm gonna go shower and get ready for Jimmie and Ashley's arrival.

> It's 2.48 a.m., G, and I just woke from the most beautiful dream. You were here, tucked in tight against me.
> We never really had much opportunity to spend whole nights

together, but when we did, it's the way we always slept. Your back pressed to my front, your head resting on the pillow, my arm tucked underneath it.

I would run my fingertips from the top of those long legs of yours, over the curve of your hip and the dip of your waist. I'd watch, fascinated as goose bumps spread across your body.

It's what I was doing when I woke from my dream, hard.

Do you ever think about us like that, G? I don't mean the sex, the closeness we shared, the intimacy? I miss it, G. I miss you. So fucking much. It's been over 3 years now since we shared a bed, since you gave yourself to me so willingly. Remember the way you used to shake, G? Whenever we used to make love, you would shake with nerves and then shake with pleasure. There'll never be anyone like you, beautiful girl. Wherever this life may take us, there will only ever be you for me. I have to keep believing that we are meant to be and one day, when the time is right and we are least expecting it, it'll happen. You'll fall back into my arms, and I'll never let you go. Until then, G, I'll hold onto dreams like tonight's, when I could smell your hair and hear your sighs and just pretend that you are mine.

It will only ever be you!

Sean and Georgia. Georgia and Sean. The way it's meant to be.

I'm done for tonight. I can't put myself through anymore of this. The girls will be here in an hour or so and I don't want them to find me a blubbering mess.

"I love you, Sean, my beautiful boy, but your words, your words just hurt my heart so bad. So I'm gonna put them away for a while. Jimmie and Ash will be here soon, and I plan on having a few wines, a takeaway, and some girl time."

Sam Smith's "Stay with Me" is playing, and I let out a long breath.

"Ok, just in case. Just in case there is the slightest chance that you're messing with my playlist, I'm gonna read one more and then

I'm gonna go shower."

>Today was both a good and a bad for me, Georgia. Today, we met our son. We listened to his heart beating loud and strong, and although they told us it's too early to tell, I know with 100% certainty, there's a Beau in your belly not a Lilly.
>
>I am so happy, G, in a way that I can't even put into words, and words are usually my thing, ya know? They're sort of what I do, but I can't come up with anything that can adequately express to you the absolute love, joy, and pride I feel when I think of you carrying our son, all tucked up safe and warm in that little belly of yours.
>
>You are, without a doubt, the most beautiful pregnant woman I have ever laid eyes on. Actually, you're the most beautiful woman I've ever laid eyes on full stop. You were pretty when you were a little girl, (I say that in a non-pervy way of course) now, though, you're simply stunning.
>
>You take my breath away. You really do.
>
>Leaving the hospital with your hand in mine, I felt like I was king of the world.
>
>And then we went to lunch.
>
>And things went to shit.
>
>It was his fucking house, G!
>
>Why the fuck would you NOT tell me something like that? Why?
>
>I know you've given me your explanation, but I've gotta tell ya, I think you're lying. I don't know why, but something in my gut just tells me I'm not getting the whole story here.
>
>And you know what else I think, G?
>
>Cameron King is bang in fucking love with you.
>
>I knew it the night he turned up at the club when we first got back together, but you had eyes for only me, and to be honest G, I just felt a little bit sorry for the bloke. I knew only too well what

it felt like to lose you, so I knew what he was about to go through.

After a while, I forgot that the man even existed. In all the years we've been back together, I've never doubted your love for me, not until last year when you lost the baby.

I thought I'd lost ya, G. I really thought we were done. You pushed me away time and time again until it got to the point where I almost stopped pushing back.

Almost.

And it was the thought of that poor fuck that made me not give up.

You remember that night you went out with the girls and ran into Haley White and you gave her a smack in that club Cameron King owns?

I saw one of the pictures from that night, G. It was a photo of you and of him. He was saying something into your ear and you were laughing, but it wasn't that that bothered me. It wasn't you or what you were doing. That wasn't what caught my attention. It was the way he was looking at you as you laughed.

It's the way I look at you.

I knew then that I had two choices.

I could continue to let you keep pushing me away until it got to the stage that I stopped pushing back. Until I just walked away and left you in your misery, loneliness, and depression.

Or I could fight for you and for us, for everything we had ever been through.

And you know what made me fight, G? I knew that as soon as I stepped aside, he would be there. He would be there to pick you up and put you back together, and I would be the broken-hearted one standing in the shadows and staring from the sidelines, just waiting for him to fuck up so I could be the one to step in and reclaim.

Because after today, Georgia, after watching him, look at you, at the restaurant today, I know for a fact that Cameron King is just waiting. He's waiting for me to fuck up or for you to just up and leave me and go back to him. He's sitting tight and biding his time.

He knows there's something there between the two of you. He knows that because you let us buy and move into his house all behind my back. You gave him hope today. When he realised I didn't know shit about him owning this place, it made him think it means something, and I'll tell you what, G, so the fuck do I.

But here's the thing, I'm going nowhere. We tried being apart, and it nearly killed the both of us, so that ain't ever happening again.

So, here we are. You, me, and a baby on the way. This is our life, and that man will never play a part in it, not all the time we're together, anyway—which will be always, because I never plan on letting you go.

In saying all of that, Georgia, I want you to know something. Like I've told you many times, you're a beautiful woman. You turn heads; you always have, but I've gotta admit, he's the only man I've seen look at you in the exact same way I look at you. It's not about sex or the size of your tits, it's about you. He only sees you. And ya know what that tells me, G? He'd love and look after you in the exact way I do. So, if we don't make it, or if anything ever happens to me and we can't be together for whatever reason and he steps up, steps in and offers to pick up the pieces and put you back together, then let it be him. It'd make me happier knowing you have someone like that to look after you if I ever couldn't.

I love you, Gia, I really do. You drive me round the fucking twist. You're spoilt and selfish and so fucking inconsiderate sometimes. You're also the most loving, caring, loyal, and compassionate woman I know. I'll take ya, whatever way I can get ya.

I'm gonna sleep now. I just needed to get all that off my chest because it's been driving me nuts since we left the restaurant.

Good night beautiful girl x Good night baby Beau x

I threw up.

I sobbed so hard that the sandwich I'd eaten at lunch time came up.

That letter, that information was as hard to digest as that sandwich had obviously been.

I splash my face with water in the downstairs bathroom, rinse out my mouth, and then head to the kitchen to pour myself a large glass of wine.

I'm shaking from my head to my toes. Even my insides shake.

All of these years, all of the guilt. If I'd have only gone through that box when I was in Australia.

What if I had, though? If I'd known I had Sean's blessing, would I have gone out of my way to seek out Cam? Would that knowledge have changed the course of our relationship if I'd gone chasing after him?

I gulp down the glass of wine and pour myself another before going up to my bathroom to take a shower. I put my music on and stand under the jets of hot water as "I Can't Feel My Face" by The Weeknd blasts out of the speaker above my head. The best thing about being home alone is being able to play my music loud without anyone moaning at me.

The kids like my music, mostly, although George had a strong aversion to The Jam, which makes me feel like I have failed as a mother in some small way, but he is, at least, a huge fan of The Clash, so I got something right with him.

For teenage girls, the twins have pretty good taste, they hadn't been into Bieber until he brought out his *Purpose* album, which even I agree is pretty good. They like certain songs by 1D, but not everything. They love Ed Sheeran, The Weeknd, Chet Faker, and Ellie Goulding. Nothing that would make my ears bleed too badly. Harry loves his rap. Eminem, Kendrick Lamar, Skepta, and Devlin are all on repeat on his playlist.

I am trying to focus on anything other than the words Sean wrote in the last letter I read. I feel like an enormous weight should've been lifted from my shoulders, but so far, I don't. I don't know how to let it go. The guilt has been around for so long that it has become embedded in my psyche, in my bones, part of my DNA.

An old song by the New Radicals comes on, and I sing "You Get What You Give" at the top of my lungs. It's a feel good sort of song, and I smile as I belt it out.

Imagine Dragons' "Demons" starts to play. I sob so hard that my legs stop working. I curl into the corner of our shower and cry until, once again, I start to heave.

That's where Jimmie finds me twenty minutes later.

Without saying a word, she turns off the water, wraps me in a towel, and helps me stand. We walk out to my bedroom, where she sits me on the edge of the bed.

Thirty Seconds to Mars's "Do or Die" is making the walls of my house shake.

Jimmie finds the remote to the sound system and turns it off.

"What the fuck happened, George?" she asks from where she's now kneeling in front of me.

I point my finger to the ceiling and can't help laughing when she says, "A song? A fucking song did this to ya?"

I smile up at her, tears still spilling down my cheeks.

"I love you," I tell her.

"You pissed?" she asks, wearing a frown.

I shake my head. "I love that you knew that I meant music when all I did was point my finger to the ceiling."

She smiles back.

"What the fuck happened?"

"Lemme get dressed, and I'll show you."

She stands and walks towards the door.

"I'll go and pour us a wine. Ash should be here soon. Paige said she'll be over once she showered and got herself together."

"How is she?" I ask.

Paige has been modelling in South America for the last two months. While she was there, she got so sick that Jim had to fly over to be with her for a few weeks. She'd apparently recovered enough to finish the shoot but has flown home to stay with Jimmie and Len for a while.

"Too skinny and absolutely exhausted. Apparently, she has news but doesn't wanna talk until she's fully awake."

She heads downstairs while I attempt to get my shit together.

TEN
Georgia

We've piled three beanbags in a circle on my office floor and are sprawled out on them. The pile of letters I've already gone through is sitting in the middle, and I have the last few I haven't yet read in my lap. Jimmie, Ash, and I drink wine as we make our way through Sean's words.

There's been tears and a few "Oh George," comments as they've read, and moments where we've each read lines aloud to each other. Sean was in Jimmie's life for even longer than he was in mine. She got him for the four years we were apart, and his death hit her hard. My subsequent suicide attempts led to Jim seeking help for the depression she was in, and she'd spent a few years on antidepressant and anti anxiety medication. She'd sought the help she needed and was in a good place nowadays.

I have no secrets from these two, except one, everything else about my life they're aware of and I have no issue with them reading the letters. The only one I haven't shown them yet is the one that caused my melt down earlier.

A lot of the letters Sean's written are just notes really. Words that are short and simple

> *I watched the sunrise over a lake in Italy this morning. I wish you were here to see it with me. One day, G, one day I'll bring you back here with me and we'll experience this together. I love, and I miss you.*
> *Sean x*

He kept his promise. We made a few trips to Lake Como over the years, and we always woke early and watched the sunrise when we were there.

> *I'm in the back of a big stretch limo. It's six in the evening and the streets of Paris are gridlocked. Our hotel is only supposed to be a half-hour drive from the airport, but we spent an hour signing autographs and posing for pictures before we could even leave, and now we've been sitting here in traffic for an hour, barely moving. I'm so over it, G. I'm sick of the travelling. I wish you'd change your mind and fly out here and meet me. I understand you don't like this city, but shit, babe, it was five years ago. We're together, all of that shit's behind us. I'll call you when, or if, we ever make it to the hotel. I miss you. I'm thinking of you. I just wanted you to know.*
> *Love ya, G.*
> *Sean*
> *X*

I tilt my head up and stare at my cloud-covered ceiling, trying to remember when he could've written this. I rarely went to Paris with him. I know it's pretty, but for me, it most definitely was *not* the city of love. For me, it was the city of Whorely.

I'd found a photo earlier, it is of no one in particular, just a wide-angled lens shot of what is obviously back stage somewhere. I'd spotted the back of Sean's head and a side view of Marley, but the face that had jumped out at me was that of Rocco Taylor. The man who had set out to ruin my life. I'd ripped the photo into tiny pieces and thrown it in the bin. Then just for good measure, I'd emptied it into the sink and set light to each and every piece.

I knew he couldn't hurt me. The evil bastard has been dead for a few years now. Accidental drug overdose all alone in a hotel room. Shame it couldn't have been something much more painful, but still, dead was dead right?

I shuddered, and just for a few seconds, I felt guilty for thinking ill of the dead.

Then I spat on the ashes that remained in the sink.

"Fucker," was only word I could think of saying as I wiped my chin.

"Unbreak My Heart" by Toni Braxton is playing over my office sound system, and I have to smile at the way every song on my playlist—no matter the era or genre seems to be relevant to my life, whether this is divine intervention or pure coincidence, I have no clue.

"Did you talk to Cam about getting a bit of tox in your chops?" Ashley asks me, while sliding across my beanbag and putting her head in my lap.

I move the pile of letters that had been sitting there before answering.

"I did."

"Blatant no?" Ash asks as I stare down at her.

"Not a blatant no. He asked me to wait until I'm fifty."

"What, why?" Jimmie looks up from the letter she's reading.

I shrug my shoulders. "He reckons I don't need it yet. He's worried it'll change the way I look and I won't be happy with the results."

"But just a little preventative won't hurt. He won't even notice." This from Ash.

"I'm not fussed; I can wait until I'm fifty. It's no biggie. Anyway, we've done a deal."

Ash smiles up at me and wiggles her eyebrows. "Oh yeah, what kind of deal?"

"You finally gonna let him have anal if you can have Botox?" Jimmie asks with a grin all over her face.

"No. I bloody will not. Ladies, his King Dick has ruined my Mildred. I'm not letting it ruin my arse as well."

"Oh, come on, George, you've never even squeezed ..." Ash trails off, but I've already worked out what she was about to say.

"No, I haven't ever squeezed babies out my vag, Ash, but I have had six-foot-five, and two hundred thirty pounds of pure male pounding a nine and a half inch dick into me for quite some time now, so no, my mildred is not as tight as it used to be, and no, that will not be happening to my arse. Can you imagine? It'd end up all loose and I'd be farting every time I bend over."

"*Meeehhh*, what's a few arse farts between husband and wife? It's the fanny farts that crack Marley up."

I spit my wine, barely missing Ashley's face.

"Oh my god, Ash. It's happened to me before, I just about died," I admit. Glowing crimson at the memory.

"What, you varted? Was it during sex?"

This time I choke on my wine. I have tears rolling down my cheeks caused by both coughing and laughing.

It feels so good to laugh.

I nod my head, because I'm struggling to talk.

"We were in Fuerteventura on holiday and it was hot and sweaty, and I was just really wet. I was mortified, but Cam just laughed."

"What's there to be embarrassed about? It's only air, and it's their fault any way for pumping it into ya. Marley just laughs and says, 'What's your next trick' or 'I'll name that tune in three'."

"I don't have that problem anymore. Got it all taken care of."

Ash and I share a look and try to straighten our faces before Ash sits upright and we both look at Jim.

"Wha'd'ya mean, 'you've had it taken care of'?" Ash asks before I can.

Jimmie shrugs her shoulders.

"That little cruise Len and I took in February? We didn't go on a cruise. We went over to the States, and I had a bit of reconstruction done."

"On your Mildred? Why?" I ask in disbelief.

"Why the fuck didn't you tell us? I would've come and had it done with ya." Ash sounds genuinely put out.

"Did it hurt?" we both ask at the same time.

"Why? Because my poor little vag has had to squeeze out four Layton and one King head. Five babies, ladies. Those kind of numbers don't leave things looking too pretty down there. I didn't tell ya coz, well, you know. It's a bit embarrassing. It's all right you girls knowing but I didn't want Cam and Marley knowing that I had a baggy fanny and could vart the national anthem."

Ash and I get the giggles again. I lean forward and pull the wine from the ice bucket sitting on the floor between us. I share the last of its contents around.

"And I wouldn't say it hurt. It was just uncomfortable for a few weeks until the stitches dissolved."

"Was it worth it?" I ask, genuinely interested.

"Absolutely," Jim replies without hesitation. "I now have a designer vagina. The Gucci of Coochies."

"The Versace of Vagies," Ash adds.

"The Louboutin of Labia," I gasp out. Fighting for breath as we all laugh hysterically.

"The Prada of Pussies," Jimmie cackles.

"The Burberry of Beavers," I add.

"It comes with a matching brolly and a trench coat for when things get too wet." I worry that Jimmie is gonna throw up as she laughs and talks at the same time.

"The Mimco of Minges."

"The Vuitton of Vulva."

"No, gag, hate that word," I gasp out at Ashley's last suggestion.

"What, Mimco?" she asks.

The noises we're making don't even sound human as we laugh and gasp for breath. I snort, which makes the other two laugh harder.

"The Saint Laurent of Snatches." I don't even know who says that last one, the voice sounds so strangled and I'm blinded by tears.

"The Cavalli of Cunts." I just know that's Ash.

We all lie back and gasp for air, the giggles and laughter still randomly breaking out.

"Oh my days, I needed that laugh," I say to no one in particular.

I sit up straight, forcing Ash to get her head out of my lap, where she's once again resting it, and take a sip of my wine.

"So come on, spill, Georgia Rae. What the fuck was going on when I got here earlier?"

I knew Jimmie wouldn't let it drop. What I don't know is how she managed to fill Ash in on my "moment" already.

"Yeah, what's going on, Slutster? I've revealed my varting abilities, Jim's revealed all about her designer vagina, now you need to spill the deets about your meltdown. What the fuck happened?"

Jimmie stands up. "Hang on, we need more wine for this." She heads off to the fridge while I retrieve the letter from my desk.

Once we're topped up and I've settled the girls side by side so they can read at the same time, I pass them the two sheets of paper.

They each take a sip of their wine and start to read.

Ashley looks up at me a couple of times. Jimmie's hand goes to her mouth, drops, and then goes back a total of three times.

"Wow," Jimmie states as she finishes.

"*Fuck!*" Is all Ash has to offer.

We all look at each other, shaking our heads.

"It's like, I dunno. It's almost like he had a premonition, but at the same time, he seemed convinced he wasn't going anywhere," Jimmie says.

"Yeah, but this is Sean. He'd do anything to protect and not worry me. If he had a feeling that something was gonna happen, he'd never have let me know."

"How'd you feel, George, after reading that, how'd ya feel?"

I move from where I was leaning against my desk and sit back down next to the girls.

"I really don't know, Jim. I had that crate shipped to Australia, but the time wasn't right, so I just packed it all up and shipped it back without reading them, well except one I think."

We're all quiet for a few long moments. Jimmie and Ash obviously trying to digest Sean's words the same way I had ...*was* still trying to in fact.

"George, if I ask you something, will you be totally honest with me."

My mouth fills with saliva, the way it does if I'm about to vomit, as I nod my head at Jim's question.

"Of course, go for it."

Jim stands and takes up the spot I was in earlier and leans her arse against my desk.

Ashley puts her head back in my lap and takes a hold of the hand not containing my wine glass.

"Did anything ever go on between you and Cam, once you were back with Mac?"

Despite having to swallow hard to get rid of the excess fluid in my mouth, it now feels incredibly dry. I take a long draw from my glass, look down at Ash, and then across to Jim.

I know I can tell these girls anything. They've loved and supported me through the worst of times and celebrated with me during the best. And they have never ever judged. This is the only thing I have ever kept secret from them. Admitting to myself what happened between me and Cam is harder than saying it out loud.

I nod my head slowly, and a very lost and lonely, stray tear makes its way down my cheek.

Ash pulls her hand from mine and reaches up and brushes it away.

"Don't cry, George, it was all a very long time ago. You don't have to tell us if you don't wanna."

I let out a loud sob. Despite the release, my jaw trembles when I try to speak.

"It was the night I kicked the shit out of Haley White."

Jimmies eyebrows raise up towards her hairline. Her eyes dart around the room, and I can almost hear her brain tick as she recalls that night.

"What? When? We all stayed at the loft that night, you came home with us."

"His office," Ash says from my lap.

"We left, he asked you to stay. You fucked him in his office."

I nod my head slowly. "That's exactly what happened."

"Fucking hell, George." Jimmie says before finishing the contents of her wine glass.

"It was just that one time. We never did it again, not even in Australia when we spent the night in the hotel room."

I was suddenly too hot and felt shaky.

"Fuck, I thought you and Maca had an epic love story, but you and Cam, that's just ... I don't even know what to say, George. You're like, magnets or something. Parts of a puzzle that just have to be together," Ashley whispers quietly.

"And Maca's letter just makes it all even more ... I dunno. What's the right word? Surreal?" Jimmie asks.

I press my fingertips into my forehead and squeeze my eyes shut for a few seconds.

"I've no clue. I'm at a loss for words really."

"Me too," says Ash, still whispering for some reason.

I pull my head back, draw in my eyebrows, and say at the exact same time as Jim, "Bullshit."

We all laugh and it breaks the tension a little bit.

"Please don't ever tell Marley," I tell Ash, now being totally serious. She shakes her head.

"Hoes Code, babe. I won't breathe a word."

I lean forward and kiss her forehead.

"So, after all these revelations, did you find anything that Marley might be able to use?" Jimmie asks. "What are these?" She picks up the pile that I'd mentally labelled "miscellaneous".

"I don't know. I set all of the song lyrics and poems over there for Marls to go through, but that was just a pile of stuff that …" I shrug my shoulders, "I don't know what they are, so I just set them aside."

Jimmie has a white envelope in her hand. Whatever's inside is quite bulky as the envelope looks like it's full.

"Can I?" Jim asks.

"Go for it."

She sets to opening the envelope carefully.

"Over the desk or against the wall?" Ash asks quietly.

"Why the fuck d'ya keep whispering? There's no one else here."

She turns her head to look at Jim, who's now reading intently.

"I know but it's just so…" She wriggles her little body. "Sexy and sordid."

"Cheers," I tell her. "And FYI, it was neither. Not, I don't mean it wasn't sexy and sordid, because it was both of those things. What I mean is, I tried to leave, he slammed the door shut, spun me around, and fucked me against the door."

"Squeeeeeeeee! It's like a scene from a book or a film. Fuck, I can just imagine TDH being all alpha and domineering."

"Oh."

I look up at Jimmie.

"What?" Ash asks before I can.

I don't miss the look Jimmie shoots her, and my stomach does a little forward roll, dragging the rest of my internal organs with it.

My eyes scan over what she's reading. There's a couple of sheets of paper in one hand and an envelope in the other.

I can't see who it's addressed to, but I can see that it's not Sean's writing on the envelope.

"Can I see that please?" In my head I ask calmly, but in reality, I just know my voice shakes.

I don't know why I feel the panic rise from my toes to my chest. Instinct? Some kind of sixth sense? I have no clue, but I'm anxious to the point where I feel sick. My mouth's dry, and I watch my hand shake as I hold it out for the letter that Jimmie is reading.

"George, I don't think ..."

"Pass me the letter please, Jim."

I feel the weight of Ashley's head lift as she sits up, but I keep my eyes on Jimmie. Hers dart to Ash and then back to me. Resignation written all over her face.

I know what's coming even before she says the word.

"No."

I nod my head slowly. My heart pumping the blood around my body so hard that a vein in the side of my neck actually aches from the pressure.

"Give me the fucking letter, Jim."

"George, if she—"

"Ash, I love you dearly, but stay out of this, babe."

I stand and take the two steps to where Jimmie leans back against my desk.

I don't ask this time, I just slide the two sheets of paper from between her fingers and start to read.

After the first few lines, the words stop making sense. The letters dance around the page, and my head begins to spin.

I close my eyes for a few seconds and wait for the world to right itself. All the while knowing, that after what I'd just read, my world will never really be right again.

Sean,

Please, please read this. You won't take my calls, and we really need to talk.

I can't believe you're going back to her. You told me it was over. You made me fall in love with you all over again. You gave me hope that finally, finally you would choose me, but just like last time, you've gone back to her. Why? Why her and not me? Is it because she lost the baby? Are you just feeling sorry for her, is that it? You can't base a marriage on pity, Sean. It should be based on love, trust, and understanding, and you two don't seem to have any of that for each other. She's pushed you away for nearly three months, and I haven't seen you doing much to stop her. She lost a baby. It happens all the time. What about me? What about our baby? You didn't care about me or that I was left all on my own to make the worst choice a woman ever has to make. Just think, if you hadn't left me and gone back to her all those years ago, we would have a ten-year-old now. A brown-eyed boy or girl that looked just like you. I suppose its Karma, really. I was forced to give up our child because you left me for her, so I suppose it's only fair that she loses her baby too. Funny how life works out.

I'd like to say that I wish you both well, but I don't. You used me ten years ago, and I stupidly let you use me again.

I thought this time was different. I was there for you, holding you tight, wiping away your tears, and making you feel better, wanted, loved. Me. Not her.

I'll give you a week, Sean. A week to see sense and come back to me. A week to see that she's nothing but a spoilt, selfish, heartless princess who doesn't care about anyone other than herself. If you don't get in touch within the week, then please don't ever get in touch with me again. Don't contact me. When we work together, just pretend I don't exist, because for all intents and purposes, you'll be dead to me.

Carla

I surprise myself with how calm I remain. My heart's galloping in my chest and my jaw feels so rigid, I struggle to speak.

I pass the letter to Ash with a shaking hand and look to Jim. "Who is she?"

Jimmie licks her lips before answering. "She worked with the producers. She was one of the sound engineers. They had a thing going on for a while, right before you two got back together. I had no clue about anything after that or about a baby."

I let out a long breath. "You never knew?"

Jimmie looks like I've just kicked her puppy. "Georgia, you're seriously asking me that?"

I feel like the biggest bitch.

"No, I'm sorry. I shouldn't have even asked that."

"I'll tell you what I do know, though, and you are not gonna believe this …"

I raise my eyebrows and shrug, urging her to go on.

"That night you got busy with Cam in his office, something went on between Maca and her at that football match they performed at in France."

"Oh my god, yes. I remember hearing something about that too," Ash pipes up from beside me.

"What the fuck ladies? And neither of you thought to tell me?"

Ashley shakes her head, and the rapid movement is making my head spin again. "It was nothing bad, George. From what I remember, she made a pass at Maca, Maca told her to fuck off, and then he changed their flights. That's why the boys came home early. It was months later that I heard about it, and you two were all loved up and pregnant again by then. It was trivial, a couple of the girls from the label gossiping when I was there waiting for Marley to get out of a meeting one afternoon. I think she was there at the meeting and that was why the two office girls were chatting about it."

I stand and hold out my empty wine glass to Jim, and she tops it up.

I want to throw the glass, as well as the bottle, against the wall. I want to punch something. I want to cry, but I'm not sure why. I don't even know for sure what, or even if, he did wrong.

"That's pretty much what I heard," Jimmie's voice brings me back to the conversation going on around me. "And like Ash said, by the time I heard anything, you were pregnant. It was a non-story. Plus, I know what you're like. I didn't want you getting upset about it or turning up at the studio, ready to knock seven kinds of shit out of the girl."

"Girl? How old is she then? Is she young?"

My paranoia is getting the better of me. It'd always been my biggest fear when I was with Sean. He was surrounded by so many women. So much very willing temptation surrounding him. Younger, slimmer, prettier.

"George, get a grip, will ya? No, she's not a girl; she's about the same age as us. He wasn't interested, George, she was a distraction. I remember talking to him about her the first time around. She meant nothing to him. The second he was back with you, it was over."

"He got her pregnant."

"Yes, by the sounds of it he did, but she got rid of it from what I just read."

My heart broke more at that news, than at the thought of Sean cheating on me. He could've had a child. Then there would've at least been something left of him.

"What about the second time? When I lost the baby? He said in that other letter that he came for me because he knew if he didn't that Cam would. Is that even true? What happened between them? Was he sleeping with her while I stayed at my mum's?"

"I don't know. I honestly don't know, George."

I let out a long breath and sit myself back down in a beanbag.

"Holy fucking fuck. Who would've thought, all these revelations were sitting in this ol' box." Ashley lets out a long whistle as she finishes speaking.

"I have no clue what to make of all this. I've put him on such a pedestal for all these years. He was the loyal, faithful husband, while I was the cheating whore of a wife, but he was just as guilty as I was. Then, to top it all off, he tells me to be with Cam. I mean, what the fuck? What do I do with all this? Everything I thought was us, me and Sean, really wasn't." I start to cry. I fight it and fight it, but I lose, and I'm so fucking angry with myself for crying that it makes me cry more.

"I've felt so much guilt. I convinced myself that I lost Baby M because I fucked Cam. All these years, I've felt so much guilt over what Cam and I did, for moving on so soon, and for going back to Cam. It was all pointless."

Ashley jumps up from beside me and stands with her hands on her hips.

"Right, stop your snivelling just for five fucking minutes and listen up."

I shoot a look across to Jim, who just frowns and shrugs her shoulders.

"You and Sean were not a fucking fairy tale couple. You were real people, with real problems. No marriage is perfect, not a single one. I don't know why, for all these years, you've thought that yours and Sean's was, but it wasn't. So, build a fucking bridge and get over it. You were two people who loved each other passionately. No one will ever call that into question, but that alone does not make for a perfect marriage. Sadly, Sean died. Sean died and you lost Beau and it was horrible, fucking awful, George. Not just for you either, I might add, it was fucking horrible for all of us. Then you got lucky. You got so *fucking* lucky. TDH did exactly what Sean predicted he would. He swept in, he picked you up, and bit by bit, he put you back together."

She pauses to take a swig of her wine, and I take that moment to draw breath. Apparently, while she was speaking, I'd forgotten to breathe.

"Where you go from here is entirely up to you. You either finally accept that what you had with Maca was beautiful, but far from perfect, and move on, enjoying the amazing and wonderful life you have with Cam and the kids guilt free. Or you ignore everything that you've discovered by reading these letters and continue living half a life, weighed down with the unnecessary guilt you feel because of past actions that can never be changed. What's it gonna be? You finally gonna give Cam everything, every little piece that makes you who you are, or are you gonna keep riding the 'I'm Not Worthy' train?"

The three of us sit in silence.

"I Will Survive" by Gloria Gaynor starts to play and totally in sync, the three of us look up towards the speakers in the ceiling. We start to laugh. I wipe the tears from under my eyes.

"It's time," I say quietly.

"Yes, it fucking is," Ash states before high fiving me.

We put the letters away and have a party for three in my office. We set my "Old Skool Club Classics" playlist up and dance the night away. The last thing I remember is singing Alison Limerick's "Where Love Lives" into an empty wine bottle. All of us finally crashing in my bed at around four in the morning.

Despite the lateness of the hour and the wine I've consumed, I can't sleep. I toss and turn for about half an hour before Ash whisper shouts, "Stop fucking thinking, George. The sound of your brain is keeping me awake."

"I can't help it."

"Yes, you can," Jimmie joins in. "Like Ash says, build a bridge and get the fuck over it. You are both the unluckiest and luckiest person I've ever known. It's about time you started enjoying the good and letting go of the bad. Life is short and then you die. You know first-hand how that one works. Time to move on, George. We're all sick of ya whining."

"Yeah, bored. Bored. Bored," Ash adds.

"Gee, thanks ladies."

"Anytime. Now, go to fucking sleep before I put this pillow over your head."

"And I help her hold it down," Jimmie offers.

I go to sleep.

EPILOGUE
Georgia

I put the potato salad I just made into the fridge. I've followed Marian's recipe to the letter and can only hope and pray I haven't fucked it up. There was very little cooking involved, except for parboiling some potatoes and frying the bacon, so I have every hope.

I know he's there before I even straighten up. The hairs on the back of my neck stand on end as his big arms slide around my waist.

He trails kisses over my neck before whispering in my ear, "I'm gonna slap that skinny little arse of yours till it's raw next time you ignore my texts and calls. Whose dick indeed." He bites and then sucks my neck. "I've missed you so fucking much, Mrs King."

I turn myself around in his arms and wrap mine around his neck. "You have no idea, baby. No fucking idea."

He claims my mouth, and it takes me less than a second to

surrender.

I waited for Dido to start playing "White Flag". But instead, it is Shine Down's "Second Chance" that comes over the hidden speakers.

"Get a room you two. Where are the beers, big man?"

I look around Cam's broad chest to see my brother trying to get around us to the fridge.

"Big brother Marley, me and you need to talk."

He stops in his tracks. "We do? About what?"

I'm not gonna hold back, I don't care that Cam is here to witness this. I don't want there to be any secrets between us, and I want the truth from my brother. What's done is done, nothing can be changed now, and I'd just like to know the truth. He either slept with her while we were together, or he didn't. Whatever the answer, I'll live with it. It'll hurt and I'll be pissed off. I am, in fact, pissed off but I'm not as angry as I should be. I don't know if that's because of my age or because I've got my head around the idea that neither of us were perfect. If Marley doesn't know the truth, well then I'll just have to live with that, too.

"Carla."

Not missing a beat or breaking eye contact with me, Marley nods his head slightly.

Cam steps to my side with one arm still around my waist, holding me against his side.

"Honest to god, George, there's really not much to tell. They were together on and off when you two were apart. They were never exclusive, and I don't think she was anything more than a warm and willing body. Apparently, she got pregnant, but because he got back together with you, she terminated the pregnancy without even letting him know. She announced it in a room full of people years later, and he distanced himself from her completely after that." I watch his throat move as he swallows hard.

"When you lost the baby on New Year's and things were a little rough between the two of you, she started sniffing around. He wanted no part of it, George. Despite the fact that you kept pushing him away, despite the fact that he was grieving for the loss of his baby just like you were, he kept her at arm's length. She turned up at your house in Hampstead and made a pass at him. I walked in."

Whoa. He knew? Marley knew and never said anything to me. The disappointment I felt at that moment almost floored me.

"Don't look at me like that, George. I walked in on him pushing her away. Things weren't good between the two of you as it was, and I wasn't about to make them worse. He told her to leave. He went to Mum's the next day and you two sorted your shit out, and that was it."

I nod my head, hating the fact that I actually understand why he didn't say anything to me. I watch as a look passes between Cam and Marley, and instantly, my suspicions are raised again. Did Cam know about Carla too? Had he also kept quiet all these years?

"What? What was that?" I ask.

"What was what?" they ask in unison. Making me even more suspicious.

"That look you just gave him? Don't even think about lying to me, Marley Layton."

He looks from me to Cam, who shrugs his big shoulders from beside me.

I watch my brother rake his fingers through his brown hair, which has the first signs of grey appearing just above his ears.

"I went to see Cam."

"What?" I ask, thinking that I've asked this question a lot lately.

"The night I walked in on Maca and Carla, me and him had a long chat. He was worried that he was losing you. He had it in his head that there was something going on between you and Cam. He'd seen photos of the two of you together at Cam's club from that night you had a run in with Haley White. He felt that the way Cam looked at you in those pictures meant there might be something going on. Anyway, I told him to man up and sort his shit out, the next day, he went over to mums and the pair of you flew off somewhere on holiday, remember?"

I nod my head. "The Dominican. We stayed for two weeks."

"Whatever. Anyway, in my infinite wisdom, I thought it would be a good idea to give Cam a visit and warn him to stay the fuck away from you."

My mouth quite literally hangs open as I step back from Cam and look up at him. He holds his hands up as if he's surrendering. "Don't go blaming me for this. I told you in Australia that your mum and brothers had all threatened me with bodily harm."

He's right, he did.

But then I remember something.

"You told me he came to see you when we first got together."

Cam shrugs. "It was a little white lie. I didn't wanna cause trouble."

"Don't blame him," Marley interrupts. "I went to see him again when you came back from Australia and asked him not to mention what I'd done."

Marley tilts his head to the side and holds out his hands, palms up. "I lost ya once, George. I didn't want us falling out. I'd lost one of my best mates, I didn't wanna lose another."

I don't know whether to bitch slap or kiss him.

"Now, you got a fucking beer or what?"

I slap him.

We spend the rest of the afternoon enjoying the company of family. My brothers, their wives, some of their kids, our kids, and my parents. We eat, we drink, and we laugh. We sit around the outdoor dining table on our back patio telling stories and we reminisce. Sean's name is remembered with affection, and I neither cry nor feel guilty.

With the help of my two best friends, I've finally accepted the path that my life has taken. Having regrets is pointless. Feeling guilty changes nothing. I need to accept that what I had with Sean, was most definitely true love but it was far from perfect. The time has finally come to love my husband the way he deserves. I don't have to divide my heart into sections. It's his, all of it. He might share it with our children, Sean, and my lost babies, but he has it all.

I reach across and run my fingers through the hair at the back of his neck. I love it when he grows it longer and down past his collar.

John Legend's "All of Me" begins to play, and I smile at the relevance of my playlist again. I wonder if I actually subconsciously choose to download the songs I do?

"What are you smiling about?" Cam asks quietly from beside me. Everyone seems to be engaged in their own conversations, except my parents. They are both snoring quietly, and my dad's hand is covering my mum's on the arm of her chair.

"You, Tiger. I'm smiling at you."

"And why is that, Kitten?"

"Because I love you so fucking much, that's why. I think I'm the happiest I've ever been in my life right now, and it's all thanks to you and everything you've given me."

His warm brown eyes dart over my face, giving me tingles in my belly. "Are you drunk, Kitten?"

I giggle. "Maybe a little, but that doesn't mean I don't mean every word I just said."

He nods his head slowly while rubbing his index finger back and forth over his top lip.

"So, you loving me enough for anal later?"

"Cam!" I say a little louder than I intend. "Seriously. Do you never give up?"

He shrugs his shoulders. "No."

I laugh at his honesty.

"A blow job then? Gwaaaan, you know you wanna." He winks. I melt.

"I think I can stretch to a blowie."

"Now. Go inside right now. Go up to our bathroom and wait for me on your knees."

My mouth goes dry as my palms begin to sweat. I won't even mention what happens in my knickers.

I stand from the table, about to make up an excuse about collecting up the empties when the alarm sounds to let us know the security gates at the front of the drive are opening.

"That'll be Paige. She just texted me for the gate code."

Paige hadn't made it over last night. Her new boyfriend flew in from America to surprise her, and she's bringing him over today to meet us all.

"Unlucky Tiger, the BJ will have to wait."

Cam pouts and drops his big soft bottom lip. I lean forward catch it between my teeth before kissing his mouth. I'm still holding the empty bottle of wine I'd cleared from the table a moment ago.

"Did we have odds on this one?" Marley asks.

"Yeah, I said a week at four to one, you said two days at three to one, and Cam said an hour at ten to one. Dad was being generous and gave him a month at a one hundred to one and Bailey plans on terrifying the poor bloke and gave him twenty-four hours at eleven to two."

"You lot are horrible," I tell them.

Every time one of the girls brings home a new boyfriend, my brothers, Cam, and my dad run a book on how quickly they can scare them off. It's funny, but mean.

"Just be nice for a little while, please?" Jimmie asks. "He lost his dad or step dad a few years back and now he's flown over here because his mum's really sick."

"I thought you said he was American?" Len questions.

"His dad's American, his mum's English. He's lived most of his life in the States. He's in a band I think she said, or his dad was. I can't remember, but any way, just be nice."

Marley and Bailey both clap then rub their palms together and make a *mwaaaahaha* sound.

"Bring it on," Marls says quietly and then makes an *umph* noise as Ash elbows him in the ribs.

Paige walks out onto the patio looking stunning. Her hair's piled on top of her head, she has minimum makeup on, and is wearing a pair of denim cut-offs with a gorgeous off the shoulder cheese cloth blouse in a pretty baby blue colour. The wedges on her feet matching her top perfectly. She looks every inch the catwalk model she is.

Holding her hand and looking a lot less nervous than he should, is a bloke of about twenty-five. He's wearing board shorts, a Led Zeppelin T-shirt, and a pair of flip-flops. Sunglasses cover his eyes.

"Hey, everyone. This is my boyfriend RJ. RJ, this is my family."

RJ lifts his sunglasses up to his head and rests them there.

"Hey, all, thanks for having me over." He smiles and they start to make their way towards the table. I watch them approach with a strange sense of unease creeping over me, the closer they get. There's something about this boy's face that looks vaguely familiar, and I'm not sure if it's that or the wine that is making me feel both sick and a little uncomfortable.

Marley stands abruptly, pushing his chair back noisily in the process.

He looks at me, his eyes wide with panic.

"What's the RJ stand for mate?" My dad, who is now wide awake and sizing up his next victim, asks.

"Oh, um, Rocco Junior. My dad was Rocco too. . ." Licking his lips, he swallows and looks around at each of us before continuing. "Rocco Taylor, my dad's Rocco Taylor, but yeah," he says with a shrug. A shrug. Like his words didn't matter.

Marley almost staggers over as he backs away from the table. I drop the empty wine bottle I was holding.

The End

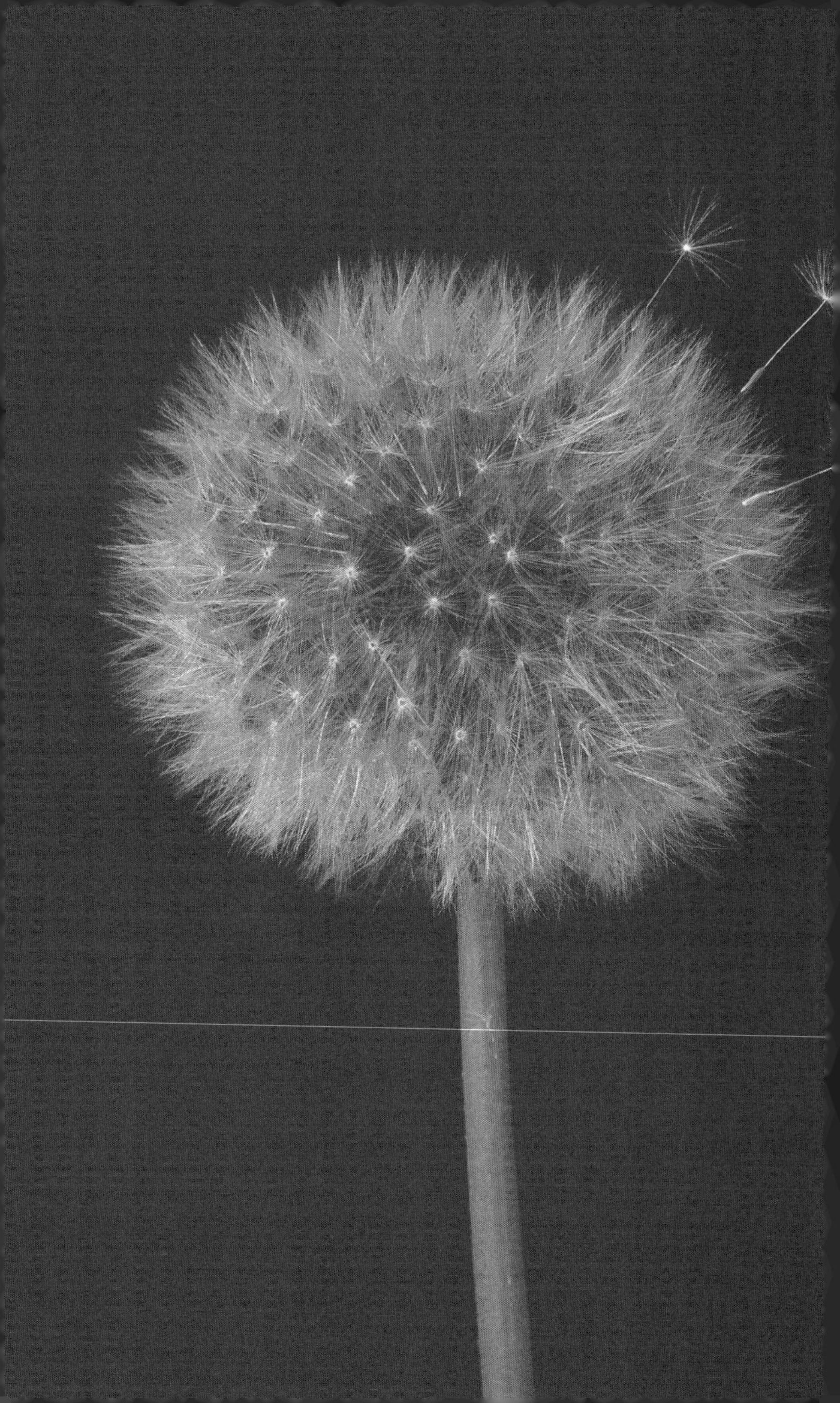

A DIFFERENT KIND OF DECEMBER

CARNAGE BOOK FIVE

LESLEY JONES

ONE
Georgia

I sit up straight, my eyes wide as they attempt to take in my surroundings. The room's dark, but I can hear at least one bird singing outside.

Cam still sleeps soundly beside me, but it's Sean's lips that I can feel on mine. I brush my fingers over them and breathe in deeply.

I both love and hate moments like this. They make me feel completely torn.

I stare down at my husband. His arms are stretched out above his head, disappearing under the pillow that his head rests on.

At my request, he's been growing his hair since last summer. He's had it trimmed a couple of times, but it's the perfect length right now. It curls where it reaches his collar, and the front is long. Though he usually pushes it back, right now it's partly hanging in his face. I want to reach out and run my fingers through it and then rake my nails over the beard covering his cheeks and chin. It's gorgeous silver grey has become one of my favourite things about him.

One of an endless list.

He's my rock. My world. He makes me who I am, a much better person than I could have ever hoped to be, and yet, here I am, watching him sleep after waking from a dream about the other love of my life.

Sean McCarthy.

He doesn't come to me often these days. But when he does, I know.

I can feel him, smell him.

On me.

I slide out of bed and head for the bathroom. I do what I need to do, wash my hands, and lift my hoodie from the hook where I left it last night as I slide my feet into my UGGs.

Our bedroom is at the very back of our house, and the kids' rooms are all towards the front. Kiks is the only one with her door open, so I take a peek inside to check on her. Kiks is our sensitive child and has recurring nightmares. They started when we explained to the kids about my past, about Sean, Baby M, and Beau. She knows about Tamara, how she died, and that Cam was shot . . . and she worries about all of it.

I feel guilty about this. The fact that my past has impacted on my daughter's peace of mind. Given the choice, I would've protected all of my kids and only told them what I felt was necessary, but there's something out there called the internet, and we felt that it was best we told them the truth and answered their questions ourselves.

Becks lifts his head from where he's curled at the bottom of Kiki's bed and looks towards me, his tail wagging while the rest of him remains still.

My daughter's dark hair is spread out around her as she lies with her face buried in the pillow. A black T-shirt covers her skinny frame, and I watch her shoulders move up and down as she breathes.

Kiks, Lu, and George will all be turning fifteen after Christmas, and our house is a hive of teenage hormonal tension. Kiks probably causes the least drama, unless of course, Lu chooses to pick a fight with her.

I make my way down to the kitchen and make myself a coffee. Our other dog, Rooney, isn't in his bed either, and I assume he's with one of the other kids. George probably, since Lu and Harry both complain when the dogs lie on their beds, which, considering I have a no dogs upstairs rule, should never actually happen. But I'm only their mum, no one ever bloody listens to me.

The whole world thinks I'm some kind of super woman who's battled on through tragedy to build an empire and become a world-renowned philanthropist. My kids and my dogs, though, couldn't give a monkey's about any of that and have very selective hearing when it comes to listening to anything I say.

I sometimes wonder if they would listen if I stamped my feet and shouted, "*Do you know who I am?*" Probably not. They'd all be wearing their noise-reducing headphones and not hear a word.

I smile to myself as I head to the mudroom, pull on Cam's quilted Barbour jacket, and grab a blanket from the basket I keep by the back door. I used to live such a rock-star life. I could never confess to my kids some of the things I'd gotten up to over the years, Lu would disown me, Kiks would pass out in shock, George would just go into denial, and Harry? Well, I might just get a fist bump from him. He usually has my back.

I collect my coffee from the kitchen and head out to the back patio. I sit in one of the swinging two-seaters and cover myself with the blanket. It's absolutely bloody freezing, but no matter what the weather's like, this is my favourite spot to come and think out my thoughts.

Today is the first of December. Seventeen years ago, I lost the then love of my life in the most horrific of circumstances.

I lost my son. My sweet innocent baby boy, who never got to take a single breath.

I almost lost my own life, and for a long time after the accident, I wished that I'd been killed too.

This year, I feel different about the anniversary of Sean and Beau's deaths. It still hurts. It'll always hurt. Not just today, but every day. I will always feel that short, sharp stab to my heart the moment thoughts of them hit my conscience, *that* will never change, and I don't want it to.

After so long, I feel like I've finally accepted that I can't change what happened on that cold icy day so many years ago. I'm not sure if I've just accepted it or if I've gotten over the guilt of being the only survivor. The guilt of being able to move on, once again find love, and have four beautiful children.

So yeah, today is a different first of December than the previous seventeen. I won't be curling up in a ball and hiding away from the rest of the world. I won't be running around our house, maniacally hanging Christmas decorations on anything that stands still long enough to let me.

Today, I'm gonna be a functioning mother to my kids and a put together wife for my husband . . . that's the plan anyway.

I pull my feet underneath me in the big chair and lean across the arm to push the button on the patio heater. It lights instantly, casting a glow all around me and competing with the sky, which is starting to change colour. There is a blackbird singing in the distance, and if I listen hard enough, I can hear the horses in the stables.

The couple buying Lu's horse are coming tomorrow. They have a ten-year-old daughter and want to get her a horse for Christmas. Lu isn't interested anymore. She whines and complains constantly about the early mornings and rarely rides these days.

She doesn't have a boyfriend yet, but I know it's gonna happen soon. I close my eyes and smile when I think about what I was getting up to at her age. I'd been obsessively in love with Sean McCarthy for four years when I was fifteen.

My stomach throws a little party inside me as I think about the fact that I was exactly the age the girls are now when I lost my virginity to him.

He was my life.

The other half of me.

A loud sob takes me by surprise as it escapes my chest, travels up my throat, and forces its way out into the cold, early morning chill.

So much for this year being different.

"I'll let you off that one, G. Now get your shit together. You've got this." I hear Sean's voice in response.

I wonder why this happens and if maybe I'm a little bit insane, perhaps I'm totally mad and no one's noticed it yet. Perhaps they have, and I'm just such a nut job that I'm delusional.

I mean, what sane person sits outside at seven in the morning when it's below zero and has a conversation with herself and her dead husband?

The timber door opens, and I jump.

"Fuck me!' Tallulah gasps, her hand goes to her chest, and she stills.

"Lula!"

"What? You scared the shi . . . z outta me. What are you . . ." She trails off and studies me for a few seconds. "You all right?"

My daughter isn't stupid, neither of them are. Lu might not be as sensitive as Kiks, but she's highly perceptive, and just like her dad, she can read people like a book.

She's also probably aware of the date.

"I'm fine," I lie.

"Should I get Dad?"

"No, let him sleep. I'm okay, I promise."

She tilts her head to the side and chews on her bottom lip.

"One day, will you tell me about him?"

Air whooshes from my lungs and exits my nose with a puff of condensation, making it visible.

"Sean?"

"Yeah."

"What would you like to know?"

"What it was like being married to someone so famous, being so young, and ya know . . . everything that happened."

I swallow.

"What do you know already?"

Her eyes dart away from mine, a move that I make when I'm either caught in a lie or about to tell one.

"I'm sure you've already read plenty online."

"Yeah, but half of that probably ain't even true, I'd rather hear it from you."

"Isn't true." I correct her.

Fuck me, I've turned into my mother.

"What ain't?"

I shake my head and let out a sigh. My kids speak far more *proper* than I ever did, but the occasional "ain't" slips in there every now and then. And where Lula is concerned, the F-bomb, too.

"I was pointing out that the correct word you were looking for is 'isn't' not 'ain't'."

"Oh, don't start."

I fight my smile while wondering how many times I've had this conversation with my own mother as I watch Tallulah roll her eyes.

Not wanting to argue with my daughter or get into a conversation about my past, I go for diplomacy and a subject change.

"Where's Kiki?"

"She's up, and nice divert by the way."

Despite the cold, I feel my cheeks heat. I've been busted by my own fifteen-year-old daughter.

"I'm not diverting, we'll talk, but today isn't the day."

She studies me for a long moment. Her blue eyes, which are so much like mine, roam my face.

"I'm sorry, Mum. For what happened to you."

My lips tremble, and my chest judders as I fight not to cry. It isn't just the date and the topic of conversation, it's the fact that I'm having it with my daughter, the one that Cam usually has to step in and stop me from throttling.

A tear slips from my eye, and Tallulah steps towards me.

"Sorry. I should've picked a better day to bring this up."

She hits me with force as she lands in my lap.

I'm shocked at her show of emotion and wrap my arms around her skinny frame. The door to the back deck slides open, and Kiks steps out while staring down at her phone. She takes a step back when she sees us, and like her sister, her hand flies to her chest.

"Bloody hell, you made me jump. I was just texting you—" Her eyes dart between us. "What's happened? What's wrong?"

"Nothing," Lu and I say in unison. Her dark eyes, which are so much like her dad's, continue their dance between our faces.

"Just giving Mumma a cuddle," Lu explains.

"Why, Wha'dya do?"

I smile at that. Lu is the one out of our four that's usually in trouble, so Kiki is right to suspect.

Tallulah lets out a huff. "It's December first, I've not done anything wrong. I just thought Mum could do with a cuddle."

Kiks licks her lips and nods slowly. "You doing okay, Mum?"

"Doing better now that I've had a cuddle."

Kiki throws herself down beside me and Lu, wrapping her arms around both of us, and sounds breathless as she says, "Sorry today is a sad day for you. I hate this day every year and just wish I could make it better."

I smile.

And I cry.

"You do make it better, Kiks. You, Lu, George, Harry, and Dad. You all make it better. Not just this day, but every day of my life."

Neither of my girls replies. We just hold on to each other while the birds sing their dawn chorus and we gently swing back and forth in the cold, early morning air. And I take a moment to appreciate how lucky I've been in my life to be loved the way that I am.

I hear the door slide open again.

"What the . . . what the fuck are you doing? What's wrong?" Cam's voice booms across the decking.

"Just giving Mumma some love on her sad day," Kiks states, her mouth still pressed against my cheek.

"George?"

He's worried. I know him well enough to be able to hear it in his voice.

I wipe my face on Kiki's shoulder and look over it at my husband.

"You all right, babe?"

"I'm all right. The girls were just looking after me."

I kiss both of my daughters on the tops of their heads. "You best get over to the stables, else you'll be late for school."

They each kiss me on a cheek, stand, kiss their dad good morning, and then walk side by side across the grounds of our home towards the stables.

I watch them for a few seconds. The emotions caused by that little moment we just shared threatening to burst out of me in the form of heaving sobs and tears.

I turn to face Cam, my eyes meeting his as he studies me warily. Eyebrows drawn down, his lips pressed together, forming a plump pink line amongst the salt-and-pepper whiskers of his beard.

My husband is so fucking hot.

"Kitten?" he questions again. Despite him having to witness me falling apart in some way on this date for so many years, I can still hear the concern in his voice.

"I love you." I know he knows this, but I want and need for him to hear me say it.

"I know. I love the fuck out of you, too." His wet tongue slips out of his mouth and slides back and forth across his bottom lip.

"What's going on?"

"Nothing. Come over here."

Cams hands go to his hips, settling just over the waistband of a pair of jogging bottoms. His broad top half is covered by a grey hoodie. He again studies me for a long moment, before relenting, and cautiously moving towards me.

My big, confident, handsome Tiger is always unsure of what mental state I'm going to be in on these kinds of days. Usually, he stands back, observes, and works out on instinct what I need from him.

Sitting down heavily in the chair beside me, the force causes it to swing back and forth. Kissing the top of my head, his arm slides around my shoulders, and he pulls me into him. I slide my own arm across his flat belly and pull myself closer, as he covers us both with the blanket I have on my lap.

"What's going on?" he eventually asks.

"Nothing much. I came out here to drink my coffee, the girls came out and caught me having a moment, and then the three of us shared another moment. Then you came out, making my morning perfect."

"Babe, it's fucking freezing. If you come back inside, I'll make you nice and warm and show you what a perfect morning's really all about."

I rest my cheek against his hard pec, and my hand against his hard dick.

"The kids have to get to school. Are the boys up?"

"Don't know. But if you don't take your hand off my morning wood, I'll be taking you back to bed and calling them a taxi."

I slide my hand back up to his belly, this time under his hoodie so I can rest it against his hot skin, saying, "Ya know what would make my day better?"

"Sitting on my face?"

I nudge him with my shoulder as I shake my head.

"The trees are getting delivered today, and Squires are coming to do the outside lights. Can we keep the kids home and just have a family day?"

He leans away so that he can look down at me. "That's how you wanna spend today?"

There is clear surprise in his voice. He's lived with my usual manic routine on this anniversary for too long not to be shocked that I want to spend it differently this year.

I've been selfish. I know I've been selfish, but in all honesty, it's the one day of the year that I've always let my grief entirely consume me. If I don't take this day, I don't know that I'll get through the rest of them.

To the rest of the world, it might look like I have this amazing, beautiful life, but I still feel the hurt caused by the events that happened to me seventeen years ago. I have scars, both physical and mental. I don't see a counsellor anymore, and I'm not on any kind of medication, but that doesn't mean I'm not still hurting. I just choose to take one day a year to grieve. When the painful memories threaten to consume me, I count the days until the first of December, when I know I can let that happen.

Yeah, it might make me selfish, but I also think it makes me a better wife, mother, person the other three hundred and sixty-four days of the year.

"Yeah," I tell Cam honestly. "That really is how I'd like to spend the rest of the day. Let's do the decorations and then go out to eat somewhere nice. All of us, together."

I've rarely seen Cam cry.

That horrible time I found him a drunken mess at his old flat above the wine bar.

When our children were born.

Our wedding day.

He doesn't cry right now, but his eyes are shining with tears. Mine just roll down my cheeks. Again he runs his tongue over his bottom lip while gazing down at me. He blinks, and a tear catches on his thick dark lashes.

"Then let's do it, Kitten."

I give him a wobbly smile. "You boys are not to touch my trees, though."

He smiles and leans forward to rest his forehead on mine. "We wouldn't dream of it. I think we're all aware of how anal you are about your decorations."

"It's just a small area of my life where I feel like I actually have some kind of control."

He buries his face into the curve of my neck, his breath deliciously hot against my skin. "You can control me anytime you like, babe."

"Yeah, I think we both know that that's a lie. You hated it when I handcuffed you."

"You wouldn't do as you were told."

"That's kinda the whole point. I was supposed to be in charge, you were supposed to do as I said. That's what being in control means."

He bites down on the soft skin behind my ear, and despite the warmth radiating from the patio heater, his body, and being under the blanket, goose bumps assault my skin.

"Yeah, fuck that. I've changed my mind. You get your way with most things, but in the bedroom, I'm in charge."

I shudder. I wouldn't have it any other way. I love that he takes charge in the bedroom. It gives me a chance to just shut out the world, shut down my brain, and do nothing but enjoy what he does to me.

After knowing each other for over thirty years and being married for fourteen, our sex life is still off the charts. Cam is as insatiable as ever, something I don't think will ever change. He can't pass me without touching me in some way—usually in a totally inappropriate way. I hope that never stops.

The patio door once again opens, and this time it's George who sticks his messy head out.

"What are you doing?"

"Just talking," Cam responds.

"It's freezing. Why are you talking out here?"

"Don't worry about it," I tell him. "We're coming in now. You can go back to bed for a bit if want. You're all staying home today."

I watch as my son's eyebrows pull down into a frown as he looks between us.

"Why? What's wrong?"

"Nothing's wrong. I just wanna spend the day with you all. We'll put up the trees and the decorations and then we'll go somewhere nice for an early dinner."

"But it's . . . that's what you wanna do today?"

I smile while watching my son's handsome face screw up in confusion. "Yes, that's what I wanna do today. Now go inside and tell your brother."

George's eyes do one more dance between Cams face and mine, before he heads inside.

"I warned them all last night to give you a bit of space today and reminded them of the date."

I wrap my arm as far around his hip as I can and squeeze us together tightly.

"Thank you."

"Thank me later. Let's get inside, I need a coffee.

TWO
Georgia

Our boys both turn in our direction as soon as they hear the door.

George, who has had a bit of a growth spurt over the last few months, is now only just a little shorter than Harry. They look more like twins than brothers who were born almost a year apart.

George turns back towards the toast he's in the middle of buttering, but Harry eyes me warily.

"Morning."

"Morning," Cam and I both respond.

"George tell you you're all staying home today?" I ask.

"Yeah, what's that all about?"

I shrug, let out a long sigh and give him a small smile.

"I've not finally lost the plot if that's what you're worried about.

A DIFFERENT KIND OF CHRISTMAS

I just want you all close today. I thought we could do the trees and decorations and then go out for an early dinner.

George turns around, and I watch as the boys share a look.

"What? Why you two looking at each other like that?"

"Mum, you go mad if we mess with your Christmas trees or decorations, so I think you're lying. You've definitely, finally lost the plot if you're gonna let us anywhere near them."

Cam passes me my coffee, but his eyes don't meet mine as his lips fight a smile. George is staring at the floor, also, it seems, fighting the need to smile. Harry's full-on grinning while my eyes dart between the three of them.

Noise travels from the mudroom, and the girls appear, talking and giggling, and then stop dead in their tracks as they take us all in.

"What's wrong?"

"Bloody hell, if I hear that one more time today . . ."

"Mum reckons we can all have the day off and help her put the trees and the decorations up," Harry informs his sisters.

"Yeah right," Tallulah snorts as she talks and laughs at the same time.

"Stop messing with me, what's really wrong?" Kiki asks.

"He's serious," George adds. "Tell them, Mum."

One pair of blue eyes and four pairs of brown are all on me.

"He's serious, I thought it'd be nice to have a family day."

"What, and you're actually gonna let us touch your trees and decorations?" Lu sounds incredulous as she asks.

I watch Cam roll his top and bottom lips between his teeth, and my hands go to my hips as I start to feel defensive.

"Are you lot all taking the piss outta me?"

They all double up and start laughing, and I feel my nose tingle and eyes burn with tears. I wanna find it funny. I know they're only joking, but today . . . today, I'm just not in the mood to be laughed at.

"Babe, we're not taking the piss, we just know full well that there's no fucking way you're gonna let any of us near your trees or your decorations."

"I'm not that bad."

"Yes you are," they all state while still laughing.

I am that bad.

"Well, this year's different, you can all have a go."

"Why? So you can change it all as soon as we go to bed like you used to when we were little?" Lu asks.

I did use to do that, I didn't think they'd noticed.

"Yeah, we knew," Harry tells me. "We always new."

Cam slides his hands around my waist and grins down at me. "Please tell me I'm not a terrible mother."

His brown eyes twinkle, and he leans in and kisses my forehead. "You're not a terrible mother, you just suffer with what the kids call CDO."

They all start to laugh again, I don't.

"I don't get it, what's CDO?" I question.

"It's like OCD, but you've got it so bad that the letters have been rearranged in alphabetical order so you don't have a meltdown of Georgia proportions," Lu informs me.

I open my mouth a couple of times.

Fucking cheek. I can't believe they all talk about me behind my back. I continue to stare up at Cam, whose eyes are watering as he attempts to suppress a laugh.

"Where'd you hear that saying? How'd you even know what a meltdown of Georgia proportions is?"

"Coz Nan says it," George informs me.

"And Marley and Lennon," Lu adds.

"And Grandad says it to Lu whenever she starts throwing a tantrum—"

"All right, all right. I get it," I interrupt Harry's input.

My kids all straighten and look at me with cautious smiles on their faces.

"Am I that bad? Would you all rather go to school?"

I get a chorus of no from everyone, and Cam pulls me into him.

"Right, well you can all stay home and pass me the decorations, if anyone touches anything, you'll see firsthand what a meltdown of Georgia proportions is really all about."

I end up burning some bacon for breakfast, we all pick at it, and then Cam and the boys go out to the garage and bring in the boxes of tree decorations while I take a shower.

When I get out, I check my phone. I have messages from Jimmie and Ash.

Just a heart from each of them.

A simple heart that says so much . . .

They want me to know that they love me and are thinking of me. They want me to know that if I need them, they'll come running.

With wine.

Vodka, too.

My girls get me. They've always gotten me.

I stand for a few long moments in my bedroom. I'm dripping wet and still have a towel wrapped around me, but I still bask in the fact that I'm loved.

I'm not the easiest person to love or even like. I'm aware that I'm selfish, whiney, and self-absorbed. I've tried to be better as I've gotten older, but traits of thirteen-year-old me still make an appearance every now and then.

Despite this, Jimmie and Ash have always been there for me, loving me like only family can, and their simple text messages have my chest feeling tight, my throat closing up, my eyes and nose stinging, and my lips trembling.

I know that at some stage today I'll get a call from my brother. Just the thought of someone else, someone that I love, feeling anywhere near the depth of loss and grief over Sean's death that I do causes a physical ache that radiates from my chest and hurts every part of my body.

Marley calls me on this day every single year without fail. I never answer, but I want this year to be different.

I go back to my bathroom, clean my teeth and moisturise. I won't bother with makeup until we're going out later, by then, I'll probably be in need of another shower.

Once I'm dressed, I sit on the edge of my bed and make the call that I should've been making every first of December. I'm not the only one that lost so much on that day.

"Little sister Georgia, what's goin' on? You all right?" There's only a slight pause between each of his questions.

I can't get my words out.

I don't know why I thought this was a good idea.

"Marls." My brother's name escapes on a shuddered breath.

"I know, Porge, I know." I hear him draw in a long inhale and let it out slow and shaky.

"I'm sorry."

"Don't be sorry. Don't ever be sorry."

"You at home?"

"Yeah, in bed with a bottle of his favourite bourbon. I was trying to get drunk enough to call ya."

"I felt brave."

"Is that right?"

"Yeah, then I heard your voice, and it all went to shit." I smile through my tears as my brother chuckles.

"So, what's happening? You're up and functioning, what's going on there?"

I let out a weighted sigh. I've spoken to Marley before about my dreams and how vivid they are, so I'm not embarrassed to tell him.

"He was here this morning. Told me its been going on for too long. He said that Cam was a dick for being so fucking perfect and that it was time for me to sort my shit out and stop falling apart on this day every year."

"I think he's right. Cam puts all of us to shame, and you do need to get your shit together, we both do."

"Agreed."

"Wanna get shit faced with me?"

"Absolutely."

"You coming to me or am I coming to you?"

"I've given the kids the day off school . . ." I trail off as I think about why I did that. "I just wanted them around me today, ya know?"

"Yeah, I know."

"I promised them a late lunch or early dinner once we've put the decorations up—"

"*We've?*" he interrupts. "As in you *and* the kids, or you and the people you get to put up your decs?"

"Well, I did mean the kids and me . . ."

"George . . ."

"Yes, I know. They've told me all about my CDO."

His laughter resonates through the phone and touches every part of me. Hearing that from my brother is exactly what I need right now.

"Anyway, you've just given me an idea. Squires are coming today to do the outside lights and decorations, I'm gonna ask them if they can do the inside, too. I cooked the kids breakfast, but they'll probably be starving again by lunchtime—"

"Wait! What? You cooked the kids breakfast? Are they okay?"

"Fuck off."

"George, seriously, what were you thinking?"

"I love you dearly, but you are gonna get a kick in the bollocks if you keep on."

"Oh and there she is. My bitch of a little sister is back."

"I'm not a bitch," I whine.

"No, you're not a bitch, you're not someone that can cook, either. You need to leave that to Christine and put your family out of their misery."

"It's her day off. She doesn't come in Friday to Sunday."

"Perhaps you should think about renegotiating her contract."

"Fuck you." I smile at his laughter again, even though the jokes on me. I've tried to be a good cook; it's just not a skill I possess.

I look up and see Cam leaning against the frame of our bedroom door, watching me intently.

"So, you take the kids for lunch, feed them something edible, and then all come over to ours. I'll give Lennon a bell and see what they're up to, sound like a plan?"

"It does."

"Right, well I'll see you then . . . and George?"

"Yeah?"

"Thanks for the call. You've turned my shitty day right around and even managed to make me laugh. I know that picking up the phone couldn't have been an easy thing to do. Fuck me, I know I have to get drunk every year before I can do it. I love ya."

I don't respond to that. Instead, I swallow the ball of emotion caused by his words and say, "Love you, too. I'll text when we're on our way."

I watch as Cam's eyebrows shoot up and then cast my eyes down at my phone as I end the call. I've had a couple more text messages while I was chatting to Marley, and I open them up.

Baily: *Thinking of you, little sister Georgia. We'll raise a glass to Maca and your babies today and have a drink with you all at Christmas. Love and miss all of you, from all of us xxx.*

The second is from Nina Reed. Despite her being younger than us by about fifteen years, Jimmie, Ash, and I have become good friends with her, and she's now one of our trusted inner circle.

Nina: *Thinking of you all on this saddest of anniversaries. With much love from the Reeds xxx.*

I breathe in deeply through my nose and watch Cam as he stalks towards me. Once again, my nose tingles, my throat burns, and unshed tears sting the backs of my eyes.

I look up into my husband's ruggedly handsome face as he nudges my legs apart with his knees and then squats down in between them.

His big hands go to my hips, and he drags me onto his lap and both of us to the floor. I bury my face in the curve of his neck and breathe in deeply. He smells like my entire world.

"Talk to me," he orders.

"I love you so fucking much."

"You already told me that this morning."

"I know, but I want you to understand just how much."

One of his hands cups the back of my head and the other slides around my waist as he holds me tightly against him.

He flexes his hips.

"I'm not convinced. I need you to show me." I smile, and my chest moves against him as I laugh.

"I showed you last night."

"That was ten hours ago. I'm old and forgetful, remember? I need constant reminding."

"You're full of shit."

He digs his fingers into my ribs and bites my neck. I squeal, and he licks a path over the teeth marks he's probably left on my skin.

He pulls on the messy bun my hairs pilled up in so that my face tilts up and my eyes meet his.

"The kids are downstairs reminiscing as they go through the boxes of Christmas decorations, we've got about fifteen minutes before Tullulah gets bored and starts bitching. Show. Me. You. Love. Me." He punctuates his words with bites, licks, and kisses to my lips, face and neck.

He's grinding against me, knowing full well that I won't be able to resist him.

I rise onto my knees, leaving a space between us and slide my hand inside his jogging bottoms and boxers.

His dick is hard and hot as I stroke him from root to tip, rubbing my thumb over his slit each time I get to the top.

He throws his head back, and I admire what I can see of his throat, but I need more.

I stop my stroking and grab at the hem of his hoodie, he catches on to what I'm doing and helps me to ease him out of it.

"Top off, I need to see you, Kitten."

He leans back on his palms and watches as I pull my T-shirt over my head. I reach behind me to take off my bra but pause when he orders, "No, leave it on. Lift your tits out, I wanna see them." My internal muscles tighten, and my thighs grip his hips. I fucking love it when he gets all bossy in the bedroom.

I look down at my peach coloured La Perla bra and then back up at Cam, who's still staring at my chest.

"You do it," I whisper. He shakes his head.

"No. You do it. Pull down the lace and play with your nipples for me."

"T." I sigh.

"Do it. Right fucking now."

I look down at my boobs. Goose bumps cover my skin, and my nipples are like bullets. I rub each of my palms over them through my bra before pulling down the cups and leaving them exposed.

"Fuck me, Kitten, you look so fucking beautiful right now. Stroke my cock baby. Grip it tight and stroke."

Again, with no hesitation, I do exactly what he says. Clear cum is leaking from the tip of his dick, and my hand slides up and down smoothly.

His hand goes to the small of my back, he pulls me closer and covers my left nipple with his mouth.

"Need you. Need you inside me."

"I know, baby, I know."

Without another word, Cam flips me onto my back, pulls off my leggings, and buries himself exactly where I need him.

We groan out our pleasure in unison. He slides his hands under my arse cheeks, tilts my hips up, and drives deeper.

I hook my legs around his thighs and dig my nails into *his* arse cheeks, pulling him into me harder.

"Fuck, I love when you do that," he pants.

"I want more."

"I know, but I love it when you show me how much."

We fuck.

It isn't lovemaking. We did that last night.

This is fucking.

This is my perfect husband fucking the sadness out of his not so perfect wife.

He knows exactly what I need, and he's delivered it with perfect timing.

He fucks me to the point of distraction. Completely senseless. He fucks me until I forget my name, the date, and the horrible events that changed my life seventeen long years ago.

THREE
Georgia

After another quick shower, I arrive downstairs to find that Harry and George have abandoned the decorations that are spread all over the hallway and the girls are sitting on the floor going through the very last box.

Tallulah is wearing a headband with a flashing star on top, and Kiki has on a *Santa's Little Helper* pixie-style hat with red tracer lights racing through it.

They're discussing a couple of Tinker Bell tree decorations we bought for them in Florida one year. They're so deep in conversation, recalling the holiday where Lu pushed Kiks in the pool over something or another, that I manage to take a couple of pictures of them on my phone without them spotting me.

"You've got to be fucking kidding—"

"Harry!" I shout.

"Sorry, but this ref needs glasses. No way was that offside," he calls out from the games room where he and George are on the PlayStation.

Every year, I promise to get a swear jar in time for the new FIFA game to come out, and every year I forget.

The level of swearing they reach would give my mother a coronary if she were to hear it.

"Okay, kids, change of plan. We're gonna go to Lakeside, do a bit of shopping, grab lunch at wherever you choose, and then go to Ash and Marley's."

"What about the decorations?" Kiki looks up from her spot on the floor.

"Dad's on the phone to Squires now, he's asking if they can do the inside as well as the outside decorations. I'll just add our personal bits and pieces over the weekend."

Lu and Kiks both stare up at me blankly, as if I've just spoken to them in Hebrew and they've no comprehension of what I've said.

Harry and George poke their heads around the game room's door and look at me in much the same way.

"What?" I question, wondering what the fuck is wrong with my kids.

"Squires?" H questions.

"You're letting someone else do the inside decorations?" Kiki asks, sounding astounded.

"Yes. All change this year. I'm handing it over to someone else and having a day out with my family. If you all keep looking so shocked, or I hear a single mention of CDO or meltdowns of Georgia proportions, you'll all take the bus to school without any lunch money for the rest of the year."

They all take turns staring wide-eyed at first me and then each other.

"Come on then, get yourselves sorted." I clap my hands as I speak, and the kids all head up the stairs.

"And remember, it's just Lakeside, not a film premiere or a fashion show we're going to."

Their mumbled responses are indecipherable as I head into the kitchen for a last-minute tidy up before we leave. Although, knowing how long my kids take to get ready, I've probably got time to wash and dry three loads of washing, so I head out to the utility room instead.

Shopping is interesting. I get asked for my autograph three times and pose for four photos. Cam makes sure to keep the kids out of the way while this happens, which is a hard and fast rule of ours.

We've been papped with the kids occasionally, but if it's possible to have any control over pictures being taken of our children, then I exert that power to the fullest.

The kids choose Wagamama for lunch, and as we wait for our table, it takes me a few moments to realise that the place has fallen quiet and people are staring.

"Dad, that woman's taking photos," Kiki whispers loudly.

We all turn in the direction that Kiks gestures, and sure enough, an overly made-up woman, who looks to be in her fifties, has her phone aimed in our direction.

"Turn your backs, kids," Cam says just as I start to make my way over to her table.

"Georgia." I'm grabbed gently by my elbow and turn to see my husband shaking his head at me. "I'll deal with it."

"But—"

"No, not today."

I let out a huff, and he leans in, kisses my temple, and leaves me with the kids.

Things like this really piss me off. My kids are not part of my past life, and even if they were, nobody has the right to take photos of them without my or Cam's permission.

In the beginning, we had to have Benny with us everywhere we went, but things have quietened down over the years and the interest in me waned. Now, we only really have security with us if we're going to a public event where we know there'll be lots of photographers.

If I am recognised, then people are mostly courteous and will ask to take a selfie or for me to sign something. I always oblige. I think they feel they're getting a little piece of Sean by getting a little piece of me, and I'd never deny his fans that.

What looks like a manager appears and heads in our direction with a smile on his face.

"Hey, I'm Brett Davies. I'm the day shift manager here." I take the hand he's holding out and shake it, returning his smile.

"Georgia McCarthy-King. We honestly don't want to be putting you to any extra trouble, we were just after a table for six and some lunch."

"Of course. We're just setting you up over in the back corner, we thought it'd be a little more private for you."

We've eaten here numerous times, it's a favourite of the kids, and we've never had a problem, but I really can't be bothered to argue, so I smile sweetly and thank the manager.

"It isn't a request. Either stop taking photos of my kids, or I'll take your phone off you."

Both Brett and I turn to where Cam is standing, arms folded across his chest as he glares down at the woman who was taking photos.

The man sitting opposite her stands.

"Shit," I whisper-hiss as Brett makes his way over to Cam.

I'm not sure what to do. We should just leave, but then, why the fuck should we?

"Is there a problem?" Brett asks.

"Yeah, there's a problem. This prick's accusing my misses of taking photos of his kids when she was just checking her phone." The man that stood up—her husband I assume—accuses.

"Bullshit, she was taking photos."

"Prove it." The woman pipes up. She's short, blonde,

and . . . curvy? She's talking to Cam but looking at me with a sneer on her face.

"Mum, let's just go somewhere else," Kiki says as she grabs hold of my hand. She hates when this kind of thing happens, whereas Lu, George, and H, all have their phones out, checking to make sure their hair looks good. Lu even pulls a lip gloss out of her pocket and promptly applies it.

"Madam, as the manager, I'm going to kindly request that you keep your phone on the table while Mr King and his family enjoy their lunch."

"Since when did you have a no phones policy?" the husband asks.

"Since I just made one."

"Oh, I see. Special rules apply just because some D-list celebrity that used to fuck a rock star—"

The bloke doesn't finish whatever he was going to add to that charming little sentence before Cam reaches across the bench-style table and drags him across it.

Chairs scrape and plates, glasses, and cutlery crash to the floor.

"Cam, no, just leave it. They're not worth bothering with."

The look he gives me tells me to shut the fuck up and stay out of it, but I ignore it and move towards him.

"Go back to the kids, George," he orders.

"Yeah, fuck off, Georgia," the woman shouts. She obviously has some kind of beef with me.

"Do I know you?" I question.

"Not really, but I know you. We went to the same school. You always did think your shit didn't stink. Then you married that Carnage bloke, and we all got to look at the lovey-dovey photos splashed everywhere of the pair of ya. Didn't mind having ya photo taken then, did ya?"

Cam's stare slices between the crazy lady and me, begging me to let him break either her phone or her husband's nose. I'd rather he did neither of those things right now. At least not while everyone else in the restaurant is watching.

"And that gives you the right to take pictures of my kids, does it? Cam, put him down," I order, he ignores me.

She stands when I reach her table, and I can see that calling her curvy was doing a disservice to curvy women. She's round like a beach ball with massive boobs, a big belly, and short legs.

I lean in and whisper in Cam's ear, "Other people are pulling out their phones and filming this, please let's just leave it." Without even looking my way, he releases the bloke, gives him a shove, and we watch as he lands on his arse back on his side of the table.

"Like I said—"

"I'm not interested." I cut her off and turn to Brett, asking, "Is our table ready?"

He looks at me and blinks—or flinches, I'm not sure which—and gives a stuttered, "Ye-yes," in response.

I call the kids over.

I could stand here and argue with these people. We could cause a scene and even demand that they be thrown out, but I've learned my lesson over the years. The press will run with whatever version of events they see fit to and rarely will it be the truth. If we make a big deal out of this, then it'll give value to whatever pictures she's already taken of us, and the last thing I want is these fuckwits making money out of images of my family.

"Follow Brett," I tell the kids, who are all eyeing me warily, waiting for it all to kick off.

I take hold of Cam's hand and smile at the couple in front of me.

"Enjoy your lunch. Thank you for ruining ours and making what is already a difficult day for me even worse. I hope you find someone to buy those pictures you've taken of my children without my permission and that your conscience allows you to enjoy spending it on something that makes your sad little life happier."

Reaching out with his free hand, Cam grabs the woman's phone off the table, and drops it into the tall glass of coke sitting in front of her. I think my mouth drops open at the same time hers does, but neither of us make a sound as the people sitting farther down the bench start clapping, then they stand and continue clapping. After a few seconds, the entire restaurant joins them.

Pulling the hand he's holding up to his mouth, he kisses the back of it before saying into my ear, "Team King for the fucking win. Love the fuck out of you woman."

He then leads me over to our table where our kids, my reason for existing, are waiting.

FOUR
Georgia

I text Marley and tell him we're about a minute away, and the gates to the grounds of "Rock Star's Retreat" are swinging open as we arrive.

We've been blown off by our kids, all requesting to be dropped off at home on our way from Lakeside to here. I wasn't happy at first, but then Cam reminded me that the last thing I probably wanted to do at their age was hang out with my parents, aunts, and uncles, so, once again, I took a deep breath and let it go. I've done so much of that today, I really should consider changing my name to Elsa.

Cam's been quiet on the drive. Well, he's been quiet since the restaurant incident. I've not pushed him for an explanation since I'm sure at some stage he'll tell me. Once he's worked it out in his own head.

We pull up on Marley's drive at a little after six.

Four minutes after six to be exact.

I don't move.

Cam doesn't move.

"Un-break My Heart" by Toni Braxton is playing through the sound system until Cam turns it off.

We sit in absolute silence as I watch the clock on the dashboard.

At eight minutes past six, Cam moves his seat back, leans across the centre consul, and lifts me to straddle his lap.

He slides his arms around my waist as I wrap my arms around his neck and bury my face in his chest and throat.

We're back to where we were this morning. Except this time, there is nothing sexual about our embrace.

This time, it's all about my husband holding me together at the exact moment my little boy was born not breathing and unresponsive seventeen years ago.

This time, it's all about me seeking comfort from the only man on this earth capable of giving me exactly what I need.

We hold each other in silence until Cam finally says, "You were fucking amazing in that restaurant today, Kitten. You blew me away."

"I wanted to cunt punt the bitch."

"Language."

"Oh, fuck off. That little troll would've deserved it."

"She did, and I know full well that was what was going through your head. Fuck me, it even went through mine. That was what made what you said to her even more spectacular. I'm so fucking proud of the way you handled things."

"Thank you. I just didn't wanna make the six o'clock news tonight or let the troll-faced beach ball make money from whatever pictures she took *and* have the kids involved."

"Love the fuck outta you, Kitten. Let's go raise a glass to Sean and your babies and get drunk with your family.

Marley's front door is unlocked, and hand in hand, Cam and I

A DIFFERENT KIND OF CHRISTMAS

walk right through to the open-plan kitchen and family room.

Somehow, despite my husband being perfect and saying the exact things I'd needed to hear out in the car, I'd managed not to cry. As I make my way into my brother's house and am greeted by the wide-eyed stares of my family, though, I feel myself wobble.

Marley has a glazed look in his eyes, and I'm not sure if it's the effects of being drunk, stoned, or sad.

The conversation falls silent as my brother walks towards me. Cam releases his grip on my hand as Marley wraps his arms around my shoulders and pulls me into his chest.

"Little sister Georgia, it's so very good to see your face."

"Big brother Marley, you have no idea."

"Oh, I think I do."

He leans around me and holds his hand out to shake Cam's. "Big man. Good to see ya."

"Likewise." Cam holds up a bottle of Pappy Van Winkles bourbon, and Marley's eyes widen.

"Well, fuck me, even better to see ya."

As Marley moves from me to Cam, Lennon steps into my personal space and pulls me in for an even tighter squeeze.

"Porge."

"Len."

He kisses the top of my head and then quickly shifts his attention to Cam, Marley, and the fifteen hundred quid bottle of drink they are admiring.

Then my girls are in front of me. Without a word, Ash reaches out and squeezes my boob.

"What the fuck!" I slap her hand away as I speak.

"Yeah, it's really her." She looks over her shoulder and informs Jimmie. Jim and I roll our eyes as Ash grabs me and kisses both my cheeks noisily. "Damn good to see ya, sluster. You still have such great tits by the way. No wonder TDH can't keep his hands off them."

"He loves me for more than my tits, I'll have you know."

"I do, her blow jobs are pretty fucking epic, too," Cam calls out.

"Dude . . . that's my sister," Marley objects.

Jim and I again roll our eyes.

"Long time coming, Georgia Rae, but seeing you like this today makes my heart happy."

"Happy to be the cause of your happiness, Jamie Louise, and I'm only here thanks to the love, support, and patience of all of you lot. Now, get me a drink, I've been sober far too long today."

Surrounded by the people that knew Sean best, I drank, I talked, I smoked a little weed, I danced, I sang, and eventually . . . I cried.

When there was no more drinking, singing, talking, dancing, smoking, and crying to be done, my husband carried me out to a taxi and took me home.

Thanks to the people that had always been unwavering in their love for me, I'd had the happiest, saddest day of my life.

FIVE
Georgia

A couple of weeks later, I'm sitting at Jimmie's breakfast bar, drinking a cup of tea.

I've had a stand up argument—well, a full-on screaming match actually—with Tallulah this morning, and it left me shaken.

She couldn't find her school shirt. She has six school shirts, but she wanted to wear this particular school shirt. I've a feeling it's because the shirt she was looking for is a size too small and makes her boobs look like they're going to burst right out of it.

When I told her I'd sent it with a bag of other stuff to the clothes bank over the weekend, she hit the fucking roof and told me I was a control freak who needed help and that she was moving out and going to live with my mother.

Yeah, good luck with that.

Good luck to both of them.

Before I inflicted physical harm on my daughter, I got in my car and drove to Jimmie's, leaving Cam to deal with the school run.

"I don't know why you let her get to you. Dealing with her is like arguing with yourself, and you should know by now you never listen to anyone."

I stare down into my tea, chewing on my lip.

"Am I that bad?" I eventually look up and ask.

Jimmie gives a small shrug. "You're a lot better now than you used to be, but when you were younger, once that red mist came down, it was always better to walk away until you'd calmed down. Lu's the same."

"Do you never row with your girls?"

"Of course I do. Harley's pretty easy going, but Paige, she's more like you, especially lately."

I watch as Jimmie reflects my actions from earlier and stares into her teacup.

It makes me feel like a shitty friend. Things haven't been great between Jimmie and Paige for a little while, and I know that it's partly my fault.

Paige is, once again, back with her on-again off-again boyfriend of the past eighteen months.

What are the odds that Lennon and Jimmie's daughter would end up dating the son of Rocco Taylor and Haley White? Considering who his parents are, RJ is actually a really nice bloke, or at least he seems to be.

I've not been around him that often, I think Jim deliberately tries to keep us apart, which I'm thankful for. I may not have issues with him, but I won't lie and say it's easy to be around him. He looks a lot like his dad, and I'll never forgive or forget what that man did to my family, what he took from me and Sean, and the way his actions changed my life irrevocably.

I know that my own stubborn pig headedness is to blame for the years Sean and I spent apart, but it all started with him—Rocco Taylor.

And as for her, his mother, Haley White? It doesn't matter that she's seriously ill with sclerosis of the liver and has apparently been dying for the past eighteen months, I would happily punch the head in and enjoy it just as much as I did the last time I did it.

Forgiveness is not part of my vocabulary where those two are concerned.

"How are things between the two of you?"

Jimmies eyes slice to mine, and her chest heaves as she lets out a sigh and shakes her head.

"Something's not right, George. She came back here Sunday with a broken wrist and a cut over her eye, she—"

"What the fuck, Jim?" I interrupt. "What happened, why didn't you tell me?"

"She reckons that she had too much to drink on Saturday night and fell down some steps." I watch as she rolls her lips together, her voice quieter, she adds, "We've been that drunk, George, we've bruised our knees and scraped our palms, but she didn't have any of those things, just a cut over her eye and a broken wrist."

I feel sick. My heart smacks against my chest like it's trying to escape.

"Where is she now? What did Len say? You think RJ's hitting her?"

She nods, and my blood feels like ice as it pumps through my veins. I can't get my breath.

Domestic violence is not something I've ever experienced, and the thought of somebody deliberately hurting my niece—or any other member of my family—sends my head into a spin. My first thought is to react with violence. I want to hunt that fucker down and feed him his own bollocks until he chokes, fucking him up the arse with his own dick in the process.

"Oh my god, Jim, I don't know what to say."

"Len went out looking for him Sunday night, but apparently, he flew back to L.A. Sunday morning with the band. She's still denying that he had anything to do with it and reckons that he wasn't even there, but I went online and found pictures of them out together on Saturday night."

Jimmie's face crumbles, and I move around the breakfast bar to where my beautiful friend is falling apart and wrap her in my arms.

"She's my little girl, George, the thought of someone hurting her, him especially. That fucking family have put us through enough."

"I know, I know, Jim. I can't believe this is happening."

"Can't believe what's happening?"

I turn my head to see Paige standing in the middle of the kitchen staring at us. She looks terrible. There's a cut and a bruise over her left eye, a slight bruise on her right cheek, and her wrist is in a plastic cast. But it's not just that; she's so unbelievably thin. She's always been thin, she's a model for crying out loud, being thin goes with the territory, but she's at least a stone lighter than when I saw her last, which was only about six weeks ago.

I watch as she slowly licks her lips and asks, "What did you tell her?"

I pull away from Jimmie so that she can wipe her eyes on the cuff of her sweatshirt sleeves.

"She told me that she's worried about you. How'd you cut your eye and break your wrist? And don't even think about bullshitting me."

"None of your fucking business," she snaps back. I'm shocked, but try not to show it.

We've always been close, and she's never spoken to me like this before. I stare at her for a long moment while shaking my head.

"You're my niece, that's my best friend, your dad's my brother. I'm *making* it *my* fucking business," I lean towards her and speak between my gritted teeth.

She flinches at the harshness of my tone, and despite being glad I appear to be making my point, the way she flinched, almost ducking away from me, has me worried.

"I tripped up a couple of concrete steps when I came out of the club Saturday night. I put my hand out to stop my fall and landed awkwardly on my wrist, kept going forward and hit my face and brow. I was drunk, it was my own fault."

I don't believe a word she's saying, but that's probably because not only does this involve a member of my family, but also it involves the son of Rocco Taylor and Haley White. As much as I'd like to consider myself a fair person and give RJ the benefit of the doubt, in reality, I don't. In my head, I'm already on the phone to Cam, telling him to track RJ down—wherever he might be in the world—and deliver a message that he's to stay the fuck away from my niece and every other member of my family.

With that message, I'd also like a little warning sent, a clue or a hint given as to what the consequences might be if he doesn't comply. Just a small one . . . nothing that hurts too much.

"Sit down," I order. "You want a tea or a coffee? You need to eat, too, you look like you're about to snap."

"Says my aunt who has less fat on her than a lettuce leaf."

"Sit down and shut up before I slap your skinny arse," I again order.

"I'll make some eggs," Jimmie says while moving towards the fridge.

"I'll do it," I suggest.

"No!" They actually both shout the word out at the same time. I hold my hands up in surrender.

"Okay, chill the fuck out. I'll put the kettle on, is that all right?"

"Can you burn water?" Paige directs her question at Jimmie, and we all laugh.

"Georgia could burn the sun," she responds, and for a little while, we drink tea, eat scrambled eggs on toast, and talk shit. Paige continues to deny that RJ had anything to do with her injuries, and Jim and I continue not believing her.

Eventually, I bring up the subject of Christmas.

"Nina, Conner, and the kids are coming to ours for Christmas this year."

I watch as Jimmie's eyes slide to Paige, and I know I've said something wrong.

"Really? Why's that? I thought they usually spent it with his family."

Jimmie plasters on a smile as she speaks, but it's as fake as a politician's promise.

"Yeah, they do, but his dad's going on a cruise and one of his brothers is doing something or another, so they all just decided to do their own thing this year. Ash mentioned that they were coming to ours, then asked me if they could come, so I called her and invited them."

Paige puts her fork down, her food unfinished. Jimmie does the same.

"What you doing, d'ya know yet?" I aim my question at Paige. When I asked her last, she said she didn't know if she would be in the country due to work commitments. Because she's just told me that she's had to cancel all of her work for the next six weeks, I'm assuming that's no longer the case.

"Can I bring RJ and his mum?" The tone she uses to ask the question tells me she already knows what I'll say, but I almost choke as I answer.

"No." I don't hesitate with my response. I feel like I've been stabbed in the heart. "Absolutely not. Never in a million years would I have that oxygen thief in my home or around my family. I can't believe you'd even ask me."

She shrugs.

She fucking shrugs as if what she just asked for is another cup of tea or for me to pass her a pen.

"Don't ask, don't get."

"But you must've known what my answer would be. Have you any concept of what that woman did to me?"

"Its ancient history and she's dying."

"Well, she best hurry the fuck up and get dead. The world'll be a much better place when she does."

"She's a human being, Georgia, one that happens to be my boyfriend's mum."

"She also happens to be the cunt who falsified a rape claim against my husband and brother and then stole four years of my life."

I stand and push back the stool I've been sitting on. I don't know where I'm going or what I'm doing. I can't fucking think straight.

"Well, then the answers no, I won't be there."

I nod. I'm wounded to the core and can't believe she'd choose her over me. I feel an ache of betrayal bloom in my belly and the burn of tears in my eyes.

"I need to go Jim. I can't be around her right now."

Jimmie follows me as I head towards the front door.

"Now do you see what I'm dealing with, George? I stayed quiet so you could see. I don't know my own daughter."

I stop at the front door and turn and face my best friend, my sister.

"I love you, Jim. I love all of you, and I totally understand if you want to have Christmas here so that you can spend it with Paige, but there is absolutely no fucking way I'm having that woman anywhere near me and mine."

Jimmie shakes her head. "I'm not generally a violent person, but you've no idea how hard it was in there not to slap my own kid. I don't want him or his mother here, and right now, I don't want to be around Paige, either." I pull her in for a cuddle. "I'm so sorry," she says into my ear.

"Don't be, none of this is your fault."

"Yeah, I keep trying to remind myself of that. Dry your eyes, I don't want you driving like that. You won't be able to see properly."

I give a small smile and kiss her cheek.

"Yes, Mum, I promise to drive careful. I love you."

"Love you, too," she responds as I head out to my car.

I feel like my head's about to explode.

What a morning.

First Tallulah and now Paige.

Perhaps it's not them. Perhaps it's me who's the total bitch.

I call Cam.

"Kitten. You calmed the fuck down?"

I smile, but still want to cry at the sound of his voice. Where would I be without this man and the way that he loves me?

"Barely. Did they all make it to school all right?"

"Yep, now I'm home all alone, sitting in my office answering emails."

"I'm five minutes away, what d'ya wanna do?"

"You in every orifice."

"I'll allow you inside two and neither will be my bum."

"You're no fucking fun."

"Take it or leave it."

"Oh, I'll take it one of these days. Drive careful, but get home quick. I love ya."

"Love you, too."

I end the call with a smile on my face. My shitty morning made better by the man who constantly rocks my world.

SIX
Cam

Marley looks up from his gift and directly at my wife, unshed tears shining in his eyes as he smiles.

"It's perfect," he says quietly.

Georgia shrugs. "I thought maybe it was time for a new one."

"Abso-fuckin'-lutely it is." He stares down at the black leather guitar strap she'd had made for him and runs it between his finger and thumb.

Georgia had explained to me that she used to buy both Sean and Marley a new one every year as a gift. She would use her dressmaking contacts and have them stitched with the band's logo. Marley's would also have the initials BBM—Big Brother Marley—stitched into it, and Sean's would have G&S TWIMTB—Georgia And Sean. The Way It's Meant To Be. When she lost Sean, she stopped the tradition, but this year, for some reason, has seen a massive turning point in the way she's dealt with the loss, and she's gifted her brother something that obviously means a lot to him.

"Ohhh, leather. You gonna tie me up or whip me with it later?" Ash leans over Marley's shoulder and asks.

His eyes dart up, and he scans the room, making sure none of the kids or his parents have heard her remark.

"Gag you with it if you don't shut up."

"Oh, Rock Star, that works, too. Can't wait."

"You're giving me a boner in front of my parents, baby."

"I got under the dinner table and gave you a bl—"

"Ash," I snap. "Little ears." I gesture towards Conner and Nina's boys, who are playing with the action figures they've just unwrapped.

While Conner is laughing, Nina, who's a lot quieter than Ash, Jimmie, and Georgia, is staring wide-eyed.

"Sorry," Ash calls with shrug out to anyone who wants to listen.

It's the end of another Christmas day.

Georgia's parents have gone off to bed and so have Bailey and Sam and their kids and Conner and Nina's boys. The younger adults and teenagers are scattered around the house doing fuck knows what, but it's Christmas, 3.20am boxing day morning to be precise, and I'm past caring.

"If I hear this song one more time, I might just shoot someone," Lennon states as I top up his glass.

"Don't let Georgia hear you say that. She's had this shit playing nonstop for the past three weeks."

"Jimmie's the same. The house has been lit up like Blackpool since the first of—" He stops and then corrects, "The end of November."

We give each other a nod, both knowing the importance of the date he was going to say.

The first of December is always a tough day for Georgia. Always has been, always will be. I've learnt over the years just to play it by ear. Some years the day goes by quietly, others it's manic. What has become a tradition is that it's the date the house gets decorated for Christmas. I think this is just a way to keep her brain occupied and busy.

This year, things changed though. It was like a switch had been flipped inside of Georgia, and she finally found it within herself to leave her guilt behind and see past the grief.

I know there will forever be a part of her that isn't just mine. A part that I will always share with Sean McCarthy and their babies. I can mostly deal with that. I have the odd moment of self-doubt, but I know that she loved me. I know that what we share is pretty fucking amazing and that we lucked out when we found each other again and then went on to have our kids.

She's the other part of me. I don't go in for all the mushy bullshit, but I am seriously not complete if I'm not around her.

Despite sometimes being a mouthy, stubborn, selfish pain in the arse, she has always loved me fiercely and with so much passion that it blows me away. To have gone through all that she has and still have that capacity to love our kids and me the way she does astounds me.

I watch Georgia now as she messes with the laptop connected to the Karaoke machine. We bought that thing as a joint present for the twins a few years back, but it's the triplets, the terrible trio of Georgia, Jimmie, and Ash who put it to most use. Tonight, they're joined by Nina.

The girls have just finished murdering "Santa Baby" and are now debating which song should be up for slaughter next.

That's a lie, actually. Georgia has a great fucking voice, the other three, not so much.

I watch my wife as she smiles towards the laptop, knocks back the champagne that's in her glass, and turns towards Marley.

"Big brother Marley, come sing with me?" The other girls boo and hiss at being outed, but Georgia just turns her beautiful smile and her glassy eyes towards me. My heart rate accelerates, the way it has done for over thirty years now. The way it always will.

She's my world.

I have a life I once never dared to hope for, but I got it, and it's all because of her.

"Top me up, Tiger!" she shouts over the microphone, and because I'm more of a pussy than a Tiger where she's concerned, I pull a bottle of the bubbly from the ice bucket on the coffee table and head towards her.

I hear a *kercha* sound from behind me as someone tries to mimic the sound of a whip cracking and turn to give Marley and Reed my middle finger before giving my wife my undivided attention.

I quickly move the bottle of Krug out of the way as Georgia wraps her arms around my neck and slams herself into me.

"Merry Christmas, T. I love you so fucking much."

"You're drunk," I reply.

"Drunk, sober, or somewhere between, I still fucking love ya."

"Yeah?"

"Abso-fuckin'-lutely, baby."

"Does that mean I get anal tonight?"

She throws her head back and laughs. My dick twitches, and I can't help but grind my hips against her.

"Easy, Tiger." She licks her lips while still grinning at me. "Nice try, but no. That thing is never going to be banging my back doors in, not ever. I can think of somewhere else you can put it, though."

She's swaying us from side to side as she speaks, and I can't help but smile at her drunken attempts to stay upright and focused.

"Yeah, you may be wanna put my baby sister down, King. She might be your wife, but she's also my singing partner."

I turn to see Marley heading towards us.

"You tell him, Rock Star!" Ash shouts from somewhere, probably two streets away with her big mouth.

I kiss Georgia's lips and then her nose. "Sing with your brother, Kitten. Your audience is getting restless."

"I'm not done with you yet, so don't go far."

She attempts to wink at me as I step away, but instead, it turns into a sort of long, drawn-out blink, and I can't help but chuckle. I love seeing her relaxed amongst her family and friends like this, but I've learned from years of loving this amazing woman, that when she's been drinking, one wrong word said, a song played, an event mentioned, anything that stirs up past painful memories and it'll be instant tears.

I retreat far enough away to be able to take in the show and stand next to Jimmie. I wrap my arm around her shoulders, pull her into my side, and kiss the top of her head.

"You all right?" I question.

Jimmie and Len have had a tough couple of weeks with their eldest daughter, and I know they've both been worried sick about her.

"Not bad, it's not been the easiest of days. We've not heard a word from her." I nod, but really, I have no clue how she must be feeling.

"Queenie doing all right?" Jim asks, obviously wanting to change the subject.

"For now." I smile down at her as I speak and notice that she too can barely focus.

"What exactly the fuck did they put in that champagne?" I ask her.

She laughs and shrugs. "Dunno, but it's fucking great."

We both fall silent for a moment as we watch Georgia and Marley break into song. It's Elton John and Kiki Dee's "Don't Go Breaking My Heart." It's been their party piece since they were kids and the reason my daughter is called Kiki.

"She's so lucky to have you, you know that, right?"

My chest feels strange, and my throat constricts. I give a small laugh.

"I think it's the other way around, Jim."

"There's no one else out there that could have saved her. No one else that could've put her back together the way you have. No one else that would put up with her shit the way you do."

"You've been her best mate almost her entire life. You never seem to have a problem putting up with her."

Jimmie gives me another unfocused, wonky grin and a shrug. "What can I say, I love the skinny bitch."

I laugh. These girls love each other to the point that I'm actually jealous of how close they are, but they insult each other like they are each other's worst enemies. Even so, God help anyone else that throws an insult in the direction of any of them, because they'll soon unite. Georgia, Jimmie, and Ash are a force to be reckoned with individually, but when they join forces, you better get your running shoes on.

"Ditto. Although, I've gotta say that my wife ain't skinny, she's fucking perfect."

"You've got your beer goggles on, Cam. I've seen more fat on a chip."

I look up as I hear Georgia call into the mic, "Tiger. This way. Now!"

She hands the mic to her brother, grabs my hand, and marches me out of the room to the sound of wolf whistles, clapping and oi oi-ing.

"Dare I ask where the fuck we're going?" I follow her swaying form out to our laundry. She pulls me into the room, slams the door behind us, and launches herself at me.

Her mouth slams down on mine, and her legs wrap around my waist, her arms around my neck.

I step forward a few paces and lift her up, sitting her back down on the edge of the worktop.

"I need you," she pleads. Her hot breath hits my ear and the side of my neck. It's all the encouragement I need.

"Lift your arms baby." Her top has buttons down the middle, but I can't be fucked wasting time with that shit and just pull it off over her head.

"Bra," I order.

"Love it when you're bossy."

"No you don't. You cop the hump when I tell you what to do."

The room is almost pitch dark, but I can just make out her beautiful smile.

"Not when we're having sex I don't. I love it when you take charge."

I know this, and even if I didn't, it wouldn't change anything. Georgia gets away with most things where I'm concerned, but in the bedroom, I'm the fucking boss.

"You gonna let me have your arse then?"

"Answers still no, and unless you have about four inches cut off that thing and lose some girth, it always will be."

Yeah, I'm the boss in the bedroom—except when it comes to that.

I help Georgia in her fumbling attempts to get my T-shirt over my head, then lean forward and draw one of her nipples into my mouth while brushing my thumb back and forth over and over.

"I fucking love your tits."

"I love your dick. Help me get my jeans off."

She undoes her belt, button, and zipper.

"Lift your arse."

I pull her jeans over her hips and then take off my own as she toes them down her legs and off. Without even checking that she's wet—I know that she will be—I pull her to the very edge of the worktop and slide inside her.

"Fuck," we both say at once.

"Feel good, baby?"

"The best."

"Tell me what you want."

"Kiss me."

I slam my mouth against hers and oblige. Our tongues tangle, dual, and taste. I pull away and bite, lick, and suck along her jaw to her ear and down her neck before heading back to her mouth.

I slide my hands under her arse cheeks and lift her slightly, which earns me a groan as I hit her at a different angle.

"Fuck, that's good," I tell her.

She leans back on her elbows, allowing me to watch myself slip in and out of her. Sliding one hand out from under her arse cheek, I brush over her clit with my thumb. Her legs tighten around me, her back arches, and I know she's almost there.

I feel her internal muscles squeeze my cock as she pants, "Coming, Cam, coming."

"I know, baby, I know. Let it go, Kitten. Give it to me."

She moans loudly, and that's all it takes. Two more thrusts of my hips, and I'm letting go inside her while she continues to squeeze and milk my cock.

She lifts herself up and wraps her arms around my neck. The sensation of her tits brushing against my chest makes my dick give a final twitch inside her, and she gives a little giggle.

"Love to hear that laugh, baby."

"And I love you. Merry Christmas. Thanks for another perfect one."

Lennon

I watch my wife flop down onto the sofa and tuck herself in between my brother and Reed. She's smashed, but just at that perfect level of smashed that she won't suffer too badly in the morning if she has a glass of water, lemonade, or anything non-alcoholic right about now.

I don't wanna kill her buzz, but I don't want her suffering tomorrow, either. With all the singing she's been doing, her throat must be dry anyway. My cock stirs as I think about the perfect cure I have for her parched throat.

I've had a semi for her all night anyway. Watching her sing, dance, and move those hips of hers has me adjusting myself constantly.

She woke me up with a blow job early this morning—it's a Christmas tradition in our house and has been ever since we moved in together, which was a lot of years ago.

I top up my glass with more of Cam's best bourbon and watch her throw her head back and laugh at something my brother says to her.

I still[A1] get a little twinge of jealousy in my gut when I watch them together. They still flirt exactly the same way they did when we were all kids. I trust them both implicitly, but still, I'm a bloke, and protective of what's mine. I just can't help it.

When we were younger, a lot of people thought that Marls and Jimmie were together, and that wasn't a bad thing. My wife was fourteen when I fell in love with her, which might sound like the stuff of fairy tales, but I was eighteen—so, not so much. Kissing and holding hands was as far as it went, and all of that had to be done in secret. We got away with it until Christmas of 1983, and then Georgia caught us.

I thought it was gonna be the end of my involvement with the band when it all blew up, but we made the best of a bad situation and got on with things. Jimmie and I still kept our relationship secret from her parents until she turned sixteen.

Jimmie's dad is mixed race, and because back in the sixties, when he first got with her mum, biracial marriages were still frowned upon by vast members of society, they went through a lot of shit to be together.

When I went to him as a twenty-two-year-old man and told him I was in love with his sixteen-year-old daughter, his wife—Jimmie's mum—had to pull him off me. He threw me out the house, barred me from ever seeing his daughter again, and threatened to have me arrested. Two nights later, he walked into the pub the band was playing at that night and asked to talk to me.

I still wasn't his favourite person, but his wife had reminded him how the whole world was against them when they first got together, and how that just made them closer. After setting down a lot of ground rules, he agreed to us seeing each other, and walked his daughter down the aisle to me wearing a smile, less than two years later.

I'm tugged from my memories as Cam walks back into the room, my sister trailing behind him. Her hair is freshly brushed, Cam's isn't. Both of them have flushed cheeks.

Ash interrupts her rendition of The Waitresses' "Christmas Wrapping" and asks over the mic, "Is that fresh fuck I smell, Georgia Rae?"

Georgia launches the bottle of water she was carrying at Ash, who catches it like a pro.

Cam heads towards me, obviously in need of a drink, while my sister squeezes herself between Marley and Jimmie on the sofa.

She leans in and kisses Marls on the cheek. "I love you dearly, big brother Marley, but your taste in women is shit. Your wife has a fat mouth."

"I know, she has no gag reflex, either. They're two of the reasons I married her."

"You know it, Rock Star," Ash states before pretending to deep throat the microphone.

"That woman seriously has no filter," Cam says from beside me.

"Nope," I agree. "Never has, never will."

We both observe our wives in silence. They're side by side, heads together, deep in animated conversation.

"Looks like Jim is getting a blow-by-blow account of whatever you two have been up to for the past twenty minutes."

Cam turns his head towards me with his dark eyebrows raised, but before he can say a word, I point my finger at him. "Don't. I do *not* want to know. She might be turning fifty, but she's still my baby sister."

He throws his head back and gives one of his big booming laughs.

"As if I was gonna tell you I've just fucked your sister in our laundry anyway."

I shake my head and walk away.

"Where'd you get the water from, Porge?" I ask my sister, using her old childhood nickname.

"Don't call me that. In the fridge in the laundry."

"Is it safe to go in there? Do I need to watch out for sticky tissues?" I joke.

"Nah, you're good. I used a tea towel out the drawer and did a thorough clean up."

"Classy, Porge, classy." I once again shake my head and walk away. My family seriously have no issues with sharing. Everything.

"Get us a bottle for Meebs please, Len?" Reed calls after me. No clue why he calls his wife Meebs, her name's Nina.

"I don't need water, there's more champagne in the fridge," Nina protests as I head off to fetch water. When I return, Jimmie's not where I left her.

George and Marley are belting out a stellar version of The Pogues' "Fairy Tale Of New York."

Cam and Reed are sitting on the edge of the sofa, watching them, and Ash and Nina have moved the coffee table out of the centre of the room and look like they're attempting to waltz around together in the space.

"Where's Jim?" I ask Cam.

"Went looking for you." He gestures towards the hallway I just came from.

I retrace my steps and notice a glow coming from under the door of Georgia's office and open it.

Jimmie's inside, standing by a shelf with a photo frame in her hand. She turns her head and looks at me. Tears fill her eyes and spill down her cheeks.

"Babe?" But I already know what it is she's looking at. She holds out the frame so that I can see it. It's a picture of Maca and Marley together. They look so young, but then, it was a long time ago. They're both wearing tuxedos, their shirts and ties both undone. Maca is swigging a champagne bottle, his eyes laughing into the camera. Marley has a big grin on his face and a cigarette hanging from his lips as he holds on to his bottle.

"I took this photo," I say quietly, placing it carefully back in its place on my sister's bookshelf.

"I know. I remember the night. They won best everything, didn't they? Song, album, video?"

"Yeah," I say, letting out a long sigh.

"Happy days."

"They were."

"We're so lucky, Len," Jimmie throws her arms around my neck, and I pull her in close to me.

"They *were* lucky, babe. For as little time it was, they had each other, and they were in love. When he died, Maca was the happiest I'd ever known him."

I don't wanna stand here getting choked up right now, and if we keep reminiscing about the past, it'll end with the both of us crying.

Things have been tense at home. Our eldest daughter, Paige, has barely spoken to either of us in weeks, and because Georgia refused to extend the invitation to Paige's boyfriend and his mum, she'd refused to spend Christmas here with us.

I can't even believe Paige would ask that of my sister. She knows the story, we've explained the connection between Georgia, Sean, Marley, and her boyfriend's parents. Yet, she still asked my sister to extend the invitation to include RJ's mum, the woman that tried to frame my brother for rape.

I don't know the person my daughters turned into since she's been with RJ, but what I do know, I don't fucking like, and that's really horrible thing to feel about your own kid.

Jimmie has been really down about it. Don't get me wrong, there's no blame on Georgia's part. I totally understand why she doesn't want the bloke or his mother in her house.

Despite the history between his family and ours, in the beginning, we set our differences aside and gave him the benefit of the doubt. Over the past year, I've seen changes in my daughter that I don't like.

I kiss the side of her neck, my hand sliding under her T-shirt. I press the cold bottle of water to her bare skin, and she gives a little squeal and smacks my chest.

"Drink some. I don't want you hung over in the morning."

Without arguing, she unscrews the cap, and I watch her throat move in the lamplight as she gulps down almost all of the contents.

My cock stands to attention as I watch her pull the bottle away from her mouth and lick her lips.

"Fancy a quickie?" I ask, hopeful.

"Here?"

"I locked the door behind me." She gives a quick raise of her eyebrows before giving me a sexy smile, grabbing my T-shirt, and pulling me towards her. My mouth finds hers, and I kiss her gently at first. Her hand makes its way into my hair, and her fingernails rake across my scalp. My girl knows exactly what I like.

"Take your jeans off and bend over the desk," I order. She moves instantly. "Take off your top but leave your bra on."

I watch her shimmy out of her jeans, wondering how the fuck she got in them in the first place.

I undo my own jeans, pull down my boxers, and begin stroking my cock. "Leave the thong," I instruct as she starts to take it off. "Lean over, baby, show me how wet you are."

She moves the chair away from the centre of the desk and leans right across it.

I move towards her. Pulling her thong down over her hips, dropping to my knees as I slide the scrap of fabric down her thighs, letting it fall to the floor.

Raking my teeth over each of her arse cheeks, I slide two fingers inside her.

"You're wet, baby."

"Always for you, Len."

Standing, I give her right arse cheek a slap.

"Again," she whispers.

I drag the tip of my cock from the crack of her arse down to her entrance. As I slide inside her, I slap her arse, pull down the cup of her bra, and squeeze her nipple.

"Fuck."

She pushes back into me as I grip her hip.

"Just a quickie, babe, remember? I've been watching you shake that arse all night; I'm not gonna last long."

"Harder. Fuck me harder." As if I'd say no to that request! I pull her back onto me as I reach around and rub my middle finger over her clit. With my free hand, I pull down the other cup of her bra and pinch and pull at her nipple.

"Len-Lennon. More, I need more."

I bite down on her shoulder, and her groan almost turns into a growl. I have to put my hand over her mouth because she's getting so loud, and then bury my face in her neck to stifle my chuckle. She reaches around both of us and claws at my arse cheek; her nails dig into my skin as she tries to pull me closer. The fact that she wants me so bad has me coming undone, I just hope she is, too.

Her loud moan and muscle spasms let me know she's there, and I let go inside her.

After a few moments to catch our breath, I flatten my front to her back, wrap my arms around her waist, and pull her close.

"Thirty-three years, baby. I never thought back then that I could love you more, but every year gets better."

"Stop trying to make me cry again."

I kiss the back of her sweaty neck and then run my tongue over the same spot. Her muscles clench around me, and my cock gives a little jerk.

"Rather make you 'come' again."

She turns her head and smiles at me. "That'd make it four O's in less than twenty-four hours. Anyone'd think it was Christmas."

"Every day is like Christmas with you, though, baby. I got lucky, you're the gift that keeps on giving . . . and taking. We should spare a moment to think of Santa right now. Poor old fucker only gets to *come* once a year."

This time she gives me a different type of groan. "That's worse than one of Cam's jokes."

"It is one of Cam's jokes; he cracked it earlier."

We're both quiet again for a moment.

"I love you, Lennon Layton. Thank you for our amazing life and another fantastic Christmas."

"Teamwork, baby, team—"

I'm cut off as someone bangs on the door.

"You better not be having sex in my office. I have security cameras in there; everything gets recorded. If you are, I'm so showing it to Mum and Dad tomorrow."

"Fuck off, Porge."

"Make me! And don't call me that!"

I lay one more kiss beneath my wife's ear. "Merry Christmas, baby, now let's get you cleaned up."

Marley

"Where's Jimmie?" Georgia asks, flopping down on the sofa next to Ash.

"Went wandering off earlier. Len went looking for her. Now, who knows. Probably shagging in your office or somewhere."

Ash then proceeds to pout her lips and look at me.

"Everyone's getting some tonight except for me. I'm not feeling the love—or your dick. Not. At. All."

"Baby, I was singing. I know I'm good, but I can't give you a live version of "Fairytale Of New York" and sex at the same time. Especially in the middle of my sister's family room with an audience."

She gives me a lazy, drunken smile. "You used to like people watching us." And fuck me if I'm not suddenly rock hard.

Now that no one is karaokeing, the only sound in the room is our conversation, but then all falls silent when we hear a loud groan coming from the hallway.

"Oh my God. They are actually having sex in my office," Georgia snaps, her head turning towards Cam. "T, they're shagging in my office."

Cam shrugs his big shoulders. "So?"

"That's... It's... No, just no."

"Calm the fuck down, Kitten. They're fucking, not killing each other." But George isn't listening. She hauls herself off the sofa and sways her way up the hallway.

"Ooops." Ash giggles.

"You better not be having sex in my office." We hear George shout as she bangs on the door. "I have security cameras in there; everything gets recorded. If you are, I'm so showing it to Mum and Dad tomorrow."

"Georgia, leave them the fuck alone," Cam calls out to her.

"Fuck off, Porge." We all laugh at Lennon's response.

"Make me! And don't call me that."

"Go sort your sister out." Cam looks at me and orders.

"Get fucked. She's your wife; you sort her out."

"You two are such a pair of pussies," Ash adds.

We are. None the men in our family are brave enough to deal with Georgia when she throws a tantrum or has a meltdown.

Reed and Nina are watching us with amusement.

"I agree with Ash, you're a pair of pussies," Reed chimes in.

"You go and sort her out then," Cam and I both suggest, just as we hear more banging on the office door.

"For fuck's sake." Cam sighs, marching out of the room like a man on a mission.

"Go get her, Tiger!" Ash shouts after him.

"You got this big man," I add.

We all fall silent, listening for how Cam's gonna "handle" her, but all we hear is George scream and then giggle.

"Surely, he isn't gonna shag her again?" Ash grumbles.

"Well, it'd be one way of shutting her up," Reed responds.

"Oh, don't bet on it. When Georgia's on a mission nothing can stop her," I tell him.

"Bet if TDH stuffs that nine-inch dick of his down her throat, she'd shut up. That thing could probably even shut me up."

Nina spits her drink at my wife's remark. I choose to ignore it.

Cam steps back into the room and has George hanging over his shoulder.

"I'm taking my wife to bed. You all know where you're sleeping, right? Help yourselves to anything you want. Thanks for a great day and night. Say good night, Kitten."

He spins around so that George is facing us. She pulls herself slightly upright and waves her hand.

"Good night, Kitten," she slurs, then giggles, and then screams when Cam slaps her arse. We're all still watching as she buries her face in his jean-covered arse and bites it.

"Ow. That fucking hurt." We all laugh at that. The fact that skinny George is brave enough to do that to a big bloke like Cam amuses the rest of us.

"Night. Love you all. See you for brunch tomorrow."

They retreat up the hallway to the sound of all of us remaining wishing them good night and thanking them for a great day and night.

"You ready for bed, Mrs Reed. The boys are probably gonna be up in about two hours."

Nina already has her eyes closed. "You can deal with your sons in the morning. I'm staying in bed."

"Yeah, we'll see. Come on, let's go. Night, you two."

Conner's wife is tiny, and he has no problem picking her up and carrying her out of the room.

I pull Ash across my body so that she's straddling me.

"Where'd you want me to fuck you, baby?" I ask as she nuzzles into my neck.

"Not up the arse, I didn't bring any lube," she mumbles. Making me chuckle.

"Noted, but I meant did you have a room preference." I continue to laugh.

"Oh, soz," Ash again mumbles, this time on a yawn. I slap her backside. "Come on, let's get you to bed."

I stand with her still wrapped around me like a monkey and make my way up to the room we're staying in, making sure to bang on Georgia's office door as we pass just to piss off my brother. That earns me a "fuck off" from both him and Jimmie, making Ash giggle into my neck.

I throw her gently on the bed and know immediately that I'm gonna be shit out of luck if I was hoping to make love to my misses. She's practically out cold already.

I pull off my jeans and socks, then pull Ashley's UGGs and jeans off. I chuckle at the knickers she has on underneath. They're like a little pair of shorts in a baby blue colour. On the front is a rather raunchy looking Alice from Wonderland, winking and pointing down between my wife's legs. Under the picture are the words: "Eat me."

I know it's wrong to take advantage of her while she's drunk, but fuck it! I blame Alice; she ordered me to do it. I lean forward and bury my face between Ashley's legs and breathe her in at the same time as I reach inside my boxers and grip my dick.

I plan to leave it at that, go to sleep with a hard-on and wait until my wife is cognizant and aware of the dirty things I'm doing to her. I might be a perv, but I'm not a fiend, after all. But then Ashley's hands are in my hair, pressing into the back of my head, forcing my face down harder between her legs.

"Take them off, Rock Star. Take off my knickers and fuck me with your tongue and fingers." And because Marley loves Ash, I do exactly that.

Within seconds, her underwear is off, my tongue is working her clit, and I'm curling two fingers inside her. I keep working at my dick with my free hand as Ash positions her legs so that they're hanging over my shoulders, tilting her hips up into my face and giving me access to her tight little arsehole.

Her knees press against my ears on either side of my head, her heels dig into my shoulders, and her hips gyrate up into my face.

"Nearly there, baby."

"Wait for me," I order. When I know I'm close, I slide two fingers inside her arse, her back immediately arches off the bed, her legs tighten around my head and shoulders, and her internal muscles grip my fingers as she groans. I push her legs away, sit up, and come all over pussy and lower belly.

Her blue eyes shine up at me.

"Thought you were tired?" I question.

She grins back at me lazily.

"Your hot mouth on my mildred woke me up."

We stare at each other in silence for a few long moments.

"Love you, Baby, Merry Christmas."

"Love you, too, Rock Star. Thanks for the orgasm."

Georgia

My head spins as Cam lays me on the bed and peels me out of my clothes.

"Teeth," I mumble.

He pulls me up, slings me back over his shoulder, and carries me to the bathroom where he sits me beside the sink.

He just has his boxers on, and I close one eye so that I can try to focus on his beautiful body and the way his muscles ripple and move.

Cam will be sixty soon but has the physique of a man half his age. He works hard at it, and the results are evident for all to see.

"You are so fucking hot, Mr Tiger Husband."

He chuckles as he passes me my toothbrush, now loaded with paste.

I take it from him and begin brushing.

"Mr Tiger Husband. That's a new one."

"Yeah. Just made it up. You like it?"

"You made it up, just for me? Then, of course, I love the fuck out of it. Spit."

I frown as I try to process what he just said.

"Mt mo malmays ma mullow," I attempt to talk around the mouthful of foam I'm now holding on to, smile, and then lean over and spit it into the sink.

"What was that?" Cam asks, handing me a glass of water.

I take it, rinse my mouth, and spit again.

"You told me to spit, but you always tell me to swallow," I explain.

"I meant the toothpaste, Kitten. You spit the toothpaste but swallow my cum."

"Oh." I laugh and then squeal as he picks me up and carries me back to bed.

Cam helps me out of the rest of my clothes and then hands me one of his T-shirts to sleep in.

We climb under the duvet, and he pulls my back into his front, my safe place.

My thoughts are an erratic jumbled mess, and for some reason, memories of when my family had me sectioned jump to the front of my mind.

"Thank you for a merry Christmas, Cameron. I'm glad I didn't die and stayed alive to share all of this with you."

"Georgia, what the fuck?" I'm flipped to my back, his big body covers mine, and his angry scowl darts all over my face.

"What?" I question.

"What d'ya mean you're glad you didn't die?"

I shrug and tears start to burn my eyes and nose.

Letting out a deep sigh, I admit, "I thought about it almost every day until you came back into my life. As soon as I realised I'd never stopped loving you, you gave me a sense of purpose, a reason to get out of bed every day." Tears are falling freely from my eyes now, running into my ears and over my neck.

I feel tired and woozy. I just wanna go to sleep.

"If I didn't have you, I think I'd probably be dead," I tell him honestly.

"Don't fucking talk like that, George. You found me. We found each other, and neither of us is going anywhere. Now go to sleep, I don't wanna hear any more dying bullshit."

"There is no more dying bullshit, that's exactly my point. It's because of you. You saved me and I know it's taken a lot longer than it should've but I'm there Cam, I'm finally there."

Thoughts and words are swirling around in my head, and I'm not sure if I'm saying them out loud or just thinking them.

He once again repositions us, and the last thing I remember is my Tiger Husband kissing the top of my head and whispering, "You are the most complicated human being I have ever met, but I love the fuck outta you and wouldn't change a thing. Merry Christmas."

The End
FOR NOW!
TURN THE PAGE FOR WHAT'S NEXT

The Definition Of Insanity

COMING SOMETIME IN THE FUTURE...

Paige

"**I**t's your sixteenth, Paige. Not your eighteenth, not your twenty-first, your sixteenth. You are not holding it in a nightclub."

I carried on walking towards my uncle's office, ignoring my mother's argument being shouted from somewhere behind me as she tries to keep up.

"Let's just talk to Cam; there may be a way around this. Perhaps if she has it on a Sunday, or holds it in the VIP area with a strictly no alcohol policy in place? Although, I'm not sure if that's even legal, so we'd have to check on that first." I heard my aunt say to my mum, using a placating tone. If anyone can win my mum around, it's Georgia.

I stopped and turned around to face them as they walked across the empty nightclub towards me.

"You're so negative sometimes, Mum. Why can't you be more like George? Instead of shutting down every suggestion I make, why can't you at least try to see if it's doable first?"

"Don't speak to your mother like that."

My eyebrows instinctively shoot up to my hairline at my aunt's words. She is the coolest person I know and usually has my back, so I am a little surprised by her tone and feel my cheeks flush.

"I'll help make this happen if it's legally possible but don't be rude to your mum. Otherwise, you'll be sitting at home on your Jack Jones for your sixteenth, or worse still, the whole family will drag you to The Harvester and make you spend it with us."

I fold my arms across my chest and glare between my mum and

my aunt. I couldn't think of anything worse than spending my sixteenth birthday at The Harvester with my insane family. We'd probably end up getting thrown out . . . again.

"I thought we were banned from The Harvester?" I question.

"Weatherspoon's then, we're not banned from there," my aunt snaps.

"I think we are actually. Remember that time we popped in for a quick drink and that woman flashed her tits at Marley and Ash threw a bottle at her?"

"You're not helping, Jim."

I let out a loud huff, and they both look at me.

"Jesus, this is like déjà vu. She looks exactly like you at that age," my mum says quietly, my aunt smiling at her words.

"It's not fucking funny, George. You're not the one that has to put up with her tantrums and meltdowns of Georgia proportions."

I just gave a loud yawn. I've heard it all before.

"Jim, you handled me just fine when we were fifteen, I'm sure you can handle her now that you're a grown arse woman."

"Yeah, just like you handle Tallulah."

"I handle Lu just fine, and if I can't, Cam does."

"Pfft, she has Cam wrapped around her little finger."

"Oh my god, are you two just gonna stand and argue all day?"

"Shut up." They tell me in unison.

"And cover your mouth when you yawn. Did your mother teach you no manners?"

My mum glares at my aunt, her mouth open in shock at her accusation.

Giving another huff, I flick my hair over my shoulder, and stomp towards my uncle's office, swinging the door open without bothering to knock.

I stop in my tracks as soon as I realise there is someone in there with him.

Cam is sitting back in his chair, his legs stretched out in front of him, crossed at the ankle, and propped on his desk.

The other person is a man, but I can only see his dark hair and his legs. He has the ankle of one resting on the knee of the other.

They each have a short, rounded glass containing an amber coloured liquid in their hands.

Cam looks up, wide-eyed with surprise at first and then he gives me a smile.

"Book, what you doing here?"

My uncle tells the worst jokes ever. Because my name is Paige, he's always called me Book, and he seriously thinks he's funny. He's not. And even when he is, I'm funnier.

"All right, Queenie, how are you?" His surname is King, so my play on his name has always been to call him Queenie, which is actually funny, considering the size of the man. He's big, like really big. Taller than my dad, my pops and my uncles and cousins. He has really wide shoulders, and I suppose you might call him good-looking in an old man kind of way . . . he must have something going for him anyway because my aunt married him, and she is beautiful. So beautiful that she was once married to a famous rock star.

"Paige, you can't just barge in there without knocking," my mum calls from behind me. I turn and roll my eyes at her.

G is pretty bad arse most of the time, except when she bangs on about being respectful to my mum. My mum has a stick up her arse most of the time though when it comes to manners, not swearing, pronouncing my words properly, knocking on closed doors before entering a room . . .

I remember that I've come to ask my uncle a favour and turn to give him my sweetest, most innocent look, but the man that is sitting in the chair on my side of the desk has turned it to face me.

My heart and my belly do this thing. It's like they've somehow become tethered inside me. My belly tries to turn itself in knots, pulling my heart down into it. My heart attempts to escape and flies up through my chest, lodges in my throat and beats erratically.

He stares at me with the bluest of eyes.

I'm just fifteen years old, but I know without a shadow of a doubt that this grown man sitting in front of me is potentially going to be my first real life crush and quite possibly, the love of my life.

Series Playlist

Marillion, *Lavender*
Simply Red, *Money's too tight to mention*
Eurythmics, *There must be an angel*
Run DMC/Aerosmith, *Walk this way*
Van Halen, *Why can't this be love*
The Clash, *London calling*
Right said Fred, I'm too sexy
Blondie, *Denis*
The Buzzcocks, *Ever fallen in love/ orgasm addict*
Joni Mitchell, *River*
The Jam, *English Rose/Butterfly collector*
Ray Charles, *Georgia on my mind*
David Essex, *Rock on*
Transvision Vamp, *Baby I don't care*
The pointer sisters, *Automatic*
Maze. Feat Frankie Beverly, *Joy and pain*
INXS, *Mystify*
Creed, *With arms open wide*
Metallica, *Fade to black*
Fatboy Slim, *Praise you*
Eminem. *Feat* **Dido,** *Stan*
Basement Jaxx, *Red alert*

Moloko, *Sing it back*
Oasis, *Wonderwall*
Nirvana, *Smells like teen spirit.*
Bone Thugs N Harmony, *Tha crossroads*
Massive Attack, *Unfinished sympathy*
Armand Van Helden, *U don't know me*
Frankie Goes To Hollywood, *Relax*
Tears For Fears, *Everybody want to rule the world*
Paul Hardcastle, *19*
The Rah Band, *Clouds across the moon*
Gloria Estefan, *Don't wanna lose you*
"The Trouble with Us" *Chet Faker & Marcus Marr*
"History" *One Direction.*
"You Get What You Give" *The New Radicals*
"Demons" *Imagine Dragons*
"Can't Feel My Face" *The Weeknd*
"Do or Die" *Thirty Seconds to Mars*
"Where Love Lives" *Alison Limerick*
"Unbreak My Heart" *Toni Braxton*
"I Will Survive" *Gloria Gaynor*
"Second Chance" *Shinedown*
"Never Forget You" *Zara Larsson*
"7 years" *Lukas Graham*
"Stay With Me" *Sam Smith*

HELPLINE NUMBERS

If you are affected by any of the issues covered in this book and need to talk, please contact:

Lifeline Australia 131114
The Samaritans UK 08457 90 90 90
The Samaritans USA 1(800) 273-TALK

AUTHOR BIO

Lesley Jones was born and raised in Essex England but moved to Australia nine years ago with her family.

Marley is her sixth novel in just under three years of writing.

She has quickly gained a reputation as a writer of gritty, down-to-earth characters, involved in angsty and emotional plot lines. Carnage having won a number of awards for 'Best Ugly Cry'

Her readers love the fact that she can switch her stories from hot and steamy, to snot bubble crying, followed by laugh out loud moments, in the space of a few sentences.

Lesley Jones

BELIEVE.

Printed in Great Britain
by Amazon